# DIARY OF AN UNSMUG MARRIED

Polly James was born in Wales, but now lives in East Anglia, which she finds unnervingly flat, and chock-full of writers.

She works as an editor, but has had a variety of different jobs, ranging from teaching dance, and designing clothes, to being an advisor for the CAB and a caseworker for two different Members of Parliament. She has found something to laugh about in all of them.

Polly is married, with two children, and a large extended family, none of whom find her half as funny as she thinks she is.

# POLLY JAMES

# Diary of an Unsmug Married

**AVON**

AVON

A division of HarperCollins*Publishers*
77–85 Fulham Palace Road,
London W6 8JB

www.harpercollins.co.uk

A Paperback Original 2014

1

A catalogue record for this book is
available from the British Library

ISBN-13: 978-0-00-754853-8

Typeset in Sabon LT Std by Palimpsest Book Production Ltd,
Falkirk, Stirlingshire

Printed and bound in Great Britain by
Clays Ltd, St Ives plc

**MIX**
Paper from
responsible sources
**FSC® C007454**

FSC™ is a non-profit international organisation established to promote
the responsible management of the world's forests. Products carrying the
FSC label are independently certified to assure consumers that they come
from forests that are managed to meet the social, economic and
ecological needs of present and future generations,
and other controlled sources.

Find out more about HarperCollins and the environment at
**www.harpercollins.co.uk/green**

# Acknowledgements

No thanks are due to the owners of the unbelievably-noisy building site at the end of my street. (*Ten years* to build a small estate? I'd complain to my MP if I thought it would do any good.) I do owe *huge* thanks, however, to those of you who were regular readers of my blog and Twitterfeed. The way you engaged with Molly's life so wholeheartedly made writing about it much more fun than I'd expected.

Even so, I don't think I would ever have believed that I could write a 'proper book' about Molly, had it not been for the incredibly generous help and encouragement of Judith O'Reilly and India Knight. I cannot thank them enough for their kindness to a stranger.

I am very grateful to the judges of the 2011 *Orwell Prize for Blogs*, Gaby Hinsliff and David Allen Green, for shortlisting me, as well as to Jean Seaton and Gavin Freeguard. Thanks, too, to all those who nominated and voted for me in the BOTY and *Total Politics* awards.

Only another writer can know what it feels like to

suddenly decide, half-way through a book, that you are *rubbish* at writing, hate doing it, and want to run away and do something – *anything* – else instead. In those moments of meltdown, I'd have imploded, were it not for the helpful advice and understanding of Sue Welfare, Ben Hatch, Marika Cobbold, Harriet Cobbold Hielte and Alex Marsh. Thank you all, very much.

I also owe a considerable debt of gratitude to others in the literary profession who have helped and supported me along the way, namely Patrick Walsh; Peter Straus; Simon Trewin; Scott Pack, and the very lovely Claudia Webb.

The same goes for people from a wide variety of fields who've been equally generous with encouragement, practical help, or advice – and sometimes all three. A big thank you, therefore, to Sean O'Mahony; Peter Black AM; Adrian Masters; Kaliya Franklin; Fiona Laird; Lily Bradic, Damian Greef; Jo and Phil Crocker; Tim O'Shea; Christopher Tuckett, Julia Kitt; Elspeth Barker; Ashley Stokes; George Maclennan; Mischa Hiller, Becke Parker, Maria Roberts, Rachel Trezise, Andrew Mackey, Charles Christian and Sally Willcox; as well as various councillors, MPs and their staff.

A number of journalists, bloggers and tweeters attempted to 'out' me, but without success (which must mean they weren't *really* trying). I'm grateful to them for being so good-humoured about it, anyway – and for continuing to take an interest in what Molly has to say. Thanks, too, to FleetStreetFox, Kit Lovelace, and Biscuit and Toast of the *Wed or Dead Wager* for inviting me to join 'Bloggers Anonymous', and for making the early days of the blog far less lonely, and a lot more fun.

I'm extremely grateful to my agent, Becky Thomas at Fox Mason, for always replying to me faster than the speed of sound, sometimes even in the middle of the night; and to my wonderful editor, Lydia Vassar-Smith, for her many improvements to my original manuscript. Sincere thanks are also due to Claire Bord and the rest of the Avon team (both for their enthusiasm for the characters I created, and the care that they have taken in publishing my book), as well as to Jo and Sabah at Light Brigade, and Rhian McKay.

Last, but definitely not least, I owe members of my family, big-time: my mum, Jenny, and step-father, Dave, for their generosity in helping me try to realise my long-held but previously half-arsed dream of becoming a writer; and my husband and children, for the neglect they've suffered during the attempt.

*For Mark, Daisy and Jack, with love*

# CHAPTER ONE

## *May*

(Or most of it, anyway. Mum didn't give me
this diary until my birthday. I think she got
it in the sale.)

**MONDAY, 10 MAY**

Max has only gone and organised a surprise party for
my so-called 'big' birthday tonight. I *bet* that counts as
grounds for divorce. I could cheerfully kill him anyway,
even though he tries to make up for it by bringing me
breakfast in bed.

'You'd better eat fast, Molly,' he says. '*And* you'll have
to leave opening your presents until tonight, otherwise
we'll both be late for work. We must have had a power
cut while we were asleep – the time on the alarm clock's
out by miles.'

'What is *wrong* with you two?' says Connie, coming
into the room uninvited, and – even worse – followed
by Josh. 'You must be the only people in the universe

1

who don't use your phones to wake you up. Apart from geriatrics, of course.'

'They're nearly geriatric themselves,' says Josh, whose opinion no one asked. 'Especially you, Mum, as now you're *another* year older.'

That's not half as funny as he and Connie appear to think it is, and I'd disinherit the pair of them if I owned anything worth inheriting. As I don't, I decide I'd better rise above the provocation and get ready for work instead. I leave Connie and Josh fighting over what's left of my breakfast, which seems to involve fencing with slices of bacon.

It's only when I arrive at work that I realise that I am wearing *exactly* what I will still be wearing when my stupid party starts, as soon as I get home again: an un-ironed dress, to match my equally un-ironed face. *And* I've left my make-up at home! This evening's doomed to be a disaster, before it's begun.

I just hope, for Max's sake, that he's at least had the sense not to invite *anyone* younger than me . . . including our children.

## TUESDAY, 11 MAY

Bloody hell, my head hurts. Thank God I'd already arranged to take today off as holiday, so at least I can lie around on the sofa this morning, groaning intermittently. I am *never* drinking gin again.

Last night was as horrendous as predicted, and now Max is sulking because I didn't look surprised enough when I came home from work to find my birthday party in full swing. So far, I've managed to refrain from pointing

2

out that his decision to tell me about it in advance may have diminished the element of surprise somewhat – but I did mention that an astonished expression would be a lot easier to fake if I'd had Botox like Annoying Ellen from next door.

Why the hell did Max have to invite *her*? She seemed quite nice when she first moved in, a few weeks ago, after her divorce came through – but before I'd downed my first gin, she'd already started swanning around announcing to all and sundry how much she *loves* sex, and how all she wants for *her* birthday is a man with a big you-know-what.

Every male in the room immediately began to salivate at this bloody nonsense, presumably imagining his particular appendage as Ellen's saviour, while we wives became ever-more invisible and murderous, particularly me. I have gone right off Ellen; and gin. Not to mention birthday surprises.

## WEDNESDAY, 12 MAY

So there's to be a ConDem[1] Coalition, and the hung Parliament is finally over – a missed opportunity, if ever I saw one. I'd quite like to have hung a few MPs myself, starting with The Boss, aka Andrew Sinclair. He's still the MP for Lichford East, by some miracle, not that he seems grateful for that.

---

[1]ConDem Coalition: Government cobbled together, during seemingly endless back-room dealings between David 'Call Me Dave' Cameron (Conservative), and Nick Clegg (Liberal Democrat). Also known as 'All Things To All Men Clegg' according to The Boss, who is not Nick's biggest fan.

He spends the whole day driving Greg and me nuts, shouting about why 'that idiot' Gordy[2] didn't resign sooner, to 'save the situation', and moaning about the Labour Party being relegated to Her Majesty's Official Opposition.[3]

We can't see what difference *that'll* make – or not to Andrew, anyway – given that he's been voting against his own party for the last decade at least. That's probably why he didn't lose his seat, though *he* puts it down to the Just for Men he applied in the run-up to polling day. I doubt he's right, seeing as his new 'hair' looks as if it's been painted on, but Andrew says it proved a much bigger asset than Gordon Brown's 'satanic smile'.

Greg and I don't argue with him, as we're just relieved that we still have jobs, for what *they're* worth – which is a lot, according to The Boss. Apparently, the country can't run without MPs' staff, 'especially not those promoted to senior caseworker[4] in a moment of weakness' (i.e. me).

[2]Gordy: Greg's and my name for Gordon Brown, also known as 'that idiot' if you listen to The Boss. Ex-Prime Minister (as of today) and ex-Chancellor of the Exchequer; and not exactly an asset during election campaigns.

[3]Her Majesty's Official Opposition: Usually the political party which wins the second-largest number of seats in a general election, and whose members sit opposite the governing party in the House of Commons. Don't ask me to explain how the LibDems won far fewer seats than Labour and yet ended up helping to run the country. The Boss can't get over *that*.

[4] Senior caseworker: If you contact your MP about *anything*, it'll be someone like me who decides what needs to be done, and then does it – while giving the MP all the credit and/or taking most of the blame. The 'senior' bit means handling the 'complex' cases. (Substitute 'nightmare' for 'complex' and you've got the picture.)

'So we'll have no more self-indulgent holidays taken to get over birthday hangovers, Molly,' he says at lunchtime today. 'All hands are needed on deck from now on – at all times – for *The Fightback*.'

Andrew is on his way out of the office when he makes this last statement – en route to his favourite watering hole – so I ask him how *he* can afford to take time off. He doesn't have an answer to that.

## THURSDAY, 13 MAY

I've been so busy planning Ellen's murder in my head all day (ever since she waved to me and Max this morning, while wearing very little) that now I've smoked a bloody cigarette, without realising I was doing it. So that's my post-birthday no-smoking resolution up in smoke.

'Bugger it,' I say, as I stub the cigarette out, and look around to check if anyone has caught me in the act.

'Bugger what?' says Connie, appearing from nowhere, as teenagers so often do. 'What have you done now, Mum?'

'I had a cigarette, by mistake,' I say. 'I need to pull myself together. What shall we do this evening?'

'Let's go late-night shopping,' says Connie – so off we go into town, where I take back almost all my birthday presents, as usual.

Maybe one year Max will buy me something I actually want, rather than whatever comes to hand in M&S at the very last minute. I do keep Connie's present, though – a copy of *Bridget Jones's Diary*. It's bloody funny, but I really can't see what Bridget thinks married people have to be smug about.

Especially not when they're parents, too. Connie insists that we go to the Topshop sale, and persuades me to spend all my refunded birthday money while we're there. I feel quite cool and trendy – until we get back home, when I try my new clothes on, only for Josh to look up from stalking everyone he knows on Facebook and say, 'Mum – you do realise you didn't get any years back for your birthday?'

I smoke four cigarettes in a row and turn all the mirrors to the wall. Max asks whether there's been a death in the house, and I say, 'Yes. My self-esteem,' but he's already turned the television on, and isn't listening to a word I say.

## FRIDAY, 14 MAY

I wish The Boss would bugger off to Westminster and annoy the London staff for a change. Thanks to the election, he's been here constantly for at least a month, using my computer and causing havoc in the process.

When I switch it on today, up comes a notification: *79 print jobs pending*. Andrew just can't seem to grasp that we connect to the Parliamentary system by remote access, the stupid man.

All you have to do is accept that there's often a delay between issuing a command and its implementation, but no – that's beyond his comprehension. He just keeps on clicking away, swearing furiously, until the system crashes; at which point he stomps off, leaving me to sort it out. And *his* is one of the brains we rely on to run the country – or did, until a few days ago!

Anyway, while I'm cancelling seventy-eight of the seventy-nine print jobs, Frank Dougan phones to demand an 'emergency' appointment at today's constituency surgery.

'I'm *really* sorry, Mr Dougan,' says Greg, sounding almost as if he means it, 'but I can't give you an appointment, emergency or not. Since you moved house, you don't live in the Lichford East constituency any more, so now you'll have to see your new MP.'

Greg manages not to add that, even if that wasn't the case, Frank is a dangerous loony that we don't want anything more to do with – and whose absence from this afternoon's surgery ensures that proceedings are blissfully nutter-free, for once. We even manage to finish on time, and then The Boss goes straight off for a meeting at the Council, so it looks as if the rest of the day is going to be quite peaceful as well.

Famous last words. I am just gathering my notes together and straightening the chairs, when who should walk in, but Frank. My joy truly knows no bounds.

'Oi, you!' he says. 'Where's your boss? No more bloody excuses – I need to see him. *Now*.'

'He isn't here,' I say. 'Surgery has finished and, anyway, you aren't a constituent any longer, so you need to see your own MP. As my colleague has already told you.'

Rational argument is sometimes grossly overrated, not to mention ineffective. When Frank finally accepts that The Boss isn't in the building, he gets me by the throat and backs me against the wall – yet again. That's the third time that he's done it this year.

I have to stand very still, look calm and try to talk him down – not easy when you can hardly breathe – until Greg finally comes to see where I've got to, and catches Frank by surprise, which causes him to lose his grip, thank God. I bet I've got broken veins all over my face.

Before Frank can re-group, I wriggle free and run out of the room, closely followed by Greg. We've only just managed to close the security door in the corridor when Frank starts banging on the glass and shouting, but we don't listen, and we don't look back.

We're too busy staggering upstairs to the office, where we collapse at our desks. I don't know which of us is the more freaked out, but Greg's voice has definitely gone up a couple of octaves.

'You'll have to phone The Boss to tell him what's happened,' he says. 'I can barely talk, I'm so out of breath.'

'*You* can barely talk?' I say. 'I'm the one who was nearly strangled. And you're miles younger than me, so you should be fit enough to handle a few flights of stairs.'

At this, Greg first points out that the Labour Government sold off the playing field at his old school, and then pretends to have lost his voice entirely, so there's no choice but for me to phone Andrew and explain Frank's latest failure to manage his anger.

Andrew waits until I've finished, and then asks me what *I* did to *upset* Frank.

I hang up on him. It's closing time, after all, and there's only so much lunacy a person can take in the course of one day before it starts to become contagious. As it is, it takes me ages to get home from work, as I have to walk sideways to make sure that Frank isn't sneaking up on me from behind.

He isn't, thankfully, so I arrive home in one piece, to find that Max is already there. I've only just begun telling him about my day when he interrupts to tell me all about a 'bunk bed emergency' he had at work, and I never get to finish *my* story. I'm sure Max thinks being a furniture inspector[5] puts *him* on a par with paramedics.

I'm counting to ten, in order to avoid pointing out that, as he works in a shop, he's therefore unlikely to encounter many incidents which would genuinely qualify as *crises*, when the phone starts to ring. It's Greg.

'Have you *heard* all the reports about that MP who was stabbed in his surgery earlier today?' he says.

'No,' I say. 'What happened? Is he dead?'

'No,' says Greg. 'He'll survive, luckily. But now everyone's saying that MPs run terrible risks, and that something has to be done to make them safer!'

'Well, that's true,' I say. 'Isn't it?'

I do *try* to be reasonable, when the opportunity presents itself. Unlike certain other people.

'Yes, but what about us, Molly?' says Greg. 'It's ten years since a caseworker was killed by a constituent, but no one even mentions that! We run the gauntlet of these

---

[5] Furniture inspector: Three jobs in one, not that you'd think so from the salary. One minute Max is selling furniture, the next he's hurtling round to a customer's house to deal with a complaint, or to repair a faulty sofa. It's probably the only job that involves crawling around on the floor wielding power tools while dressed in a suit. (Costs a fortune in dry-cleaning, too.)

loonies every day: get threatened, get assaulted, but that's all okay – because *we're* just the little people. We're *dispensable*!'

'It's worse than that,' I say, all attempts at reasonableness abandoned. 'It's *our* fault we upset the nutters in the first place, remember?'

There is a noise as if Greg is being strangled, and then the phone goes dead. I call him every half-hour for the next two hours, but don't get any reply until, eventually, he sends me a text:

"Molly, I am so filled with hatred that I am dangerous. I am therefore getting drunk enough to post dog poo through the letter-boxes of every mad constituent I can find on my way home from the pub. I may save the biggest piece for The Boss' house."

I've been trying to phone him ever since then, but he still won't answer. Now it's nearly midnight and God knows what he's done. There *have* to be easier jobs than this.

## SATURDAY, 15 MAY

Thank God it's the weekend. I really need a lie-in after yesterday's shenanigans, so of course Dad phones first thing.

After he's given me the usual lecture on immigration – I'm sure he thinks *I'm* the Home Secretary – he finally gets to the point. He's bought himself a laptop on special offer at PC World and is 'planning on becoming a silver surfer'. He says that, if Max and I can use a computer, it *must* be simple.

Over the course of the day, he phones a further fifteen times, demanding to know why he can't send me an email. Each time, I have to turn our computer on to try to replicate what it is that he says that he is doing. We get nowhere, and the whole day is wasted.

At 10.30pm, I realise that he can't send emails because he hasn't got an ISP.[6] Bloody hell, now I have to try to explain to him what *that* is.

## SUNDAY, 16 MAY

I spend the day doing the usual mundane household tasks. Then, by virtue of shameless bribery, I force Josh and Connie to make their duty calls to the extended family.

When I hear Connie earnestly explaining oral sex to Aunty Edith – presumably unasked – I decide to see if I am able to tolerate gin again. Sometimes I think we should have Connie tested for Asperger's, but I'm not sure I'd really want to know the result.

I don't know if Max was listening to Connie, so it *may* be a coincidence but, when we finally fall into bed, we somehow find the energy for our bi-annual shag. It's very nice, and Max wonders aloud why we don't do it more often. I reply that it may have something to do with his love affair with the TV, at which he laughs, as if I was joking.

---

[6] ISP: For other computing incompetents like Dad, an ISP is an Internet Service Provider. If you don't have one, it's a bit like trying to use your phone when you haven't signed up with a phone company, i.e. futile.

Afterwards, there's some blood on the sheets.

'What's this? Have you got your period?' says Max.

'No,' I say, while trying not to panic. 'My hymen probably grew back.'

He doesn't laugh this time, and all restored closeness evaporates at one lash of my tongue. There must be a market somewhere for that kind of deadly weapon.


## MONDAY, 17 MAY

Monday morning, oh joy. God knows why the public think working for an MP must be glamorous.

When I arrive at work, I'm greeted by the sight of a hideous new office-calendar bearing the logo: *Andrew Sinclair MP: Working Hard for Hardworking People*. It features The Boss grinning inanely in front of a block of flats in Easemount.

You can't see the other block, which got burnt out just before Christmas by our regular nutter, Steve Ellington, on the basis that, if *he* was going to have a miserable festive season, then so were all his neighbours.

Greg has Photoshopped the picture to show a bevy of obese, naked women standing behind The Boss. They are also grinning inanely, and improve the photo no end; though it's lucky that Andrew's gone back to the House[7] today, so I won't have to cope with him in the flesh. There's quite enough of *that* on the calendar.

---

[7]House: One way of referring to the House of Commons, which is by far the best place to keep MPs – as far as constituency staff are concerned.

I concentrate on opening the mail. The first letter I open sets the tone for the day:

*Dear Mr Sinclair,*

*I am writing to you because there is a serious problem on Broad Street. I walk down there every day to my job at Economyland, (a girl needs her pin-money, after all), and what should I see at the side of the road today, but a dead rat!*

*This is bad enough, but what I want to know, Mr Sinclair, is what would happen if, when I was walking past one day, the rat were to be struck by a car, be hurled up in the air, and then strike me in the face? Something needs to be done before this happens.*

*Thanks for all you do for hardworking people.*

*Yours, etc.,*

*Pauline Harpenden (Miss)*

Greg thinks it's funny, but I despair: what the *hell* am I supposed to reply to that? There's no one else that I can ask, unless you count The Boss – which I don't, not even when he phones to check if we need him.

After I've said, 'No, thanks,' it turns out that he has a question for me:

'Am I for or against cycle helmets?' he says.

Honestly, no wonder the country's in such a mess when MPs can't even remember where they stand on the simplest issue. Mind you, I bet the Tories and LibDems have no idea where they're supposed to stand on *anything* now, given all the horse-trading over the last few days. Whenever Nick and Dave pop up on the TV, they look knackered and unshaven – though at least they're *supposed* to be able to grow a beard. *I'm* not but, when I get home, I look closely in the mirror for the first time in days, only to see hairs sprouting from my chin. I start plucking them out, but seem to grow another two for every one that I remove, and I can't even see the damn things properly, despite the x25 magnification.

I suppose I'll be able to work as a circus freak when Max notices them and leaves me for someone less hirsute – not that he seems to be concentrating much on me at the moment, anyway. Since Ellen's comments at my birthday party, he's taken to doing sit-ups, every night – much to Josh's amusement, if not to mine.

I think it'll take more than sit-ups, but wisely say nothing, as I am endeavouring to become an enigma. Mum, however, sadly isn't. She phones just before I go to bed to announce her latest affliction – something to do with a painful buttock.

I endure an hour of symptom discussion before she rings off, and then I instruct Josh to shoot me if I *ever* become like my mother. He just raises a meaningful eyebrow.

## TUESDAY, 18 MAY

Our phones don't stop ringing *all day long*. It pains me to admit it, but one of the legacies of thirteen years of a Labour Government seems to have been a huge increase in victim culture. Honestly, the amount of complaining I hear from people with minor problems is incredible.

Mr Franklin phones first thing this morning, to tell me that it's my job to get him his emergency benefit payment 'asap' – as he's going on holiday tomorrow and needs to buy new clothes to take with him. He takes the opportunity to remind me several times that he is 'severely disabled'.

I can't remember the last time Max and I could afford a holiday, but it *must* be more than ten years ago – and yet here's Mr Franklin off on yet another bloody jaunt. I wouldn't mind so much, but the *only* thing wrong with him is that he's hugely fat. I do wish he wouldn't talk with his mouth full, too.

God knows how many meals he consumes during today's conversation but, eventually, I manage to get rid of him by agreeing to phone the Benefits Agency to emphasise his need for outsized Hawaiian shirts.

'Make sure you do it today,' he says. 'It's an emergency, after all.'

Then he hangs up, and the phone rings again immediately, but this time the caller is an elderly man who introduces himself as George Bradley, from Silverhill. Then he apologises profusely for 'bothering' his MP, but says that he wonders if there is anything we can do to help him, as he's getting nowhere by himself. Both literally and metaphorically, as it turns out.

The poor man had his leg amputated months ago, but the hospital seems to have forgotten to arrange ambulance transport to take him to his follow-up appointments

15

– which means that Mr Bradley hasn't even been able to get his prosthetic leg fitted yet.

'It's not *all* bad,' he says. 'The grandchildren love it when I fall over, but it is making caring for my wife a little tricky. She's got Alzheimer's, you know.'

Honestly, first Mr Bloody Franklin describes his lack of holiday clothes as an emergency, and then someone like Mr Bradley is embarrassed to have to ask The Boss for help. Sometimes I think the world is going mad. How much people complain seems to be in inverse proportion to the severity of the problems that they face – and this includes The Boss, who's doing nothing *but* today.

He phones every few minutes to moan about everything: having to sit on the 'wrong' side of the Commons Chamber;[8] the Speaker ignoring him, and the fact that he still hasn't managed to persuade the Commons authorities to move his office out of Portcullis House,[9] and back into the HOC[10] itself.

[8] The 'wrong' side of the Commons Chamber: The government sits on the benches to the right of the Speaker of the House of Commons, so when a party loses an election, they have to switch sides from right to left. The Boss isn't enjoying being on the left half as much as his political views might suggest.

[9] Portcullis House, also known as PCH: A fancy new building to house MPs and their staff, after they ran out of space in the Palace of Westminster. The Boss feels very cheated to have been allocated a 'pathetically small' office in PCH, and retains a fondness for the additional leg-room offered by his old office in the HOC. Some people are never satisfied.

[10] HOC: Usual way staff refer to the House of Commons in writing, for example in diary entries, such as, 'Boss to HOC today. TG.' (TG stands for 'thank God', though The Boss is unaware of that.)

He even starts complaining that the girls in the London office take up too much room, because their legs get in his way. As far as I can remember, it was primarily the length (and shape) of their legs that persuaded him to employ them in the first place, so I don't exactly have much sympathy, especially when he makes it sound as if they should get *their* legs amputated to avoid causing him further inconvenience.

'You should think yourself lucky your office hasn't been moved into a broom cupboard,' I say. 'Given the Party's less-than-resounding success in the general election.'

'Well, that's where that bloody idiot Gordy's new office should be, then,' says Andrew, who never hesitates to apportion blame. 'And, anyway, I can't spend all day talking to you. I have a cunning plan to disrupt the Coalition.'

When he explains that this involves nothing more than giving disorientated new MPs misleading directions, I congratulate him on his maturity – and he hangs up on me.

'Hopefully, he's the *only* delinquent we'll have to deal with today,' I say to Greg, who replies, 'Don't tempt fate.'

Ten minutes later, I get a call from Josh's tutor, who says that Josh is to be in detention this afternoon, 'for leaving class mid-lesson for no reason, and being obstreperous when told off'.

I demand an explanation from Josh when I get home from work, whereupon he informs me that the teacher

17

is a 'f*ckwit who doesn't understand the meaning of the word "emergency"'.

'Tell me about it,' I say, which Josh misinterprets as a sign that he should continue to explain.

Apparently, he had 'no choice' but to rush out of the classroom when he noticed the words '*Josh Bennett is gay*' written in large letters on the wall outside the window; and he obviously considers this slight on his heterosexuality to have more than justified his impromptu exit. He is incredulous that anyone should have found a reason to object.

'I went straight back to class, anyway,' he says. 'As soon as I'd finished painting it out.'

*Painting* it out? Am I raising a member of the underclass? Why would Josh even *possess* a can of spray-paint, let alone keep one in his rucksack for so-called emergencies? On this evidence, my son could be a vandal, or involved in a gang war – not that Max is any help with either scenario.

'Can you please deal with your son?' I say, at which he laughs, and pats Josh on the shoulder. Things are rather frosty after that, until Max falls asleep on the sofa, and I begin to check my emails.

Greg has sent me a link to an old article about the cost of air-lifting an extremely obese man from his home, to enable him to attend a hospital appointment. 'This'll be Mr Franklin next, Molly,' he says. 'And we taxpayers will be the ones paying for it!'

Oh, good God. Are Greg and I becoming fascists, or worse, Tories? It's *very* worrying indeed.

## WEDNESDAY, 19 MAY

I risk the country being unable to cope without me and leave work early, because I have to go to the doctor's for a smear test on my way home.

How on earth are you supposed to make conversation in a casual, relaxed way with your knees apart and your bits on display? I chat about the weather for a few minutes, but then my voice just trails away to nothing, while I try to pretend that I am not talking to someone while wearing nothing at all on my bottom half.

I don't think this is what the nurse is referring to when she asks me whether I've noticed anything unusual, though – so I decide I'd better mention the blood last time Max and I had sex. I suppose I could have just mentioned the *sex*, but that doesn't occur to me at the time.

'How often has this happened?' she says.

'Once,' I say, which is a dual-purpose answer, as I'm not quite sure whether she's referring to the blood, or the sex. You can't work for a politician for ten years without learning the value of the dual-purpose answer.

'Oh,' she says, in a meaningful way, and then tells me that she'll refer me to a gynaecologist for further investigation. *There's* something to look forward to.

When I eventually get home, I'm still so distracted that I put a pack of sanitary towels in the fridge, and forget to be cross with Josh, the nascent gang lord. I even wave to Annoying Ellen by accident so *that'll* just encourage her and, before you know it, she'll be popping round again to 'borrow a corkscrew'. How an

19

alcoholic can manage without one of their own, God only knows.

I quite fancy a gin myself, but Max looks disapproving when I suggest it. *He's* still on his keep-fit mission, though I can't say I've noticed any difference so far.

## THURSDAY, 20 MAY

Good God, I wonder how many other candidates there'll be for the leadership of the Labour Party by the end of the week? They're coming out of the woodwork in droves, while trying to pretend that they're all part of one big happy family, which I don't think anyone believes.

I don't, anyway – not considering the state of mine. Honestly, the press have no idea what they're talking about. They keep bemoaning the death of the extended family, but what they don't say is that it's just become *over-extended*, due to divorce, leaving people like me with no choice but to spend all our leisure time phoning parental figures, in an endlessly repeating loop.

First you feel guilty for not phoning any of them, but then you phone one and immediately feel guilty that you haven't phoned the other. Before you know it, that's the whole evening gone. I sometimes think it would be much easier to be an orphan; but then *that* makes me feel guilty too.

I wouldn't mind so much, if feeling guilty didn't always give me hiccups – and, anyway, when your job involves spending all day taking calls from the usual suspects, you don't perceive having a 'nice long chat on the phone' during your time off as a good thing, no matter *who* it's with.

Today's been fairly quiet on the call front, though, so by the time I get home from work I am less horrified by the sight of a phone than usual. I'd better call Mum and capitalise on this rare state of affairs – or, on second thoughts, maybe not. It's Dad's turn, so I try him first.

'I went to B&Q today,' he says. 'Never going there again on a Thursday. Bloody awful, it was.'

'Why?' I say, somewhat bemused.

'Full of bloody wrinklies,' he says. He is *seventy-five*, for God's sake.

After he has explained to me exactly what is wrong with the country – *and* asked me a hundred incomprehensible questions about the apparent foibles of his new computer – I finally manage to get him off the phone. One hour and forty-five minutes exactly.

I need three consecutive cigarettes before I can handle phoning Mum. She is unavailable – something to do with the painful buttock again – so Ted chats to me for five polite, step-fatherly minutes, and then that's it. *Result*!

It's only 10:45pm. If I put off calling Stepmother Mark II until tomorrow night, I might catch the end of *Question Time*[11] and be able to vent the day's aggression by shouting at the TV.

So much for best-laid plans, that's all I can say. I miss *QT* when Dad phones back with 'a quick computer

---

[11] Question Time, also known as QT: Weekly BBC television programme in which various ministers and MPs debate the hot political issues of the day. Or not. Compulsory viewing for MPs' staff, as all constituents watch it and want to discuss its high and low points the following morning. Usually forewarned is forearmed.

question'. Two hours later, I log on to Amazon, and buy a copy of *PCs for Dummies*.

I arrange for it to be sent directly to Dad, labelled: 'A gift from a well-wisher.'

## FRIDAY, 21 MAY

Greg says he ran into his ex-girlfriend last night, so he spends most of the morning in a decline in the Oprah room,[12] before returning to his desk and typing 'creative methods of revenge' into Google.

'You need to get over her,' I say. '*And* move out of your mum's house, while you're at it. No wonder you haven't had a girlfriend since.'

'Recovering from a broken heart takes time' says Greg, 'as does getting rid of a hint of man-boob. I still can't believe she dumped me for *that*.'

'I thought it was because she was cheating on you,' says The Boss, ignoring my warning glance. 'And, anyway, being single's great. It's the best guarantee of an active sex-life, isn't it, Molly?'

There should be a law against mocking the afflicted. We *do* have feelings, too.

## SATURDAY, 22 MAY

Sam arrives first thing to stay for the weekend. We haven't

[12] The Oprah room: The political equivalent of a green room, though ours is a shade of bilious yellow. (The Boss chose the paint, which proves he's colour blind, as if you couldn't already tell that from his hair.) It's supposedly used for holding informal meetings with journalists, lobbyists and the occasional sane constituent. Supposedly.

seen him since my ghastly birthday party, and of course Max hasn't phoned him at all since then.

How can you call someone your best friend when you never bother to contact them? Not that this stops Max acting as if he's delighted to see Sam, and slapping him on the shoulder in the weirdly repressed way that men do.

Sam slaps back, but I reckon he only puts up with Max's neglect because he *still* hasn't got a girlfriend. Now he's joined an internet dating site and wants me to check his profile for its woman-appeal.

I'd rate it at zero, unless honesty is no longer a desirable quality. Sam's claiming to be a non-smoker (!); a moderate drinker (only true if compared to Annoying Ellen), and he's put 'University' in the education section. In response to my raised eyebrow, he mutters, 'University of *Life*.'

His photograph is terrible too – he looks like a middle-aged woman with a really bad haircut. Why do so many men insist on growing their hair once they get to a certain age? Thank God Max isn't one of them – I'd wield the scissors while he slept, if necessary. (I've always quite liked the name, Delilah, now I come to think of it.)

It's not just Sam(son)'s hair that ruins the photo, either. For some unaccountable reason, his neck is swathed in a scarf that could almost be one of those hideous pashmina things that everyone but me seems to be wearing. (Everyone female, and of my age, that is.) Maybe this is part of his attempt to appear metrosexual? In the 'About Me' section, he's written a load of pseudo-sensitive stuff that completely belies the fact that he's about as un-reconstructed as you can get.

I'm still trying to find a subtle way to tell him that his profile and photo are rubbish, and that he's doomed to permanent bachelorhood, when he announces that fifteen women have already contacted him in the three days since he registered on the site. *Fifteen!* Why do I find that so depressing? (And, talking of middle-aged women – which I was, though admittedly ten minutes ago – does my birthday mean that *I've* officially become middle-aged?)

If I have, I bet no one would be interested in dating *me*. I'd have to lie about my age, and smear Vaseline all over the camera lens before I took the picture for my profile. It's different for men, obviously. They can be as old as the hills and women still want to date them. Even men as old as Dad – according to Dinah, anyway.

She calls to tell me that she's positive that *he* has taken up internet dating now, and says she bases this assumption on the fact that he seems to be sending emails very late at night. 'And he sounds suspiciously cheerful when you talk to him, too,' she says. 'So it's either that, or he's becoming obsessed with online porn.'

Good God. Is everyone having sex, apart from me? (Rhetorical question – don't answer that.)

### SUNDAY, 23 MAY

Some excitement at last! When I log on to the computer this morning, I find a private message on Facebook from someone called Johnny Hunter – who seems to remember that we had a night of passion behind the Science block, after the fifth-year end-of-term disco.

There's no photo on his profile, and the 'about' section is helpfully blank, so I send a brief reply, in the hope that it won't be too obvious that I can't remember who the hell he is.

I forget to tell Max about it, as he and Sam have been to the pub for a so-called quickie before lunch and are incapable of intelligent conversation by the time they get home. They don't seem to realise this, though, so I leave them to bore each other to tears while I walk into town. I shall have a sober wander around the shops instead.

Mainly stationery shops, given that I want to buy a packet of gold stars, like the ones that Connie and Josh's primary school teachers used to stick in their school books, in recognition of particularly good pieces of work.

I'm not intending to reward quality so much as quantity, myself. The latter's as important as the former in some situations – like how often Max and I are having sex. So, when I get home, I open the dog-eared packet of stars I finally found at the back of a shelf in Ryman, stick one onto the calendar and put the rest in the kitchen drawer.

There seem to be an awful lot of stars left unused but, luckily, Mum distracts me from thinking about this when she phones with an update on her health. She's getting Ted to tow her around the house on a tea-tray now, as her buttock hurts if she walks. I *really* hope it's not hereditary.

## MONDAY, 24 MAY

In the morning, Greg and I are under orders to represent The Boss at a public meeting to reassure constituents that the powers-that-be are *tackling* anti-social behaviour – as opposed to simply wringing their hands and despairing about it.

Greg arrives before I do, and sends me a text:

"Molly, you're late. Meet me in the lobby. I will be staring intently at the circus of freaks, losers, the mad, the bad and the weak who pay our wages."

Even though this description doesn't really apply to most of the audience, for once, the meeting's ghastly anyway. It's impossible to answer hostile questions realistically while constrained by political correctness, let alone while having to contend with Greg's increasingly demented texts. I can't even kick him, because he's sitting four places away from me, holding his mobile underneath the table and typing away furiously while wearing his usual angelic expression. I do wish he'd cut that out whenever we're on public display.

He stresses me out so much that, eventually, I'm driven to my own version of anti-social behaviour and sneak out for a cigarette, joining the crowd of teenagers hanging around outside. I end up chatting to them – *hug a hoodie*, as Dave Blancmange Face[13] would say – and they tell me that they aren't too happy about recent calls to ban smokers from standing outside pubs.

[13] Dave Blancmange Face: Connie's name for David Cameron. What it lacks in respect for one's elders, it makes up for in accuracy, or so Max claims.

They want to know why drunks aren't to be banned as well.

They've got a point, now I come to think of it. Smokers don't go around beating people up on their way home from a night's smoking, *or* vomit all over the pavements. So that's decided it – I'm definitely not giving up my bad habit, just because a hypocritical ex-government has told me to.

Especially when The Boss hasn't given up either, and he *voted* for the smoking ban.

## TUESDAY, 25 MAY

Why, why, *why* don't I work at Westminster? Everyone there is spending today basking in the excitement of the State Opening of Parliament. Meanwhile, it's Groundhog Day here in the provinces.

All the usual suspects phone first thing, including Miss Chambers. We need noise limiters like they have in call centres, because that woman is slowly but surely wrecking my hearing.

Now she thinks her next-door neighbours are stealing her electricity. She wants them arrested, and if she doesn't get what she wants, she'll scream and scream until she makes herself sick – and renders me deaf. That is, if I listen to her, which I have absolutely no intention of doing. Unlike some people, I learn from experience.

So, while Miss Chambers works herself up to full volume, I put the phone down on the desk and head for the kitchen, where I make a coffee and eat one of Greg's chocolate biscuits – but she's still screaming when

I've finished that, so then I go outside and have a cigarette.

I take my time but, even so, she's still at it when I
stick my head back into my office to check; so then
I decide that I may as well go to the loo and experiment
with my new miracle-working mascara while I'm there.
(It doesn't work miracles at all, I'm disappointed to
report.)

Anyway, when I've finally run out of places to go and
things to do, I resort to blocking her out by listening to
Greg's iPod, which I've just found under the sofa in the
Oprah room.

I'm having quite a good time, dancing around my desk
and miming into the stapler, until Greg comes in from
the outer office, removes one of my headphones and says,
'For Christ's sake, Mol – is that Miss C? Can't you get
her off the phone? I can hear her at my bloody desk.'

'Oh, sorry,' I say. 'Hang on. I'll put Plan B into
operation.'

I approach the handset – with extreme caution – and
pick it up, while holding it well away from me. Then I
start making whistling and chirping noises, which I follow
by banging the phone on the desk a few times.

After that, I put the mouthpiece carefully to my lips
while swivelling the earpiece away from my ear. 'Hello?
*Hello?* Miss Chambers? I can't hear you, I'm afraid.'

This is a complete lie, as the whole building can hear
the damned woman by now. No wonder most agencies
have stopped accepting her calls. I'd ban them, too, if
The Boss wasn't so worried about losing a vote. (He

never believes me when I remind him that Miss C always votes Conservative.)

I put the phone down again, just in time. It's a fine art, but then I've had a lot of practice.

'Listen to me, Molly Whatever-Your-Name-Is – you *stupid* woman!'

The phone vibrates and rattles against the desk with that last statement, delivered in Miss Chambers' convincing version of a sonic boom. Greg looks at me, then I look back at him and nod. It's time for the last act in this all-too-familiar performance.

'Oh,' I say, into the receiver. 'This phone's not working. We've been cut off.'

Then I slam the phone down, and switch it to answer-phone, quickly, before Miss C rings back. There is a loud chorus of '*Barking!*' from all the surrounding offices, coupled with sustained applause. It's satisfying, but only momentarily, and I wish, not for the first time, that I had a nice little job somewhere like Tesco.

Maybe I could *get* a job at Tesco? At least then I might meet some people during the working day who weren't actually certifiable. I decide to take an early lunch-break, to explore my options. It is nearly 11:00am, after all.

So much for *that* idea. Apparently, Tesco don't need any new employees, so I cheer myself up by spending far too much in Primark, as per usual. I often wonder if it might be an idea to buy fewer clothes at a higher price, but always rule this out pretty quickly. Miss Chambers equals daily stress, which equals the need for immediate retail therapy – so shopping anywhere other than Primark would bankrupt me. Maybe I could get a job *in* Primark, and cut Miss Chambers out of the equation?

I am cheered by this prospect until I return to my desk, to find twenty-eight messages on the answer-phone. I was only gone for an hour, for God's sake! Nineteen are from Miss Chambers, becoming ever more glass-shattering with every one.

The other nine are from The Boss, who wants to know if there's anything we need to speak to him about. There isn't, as always – so I'd better find him something safe and uncontroversial to do for the rest of the day, before he gets bored and starts giving opinions to the press on anything they ask.

With the thought of *that* terrifying possibility, today is fast shaping up to be a double Primark day . . . I wonder what they pay their staff? It can't possibly be much less than I earn now, but I suppose I really ought to check.

I phone the union, and ask how my earnings compare to shop work.

'Well, as you're one of the very lowest-paid employees on the House of Commons payroll, Molly, I'd get that Primark application in pronto, if I were you,' says Martin, rather too brightly if you ask me.

I'm so stunned that I put the phone down without even remembering to say goodbye. One of the lowest paid? *Lowest* paid? In the *whole* House of Commons? A place full of cleaners and catering staff, many imported from the Philippines, and yet I have the honour of being the *lowest* paid? For putting up with the likes of Miss Chambers all day?

I am collecting a Primark application form on my way home, if they're still open then. I have a degree and specialist training, and I am too damned good to be working for an MP.

## WEDNESDAY, 26 MAY

I'm almost too depressed to write. Primark has no vacancies – and all that discount's gone out of the window as well. It looks as if I'm stuck with The Boss for the foreseeable future, or at least until IPSA's[14] cuts cost me my job.

To make things worse, Mr Beales writes in with yet another problem – the third one in the last ten days. One of his clients won't pay for her wedding photographs, and Mr Beales encloses copies to illustrate his point. After I've taken a look at them, I'm not surprised the poor woman won't pay: a number of the guests are headless, along with the groom.

I *am* surprised by one new development, however – Greg and I have always thought that Mr Beales was a *school* photographer. He seemed well suited for this, in that he most closely resembles a paedophile or, at best, a serial killer. (Greg says that all paedophiles are easily identified by the double bar across the bridge of their metal-framed glasses.)

Anyway, whatever he is, I really can't be bothered with Mr Beales today, so I just dump his letter and photos into the otherwise-empty filing tray marked 'Show to The Boss'.

[14] IPSA: Independent Parliamentary Standards Authority, set up in the wake of the MPs' expenses scandal, with the sole purpose of making life difficult, according to The Boss.

The rest of the day passes without incident until, in the evening, I get another email from Johnny Hunter. A long one, this time suggesting I reply to his email address at work – and the tone is very friendly, if a little boastful. He's only an *International Director* for a global oil company!

He's also married, with four children much younger than mine, which is presumably why he and his wife have managed rather more impressive careers than working for a backbench MP.

Johnny goes on to say that it is 'the help' that enables him and his wife to keep flying across the globe with their demanding jobs, by ensuring that their children are well-cared for at the same time. He also says that he can't afford to downsize to spend more time with his family, as 'you know what school fees are like'.

I am a gutless hypocrite. I do not say in my reply that of course I do *not* know, because I am politically (and financially) opposed to private schools; work for a *Labour* MP, and have put both my kids through the wringer of the state school system *because it teaches them important life skills*. (Well, that's what Max and I always tell our posh friends anyway – we don't mention Josh's gang lord credentials.)

In response to Johnny, I just wimp out and sympathise with his difficulty, as if I understand it all too well. What on earth is *wrong* with me? I have about as much idea of what his life is like as he probably has of mine, though I bet *his* wife doesn't shop at Primark.

I still have no idea what he looks like, either – though I'm hoping he was that nice one with the dark hair and really blue eyes who used to catch the school bus with me. I'd better check if he wears glasses now, though, and – if so – what the frames are like. You can't be too careful, in this day and age.

## THURSDAY, 27 MAY

I have cheered up slightly. One of the girls in Primark tells me that they don't get staff discount, because the clothes are so cheap already.

However, my good mood doesn't last past lunchtime, when Greg throws a dart at The Boss' picture (displayed on the dartboard hidden in the archive cupboard) and it misfires, leaving me with no choice but to take him to A&E.[15]

Now he has an eye-patch, and sang Gabrielle songs in the car *all* the way home. My ears feel as if they're bleeding. I wouldn't mind, but that's not the end of today's medical emergencies.

'I had to go to the doctor today,' says Dad.

'Good God, what's the matter?' I say.

You can say this to Dad. You never, *ever*, say it to Mum, unless you have nothing to do for the rest of your life – but Dad never goes to the doctor.

'Well, I had an erection when I woke up—' he says, before I manage to interrupt.

'*Way* too much information,' I say.

'Well, your father's all man.' Dad pauses while I make

[15] A&E: Accident and Emergency, the equivalent of a home-from-home for me, what with a colleague like Greg and a son like Josh.

a vomiting noise, and then continues, 'And, anyway, when I looked down, there it was – all bent.'

'What?' I say. (I really should know better by now.)

'Bent. My pe—'

'Yeah, okay. Do we *have* to go into this?' I say, feeling somewhat desperate.

'Just listen now, Molly. This is interesting, especially as you work in politics.'

Dad might be right, actually. I'll be *fascinated* to know what a bent willy has to do with politics. Not to mention how it persuaded him to visit his doctor on the day it occurred, unlike any of the genuine emergencies he's ignored in the past.

'Well, the angle it was at made my penis look foreshortened,' says Dad, as if that explains everything. Which I suppose it probably does.

'So what exactly is wrong with you?' I say.

'Peroni's Disease. That's what Bill Clinton had, so I'm not too worried now. It obviously doesn't affect performance.'

On that pseudo-political note, Dad rings off, while I wonder why a bent willy would be named after a fizzy beer.

I look it up online and, having discovered that the correct spelling is *Peyronie's,* I'm hoping that this will be the last that I hear of Dad's bent appendage tonight, but Dinah makes sure there's no chance of that.

'Have you *spoken* to Dad?' she screams down the phone. 'Disgusting! He's *disgusting*. You'll never guess what he's just told me—'

'Yes, Dinah, I know. He's already phoned me,' I say. 'So you really don't have to—'

'But don't you think he's *disgusting*?' she shrieks.

Honestly, I may as well not have said anything at all. Nothing stops Dinah when she's in full flow.

'We should bloody well report him to someone. Imagine ringing up your daughters and telling them about your bent willy! Don't you think we should report him for child abuse, or something like that?'

'Dinah,' I say, lighting yet another cigarette, 'has it occurred to you that both you and I are technically middle-aged? I don't think child abuse would apply.'

'*Middle-aged?*' she yells; and then she hangs up. Sometimes you'd swear my sister's in as much denial about the passing of time, as she is about the absence of her husband, John. She says he'll be back, 'as soon as he's accepted the need for self-improvement', but I doubt he will. He told me he'd had more than enough of Dinah's 'helpful hints'.

Imagine being interrupted every five minutes while you're having sex, by someone saying things like, 'Top tip: get your bearings first'! Max says he'd rather not.

'It's no wonder Di and John only had one child, is it?' he says, as he makes room for me on the sofa with an obvious sigh – initially of relief, and then of irritation, when the phone starts ringing yet again.

'My buttock's still terribly painful,' says Mum, apropos a greeting.

*Christ!* Both parents obsessed by their rear ends. It's all too much.

**FRIDAY, 28 MAY**

God, I'm depressed. Not only is it Friday, which means that The Boss is here almost all day for his surgery and a seemingly endless series of largely pointless meetings, but I have just worked out that, if I am one of the lowest-paid members of staff on the whole HOC payroll, then that must mean that *Greg* is being paid more than me.

He's half my age, *and* a f*ckwit – a lovable one, admittedly, but I still have to open all his supposedly finished letters when he's not looking and vet them before I take them to the post.

This is a precautionary measure, brought in after last year's debacle when Greg libelled the LibDem councillor, and then gave the poor man's home address to our most violent constituent; and yet *he* is worth more money than me? I think I may have to go on strike.

I'm a little reluctant to risk direct action, given that there *is* a recession on, but that doesn't seem to be stopping everyone else – so I phone Martin and ask him if the union will support me with a mass walk-out if I do strike for a decent wage.

The answer's not exactly what I hoped. Martin will apparently be behind me 'one hundred per cent in spirit', but asks if I realise that the union has *no* authority over individual MPs – as they are each, effectively, separate small businesses.

When I've stopped hyperventilating at this unexpected news, I ask Martin a number of questions, not least of which is why I've been bothering to pay my union subs for all these years. He seems oddly reluctant to answer, but says that, as The Boss is a left-wing socialist, I surely don't need the union to persuade *him* to do the right thing, anyway. How can a union rep be so bloody naive?

The only highlight of the day is another email from Johnny Hunter, even though he sounds very unimpressed with my job. So am I at the moment, but I would like him to *pretend* that my working life is slightly more significant in the scheme of things.

I suppose working for an MP isn't ever likely to sound very impressive to an International Director of a Global Oil Company – I do like that phrase, hence the random capital letters. Johnny probably has hundreds of MPs in his pocket, metaphorically speaking, of course.

It's just a shame that The Boss is unlikely to be powerful enough to merit being one of them, otherwise Johnny might be able to use his influence to get me a pay-rise. It doesn't look as if the union's going to be much help with that.

## SATURDAY, 29 MAY

I do wish The Boss wouldn't phone me on Saturdays. Or at least not ten times, and not in order to say the same thing on every occasion, even if he *is* enjoying gossiping about the latest parliamentary sex scandal more than is good for him.

If Nan was still alive, she'd tell him that pride comes before a fall, but I can't be bothered to advise him not to tempt fate – I'm too busy worrying about the night out that Max has planned, even though it's all my fault for complaining that we have no social life.

I've just found out that we're due to meet his colleagues at a bar, which coincidentally happens to be Josh's favourite drinking place. This is not promising, as it means that all the women there will be significantly younger than me, if not under-age; and there'll be acres of highly toned flesh scattered with strategically placed piercings. I shall look like an ageing fish out of water, and Josh will probably mention that *no years back for your birthday* thing again.

'What do you think I should wear?' I say to Max – without much optimism, if I'm honest, but you never know.

'Oh, anything, darling,' he says. 'You always look nice.'

This feels like shorthand for *I can't be bothered to think about it*, and is no help whatsoever, so there's nothing for it but a trying-on session. Also known as a triumph of hope over experience, like all Dad's marriages so far.

The first outfit I try is too dated, even for me; and the next causes *mutton* and *lamb* to spring to mind – simultaneously, which takes some doing – and that's just the start of the horror. My knees seem to have become baggy overnight, so that rules out most of my dresses; half of which are also too low-cut. When did my *chest* develop wrinkles?

I keep going in the face of adversity, until I have ruled out almost everything I own, by which time all my clothes are in a heap on the bed, and we are already late. So I cobble together an outfit designed primarily for invisibility, and then slap some make-up on my face. Never

38

experiment when you're under pressure. A sample sachet of foundation that I found in one of Connie's magazines causes hundreds of new wrinkles to erupt, so then I wash it off again.

Connie phones, Dad phones, and Mum phones. One eye is still without make-up, and now it's almost 9:30pm.

'How does this look?' I ask Max.

He doesn't move his eyes from the television. 'Fine, darling.'

Oh, *honestly*! I have a large gin, and then Max looks at his watch, says, 'Christ!' and rushes upstairs, shouting, 'What do you think *I* should wear?'

'Anything will do,' I say, as innocently as I can. 'You *always* look fine to me.'

This is rapidly revealed to be untrue. Max puts on everything that happens to be clean, which results in a strange, multi-seasonal mix of linen, denim and wool – all in completely different shades of washed-out black and navy. He looks almost as bad as me.

It takes him a further ten minutes to find his shoes under a pile of smelly laundry. By now, it's 10:30pm, and I decide to lie on the couch and watch television instead. I suspect my partying days are over.

### SUNDAY, 30 MAY

I want to be a teenager again, especially since last night's disaster. They have so much more fun than adults, despite their superficial angst. And it's not just the constant sex and the taut bodies that I envy, but also the things that they think of to do – *and* have the nerve to carry out.

Josh can create anarchy from the most mundane of tasks.

He decides to join me and Max when we go food shopping today and asks if his best friend Robbie can come along, too – presumably because they're both intent upon what they apparently call 'Shopping for Others'.

Max and I watch in disbelief as the boys spend the next hour or so happily putting things into the shopping trolleys of complete strangers when the latter aren't looking. We don't know what to do with ourselves when an elderly spinster heads for the checkouts with twenty packets of condoms and some Durex Play gel in hers; and a butch body-builder type looks puzzled at finding lipstick, eye shadow and tampons amidst his other purchases.

The most stressful moment comes when I notice a large leg of pork being covertly added to the contents of a trolley belonging to a hijab-clad middle-aged woman, at which point Max decides enough is enough and calls a halt. I think he secretly enjoys the whole experience as much as I do, though, because he's still laughing when we reach the car park.

'That's what *we* need,' I say. 'More excitement in our lives.'

Max nods in agreement, rather too vigorously for my liking, but doesn't make any suggestions as to how this laudable aim might be achieved. Then, once we've unpacked the shopping, he turns the television on, and is fast asleep within ten minutes.

Just the *thought* of excitement is probably enough to

have tired him out, unlike Johnny *International Director of a Global Oil Company* Hunter, who tells me that *he's* been away for the last few days, globetrotting across Eastern Europe again. Apparently, this wasn't as enjoyable as it sounds, or so he claims.

He says that Johnny *hates* hotel rooms, and wonders whether I do too. I've only ever stayed in a really posh hotel once, and that was on my wedding night, when Dad accompanied Max and I upstairs to our room after the reception, and then waltzed inside when we carelessly opened the door a little too wide.

After he'd made himself comfortable on the bed, he proceeded to order blithely from room service, while asking our advice on how to 'manage Dinah and her tantrums'. Max and I finally got rid of him at 3:00am, so we weren't even earning gold stars on our wedding night, which probably should have been seen as a portent of things to come. Or not, if you'll forgive the pun.

It's not as if I even get to stay in decent hotels because of work. At conference,[16] we're lucky to get booked into a broom cupboard – so I have no experience of the high-life at all, which does rather lessen the sympathy I feel for Johnny.

He and I have nothing whatsoever in common, now I come to think of it; and, to make matters worse, he wants to know what I look like these days, and whether I still have 'that amazing hair and those incredible legs'.

---

[16] Conference: The Labour Party Conference/bunfight/scene of some of The Boss' worst social faux pas.

I seriously doubt it, but I'm more worried by the fact that I still can't remember who on earth he is.

He could turn out to be the human equivalent of a surprise leg of pork: a crazed internet stalker or – even worse – a constituent playing mind games. That *would* be far too much excitement, even if it would be just my luck.

## MONDAY, 31 MAY

The weather's getting warmer, so now we have to listen to Annoying Ellen's sex-life on a regular basis. She *must* be pretending she's enjoying it. I've never heard anyone make so much noise in my life.

I thought one of her toy-boys was killing her the first time she started yelling like that, but now I think she's just doing it to get attention, especially as she's pushed her bed in front of the window – which she makes a point of opening before she *entertains*.

Max seems to be spending a long time in the garden in the evenings, watering the plants – or so he says. He comes back indoors with a stupid, dreamy look on his face. Honestly, men are such suckers. Why can't Ellen just die – preferably in silence?

At least she's reminded me about the gold stars, though, so I decide to have a very early night in the hope of persuading Max that we should earn another one. My plan is going very well too until I make the fatal mistake of mentioning the stars, after we get into bed.

'What?' he says. 'You're awarding marks for performance now?'

'No, of course I'm not,' I say, though I'd probably have done better to omit the 'of course' from that sentence. Max glares at me, then waits to hear what I come up with next.

'I'm carrying out a sociological study,' I say. 'Which will be of immense value to market researchers who have to assess how often the nation is having sex.'

'For God's sake, Mol,' he says. 'I bet other people's wives don't keep records.'

'Probably too busy doing it,' I say – at which Max emits an unfeasibly loud sigh, and then turns his back on me. He starts snoring almost immediately, so no stars are earned tonight for any reason.

It takes me ages to fall asleep and, even when I do, I doze fitfully for an hour before waking up in a panic. *Now* I know who Ellen reminds me of – a blonde James Blunt!

It's a question that has been bugging me for weeks, but sometimes ignorance is bliss. If Max fancies Ellen, and Ellen looks exactly like a man, does this mean that Max is gay, and is *that* why we have no sex? Oh, my God.

# CHAPTER TWO

## *June*

(Which, appropriately enough, rhymes with 'loon'.)

**TUESDAY, 1 JUNE**

Greg tries very hard to distract me from worrying about Max and the blonde James Blunt by spending the morning holding forth about how badly MPs' staff are paid. (Some of us rather more than others, actually.) Then, in the afternoon, he proposes his latest economic theory: that every pound he pays in tax goes direct to Liverpool to be spent on shell-suits.

'Maybe you should check that with the Chancellor of the Exchequer before you broadcast it to anyone else,' I say. 'Just to make sure that you're right about it.'

'Don't be silly, Molly,' says Greg. 'I'd be accused of being politically incorrect if I did that. Which I'm not – am I?'

'No,' I say, not because he isn't, but because it's obviously the answer that is required. Never say I don't try my best to give people what they want – unless their name is Mr Beales.

*He* phones just before the office closes for the day. 'Has your boss written my reference for the court yet?' he says.

'What reference?' I say, but then wish I hadn't. There are some things a person is far better off not knowing. Such as the fact that Andrew has – apparently – agreed to write to the judge on Mr Beales' behalf.

'But why?' I say. (I can't help myself.) 'What on earth has he agreed to do *that* for?'

'To confirm the excellence of my photographs, of course,' says Mr Beales, who may be the world's worst photographer, but who still knows far more about the subject than Andrew does.

## WEDNESDAY, 2 JUNE
I am reading the local paper for references (favourable or otherwise) to The Boss, when I come across the wedding photographs section. There are twelve photos, mainly of plumpish, blonde-streaked women marrying shiny-faced, gel-haired men. Four couples are, however, headless.

I look at the picture credits. Sure enough, the decapitated newly-weds are attributed to one Edmund Beales, so I photocopy the page and fax it to the House of Commons – marked for the urgent attention of The Boss – together with a copy of the draft reference for Mr B. I scrawl, 'Re-think advised' across the top.

Then Greg takes the original page from the paper,

masks out the credits with dollops of Tippex, and sticks it onto the wall. He says that, from now on, our team-building activity will no longer be darts, with a photo of The Boss denoting the bull's-eye, as this is 'too dangerous to hardworking people'. (Greg's eye-patch is still in place.) From now on, the game is to be: *Guess which Photos Are the Work of Mr Beales?*

After the next five people to visit the office identify the correct photographs without any hesitation, Greg admits defeat, and heads for the pub for a medicinal gin. Upon his return, he decides to avoid further references to the abject failure of the Mr Beales game by decreeing that we will watch PMQs[17] online.

The whole Commons Chamber is already full of MPs hoping to appear dynamic in front of their constituents on live television. We can't find The Boss, though, until I finally spot him half-way along the opposition benches. He is sitting slumped in his seat.

'Oh, Christ,' says Greg.

We both know all too well what usually happens next, so I send Andrew a text saying, 'Sit up straight!'

Within the next five minutes Mr Beales, Miss Chambers and Miss Harpenden all phone to complain that The

---

[17] PMQs: For those of you lucky enough to be uninitiated, this stands for Prime Minister's Questions. Misleading, as the Prime Minister (PM) doesn't get to ask any questions, other than rhetorical ones. Instead, his acolytes ask him prepared questions along the lines of, "Would the PM agree that he is the best thing to happen to the country since sliced bread?" while the opposition ask him the most awkward ones they can think of, in an often-successful effort to make him look stupid.

Boss is not taking his duty to the taxpayer seriously, as he is 'obviously taking a nap'. Miss Harpenden adds that, in such an old building, there could easily be rats running around his feet while he sleeps, putting him at risk of plague.

Meanwhile, there is no reply at all from Andrew to my text, so I send another five in quick succession. They all say the same thing – 'Wake up!' – but have no discernible effect, as he sinks lower and lower in his seat, and the calls from disgruntled constituents continue.

After half an hour or so, I'm pretty sure I can see a trickle of drool on The Boss' chin. That man's becoming more of a liability by the day, though there are people far more dangerous than him on the loose. While the Prime Minister has been taking questions, a man armed with a shotgun has run amok in a small town up north, and has already killed several people, and injured considerably more.

'Greg,' I say, 'we have to wake The Boss up now. It looks terrible when he sleeps through an event of national significance.'

'Ssh, Molly!' Greg waves at me to go away. 'I am waiting to see if the new Minister to the Treasury is going to use the question I proposed he should ask the PM. He invited suggestions on Twitter, you see.'

'Let's hope The Boss never starts doing that,' I say, refusing to budge. 'And, anyway, Greg – you don't even live in the Minister's constituency, so what did you want him to ask on your behalf?'

'I merely required specific details as to the percentage

of my tax that is spent on shell-suits,' says Greg. 'I changed my mind about wanting to know. It's an important issue, after all.'

He leans forward and turns up the volume on his computer, as a subtle hint that I, less subtly, refuse to take.

'Oh, for God's sake, Greg,' I say, 'Don't you think today's terrible events should take precedence over clothing?'

'I bet the man with the gun is wearing a bloody shell-suit,' says Greg, to whom the concept of political correctness is becoming ever more alien by the day.

## THURSDAY, 3 JUNE

What on earth do the girls in the Westminster office *do*? Are they *completely* hopeless? Just before lunchtime, I receive an email from Carlotta saying that she's booked Mr Beales in for tomorrow's surgery, as Greg and I aren't answering the phone.

Wrong, you dingbat. Greg and I are *screening* the calls – which is a completely different thing – with the sole aim of avoiding having to give Mr Beales yet another surgery appointment so soon after the last one.

We do try to leave the odd slot free for people with *real* problems, but it's a constant battle, even without the 'help' of the girls in London. Not that Carlotta accepts that this is the case. She says she is going to complain about us to The Boss – for abdicating our responsibilities.

'I should not have to speak to people who are so rude that they make me cry,' she says.

It turns out that she doesn't mean Greg, but Mr Beales, though I can't believe that she thinks *he's* rude. He's a rank amateur compared to most of the usual suspects – and doesn't she realise that she wouldn't have a job if it weren't for those 'nasty constituents' anyway?

'Those people are for you and Greg to deal with,' she says. 'I have Andrew's speeches to write, as well as important research to do.'

'Carlotta, Andrew's a backbencher, for God's sake, and no one in the Commons ever listens to a word he says,' I say. 'He doesn't really need a researcher, let alone one who writes speeches. Or he *wouldn't*, if he'd shut up occasionally. He could easily manage with just Marie-Louise in London, doing his diary.'

This doesn't go down very well, and Carlotta does one of those exaggerated Spanish sighs that she's so good at.

Sighing's one of the few things she *is* good at, now I come to think of it – the value of Andrew's London-based staff being mainly decorative as far as anyone can tell. And I do wish both she and Marie-Louise would use pseudonyms when they talk to constituents. At least that would stop the usual suspects moaning that The Boss only employs 'foreigners' in his Westminster office. He doesn't, though he *does* insist on long legs and an appearance which won't embarrass him at the Cinnamon Club. (It may be a coincidence, but I've just realised that neither Greg nor I have ever been invited *there*.)

I probably shouldn't have mentioned this inexplicable oversight to Greg, as he's already furious with Carlotta, not just because she agreed to give Mr Beales another surgery appointment, but also because she apparently claimed to be in charge of *all* Andrew's staff while doing so. Now Greg's even more determined to get his own back, to teach Carlotta to know her place in what he calls 'the complex hierarchy caused by Andrew's anarchic staffing arrangements'.

'What do you mean, "complex hierarchy"?' I say. 'It's simple: Carlotta's in charge in London – of herself and Marie-Louise. I'm in charge in Lichford. Of you and me. No one's in overall control.'

'Just like the Coalition,' says Greg, 'but that's not what I mean and, anyway, you're only nominally in charge of me. Whoever is *Goldenballs* is really the person in charge, and – as we both know – *that* title can change hands at a moment's notice. You may be Andrew's favourite at the moment, Mol, but you know the good times can't last forever.'

On that chilling note, Greg decides that now is the perfect time to phone the Westminster office – while both girls are out for their no-doubt glamorous lunch in the House. Then he leaves twenty-five 'messages' on their answerphone.

These involve little more than bouts of heavy breathing, coupled with the odd menacing grunt and barking noise. I really, *really* hope Greg remembered to press 141[18] before dialling each time.

---

[18] 141: UK number to dial, prior to the rest of someone's phone number, if you don't want them to be able to identify yours. An absolutely vital service for those whose names are Greg or Josh.

'Very satisfying,' he says, when he's finished. 'That'll teach Carlotta to think she's in charge of me. I suppose we'd better turn *our* answer-phone off now.'

Big mistake. The first call is from Miss Chambers, complaining that the police aren't taking her latest incident report seriously and are trying to imply that she 'should stop making enemies'.

She goes on to say that she has never upset *anyone*, which is so delusional as to be almost funny – until she asks 'what kind of madman' would post dog poo through her letter-box? I don't tell her that I am sitting in the office with *exactly* such a man.

I know you can lie by omission, but it doesn't feel as bad as the proper out-and-out kind of lying, does it? And, anyway, Miss C deserves it – though I'm not quite sure that Max does too.

I still haven't got round to telling him about Johnny Hunter, though I don't know why, other than I keep forgetting to. But now, I'm not at all sure that I should – not after reading the email that Johnny sends me tonight. I have a very odd feeling he may be *flirting* with me.

He's finally sent me a photograph of himself, too, but that's a bit of a disappointment. He's definitely *not* the dark-haired, blue-eyed one from the school bus but (just my luck) the mousy paper-boy. He's sitting in a mid-life crisis-style car, looking disturbingly like President Putin; though I suppose if you live and work in Russia, it's quite a good idea to look like someone who's well-connected. I wonder if Johnny looks as good as Putin in a judo suit.

Even if he doesn't, my life still seems horribly pedestrian

in comparison to his. (Johnny's, I mean, *not* the President's, though I suppose that both would apply.) He seems to be on a plane almost as often as he is on land; and says that he's working flat-out so that he can retire at fifty-five.

I haven't even decided what I want to do when I grow up yet, and my pension's going to be worth nothing, especially now that IPSA's making The Boss pay for it.

On top of that, I bet Max will trade me in before much longer – probably for Annoying Ellen, if the sit-ups and mooning around in the garden are anything to go by. Then I won't even get half of *his* lousy pension, and will have to work until I drop (or The Boss does – whichever comes first).

At that point, I'll probably have to opt for some DIY euthanasia when I can't face another day without heat or food, spent wrapped in a blanket and wearing an incontinence pad.

It's quite nice to have an *International Director of a Global Oil Company* flirting with me in the meantime, though. It makes a change – though I do wish I could recall what the *hell* we did behind the Science block.

### FRIDAY, 4 JUNE
Oh God, I *hate* Fridays. I bet other people love them, but then they don't work for an MP, do they? Whoever thought it would be a good idea to designate Friday as 'spending time in your constituency day' ought to be shot. Several times, if possible.

I'm on the phone to DEFRA[19] this morning when The Boss arrives, dumps his briefcase on my desk and opens it. A crumpled shirt and five pairs of obviously dirty Y-fronts fall out. He fishes around for a folder, and then buggers off to do an interview, leaving me staring at skid marks. I have a degree, for God's sake!

It takes me the rest of the morning to get over the shock, and I still can't face eating my lunch, though Andrew kindly saves me the bother upon his return. He finishes my sandwich just in time for today's surgery – which is attended by the usual collection of total nutters, interspersed with the odd sane person with a really serious problem.

I'm disturbed by yet another case where a middle-aged woman has apparently died unnecessarily while a patient at the local hospital. From *dehydration*. That's the fifth or sixth case in the last three months, so I'm getting a bit worried about what's going on now. I know that nurses have degrees these days (like me, not that mine does me any good), but lots of people don't, and most of *them* can manage to remember to give their children (or pets) enough to drink. It's not exactly rocket science, after all.

Anyway, talking of pets, The Boss doesn't seem half as exercised by people dying of thirst as he does about the ban on docking the tails of some pedigree dogs. This

---

[19] DEFRA: Department for Environment, Food and Rural Affairs. Also known as 'the kiss of death to political ambition' by Greg, who doesn't believe anything much happens in the country, other than the chasing of foxes by 'half-crazed posh people, wearing red coats'.

probably has less to do with a fondness for canine mutilation than with the fact that the constituent in favour of it turns out to be a reasonably attractive woman in her late forties.

She flirts outrageously with The Boss, who flirts outrageously back, and – before I can get a word in edgeways – he's agreed to consider bringing a Private Member's Bill to reinstate docking, and she leaves in a presumably hormonal tizz. If she had a tail, I'm sure she'd be wagging it, and Andrew's looking pretty perky, too.

In fact, he's still flushed with success when I show the next constituent in: Mr Beales, yet again – though Andrew greets him as if he were a long-lost friend. Why the *hell* does The Boss insist on doing that? The usual suspects need *no* encouragement.

Grinning like an idiot, Mr Beales pulls a piece of paper out of his pocket, then passes it to The Boss, completely ignoring my outstretched hand. 'If you could just sign that, Andrew, then I'll be on my way,' he says.

Since when does Mr Beales call The Boss *Andrew*? Not that it seems to bother anyone but me. Andrew just smiles, and flourishes his pen.

'At least *read* it first!' I say – sotto voce – or at least that's my intention, but Big Ears Beales hears me anyway. He pushes his double-barred paedophile glasses to the end of his nose, and peers at me over the top. His eyes are unnervingly cold.

'It's just my shotgun licence application,' he says. 'Your Boss *knows* me, after all.'

'Indeed he does,' I say. 'That was rather my point.

Andrew, are you *sure* you don't want to wait and think about this first?'

The Boss notices my expression – which Greg says is the one that makes me look like a member of the Infected in the film *28 Days Later* – and finally reacts.

'Ah, Edmund,' he says. 'Molly's right, you know—'

'Thank God for that,' I say, under my breath, but then Andrew carries on where he left off:

'She's forgotten to type up that reference for the court. Tell you what, she can go and do that now, and I'll sign this while you wait.'

Of such incidents are armed serial killers made. I give up, I really do.

## SATURDAY, 5 JUNE

Sam arrives for the weekend, and brings a new girlfriend with him. He says that he met her via *Guardian* Soulmates and that he wants her to meet Max and me so that she can see that he does know '*some* married people'. She's six feet tall, wears trainers and says nothing. Really. *Nothing*.

After dinner, Sam suggests that we all go to the pub for a drink, but I can't face it – the idea of spending the whole evening with a woman who's taken a vow of silence is far too much for me, so I claim that I have an urgent report to write for work and send Max off to entertain the lovers by himself.

He's *much* more tolerant than me, anyway, as well as being far closer to the girlfriend's height. I already have a crick in my neck.

As soon as they shut the front door behind them, I curl up in front of the television with the bottle of wine left over from dinner, on the basis that alcohol is a muscle-relaxant.

After one glass, I fall asleep in a neck-paralysing position on the couch, only waking when Max, Sam and the Tall Enigma come in and catch me drooling all down the front of my TV-watching fleece.

They're all roaring drunk, and the lovers are eager to get to bed – so I wait until they've gone upstairs, then ask Max, 'How did it go?'

'Never been so bored in my life,' he says.

'Did she speak at all?' I say. They've been gone for four hours, after all . . .

'Well, she told a few rude jokes, and then they spent the rest of the night talking about rugby. It was like a night out with your dad,' says Max.

'Oh God, that's *it!*' I say. It's all become crystal clear to me now, if not to Max.

'What's it?' he says or, rather, 'Whasht-it?'

'What Sam sees in her,' I say. 'She shares his *interests*.'

'Too true,' Max says, then passes out attractively on the couch.

I wait until *he* starts drooling, then cover him with a blanket and go to bed. At least our house is going to bear witness to *some* sex tonight, I suppose – though I hope the Tall Enigma doesn't bring any rugby moves into the bedroom. That spare bed has a wobbly headboard.

## SUNDAY, 6 JUNE

My toes have suddenly gone all funny, like my mother's: white, wrinkly slugs attached to my feet. *Repulsive*. I had no idea that was due to age but, now that I know that slug toes aren't just a peculiarity specific to Mum, I suppose sandal-wearing's well and truly out of the window.

Is there *no end* to the parts of your body you have to keep covered, once you pass a certain birthday? Whole chunks of your anatomy consigned to obscurity overnight: the tops of your arms, any leg above the knee – not to mention the baggy knees themselves. And the same goes for wrinkly necks, ageing hands and, now, for bloody toes as well.

I might as well become a Muslim and wear a burka. At least that would cover everything in one fell swoop, whereas, if you used all the cover-ups the magazines suggest, you'd look a right twit: gloves; an artfully draped scarf or a huge necklace; a long skirt (with opaque tights), and long-sleeved tops, segueing neatly into the aforementioned gloves. Soon I'll need a hat to obscure the bald patch, or a balaclava to cover the incipient beard.

And wearing trousers will be out, too: as Mum says that, one day when you're least expecting it, your arse suddenly slips sideways and becomes flat and wide, just like that. Talk about something to look forward to.

God knows what Johnny would think if he ever laid eyes on me – which is all the more bothersome a thought since he started emailing me so much more often. He says talking to me 'puts a smile on his face' and that even his staff have commented on his change of mood. I suppose anyone working for an oil company would be glad of a distraction from the horror of the Deepwater blowout[20] at the moment – but it's flattering, all the same.

I do wish Johnny wouldn't keep referring to that business behind the Science block, though. I still can't remember what it was, but he says that he had to take his watch off because it was getting in the way. God knows what he means, but I bet it'll turn out to be even more embarrassing than my toes, if I can ever find the diary where I wrote it down.

Bugger – I'd nearly forgotten about those bloody toes. What's the point in flirting with someone when you'd have to keep *everything* covered if you ever met up and took things further? I bet that's why people stay married – to avoid the horror of having to disrobe in front of someone who isn't inured to disintegration via familiarity..

Now I'm even *more* suspicious of Max's half-hearted attempts to get fit.

## MONDAY, 7 JUNE

This morning's postal delivery is interesting, I don't think. Fifty-five letters and twelve campaign postcards: save trees and/or whales; bring back imperial measures; ban

---

[20] Deepwater oil spill: Disaster in the Gulf of Mexico, described by Johnny as "that massive cock-up", but only off the record, of course. It started back in April, when the Deepwater Horizon oil rig exploded and then sank, killing eleven people, and gallons of oil are still gushing into the ocean now, in June.

fireworks; introduce a bank holiday for St George's Day; make cycle helmets compulsory; don't make cycle helmets compulsory; and sign the declaration in support of religious broadcasting. There is also a parcel containing five one-litre bottles of urine, beautifully packaged, but with no return address.

## MONDAY, 7 JUNE (EVENING)
Success! Finally found my fifth-form diary. I'm going to read it in bed as I haven't had time until now.

Johnny Hunter's name is scrawled on the front: 'Johnny Luvs Molly 4 Eva'. Spelling obviously wasn't a priority at the time.

## MONDAY, 7 JUNE (LATE EVENING)
Oh God, now I *definitely* know who Johnny Hunter is. *And* what he's talking about.

## TUESDAY, 8 JUNE
This morning's post is even less enthralling than yesterday's – as if to rub in how boring my life is, now that I'm no longer fifteen and getting up to God knows what behind the Science block – although The Boss does have a new batch of death threats, written in bright red ink, for a change.

I'm inclined to ignore them as, apart from the distinctive colour, they're not much different to those he gets all the time. (Greg denies any involvement on this occasion, and claims not to own a colour printer, anyway.) So I'm just about to throw the letters into the bin, when someone from Special Branch phones to say that they've infiltrated a group of animal-rights extremists and think that we should step up our precautions against attack.

The officer wants to know what our security arrangements are and, when I tell him we don't have any, he suggests we get some, preferably yesterday. He sound even less impressed when I tell him that The Boss doesn't agree with security arrangements as they are a 'threat to democracy'.

'Doesn't Mr Sinclair realise that, while *he* is protected for most of the week by the security at the House of Commons, you and your colleague are totally vulnerable?' he says, in the sort of voice that you'd get if you crossed Alan Rickman with Barry White.

He sounds so sexy that I resist the temptation to sarcasm, and somehow avoid saying, 'Gosh, officer, we hadn't thought of *that*!' Instead I surprise myself by flirting a bit – the mutilated-dog-tails woman must have been contagious – and I end up confiding that The Boss isn't the easiest person to manage sometimes.

It's a good job the officer can't actually *see* what I look like, otherwise I'm sure he wouldn't then have offered to carry out a security inspection, and to tell The Boss what needs to be put in place to protect me and Greg.

'I'll come and see you later this afternoon, if you like?' he says, which would be very good news if I didn't have to leave work early for my appointment with the gynaecologist – though I don't tell *him* that, of course. A woman must protect what remains of her dignity, after all.

On that note, I have insisted that Max comes to the hospital with me, in case I am asked how often we have sex, so that he can share the embarrassment if I tell the truth. Even so, he's really not amused when I answer the gynaecologist's question about whether I can think of anything that might be causing the problem by suggesting: 'Rust?'

*She* laughs, though, and then says there's nothing to worry about – but Max is still not talking to me when we get home, and things are frosty until the doorbell rings. It's Annoying Ellen, oh joy. That's three times she's borrowed the damned corkscrew this week.

After she left last time, Max said, 'She's always so *cheerful.*'

I said that I'd be bloody cheerful, too, if I had a huge house, all paid for, tons of alimony and the kids home for only one week in two – not to mention a succession of toy-boys. Max looked even more pained at the mention of toy-boys than he did at the rust.

**WEDNESDAY, 9 JUNE**

The morning's post brings more death-threat letters, still addressed to The Boss, and still written in red ink. He's being so annoying that I'd write some myself if I thought there was the remotest chance that he'd ever *read* the buggers.

He phones first thing this morning, to tell us to keep Friday lunchtime free: 'I've re-booked the restaurant for our work Christmas lunch,' he says. 'Be there, or be square.'

For God's sake. This is the lunch that was originally scheduled for the day before Christmas Eve – the one that The Boss cancelled at the last minute, after deciding that Greg and I had far too much work to finish to be able to spare two hours to celebrate. Which we did, but only because Andrew had just *created* it.

Then, to add insult to injury, he said he'd pop into the restaurant while he was passing, and cancel the reservation in person. Two hours later, he phoned me to say that he'd met 'two lovely ladies in the street' and had asked them to join him for lunch, seeing as Greg and I 'couldn't make it'. When he started to enthuse about what they were all eating, I'd had enough, so I hung up.

So now Greg and I aren't exactly in the mood for Christmas dinner, especially not in June, but Andrew hangs up on *me* when I tell him so. Then Greg does a lot of creative swearing about unreasonable bosses, while I decide to re-think my position on the red-ink letters and fax them through to Westminster, implying that I think they are far more serious than usual.

I even contemplate forging one which suggests that the author knows The Boss' home address, but chicken out at the last minute. You never know – I might have to hand them over to Special Branch at some point, and then I'd probably get the blame for sending *all* of them. If I'm still alive to hand anything over, that is – which Officer Sexy seems to find an unlikely proposition.

He arrives mid-afternoon, but his appearance doesn't

really live up to his voice. This is almost as disappointing as he seems to find our non-existent security arrangements, though at least he writes a report recommending lots of changes, so I suppose that's something.

He even says that, if The Boss doesn't comply with the recommendations, the police will have to think carefully about whether they can be held responsible for ensuring our safety in future.

'Oh, God,' I say. 'There's a bit of a problem with *one* of your suggestions, at least. The Boss considers CCTV an invasion of constituents' privacy.'

Officer Sexy just stares at me for what feels like ages. Then he gives a little shake of the head, and says, 'This *is* Andrew Sinclair's office, isn't it?'

When I confirm that it is indeed, he says that he would never have thought that The Boss was camera-shy, given that he appears on local television at every opportunity. There is no denying or explaining this, of course, not without casting further doubt on The Boss' sanity.

'Well, I hope Mr Sinclair is grateful for the risks you people run on his behalf,' says Officer Sexy, as he gathers up his paperwork in readiness to leave.

'No, he isn't,' says Greg. 'Molly and I have no idea what it is to be appreciated.'

Normally this would be all too true but, when Max and I get home this evening, we find that we have run out of toilet roll – thanks to a bizarre papier mâché experiment by Josh – so Max has to make an emergency trip to Sainsbury's.

He brings a bunch of flowers home for me and,

although he forgets to take the 'reduced' sticker off, it's the thought that counts. Isn't it?

A warm glow lasts for all of ten minutes, until I show Josh, who claims that husbands only buy their wives flowers when they are feeling guilty about something, in which case – if I'm about to be put out to grass in favour of Annoying Ellen – I suppose I may as well send Johnny the photo he keeps asking for. With any luck, it'll distract him from wanting to know whether I've found my diary yet, seeing as I don't even want to *think* about that. Talk about exhibitionism!

At least there isn't any photographic evidence of the Science block escapade, so things could be worse. Not that there's much photographic evidence of my existence, either. There are virtually no pictures of me in the family photo box at all, though there are *hundreds* of Max and the kids – all taken by me, of course. (If I died, within a week my family would be completely unable to recall what I looked like.)

So, given that I'm not exactly spoilt for choice, there's no alternative but to select a picture in which I am gurning furiously, during a face-pulling contest I had with Josh and Connie over Christmas. I'm almost too embarrassed to send it, but then I realise that Johnny won't have a clue whether I am genuinely hideously disfigured or not, so I'm looking forward to seeing how he'll cope with framing his response.

I seem to be becoming far more 'fun-loving' (ghastly phrase) since starting to correspond with him. I wonder if *that* attitude will survive the rest of the week.

## THURSDAY, 10 JUNE

Greg is wounded today or, rather, his ego takes a knock-out blow. I've just started opening the mail, when Mrs Nudd comes bursting into the office like a madwoman, presumably thanks to the so-far unidentified idiot who left the security door on the catch.

She's already reached my desk before I've had a chance to react, and is waving a letter in my face while screaming at the top of her voice: 'What the *f\*ck* do you mean that there's nothing more you can do for me?'

Then she starts throwing files and chairs around, and ends up holding a letter-opener to my throat. (Why do the nutters always go for *my* throat? Is it because I am almost a midget?)

Greg is surprisingly butch (for him). He attempts to take hold of Mrs Nudd from behind, but then she grabs me and hangs on tight, so Greg tries a little harder and manages to yank her backwards, though she still doesn't let go of my neck. When he eventually succeeds in throwing her off-balance, she dislodges me from my chair and we end up in a heap on the floor.

'Phone the police!' says Greg, while manhandling (or possibly boy-handling) the still-struggling Mrs Nudd towards the door.

She calms down a bit when she hears me reporting the assault, and Greg seizes the opportunity to push her over the threshold and slam the door – but not before she's hissed, right in his face, 'You are the ugliest f\*cker I've ever seen in my life.'

Then she goes off into the sunset to pick yet another

fight with her daughter-in-law. How on earth does she expect *us* to make her son 'see sense and get a divorce'?

About forty minutes later, a police constable saunters in; says something about being unavoidably delayed, and then goes away looking relieved when we can't be bothered to press any charges.

In retrospect, this may have been a mistake, as Greg is too traumatised to do any work for the rest of the day. He just keeps wandering off into the men's loo and staring hopelessly into the mirror, while mumbling that he'll never get another girlfriend.

I try to cheer him up by pointing out that *no one* is as bonkers as Mrs Nudd: an over-optimistic theory which Dinah succeeds in disproving, when she phones just as Max, Josh and I finish eating dinner. *She* sounds as mad as a hatter.

'Dad's joined bloody Facebook now,' she says.

'And?' I say. There's always an 'and'.

'He's got six friends already, apart from me – and they're *all* women. I *told* you not to teach him to use that computer!'

'Well, maybe they're old school-friends or something,' I say – with an optimism that I do not feel. (My Mrs Nudd theory didn't exactly stand up well to scrutiny.)

'They're all about twenty, and look Thai! Silver surfer, my arse.' Dinah sucks noisily on her cigarette for emphasis, says, '*F\*ck's sake!*' and then hangs up.

Sometimes I think it wouldn't matter if I walked off when she phones, like I do with Miss Chambers. I am nothing more than a receptacle for the venting of others and it's *very* tiring indeed.

I'm not the only one who's knackered tonight. Both Max and Josh have already gone to bed by the time that I check my email, before I hit the sack myself.

There's a message from Johnny, who negotiates receipt of my challenging photo with consummate ease, by the simple trick of restricting his response to '*Very* attractive!' He has more political awareness than The Boss, that's for sure – so I feel compelled to send him a proper picture as a reward.

I end up sending one that Josh took by accident earlier this evening, when he wanted to check whether the batteries in the camera were still working. It shows me with my eyes closed, thus allowing me to retain an air of mystery. Or that's what I tell myself, anyway.

When I finally get into bed, Max asks me what took me so long, and I say that I've been working on a report for one of the Select Committees. I don't *think* he knows The Boss isn't on any of them since the election, but he does go a bit quiet after that. Now I'm not sure if he doesn't believe me, or if he's just asleep. He's not snoring yet, so it's hard to tell.

### FRIDAY, 11 JUNE

Thank God Greg and I refused to go out for the Christmas meal at lunchtime, as surgery proves quite stressful enough on its own. I try to persuade Greg to go in with The Boss for a change, on the grounds that I've already been lumbered with doing tomorrow's supermarket surgery, but Greg is having none of it.

'I am still suffering from Post-Traumatic Stress Disorder,' he says, taking a long look into his pocket mirror to add an air of *verité*. 'The ego is a fragile thing.'

That's undeniable – so, as usual on a Friday morning, I'm the one who has to sit listening to The Boss promising the impossible to each constituent who has an appointment, before he leans back and basks in the love in the room. Later, it'll be down to me to tell them that what he's promised is unfeasible, or against regulations, or whatever – and then the constituents will phone *him,* to complain about *my* attitude.

Today he assures a single woman with one small child that he can get her a four-bedroomed Council house in the same street as her mother, 'no problem.' This is despite my resorting to kicking him under the table, and making my 'Infected' face.

Then he promises a slimy old man, who's just got out of prison for an unspecified sexual offence that 'of course' we can get him a visa for his Thai bride – whom the man hasn't even met yet. (This leads to me fretting about Dad, and briefly losing concentration, so I can't recall *what* the next constituent is promised.)

We do have one case that gets me really 'exercised', as The Boss would say. A sweet little guy, called Mr Something-or-other-totally-unintelligible, but which sounds like Mr Meeeeurghn, wants us to see if we can get his passport back from the Home Office, as he wants to go home to visit his family.

He gives his address as the bail hostel on Seymour Road. For God's sake, what is this country coming to when we put traumatised refugees up in places like that? Dad would approve though – as long as the refugees weren't young and attractive. And Thai, of course.

I block that thought for the rest of surgery, after which The Boss heads for the Oprah room to do an interview with a reporter from the local paper. (We normally use this room when Andrew needs a lie-down after a particularly hard-drinking lunch, as it contains a comfy couch and is soundproof enough to dull the sound of snoring, but this is one of the rare occasions when it's being used for its proper purpose.)

Leaving Andrew unsupervised during an interview is a bit of a risk, to say the least – so Greg and I keep our ears pressed to the door as a precautionary measure, only to hear Andrew say that he's had enough of the red-ink letters, and has decided to 'speak out'.

In response to the reporter's murmurs of encouragement, he continues: 'I refuse to be intimidated and will not be prevented from opening my mail, which consists of important letters from constituents.'

Local vox pops later applaud his courage. The Boss doesn't open his letters. I do.

## SATURDAY, 12 JUNE

Gah. It's supermarket surgery this morning, and this one is as bad as usual. Constituents who have nothing whatsoever to complain about – which is why they don't bother to contact the office during the week – spot The

Boss sitting under his banner in Tesco's foyer when they walk past on their way to buy groceries.

As soon as they recognise him, they start racking their brains in an attempt to dredge up a minor irritation to talk to him about, purely to be seen by their neighbours in the company of an MP, however unkempt and hungover said MP may look.

So, today, we are presented with complaints about: uneven pavements; puddles at the end of driveways; overgrown hedges; and litter. Each one will require me to write a letter to whichever is the most relevant agency, and to send a copy to the constituent – together with a covering letter saying how nice it was to meet them (which it often wasn't, if I'm being honest).

Then, when we eventually receive replies from the County or Town Councils, *they'll* be sent out with another personalised covering letter. And so on, and so on, ad infinitum.

What with the weather we've been having, there are four hazardous puddle complaints alone; not to mention all the beer-toting, polyester-clad, World Cup-crazed constituents who just want their photographs taken with The Boss – who insisted on wearing an England shirt this morning.

There *has* to be more to life than this, not that I'm suicidal, of course – unlike The Boss. Taking me home at lunchtime, he drives even more erratically than he usually does.

'Are you still drunk?' I ask.

'No,' he says. 'I have a lot on my mind.'

I somehow doubt that, but I know a cue when I hear one. 'What's the matter, Andrew?'

'Do you think I'm too trusting for my own good?' he asks.

'Um, I don't know,' I say. God knows where this conversation is going and, more to the point, is Andrew looking where *he* is going? I do wish he'd keep his eyes on the road.

'I think those shits in the local Party are out to get me again,' he says. 'I was set up at GC[21] last night. Oops.'

He steers the car off the inconsiderate stretch of pavement that has had the temerity to get in his way; and then continues:

'Bastards wanted me to confirm that, now we're finally in opposition, I can – *at last* – be relied upon to toe the Party line. Outrageous. I think I may have to take steps to deal with them. I'm sure that swine Peter Carew is angling to steal my seat.'

I don't quite know what to say to this. The Boss has recurrent bouts of paranoia anyway – like all the politicians I've ever met – but he doesn't usually look and sound *quite* so unsettled. I can't actually think of anyone in the Party (Pete Carew included), who'd have either the energy or the desire to usurp him, but then I don't

[21] GC: General Committee, regular meeting of local Labour Party big-hitters, to whom The Boss has to present his GC report, explaining what he's been up to at Westminster. Usually drafted on a napkin from the buffet car during Andrew's journey home on Thursday evenings, and then given to me to decipher, completely re-write to remove all references to jollies, and then pass to Party staff to print and disseminate at the start of the meeting.

share Andrew's long-standing belief that they'd *all* stab him in the back as soon as look at him.

'I don't want you or Greg talking to *anyone* from the Party from now on, Molly,' he says. 'Not even the staff – you can't trust any of 'em.'

'But they're in an office in the same building as us.'

Andrew glares at me and almost crashes into a woman with a pushchair standing at a zebra crossing. I decide it's safer to shut up, to prevent the deaths of innocent pedestrians, and live to enjoy what remains of the weekend.

Now I wish I hadn't bothered, after Max and I have dinner with Susie and David this evening. We're celebrating David's company having just been sold – for three million pounds.

To give him his due, David does resist the temptation to remind me that I warned him he'd never make a penny if he set up a courier company, on the basis that the market was already saturated; but he does say, 'Molly, you are the biggest waste of potential I have ever known.'

I may not see David very often since he became so bloody successful, but he's still *supposed* to be my best friend. Max says I should have asked him what he meant, but I say I don't *want* to know.

## SUNDAY, 13 JUNE

I'm feeling a bit fragile after last night's drinking session with David and Susie, and this isn't helped by a newspaper article that Dinah sends me in an email.

The report refers to the mass-murderer who went

berserk with a shotgun, the one that Greg was so sure would be wearing a shell-suit at the time; and seems to imply that the man was driven to the brink of insanity by falling for a young Thai woman, who allegedly encouraged him to send her loads of money and then dumped him when he ran out of cash.

Dinah doesn't go into any more detail herself, except to say, 'There goes our inheritance, *and* our social standing.'

I don't bother to reply, as Dad doesn't own a shotgun as far as I know, and God knows what Dinah expects to inherit anyway. When a man's been married as many times as Dad, there's not exactly a limited number of children and step-children to share the proceeds of one small bungalow and a (probably fake) Rolex watch.

My mood doesn't improve when Josh informs me that today is the day that he and his girlfriend Holly celebrate their third anniversary. What is *wrong* with young people these days? Why don't they make the most of their freedom?

I say as much to Max, who agrees rather too wholeheartedly, though cunningly out of earshot of Josh. I can't stop once I've started, though. Since when are you allowed to even *have* anniversaries of when you started going out together? Anniversaries are supposed to be treats in recognition of hard labour at the coalface of marriage, not trivialised in this way!

The one thing that I do not say is 'Congratulations', and now Josh is in a mood with me. Max *does* and is, as usual, the favourite parent. Creep.

I assume that this craven behaviour is what Max is

referring to when, much later, he sidles up to me in bed and tells me that he's sorry – but, as usual, I'm wrong. He's trying to prepare me for bad news instead: that he will be away on a business trip to Germany on *our* anniversary. I go ballistic, but he says he doesn't have a choice, and that the company are talking about redundancies.

He seems so worried that I don't have the heart to keep moaning. I wonder if *that's* why he's off sex?

## MONDAY, 14 JUNE

My first priority this morning is to make a few calls to see what I can do to help poor little Mr Meeeeurghn – who turns out to be in a bail hostel because he has just got out of prison. More details are being sent by post, and are designated *strictly* confidential.

I have no one to share this development with, as Greg has decided to take the day off sick with his self-diagnosed Post-Traumatic Stress. He might as well have come into work, seeing as I seem to be the psychiatrist on call, at least as far as the usual suspects are concerned.

Honestly, when Mrs Thatcher's government got rid of long-stay wards for the mentally-ill, to be replaced by 'Care in the Community', it didn't seem a bad idea at the time – until it become apparent that the two central planks of this new approach were conspicuous by their total absence: Care *and* Community.

Now we – MPs and their staff – seem to be expected to plug the gap left by this minor oversight, so I decide to keep a tally of how many sane enquiries we get in a day.

Today's result is nine. Out of a total of thirty-three phone calls, and thirty-nine letters – and not including any emails at all. I don't count the five Greg sends me, asking whether he really *is* the ugliest man in Lichford, so I think it's pretty safe to rest my case.

## TUESDAY, 15 JUNE

Mr Meeeeurghn has been convicted of *murder*. To add insult to my injured faith in human nature, it transpires that he can't have his passport back because he is on bail and, anyway, he doesn't need it to go home – because he *can't* go home. His country of origin won't let him back in. God knows what he did there, but my faith in the public has taken yet another blow.

I email Greg and tell him that I don't care if he *is* still traumatised, I need him back at work tomorrow to save me from plunging into a suicidal depression, caused by dealing with people with unpronounceable names who turn out not to be half as nice as they appear.

It's much harder to cope with such disappointments when you're on your own – although there is *one* piece of good news today: The Boss has approved a new security door! Admittedly, it's only a replacement for the one that Steve Ellington broke on his way out this morning, but even so.

The viewing panel's shattered, and the frame is all bent out of shape – but there wasn't a *mark* on Steve's forehead. God knows what his head is made of, but it's something a hell of a lot stronger than my nerves. *They* are feeling completely shredded, especially after Johnny sends me an email in which he says that he *loves* my photo, but that I look tired and 'in need of a massage'. What on *earth*? Maybe the oil spill saga's starting to mess with his mind now, or he and I are locked in a delusional co-dependency.

I have no idea *what* the last part of that sentence means, but I quite like the sound of it. I got the bit about co-dependency from Sam, who told me that one of his internet dates had said it about *their* relationship, just before she dumped him for a used car salesman. (I've warned him over and over again to rule out any woman who lists 'self-help books' in the *Preferred Reading* category of her dating profile, but he never listens to a word I say. Like some other males that I could mention.)

Max is about as far from being co-dependent as it's possible to be this evening – with me, anyway. He barely says a word and looks very tired, so I leave him in front of the TV and catch up on personal correspondence at the computer instead. This doesn't include emailing Johnny, as I still haven't decided how to respond to him yet, but Greg replies to my earlier suicidal message thus:

*What about drinkypoos and a little outing after work tomorrow night? To include pizza and gin, then gin, gin and gin? I have a pent-up rage that needs dealing with, and minority groups will no doubt suffer.*

I ask Greg where we're going, but he won't say, and just tells me to put together a list of all our craziest constituents. (He defines these as the people in whose

76

company I hear *The Twilight Zone* theme, which means it'll take me *hours* to comply.)

I tell Max that I have a date with another man, to see how he reacts – but he seems unbothered, presumably on the basis that he thinks I wouldn't be tempted by an *American Psycho* lookalike half my age. Maybe he'd think the same thing about Johnny, the oil-rich Putin lookalike, too – but Max doesn't know about *him*, yet, does he? Oh.

That's a bit of an uncomfortable thought but, even so, I don't know whether to find Max's faith in me touching, or arrogant. Maybe he thinks it's irrelevant whether I'd be tempted or not, as no one would ever be tempted by me?

**WEDNESDAY, 16 JUNE**

After we finish work, I find out why Greg wanted the list. He insists we wait around in the office until it's almost dark, and then he says, 'Here are the keys to the Gregmobile – you go and get in. Won't be a minute.'

Five minutes later, he reappears and dumps fifteen manila folders in my lap, together with a map and a torch. I get really worried. Is Greg's Patrick Bateman exterior an unsubtle indicator that he is a menacing rapist who carries a chainsaw around? Should Max have been more concerned for my safety, and when will he notice that I'm missing? *Will* he notice that I am missing?

'What's number one on the map?' says Greg, swerving wildly to avoid a cyclist.

'What?' I ask.

'Map,' says Greg. 'On your lap. What's number one?'

I open the map, but can't see what I'm doing, so then I start dropping files all over the place.

'Torch,' says Greg, and then, 'F*ck's sake!'

I direct the torch at the map and find fifteen small, coloured dots affixed to various parts of East Lichford. These are cross-referenced to a list of numbers stuck at the side of the map. I cheer up – surely Greg wouldn't have gone to all this trouble to rape someone (almost) old enough to be his mother?

'Number one – Eleanor Road,' I say. 'Why?'

'Find the file with number one on it,' says Greg.

I do as he says. The file is labelled 'Edmund Beales'. Oh, *Jesus* Christ.

'Gregory,' I say, 'I *thought* we were going for a drink. What the hell *are* we doing?'

'Our DIY version of a CRB[22] check,' says Greg. 'I am sick of waiting for a mad constituent to chop my head off with a samurai sword, so you and I are going to make a pre-emptive strike.'

'Huh?' is my considered response.

'We are going to check out what little we actually know about the crazy f*ckers we have to deal with every day – without security – and see if any of it stacks up. We could get killed waiting nine months for the Criminal Records Bureau, and Special Branch only ever seem to

[22] CRB check: Vetting procedure carried out by the Criminal Records Bureau. Far too slowly, according to Greg, who has a problem with deferred gratification of any kind.

notice the animal-rights loony tunes. First stop, the home of Edmund Beales.'

## THURSDAY, 17 JUNE

I have a very bad hangover from the bottle of gin that Greg and I drank when we got back last night, after our narrow escape from the dog in Mr Beales' garden, so I'm taking today off as a holiday.

At lunchtime, I get an email from Greg who says:

*The carpenter is here, working away on the security improvements. He tells me that he hasn't bothered to fit bulletproof glass to the new door he has just installed. The consequence for me, if anyone needs reminding, will simply be* this.

I open the attachment to find a video clip of JFK's assassination.

## FRIDAY, 18 JUNE

God, I'm so glad that Connie's coming home from uni today for the summer holidays. I've had about as much testosterone-related craziness this week as I can take. Mainly from my lunatic son.

I have to ask Greg to take over for the second half of this afternoon's surgery, as Max and I have been called into school to see Josh's tutor, Mr Bowen. When we arrive, we discover that Josh is *furious* that we've been contacted, and he doesn't even calm down during the lengthy period we spend waiting outside the tutor's office. He spends the entire time ranting, just like a mad constituent.

'That bloody man's got it in for me. He just picks on

me – *all the time*. It doesn't matter what anyone else is doing, it's always, "Joshua Bennett. My office – *now*!" He's just jealous because I haven't got a disability,' announces Josh, with venom.

'Disability?' I ask.

'We call him Mr Thumb,' says Josh. "Cause his thumb's five times the size it should be.'

Josh draws various illustrations of Mr Bowen's affected appendage to support his claims, and his outrage seems so genuine that Max and I are feeling really hostile by the time we enter the office. I will *not* have someone picking on my youngest child, just because his digits are undamaged.

I put on my best MP's office voice and walk to the desk, my hand outstretched. 'Mr Thumb? I'm Molly Bennett. Pleased to meet you.'

Max and Josh collapse in hysterics, while Mr Bowen looks at me in disbelief. I realise what I've done and have to excuse myself. I clutch at my forehead and say, 'I am *so* sorry, I'm unwell. I think I may be going to be—' and then I run for the door, making (very convincing) retching noises.

Max tells me later that things didn't get any better after my departure. Apparently, when he complained that Mr Bowen was picking on Josh, Mr Bowen replied that Josh was in the sixth-form common room all morning – and all afternoon – of every day, playing *poker*. Max didn't believe this, so Mr Bowen made him watch a CCTV recording of Josh in action.

Max then tried to argue that Josh was probably only

relaxing during free periods but, again, Mr Bowen's response wasn't exactly helpful. He demanded Josh's homework diary, to enable him to show Max the lesson timetable. The entire cover was decorated with extremely realistic, outsized thumbs.

Max says there's nothing for it but to kill Josh. Connie's (unsurprisingly) in favour, and even I agree to think about it. We don't ask Holly her opinion, in case she objects.

## SATURDAY, 19 JUNE

Ouf, I don't think Connie's got the H&M job she was interviewed for today, although she says that everything went well until the manager asked her whether there was anything that really annoyed her about people. (The Boss never asked *me* that!)

The trouble with Connie is that she's so truthful that she can't understand the point of those interview questions to which the only correct answers are lies, such as what she *should* have said on this occasion: 'I am very tolerant, and *really* like dealing with the general public.'

Connie doesn't say anything of the sort. Her argument is that any interviewer worth his or her salt would assume that a candidate who answered with such bullshit must be a compulsive liar, and should therefore be avoided.

She takes the same approach to interviews as she does to life in general: tell the truth, the whole truth and nothing but the truth. (I have strong suspicions that this characteristic may also be linked to Asperger's, along with a pathological inability to judge when to explain oral sex to an elderly relative.)

81

Anyway, Connie's answer to the H&M manager apparently goes like this: 'Well, one thing really, *really* annoys me . . . '

'What?' says the (presumably incredulous) manager.

'When someone has thin hair, and their ears poke out – right through it.'

Connie says the interview ended shortly thereafter.

## SUNDAY, 20 JUNE

I bet you can tell a married woman from a single one, just by the state of her underwear. Mine is tragic. Rather worryingly, this thought occurs to me while I am trying to draft a reply to Johnny's last email – the one in which he mentioned massage.

I'm hoping that he was so distracted by the oil spill that he forgot that he was writing to me, and thought he was emailing his wife instead – but now I have no idea whether to respond to his suggestion, or whether it's safer to ignore it altogether.

I draft several clumsy attempts at suitable replies, but my political skills seem to have deserted me entirely so, eventually, I give up and decide to phone Dad instead. It *is* Father's Day, after all – even though Connie seems oblivious to the fact that this also applies to Max. She's still in bed, moaning to her friends on Facebook about retail managers with no sense of humour.

I, however, am in my father's good books, due to being the only one of his many children who has remembered to send a card, or to phone – or at least I am, *until* the subject of Facebook comes up again. Along with a mention of Dad's young Thai women 'friends' who are all, without exception, 'neighbours', or so he says.

He gets quite cross when I question the likelihood of this, on the basis that: a) he lives in a really small village, and b) it's in Dorset. Then he says he's not interested in women since Stepmother Mark III left him, anyway – so I have to phone Dinah as fast as I can.

'Di,' I say. 'Can you set Dad up with one of your friends' mums?'

'Why? What's he up to?' says Dinah.

(We have a sisterly shorthand which avoids the need for a lot of explanation, which is lucky as she talks so much that I often can't get a word in edgeways.)

'He says he's *not interested in women* again,' I say. '*And* that the Thai girls are all his neighbours.'

'Christ!' says Dinah. 'I'll get onto it straight away. In the meantime, why don't you write something off-putting on his Facebook wall?'

'Like what?'

'Like asking him if his willy's still bendy, for a start.'

There's a distinctly triumphant tone to Dinah's last comment. I wonder if this is how most daughters discuss their fathers? Mind you, I also wonder how many fathers have women friends as young as *those*. Maybe Max fantasises about starting all over again with someone new, probably half my age, and from another continent.

I don't think I want to know if he does, but I'm unsettled for the rest of the afternoon now that the thought's occurred to me. I keep finding myself staring at him, until he notices and says,

'What's up? Have I got a bogey hanging from my nose or something?'

He hasn't, but it's odd how you don't really notice the person you've been married to for aeons, until you start to consider how attractive they might appear to another person – which is a bit alarming, not just because I bet *I* look terrible, but also because I suspect Max doesn't. And, as if that isn't quite depressing enough, Josh is taking Max out 'for a Father's Day drink' – at a lap dancing club, or so he says.

Honestly, is there no end to the pressure? First, I need new underwear, and now I shall have to learn to pole-dance, too.

**MONDAY, 21 JUNE**

God, why do I look so different in photographs to how I *imagine* I look?

The Boss' website is being updated, to allow him to blog – talk about asking for trouble – so I have to have a new photo taken. The result makes me look like Mr Burns in *The Simpsons*. When did I become a hunchback?

I blame it on the weird position I have to adopt, in order to preserve an ear-protecting distance from the receiver while talking to Miss Chambers on the phone – and last night's misguided attempt at pole-dancing didn't help much either, but what are you supposed to do when your husband and son spend five hours in a lap dancing club on Father's Day? (Max claims they only went to the pub and that Josh is winding me up, but he looked suspiciously cheerful when he left for work this morning.)

I suppose my photo could be worse, though – Greg looks even more like Patrick Bateman in *American Psycho* than usual in his. He says he thinks he looks 'damned attractive' and 'will scare off lunatics', so I can't persuade him to change it – but I'm not letting mine go anywhere except into the virtual trash.

I'm going to suggest the web designer uses the most recent photo I sent to Johnny instead. The constituents probably won't notice that I have my eyes shut or, if they do, they'll think I'm wincing with empathy for their plights.

Actually, I *am* feeling rather uncharacteristically empathetic today, seeing as Anti-Social Behaviour is on the agenda. Such an *idiotic* term, which doesn't at all reflect the utter misery that is wreaked on so many by so few.

If there's one thing I blame the Labour Government for, it was their complete inability to call a spade a spade. ASB sounds like a toddler tantrum, which drastically understates the case if our constituents are anything to go by. Whole neighbourhoods are being terrorised, by one or two nightmare families who are out of control.

Whenever the subject comes up at dinner parties – which is pretty rare, anyway – our friends look at me as if I'm making up examples for the sake of entertainment. East Lichford might as well be *A Tale of Two Cities*, given how little awareness of the underclass those who live in its richer parishes seem to have.

When I mentioned the horse and the burned-out cars Steve Ellington keeps in his front garden, David said, 'Oh Molly, you *are* funny.'

He should have seen Edmund Beales' bloody Doberman the other night; and I bet there were three pit-bulls inside that house as well – Greg and I escaped by the skin of our teeth. I didn't even recall Mr Beales' shotgun licence until afterwards, so I suppose things could have been even worse.

Anyway, I'm getting sidetracked now, which is what empathy always does to the brain. You can't afford too much of it in my job but, getting back to ASB, there seems to be no meaningful deterrent at all. If the night-mare neighbours have children, they'll be re-housed straight away if they *are* evicted – in order to protect their children; and then their new neighbours will quickly end up as frantic as the old ones were.

What's even more depressing is the way that so many of the Council's Housing Officers seem to view desperate, but otherwise reasonable, residents as 'moaning minnies'.

I'd find this rather less irritating if almost everyone who worked in the Housing Department didn't live miles away in rural bliss, as evidenced by their complete inability to get to work at the first hint of snow.

I wonder if they have ASB in Russia? It seems unlikely that Putin would tolerate anything like that, but I forget to ask Johnny about it when he emails me, just before I leave the office. He asks if I'm not talking to him, seeing as I haven't replied to his offer of a massage yet – so that *must* have been directed at me, and not his wife!

Now I don't know *what* to say, especially as I really

fancy a back rub. I'm sure I pulled something, trying to spin around the curtain pole Max left propped up in the hallway. I *told* him it would cause an accident if he didn't put it in the shed.

**TUESDAY, 22 JUNE**
I'm getting really tired of Mr Meeeeurghn now, and not just because his name is so bloody hard to spell.

At lunchtime, he phones and starts screaming that he is being mistreated. 'You protect me, *now*!' he says. 'I am *refugee*!'

Then he puts me on to someone else, who identifies herself as a member of staff at Primark. It turns out that Mr Meeeeurghn is trying to claim a refund on a pair of jeans that he insists he's never worn.

The weary-sounding girl says that the jeans are *covered* in bleach; and that Mr Meeeeurghn is threatening to kill all the staff if she does not give him his money back immediately. He apparently told her that he would phone his MP who would *make* her do it.

Meanwhile, the queue of waiting customers is now so long that it reaches down the stairs, and out of the shop, but none of *them* can be served until Mr Meeeeurghn has been dealt with – by me, presumably. Some people have all the luck.

So, I tell her to put the screeching Mr Meeeeurghn back on the phone to speak to me; tell *him* that I cannot help him, and then go and check that the new office door is double-locked. Primark have security staff. We don't – and nor do we have bulletproof glass.

**WEDNESDAY, 23 JUNE**

Greg is out of the office in the morning, 'raising awareness'. He texts me at 11:30am to say that he has found a solution to all our problems with difficult constituents. 'Nuke 'em', is his measured response.

He comes back shortly afterwards, but tells me that he is so traumatised by his run-in with Miss Harpenden and her hypothetical rats that we need to treat ourselves by nominating lunchtime as *Writing Honest Letters Hour*.

This is a luxury in which we occasionally indulge. A typical example would be my reply to Mr Ellis' repeated threats to kill himself, if we don't get him what he wants:

> *Dear Mr Ellis,*
>
> *Thank you for your letter threatening to throw yourself off the multi-storey car park if we do not stop your next-door neighbour from turning off her light switch so noisily.*
>
> *I regret that I will not be able to be present tomorrow at 4:00pm as you requested, as I have to be in the House of Commons from Mondays to Thursdays. However, if you could possibly arrange to reschedule the event for 4:30pm on Friday, I shall be more than happy to attend.*
>
> *Yours sincerely,*
>
> *Andrew Sinclair, MP for Lichford East*

Meanwhile, Greg is composing a response to Mrs Underwood, who has written in to ask whether there are plans to increase spending on public benches on the short route between her house and the betting shop:

> Dear Mrs Underwood,
> Further to your recent letter, I regret that there are currently no plans to increase spending for accessible seating in your area, as any additional funds are earmarked for tax cuts for me.
> Yours, etc.,
> Andrew Sinclair, MP for the hardworking people of Lichford East

It's almost heartbreaking to have to shred our literary masterpieces as soon as we've finished reading them out but, even so, WHLH has cheered us both up no end. I've even managed to forget that Max has jet-setted off to Germany on his business trip, and that he won't be home tonight – until I get home, and have to deal with Josh and Connie all by myself.

Do kids *ever* grow out of sibling rivalry? As I let myself in at the front door I hear yelling and incredibly loud banging, only to find Connie calmly listening to her iPod, while Josh is kicking the hell out of the back door. From the outside.

It turns out that he has been stuck in the back garden for the last two and a half hours, and has missed the whole of the England match as a result. It probably serves him right, though, if he really *did* call Connie 'a freak who has no friends' before she decided to lock him out.

God knows what the neighbours must have thought. The air was positively blue.

Josh used to be able to escape when this sort of thing occurred, but now he can't – not since we added barbed wire to the six-foot walls around the garden and padlocked the gate, to which Max has the only key. (I'm *sure* it was Steve Ellington who burgled us both times, but still can't prove it.)

So Josh is in a foul mood; while Connie says that she is depressed as, not only does she have the most vile brother on the planet, she didn't get the H&M job either – even though the manager did write and thank her for a 'most entertaining interview'.

She and Josh spend all evening in their respective rooms, each furiously complaining about the other to their friends on Facebook. The only thing they are agreed on is that I am guilty of outrageous favouritism, though they disagree on which of them I apparently prefer.

I'm not too keen on either of them tonight, if truth be told; and I'm positively *dreading* tomorrow evening – Max and I have always spent our wedding anniversaries together until now. He's left me a note on my pillow, though, so that cheers me up. For a second or two, until I read what it says:

*Darling, we're out of milk. Can't find details of hotel but will phone you tomorrow and let you know then. All love, Mx*

*Can't find details of hotel?* What sort of stupid statement is that?

**THURSDAY, 24 JUNE**

I'm a bit surprised today when Johnny emails to tell me that he's back in London, 'standing in for an embattled colleague caught up in the oil spill fall-out' – and to ask whether I'd like to meet up while he's there.

When I hesitate, he says what a shame it is that Max and I can't be together for our wedding anniversary, and then asks whether I don't think I am being taken a little for granted. I forget to ask him what he and his wife did for *their* anniversary in my rather non-committal reply, but I bet it was preferable to the way I spend my evening: completely on my own.

Both kids are still in self-imposed exile upstairs, and I haven't got any friends to go out with, or none who won't insist on making me feel like a poor relation, anyway – and even Annoying Ellen isn't in when I pop round to check she doesn't need to borrow the corkscrew again. (I think she must have gone away, as I don't seem to have seen her for a couple of days.)

I do speak to Dinah on the phone, which cheers me up a bit – especially when she tells me that she has found two women who might be suitable for Dad amongst the mothers of her friends.

'Brilliant,' I say. 'That's the best news I've had all day. At least we don't have to worry about a Thai bride now.'

'Hold your horses, Molly,' says Dinah. 'I haven't finished yet. You really must learn not to interrupt.'

Then she goes on to explain that Dad has ruled both women out, without even taking either of them on a date. Apparently, he told Dinah that they were 'too old' for him.

'Well, I suppose Dad *is* quite youthful for his age,' I say. 'How old were these women, anyway?'

'The oldest one's fifteen years younger than him.'

By the time I'm capable of a response to that, Dinah has lost patience and hung up on me – which is what I feel like doing to Max, when he finally phones me some time after midnight, and then forgets to say 'Happy Anniversary' anyway.

He sounds as pissed as a fart, and is still claiming that he doesn't know the phone number, or even the *name* of the hotel he's staying in. When I say that I need it, in case of emergencies, he says there's nothing I can't handle, given my job – and that he'll see me tomorrow night. Then he rings off, as if that was that.

What kind of halfwit doesn't know the name of his hotel – when he's been *staying* in it for the last twenty-four hours?

If anyone told me that their husband had told them that, I know *exactly* what I'd think was going on – but I don't want to think the same thing about mine. Though a weekend in London is starting to sound very attractive, all of a sudden.

## FRIDAY, 25 JUNE

Sometimes it feels as if Fridays occur *much* more often than other days. It certainly doesn't feel as if a whole week has passed since The Boss was last in the office, sitting with his feet up on my desk and helping himself to my breakfast. I do wish he wouldn't swear so loudly while I'm on the phone to constituents. They all know it's him, because of his Birmingham accent.

He's being particularly demanding today, which is really saying something. 'Molly, get me Paul Whatsisname on the phone.'

'Andrew, you have the phone in front of you,' I say. 'Have you lost the use of your hands?'

'Find me his number then.'

So much for manners maketh man – but I rise above all provocation. 'Andrew, I have never heard of Paul Whatsisname. *Who* is he?'

'*I* don't know. You'll have to write to him instead. I've got *totally* incompetent staff.'

The Boss rolls his eyes and finishes my croissant. There are crumbs absolutely everywhere, but unfortunately he doesn't choke on any of them.

I'm starting to worry about him a bit, actually. Not just because he's becoming so rude that someone is *bound* to punch him fairly soon; but why he's got this notion that someone from the Party is spying on him, God only knows. He can't possibly have any secrets which would make it worth the effort – given that he makes his views known to anyone who stands still for more than a second. But there's no reasoning with him this week, at all.

He insists that we hold our usual Friday briefing in the corridor today, and that only *I* attend. Then next week will be Greg's turn. The Boss reasons that, this way, Greg and I will be less dangerous if we turn out to be moles, as we will only know *half* of what is going on. I suspect that the person who *actually* only knows half of what is going on is The Boss himself, but it's probably wiser not to point this out.

It's an effort not to, though, when Roger Fennis comes in for his surgery appointment. Apparently he is being paid far less than his much-younger colleague, whom *he* trained to do the job. You'd think that would sound familiar to The Boss – but of course it doesn't. Instead, he's shocked to the core.

'That's bloody *outrageous*, Roger. I'm not having that. You leave it with me and we'll get it sorted.' He pats Roger on the back, then says, '*Disgusting*. Oh, and make sure you join the union too.'

'I will,' says Roger. 'And thanks very much. I knew you'd see my point of view.'

I don't know *how* I don't push Roger out of the door when I show him out. Though I do slam it behind him, just a little.

'Molly,' says Andrew. 'Get onto that case, straight away. I can't *stand* bloody bad employment practices.'

Honestly, I can't believe it. The Boss is a Marxist where other people's employers are concerned, but a veritable Thatcherite when it comes to staff of his own. I wonder if Roger will have any more luck with his union than I've had with mine? I haven't heard a thing from Martin about my latest idea to work to rule.

I don't hear anything from Max, either, until I get home from work, at around the same time as his plane lands at Heathrow. Then he suddenly seems to recall that he is married; and begins sending a flurry of texts which give a blow-by-blow account of the rest of his journey home. He chooses that moment to share the name of the German hotel, too – now that the damn thing is bloody irrelevant.

I *had* been intending to keep his meal warm, but after that I burn it to a crisp by 'forgetting' to turn the oven down; and then I go upstairs to take an exceedingly deep bath. This ensures that Max will be both hungry *and* unable to have a shower, as I have used up all the hot water. I can't take the plant back that I bought him for our anniversary, though that's what I feel like doing – so I tell Connie where his secret stash of Ferrero Rochers are kept, and authorise Josh to drink the only can of beer that's left in the fridge, instead.

I even go to bed before Max finally arrives. I can't get to sleep, though, so I watch him fall over the pair of shoes I deliberately left in our bedroom doorway – and the subsequent trouser dance – through one sneakily half-open eye. Then I do a very convincing *stretch and turn* manoeuvre so that my back is to him, just as he tries to snuggle up.

Half an hour later, he's snoring like a steam train and I'm back downstairs making cocoa. I look everywhere for the Valium that Dad left behind when he came to stay after Stepmother Mark III left him, but I can't find it anywhere, so it's shaping up to be two sleepless nights in a row.

The phrase, 'I don't know the name of my hotel' will *not* stop running through my head.

## SATURDAY, 26 JUNE

I'm quite glad there isn't a supermarket surgery again this week, as it allows me a lie-in and postpones the moment when I have to talk to Max.

When I do get up, he's weirdly attentive, and jumps around making cups of tea and a cooked breakfast. He doesn't even mention Germany. I really hate how he does that – makes *me* have to broach any subject that he knows is going to lead to an argument. It makes me look *so* confrontational.

I'm determined not to fall into that trap today, though, so I decide to get the parental phone calls over and done with instead. Mum and Ted aren't in – probably on the first of their twice-daily visits to Waitrose. Dad *is* at home, but says he hasn't got time to talk to me, because he's about to leave on a trip: he's going away for a few days to Cousin Mike's.

I thought Cousin Mike was dead, but Dad assures me he's alive and well, and living near Heathrow with his second wife.

'I'm at the age when family becomes more important,' he says, when I ask why he's suddenly taking an interest in second cousins, once removed – if not departed. Then I ask for Mike's phone number and he gives it to me, though he says he thinks they'll be 'out and about' for most of the weekend.

The duty calls have taken a fraction of the time they usually take, and now the rest of the day is stretching unappealingly ahead – so I ring Dinah, just for a chat.

'Dad's gone to visit Cousin Mike,' I say.

'Thought he was dead,' says Dinah. 'We went to his funeral. Remember?'

'That's what I thought too, but Dad says *that* was Cousin Fred.'

'Christ,' says Dinah. 'We have far too many bloody relatives, living *or* dead. Why's Dad suddenly decided to visit him?'

'He says family's becoming more important to him,' I say.

'Don't be stupid,' says Dinah. 'Give me Mike's phone number and hurry up.'

Dinah is *so* bossy sometimes – but I don't *have* to do as she says, do I? Not without question, anyway.

'Why?' I say, mainly because that's the best I can do.

'Well, Dad's obviously up to something,' she says. 'God, you're dim, given what you do for a living. No wonder the country's in such a mess.'

I give her Mike's number, but I don't want to know what's going to happen next. Why are women automatically suspicious of men? Is it because we're genetically paranoid, or is it actually because of the stuff they get up to, if left unsupervised?

When I finally crack and ask him about his trip, Max makes his inability to recall the name of his hotel, for the whole of the twenty-four hours that he was staying in it, sound perfectly understandable. It was booked for him; the company guide had all the details; they were driven there from the airport by coach; and it was dark by the time that they arrived. Then he couldn't read the name from the hotel signage or stationery because it was in a completely over-the-top Gothic script. Or so he says.

When I still look a little dubious, he gets cross and falls back on that positively *antique* old chestnut: 'If you don't trust me after all these years, then what the hell is the bloody point?'

The 'after all these years' bit *is* the point, but I'm now so confused that I drop the subject. I almost wish there had been a surgery today. I know exactly what to do to help constituents with *their* problems.

## SUNDAY, 27 JUNE

Max still isn't talking to me after the 'after all these years' conversation, so I spend the day helping Connie with some job applications. She's decided she'd be better off in a call centre job, as she wouldn't be able to tell whether people had thin hair and poking-out ears over the phone.

I can't believe the hourly rate that some of them pay – it's almost as much as Max gets, since the two pay cuts he's had to accept during the last year; and yet he is *twice* Connie's age, if not more. I sometimes wonder if we wouldn't be better off if we separated, especially as all my single parent friends manage a holiday at least once a year. I have no idea how they do it.

Talking of single parents, Dinah phones in the evening – to discuss the one she and I are lucky enough to share. 'Dad *was* up to something, the bastard,' she says.

'Why?' I say. 'How d'you know?'

'I phoned him on his mobile at lunchtime – pretended

I'd just remembered it was Father's Day – but he sounded a bit flustered, and didn't try to guilt-trip me. *At all.*'

'Unusual, I grant you, but what's your point?'

I want to finish waxing my upper lip, and I'm a bit worried the strip won't *ever* come off if Dinah doesn't hurry up.

'Well,' she says, taking a deep breath as if in readiness for a very long explanation. 'He said he was in the pub having lunch with Cousin Mike, so I said, "Put Mike on, then, so I can say hello." Then Dad says, "I can't, because Mike is in the loo"!'

'Still clear as mud,' I say. 'Mike's allowed to go to the toilet, like the rest of us.'

'Shut *up*, Molly! You don't know what you're talking about. Just stop interrupting and listen for a minute!'

Honestly, unreasonableness runs in the family but, even so, no one *ever* manages to interrupt Dinah, so that is really, really unfair of her. Not that she's bothered – she just carries on: 'So I get off the phone to Dad, and then I phone the number you gave me for Cousin Mike's house and—'

'Oh, God,' I say, as Dinah shrieks, 'It's Mike who answers!'

Sometimes Dinah is *so* tiring. Now she's not speaking to me, because she wants *me* to phone Cousin Mike and ask to speak to Dad, and I just can't be bothered. We'll know eventually if we're going to get a Stepmother Mark IV, seeing as the whole family always has to attend Dad's weddings. The most recent one was when I last saw Cousin Mike, now I come to think of it.

Max seems to find the whole thing funny when he overhears me telling the kids about it, but Josh doesn't, much to my surprise. He's *disgusted* by his grandad's carryings-on. Maybe I should ask *him* what he thinks about Max and the mystery of the hotel without a legible name?

Oh, but parents can't do that sort of thing, though – can they? *Their* relationships are supposed to be rock-solid, as well as entirely platonic, so I'd either just worry Josh or make him squirm with revulsion. And anyway, I can't do it at the moment. I've still got to get that wax off my face somehow or other.

## MONDAY, 28 JUNE

Today sees the arrival of the first contender in The Boss' long list of summer interns, who usually fall into one of three distinct categories: purely decorative additions to the scenery; sixth-form leavers with their sights set on PPE[23] at Oxford and then government; and/or those repre-senting favours to Andrew's mates who want us to babysit their recalcitrant teenagers.

Today's is one of the PPE batch: James. He's expected to get five A*s at A-level, and appears to be quite without a sense of humour. This may be because he expected the constituency office to be a little more impressive than it is.

I think he was hoping for something less depressing than a view of the YMCA, not to mention his encounter

[23] PPE: Politics, Philosophy and Economics. De rigueur combination for would-be politicians, in these days of professional MPs. Or so Greg says.

with the bus driver from South Park, also known as Joan who works in the Labour Party office. She does take a bit of getting used to, but there was no need for James to demonstrate *such* an exaggerated startle response.

I always get saddled with inducting interns, though I'm not sure why. Greg's far closer to them in age, if not degree of earnestness – but much better than me at getting out of things. So it's down to me to obtain James' signature on the usual confidentiality agreement, and then to explain the security measures.

Which wouldn't take long, if I only mentioned those that The Boss has put in place but, of course, I don't. I am *far* more responsible than that – *and* I have kids of my own, so I always feel obliged to look out for other people's too.

First I explain that you never exit the security door before checking that there isn't anyone lurking to either side of it; then I move on to Special Branch's advice that we always look under our cars before getting into them, and check for people following us either to or from our homes. James starts looking a little concerned at this point.

I've just begun to detail the various personalised arrangements for handling the usual suspects when I'm interrupted by the phone. It's Miss Chambers, so James is exposed to the *risk to hearing* issue rather more quickly than I'd intended. When I glance up at him, he's already copying Greg, who has both hands pressed against his ears. I'm impressed. This kid learns fast.

Even so, I'm not sure what to do with him for the rest

of the day, as we don't have a spare computer and now he seems oddly reluctant to answer the phones. The Boss never thinks about this sort of thing when he accepts applications – but James looks to be an intelligent person, so it should be safe to entrust him with some filing. Not that he seems any more impressed by that than he does by the office. Or by Joan, for that matter.

He seems even less keen when he sees the number of live files that we have; and the sight of the archive cupboard makes him blanch. But he gets on with it without complaint, though he does seem to go to the loo an awful lot – which may be due to the weird healthy tea he brought with him in a Tupperware box.

On that basis, I can't help feeling he'd be better off at the Council. The staff there *all* drink fruit tea which, along with the wearing of Ecco sandals and long swishy skirts, is an accurate predictor of woolly-headed liberalness and Council employment, at least in the case of women. Or so Greg says, anyway.

While James is filing, I check my email, only to find a message from Johnny. He's back in Russia, but wants us to meet the next time he's in the UK. Then he asks whether I have any more photos I can send him, preferably ones with my eyes open, to 'keep him going' until then. (Going *where*, he doesn't say.)

My arse would take a much better photo than my face, but that's hardly helpful, is it? Someone once told me that, after forty, you can either have a great face or a great arse, and I fall into the latter category – which does make sending anyone a flattering, but

102

non-pornographic, photo rather challenging. Like a fool, I mention this in my reply.

Johnny's response arrives with indecent haste – he would be 'very happy to receive a photo taken from whatever I deem the most flattering angle, and of any body part I think he'd appreciate'. *Now* what the hell have I done?

At least someone doesn't object to looking at me, though – unlike Max, who's avoiding all eye contact this evening. One minute his explanations for his hotel name amnesia ring true, but then the next minute I think I must be insane to believe them. I'm just about to google 'How to tell if your husband is being unfaithful' when I'm distracted by yet another call from Dinah.

'He's f*cking incredible,' she says, without preamble.

She can only mean Dad – so there's probably no need to respond.

'He *was* up to something, as usual! Visiting Cousin Mike, my arse.'

'Up to what, though?' I say. It could be almost *anything*.

'He was on a date,' says Dinah. 'With my friend Annie's *mother*! He spent the entire weekend shagging her, the bloody hypocrite – she's one of the ones he said was too old when I first gave him her number.'

'So what happened?' I say.

I may as well know the worst, I suppose. Max obviously wants to, seeing as Dinah's yelling loudly enough for him to hear every word.

'This morning, Dad told her he didn't think it was

103

meant to be, and just got into his car and left,' says Dinah, taking the volume up a notch. 'I don't know how I'm going to face her, I'm *so* embarrassed. Apparently she thought he was *the one*.'

'Good God,' I say. 'Poor woman's obviously unwell. What does *Dad* say about it? I assume you've asked?'

'He still says he was at Cousin Mike's. Denies absolutely *everything*.'

'That man wouldn't know the truth if it jumped up and bit him on the arse,' I say, staring hard at Max.

*He* remembers that he needs to clear out the loft – urgently – and disappears. It's a startle response worthy of James.

**TUESDAY, 29 JUNE**
Honestly, I can't bloody well believe it. What kind of f*ck-witted, supposedly-A*-pupil thinks that you only file by the *first* letter of someone's name? It's going to take months to find anything now.

Once I've stopped swearing under my breath, I ring The Boss and demand that he finds James something totally harmless to do – so he thinks up a 'special' project: something to do with finding out how many teenage pregnancies there have been in Lichford in the last ten years. James brightens up for a minute at the prospect. He probably thinks this will gain him access to my computer, but I send him to the library instead, much to Greg's relief. At least *they've* got more than one male loo.

I tell James to be back in time for a meeting I've

arranged with a local manager from the Mental Health Trust, on the basis that it will be educational. He reverts to looking distinctly unenthusiastic, and becomes more so once the meeting starts.

I am trying to establish exactly the point at which our duty to protect staff and others would take precedence over our duty of confidentiality, and am a bit astonished to discover that several of the constituents that Greg and I deem the most dangerous have already been the subjects of a number of multi-agency meetings and risk assessments, *none* of which we have been included in. We deal with these nutters *daily* – and without any security at all!

After I point this out, there's a lot of embarrassed clearing of throats, and then it is agreed that we will be faxed copies of the relevant risk assessments this afternoon – on a 'need to know' basis – and we'll also be invited to attend the meetings in future. Greg and I are well-pleased at this development, but James looks decidedly pale.

I'm not looking much better myself by the time I've read the risk assessments. It's amazing how many of our usual suspects have convictions for ABH,[24] are known to carry weapons, and are considered to pose a high risk to any staff who have to deal with them.

I'm not sure I wouldn't rather have remained in blissful ignorance, relying on *The Twilight Zone* theme to protect me. (It hasn't served me too badly so far,

[24] ABH: Actual Bodily Harm. Does what it says on the tin.

after all. Apart from Frank Dougan, I suppose. Oh, and Mrs Nudd.)

Anyway, the only useful information is a list of those things which are known to trigger certain constituents to commit acts of violence. In Mr Meeeeurghn's case, this is almost anything, but I had no *idea* how dangerous Mr Humphries can be.

A paranoid schizophrenic with a persecution complex, I already knew that he's convinced that all government agencies are spying on him. What I didn't know was that he believes that other people's unconscious tics are *codes* to alert the authorities, and switch on surveillance.

It's only by the grace of God that Greg and I haven't ever scratched our noses, fiddled with a stray hair, or chewed the end of a pen while talking to the man! I'm starting to think that a degree in psychology would have been far more useful than one in politics. Even with the addition of another P and an E.

Once I've finished reading the risk assessments out loud, James says that he feels unwell, because his irritable bowel syndrome is causing him a problem, so I let him go home early. I'm not entirely sure about *his* sanity, if I'm honest. I keep hearing snatches of familiar music whenever he passes by.

Greg says this is probably a sign that I am losing the plot, so he suggests we go and get drunk to obliterate the memory of what we've been told about the usual suspects. I can't handle it tonight, though, as I haven't slept properly for days, so I opt to go home instead.

I soon wish I hadn't, because Max is in a really bad

mood, seemingly because Connie's got an interview for that call centre job. He overhears her telling a friend that it 'isn't brilliant money' and then doesn't speak to any of us for the rest of the night. Apart from Max, I'm the only one who knows that the sum in question is barely a thousand pounds a year less than he now earns. And not that much less than *I* earn, either.

Honestly, could Johnny and I inhabit worlds that were any more different? I just hope he's forgotten *I* was the one our class voted 'most likely to succeed'.

## WEDNESDAY, 30 JUNE

Oh, dear. That has to be the record for the shortest stay by an intern – ever. Mr Humphries proves too much for James, who has disappeared in a cloud of loose bowel movements. He hasn't even been back to collect his stuff. (Let's hope he has plenty of that disgusting tea at home.)

The morning goes suspiciously smoothly until almost 10:00am, funnily enough, but then Mr Humphries makes the first of what turns into a series of visits to the office. He becomes more agitated with every one.

I deal with the first few, which involve something to do with him being spied on, as usual, but I'm busy when he comes in again just before lunch – at which point Greg receives a frantic call to say that Mr H is holding Joan at knifepoint in reception.

We hadn't got round to telling Party staff that they mustn't rub their noses while talking to him, and Joan suffers from hayfever. Incensed by her apparent use of the code to activate government surveillance, Mr H has pulled a Stanley knife and locked her into the room.

The whole building is sent into lockdown mode as I try to contact the police – which is a thankless task, if ever there was one. Dialling 999 achieves nothing more than my being put on hold for eighteen minutes – *eighteen minutes!* You could walk to the police station quicker than that.

Having worked this out, Greg finally loses his patience and legs it over the roof, climbs down the fire escape and runs there, then pushes to the head of the queue and demands a police escort back to the office immediately – or he will 'tell the Home Secretary'.

Meanwhile, James has gone green and is more than usually desperate for the loo. He can't get there, though, because that would involve passing reception, where poor Joan is still stuck with a known madman, and a bad case of paroxysmal sneezing.

It takes until almost 3:00pm for the police to storm reception, arrest Mr Humphries and take him away – and for the building to be finally open for business again. This seems an opportune moment to send James off to get a late lunch, and to calm down while he's at it.

He makes *me* escort him out of the building, despite the fact that he is almost six feet tall, while I'm at least a foot shorter, but hey, whatever – as Josh would say. Not that that's what *I* say when this turns out to be the last that we will ever see of James, who doesn't come back to the office and ignores our calls for the rest of the day.

As if that isn't bad enough, it turns out that he also

made life difficult before he left, as well – by answering the phone to The Boss while Greg and I were otherwise occupied, and telling him what was going on. What an idiot. Greg can't get over it.

Now Andrew has left a message instructing me to call him back 'as soon as the misunderstanding with Mr Humphries is resolved'.

Misunderstanding? *Misunderstanding?* It was more than a bloody misunderstanding. Joan is a wreck, and James looked even worse than she does, before he did his disappearing act.

The staff of all the other offices in our building are *incandescent* with fury, too. They blame us for 'attracting undesirables' and 'failing to manage them properly' – as well as for having effectively lost them the output of an entire working day.

I don't have time to pour oil on any of these troubled waters, though; or to respond to Johnny's email reminding me that he is still waiting for a photo of my arse. I still have to give a statement to the police – once Greg and Joan have finished giving theirs.

It's almost 8:00pm by the time I get home, where I find Ellen sitting at the dining room table with Max. No wonder he hasn't called to see where I am.

'Molly,' she says. 'Try this wine. I came to borrow your corkscrew, but then I thought Max might enjoy a glass while I was here.'

'Oh,' I say. 'I'm sure he would.'

Max doesn't meet my eyes, as he fetches me a glass and begins to pour.

'It's my new discovery,' says Ellen, twisting the bottle to show me the label. 'Dornfelder-Würzgarten Kabinett.'

Her German accent sounds faultless to my untrained ear. I breathe in, then take a sip, though I'm pretty sure I'm going to choke.

'What does "*trocken*" mean?' I say, trying very hard to swallow.

'Dry,' says Ellen, which could also be said to describe my mouth.

# CHAPTER THREE

# July

(Which doesn't rhyme with anything.)

**THURSDAY, 1 JULY**

I can't find that wine for sale anywhere – not online, nor when I spend my lunch-hour checking all the off-licences in the centre of town. I'm sure the staff of Majestic Wines think I'm unusually fussy for an alcoholic, when I burst into tears after they say you can only buy 'that Bornfelter stuff' in its country of origin. Bloody, bloody Germany.

After I've stopped sniffling like an idiot, I decide that, if Max can get up to God knows what during a so-called 'work' trip, then I can do whatever I like, too. So now I have new underwear – a *lot* of it. It doesn't feel great (a bit cheap and scratchy) but at least it'll look okay in a photo for Johnny, so I suppose what it feels like doesn't matter. It's not as if he'll ever get to touch it, after all.

It makes me feel miles better, though, and helps my blood pressure normalise after The Boss gives me a bollocking: first for 'breaching Mr Humphries' confidentiality' by phoning the police, and then for giving them a statement about what happened to poor old Joan.

She still looks as if she's been electrocuted or at least over-Botoxed – while Mr H is now in hospital on a section and hopefully getting some help at last. The police say there is to be an injunction against him returning to the building, so everyone's relieved, except for The Boss, who rants as if he too needs to be sectioned during his phone call, made from his nice, secure office in Westminster. He hasn't even *met* Mr Humphries!

Greg phones James to tell him it's safe to come back to work, but James' mum isn't having any of it. She says James is far too shocked by yesterday's events to ever return to the office, and that The Boss should know better than to expose his staff to 'such outrageous risks'.

Greg says all he could think of in response was, 'True.'

'Perhaps James has been put off politics for good, and will get himself a proper job instead,' I say. 'He'll thank us for it, in the long run.'

'Maybe so, but what shall I do with all this in the meantime?' says Greg, gesturing at James' dietary paraphernalia and his bowel medications. 'And what the hell is *Chai* supposed to be?'

'No idea,' I say. 'Some sort of bowel-enhancing tea, I think. And no, of course I don't want it. You'll just have to pack everything up and post it all back to James.'

'Or I could offer it to Joan,' says Greg, continuing to rummage around in the kitchen cupboards. 'She still looks a bit bilious. Ooh, what's this I've found?'

Honestly, there's *no* privacy, is there? Not even when you hide something right at the back of a cupboard. Greg has spotted my Primark carrier bag and, before I can swipe it out of his hand, is wearing my new lace boxer shorts. On his head.

The sight makes listening to the next call oddly bearable, even though it's from Mr Beales, who goes on and on for hours about something so boring I can't even remember what it was. I think I may suggest that cranial knicker wearing is introduced nationwide, as a contractual requirement for constituency staff. Greg reckons it would really help to minimise stress at work.

'I felt great, wearing them while I talked to the Chief Whip,'[25] he says, as we lock up for the day. 'I'm almost sorry to have to give them back.'

'Well, I don't want them now,' I say. 'I'm not going to wear them after they've been on your head all afternoon. I'd never get the hair gel out.'

'They *are* a bit sticky,' says Greg. 'And a bit glam for you, anyway, now I come to think of it. Maybe you should post them through the letter-box at the Relate shop on your way home. Help someone in marital difficulties, and all that.'

I stare at him, hard, but he doesn't react, so maybe he isn't being ironic. I do as he says, though, just in case.

My donation doesn't seem to bring any immediate

---

[25] Chief Whip: Not what you may be thinking, having read tabloid reports into the sexual proclivities of some MPs, but the person responsible for Party discipline. Also known as 'the enforcer' by The Boss.

benefits, as Max does double the usual number of sit-ups as soon as he gets home from work, and then goes outside to water the garden, yet again – even though it's pouring with rain.

I leave him to it, and am in the bathroom, trying to photograph my own arse in the mirror – much trickier than it sounds – when I'm interrupted by a phone call from Mum, who says that Dad phoned to wish her a happy birthday for tomorrow.

He hasn't mentioned anything about it to me, but Mum says that he told her that he got her number from Connie – who'll tell anyone anything, the idiot. *Now* what the hell is going on?

I like both my biological parents to stay nicely in their separate boxes, along with their matching and various new spouses. It's the bloody least they can do to compensate for making me the insecure maladjusted child of a broken home.

I suppose it's too much to expect the proceeds of a pair of secondhand lace pants to fund effective help with that.

**FRIDAY, 2 JULY**

Maybe it's a good thing that long-serving MPs become so disconnected from their constituents. How else would they retain any certainty about their own political ideology? The more I hear and investigate constituents' real-life stories, the more confused I get. It's like trying to work out the guilty party during one of Josh and Connie's arguments: absolutely bloody *hopeless*.

Mrs Hetherington attends surgery today. She's a mature student at university, has teenage children like me (poor woman), and previously worked full-time for twenty years. She's also furious, having discovered that she won't be entitled to sign on during the vacation if she's unable to find a job. To add to the problem, her husband's self-employed and his business is collapsing.

The Boss nods sympathetically, as he tries to think of a way to blame Mrs H's situation on the Coalition, but then she hits him with it: 'There's a single parent on my course who's allowed to sign on during vacations,' she says.

'Ah, well, obviously *someone* has to care for her children, and she does only have one income,' says The Boss, looking relieved.

'*Benefits*, not *income*,' says Mrs H. 'And her daughter is *fifteen years old*.'

'Um,' says The Boss. He looks helplessly at me.

I'm in no mood to help out and, anyway, I want to hear his answer.

He says, 'Ah.'

'*And* she's never worked a day in her life,' says Mrs H. 'Whereas I've been paying tax ever since I left school. Explain *that*, if you can!'

The Boss looks relieved. There's a Party line on this one.

'But surely you'd agree that it's in everyone's interests for single parents to be encouraged to train, and then find employment, wouldn't you?' he says.

'No,' says Mrs H. 'Be bloody nice if you politicians

encouraged people to work and to stay married, for a change.'

The Boss has no answer to that. Nor do I, though at least there won't be any letters to write on the back of this particular appointment. I have no idea to whom I'd address Mrs H's enquiry, *or* how I'd word it.

The Boss isn't very happy, though. 'You were no help, Molly. No bloody help at all,' he says, as Mrs H takes her leave.

'Well, I don't know what I think about what she said,' I say. 'Do *you*?'

'She's a bigot,' says Andrew, with no trace of irony.

He goes off in a huff – to get the early edition of the local paper, or so he says. That's usually code for a 'restorative' drink.

While he's gone, I email Johnny the best of the photos I finally managed to take last night – by waiting until everyone else had gone to bed, then locking myself in the bathroom again.

I had to keep flushing the loo and groaning so Max would think I had a stomach upset, while twisting around like a lunatic to make sure that my arse was actually in the frame. The whole thing took ages, and it was after 4:00am when I finally got to bed. *How* have I come to this?

Of course, as soon as I hit *send*, I change my mind. Then I spend the rest of the afternoon panicking, especially when I get an out-of-office reply from Johnny. I bet his PA is showing my arse to everyone at the Global Oil Company water cooler right this minute.

I'm still trying to work out how to get an email back when there's another call from Josh's school. For God's sake. Josh has apparently 'failed to control' his skateboard, which has flown up into the air and smashed the window of the Deputy Head's office.

Mr Thumb says that he *had* intended to confiscate the skateboard for a week, but has now changed his mind.

'Why?' I ask.

I'd have confiscated it for ever, given half a chance. Josh's teeth looked perfectly normal until he took up skateboarding, and I'm sure he was more reasonable before all the blows to the head.

'Because of the championship,' says Mr Thumb.

'Pardon?' I say. I have no idea what he's talking about.

'Well, Josh was saying that he's in the National Skateboarding Championships this weekend, so I felt it would be only fair to delay his punishment until next week.'

Josh can't stay upright on that damned thing for more than twenty seconds without having an accident. No way is he capable of participating in a National Championship, unless it's the *Unintentional Comedy on a Skateboard Championship* – which I don't think exists, though it certainly *should*.

'Don't you agree?' says Mr Thumb.

I'm barely capable of speech, so just mumble a pathetic 'Thank you', and then hang up.

How the hell did Max and I raise a compulsive liar? And why didn't I expose Josh's dishonesty, to teach him a lesson? This abdication of parental responsibility and

117

discipline is probably how serial killers are made – as well as gang lords.

At least Connie's unlikely to become either of those things, as she's got the call centre job, which sounds fairly harmless. She's very excited about it – particularly at the thought of flexi-time – though I forget to ask her why, as just then Max arrives home, looking thoroughly fed up.

He feigns enthusiasm for Connie's achievement pretty well, but later tells me that *his* boss warned of further branch closures this morning. I try to reassure him, but God knows how we'd manage on my pathetic salary alone. We'd probably have to separate to survive. According to Mrs H, that's what all married people should be doing, anyway . . .

## SATURDAY, 3 JULY

Josh does not take well to Max and I taking the piss about the National Skateboarding Championships. In fact, he goes so far as to say that it is our failure to encourage his talents which has made him the way he is. Then he storms off into town with Robbie.

Max laughs, while I fall into a guilt-ridden slough of despond, which isn't helped by the fact that I won't get a reply from Johnny until Monday at the earliest.

God knows how many copies of my photo his PA will have disseminated around the typing pool by then. I will be his staff's equivalent of Mr Beales – my buttocks might even adorn their dartboard, as Andrew's face does ours.

This thought is so horrendous that even Max notices that I'm looking a bit stressed-out, and suggests we go and have a coffee somewhere – so we plod down to Caffè Nero, where I ingest so much caffeine that I give myself a bout of palpitations.

Max wants to know if I think The Boss will give me a pay-rise now that I can prove that I'm so badly paid in comparison to the employees of most other MPs. I say I rate my chances of that at zero, to which Max says he has now developed palpitations as well. The way our working lives are going, we'll have to rely on Connie to keep us soon – and *she's* only back at home for the summer!

Anyway, if Max's job's in such jeopardy, we can't afford to buy anything other than a coffee, so we decide we may as well go home again – and I feel even more guilty about the twenty quid I spent on underwear than I already did. It's not as if you can take *that* back for a refund, unlike your wife.

So now I've got stress hiccups, and Max and I are heading home, less than an hour after we left the house. We walk along in silence most of the way – me holding my breath and trying not to think what he'd say about the underwear if he found out about it, while he could be thinking about Ellen, for all I know – until we reach the underpass.

We've just passed through one of its steepish, sloping arms when we're stopped in our tracks by a sudden loud, rumbling noise, which startles me so much that my hiccups stop. As we stand still in the central circle, a skateboarder suddenly shoots out of another of the arms, waves, spins a few times, then roars gracefully past – out into the other arm that leads in the direction of our house.

We just manage to spot that it's Robbie, but honestly, *blink*, and you'd have missed him: it was all over in seconds, even though he was going uphill on the way out.

The rumbling doesn't diminish as much as it should, though, seeing as Robbie should be a fair distance away by now, given the speed he was going. Instead, it's intensifying, though it isn't half as rhythmic as the earlier sound.

Unnerved, Max and I continue to stand still in the central area, in case we're about to get taken out by a runaway trolley or something.

We seem to wait for ever until, eventually, another skateboarder appears. He's veering all over the place, and wobbling like a maniac.

It's Josh – and watching him is *agonising*.

Max and I look at each other, both close to hysteria, then back at Josh, who doesn't acknowledge us at all. He's too busy concentrating on wobbling his way slowly – *very* slowly – out of the underpass.

Just before he's out of earshot, it all becomes too much. Max lets out an explosive volley of laughter, and I sink against the wall, shaking. I may need an incontinence pad.

'Our son, the skateboard champion,' says Max.

I just nod. Honestly, we are *terrible* parents.

## SUNDAY, 4 JULY

Josh doesn't speak to Max or I all day, but he does leave the skateboard behind when he goes round to Holly's. Connie's also out, with her new boyfriend, so it's very quiet, even for a Sunday.

Max and I are sitting in the kitchen, in a fairly companionable silence, while he tightens the wheels on Josh's skateboard to improve the steering and I read the Sunday papers – which for once don't include a single quote from The Boss. We're having quite a nice time, until Annoying Ellen turns up, to borrow the corkscrew yet again.

After another of her overly vocal performances late last night, I ask her whether she's aware of how sound travels between our houses. Honestly, I'm *so* stupid sometimes.

She doesn't even look me in the eye, but does a silly little giggle, then simpers – right at Max – and says, 'Oh, sorry – it's just that I do *so* love sex.'

I say nothing, while I envisage beating her to death with a blunt object. I doubt Max is picturing the same thing, though he doesn't look any more amused than me.

'I didn't hear anything last night,' he says, looking up at Ellen, and cutting his finger on the chisel he's using to straighten Josh's wheels.

'Don't worry, Max,' she says. 'You didn't miss anything. Only me and some batteries.' Then she winks at him.

Max blushes, gets up to fetch the corkscrew, then presses it into her hand – just a little more slowly than necessary, though he claims that's because his finger's bleeding.

I'd have drilled the damn thing right through her palm, if I'd had the chance. Then they'd both need medical attention, not just Max.

He still looks a bit flustered when Ellen leaves, though that may be due to it being rather tricky to put a plaster on your right hand with your left, when your wife says she's too busy to help you do it.

I'm not sure if he realises 'busy' is a euphemism for 'annoyed', but things are tense for the rest of the day and I'm relieved when the phone rings, for once in my life.

It's Mum, who says that Dad has phoned her again, and she thinks that he is flirting with her now: too horrible a thought to contemplate. Wrong, wrong, wrong, wrong, wrong, wrong, *wrong*. Divorced parents should know that you don't suddenly start flirting with each other when you're in your seventies, and when your offspring have only just come to terms with being from a broken home.

Now I suppose I'm going to have to do something about it, and God knows what Dinah will say. Or *would* say, as *I'm* not going to tell her. I'm not that stupid. I just hope Dad's not chatting her mother up too, otherwise chaos could ensue.

What happened to women over thirty being 'too wrinkly'? That man's a hazard to the whole of the opposite sex, bendy willy or not. He's basically the Annoying Ellen of Dorset – with the addition of a foreshortened penis.

I'm so worn out by all these sex-crazed divorced people

122

that I've just decided to go to bed for a very early night, when my phone emits a beep. I have a new email – from Johnny! I forgot not everyone's like The Boss, who turns his phone off whenever he can and who has been known to throw it into the Thames – along with his pager – whenever he starts feeling persecuted by the Whips. Johnny keeps *his* BlackBerry turned on. (I wonder if this is some sort of omen?)

He doesn't say much, just, 'Fabulous arse. When can I see it in the flesh? Name the date, and don't keep me waiting too long.'

Oh, my God. I bet *I'm* the one who's blushing now.

**MONDAY, 5 JULY**
I seem to be surrounded by compulsive liars. All male, apart from Miss Chambers. What are the odds Johnny isn't another?

At work, the new website's almost finished, and the designer asks for a copy of The Boss' CV for inclusion. Greg finally finds a dog-eared old copy under a pile of photos of Andrew, all dreadful, even though he still had real hair in some of them.

I give the designer the least horrific, while Greg chooses the worst one for use on the dartboard, then reads the CV aloud. Neither he nor I can ever remember seeing it before.

Buried at the bottom of page two is the news that Andrew used to play cricket semi-professionally. For a fairly well-known team, in his home town. I don't pay much attention at first, as I am otherwise occupied in re-reading Johnny's email from last night; anyway, The Boss is a sports fanatic, which is why most of his jollies – sorry, *fact finding trips abroad* – take place at exactly the same time as major sporting fixtures. Greg is just suspicious by nature.

Before I know it, I hear him say, 'Just wondered if you could confirm the dates that Andrew Sinclair played for the team?'

*Now* what the hell is he doing? I leave my office and stand in the doorway to Greg's, raising my eyebrows in enquiry. Greg waves me away and swivels his chair so that his back is facing me.

'Are you sure?' he says. There's a pause, then he continues, 'You're *positive* there's no mistake?' He gestures furiously at me to approach his desk.

I wish he'd make his bloody mind up which direction I'm supposed to go in, and am about to say so, when he slams the phone down and punches the air. He looks even more like Patrick Bateman when triumphant.

'He's *such* a tosser sometimes,' he says.

'Who?' I say.

'Our lord and master, the keeper of the socialist flame and all-round good egg. That was the Secretary of the Cricket Club,' Greg says, as if that makes everything crystal-clear.

It doesn't. 'And?' I say.

'And they have never – *ever* – heard of Andrew Sinclair!'

'What?' And there was me, thinking that all my illusions had already been shattered. 'You mean—'

'That's *exactly* what I mean, Molly. The Boss' CV is

total bullshit. He never played for the team. Probably never did *half* the stuff he's got on here.' Greg screws up the CV and lobs it into the bin.

I don't know what to say, so I return to my desk and delete the email I'd started to draft in reply to Johnny's. I don't feel like flirting with him now – not when all I know about him is what he's told me himself.

'A drinkypoo at lunchtime?' says Greg.

I nod. Vigorously.

After lunch (one G&T for me, three for Greg), we pop into WH Smith, at Greg's insistence, where he buys a large, red box file and some new labels – and pays in cash. When I point out that we already have folders and labels in the stationery cupboard, he says that his purchase is 'for personal use'.

When we get back to the office, he retrieves the balled-up CV from the bin, smooths it out as best he can, then shoves it into the new folder. He winks as he does so. (I *do* wish people wouldn't keep doing that.)

The rest of the afternoon's not too bad, at least from a constituent point of view. Miss Chambers rings, but only once – to complain about a letter she's received from the local Council, telling her that their staff have been instructed not to take her calls any longer, and to insist that she writes in with her complaints instead. The hearing of Council staff is obviously *much* more important than mine.

Anyway, I'm deafer, but quite calm when I close down my computer and prepare to go home – until I spot Greg, who's precariously balanced in the depths of the archive cupboard, his feet straddling two of the shelves, half-way up. (There's a certain amount of wobbling going on, which reminds me of Josh.)

'Give me a hand, Molly, before I break my neck,' Greg says. 'Pass me that new box file, will you?'

I pick it up from his desk. It now bears the label 'Staff Insurance Policy'.

*What on earth* are we becoming?

## TUESDAY, 6 JULY

Mum rings me at work. Her preamble is not promising.

'Sorry to bother you at work, dear. I just wanted to ask you whether you'd noticed my eyelid last time you saw me?'

'What eyelid?'

I am trying to scroll through my inbox, which already contains two hundred and twenty-seven emails received overnight.

I have no idea why the House of Commons spam filter picked up an email in which I described a local councillor as 'disappearing up the arse' of a certain MP, when it seems incapable of removing the forty-eight adverts for Viagra I receive daily, not to mention those for fake watches and penis enlargements.

'My right eyelid. I've been looking at it in the mirror, and it looks a bit droopy,' continues Mum.

'Was that the twenty-five-times magnifying mirror like mine?' I say.

'Well, *ye-es*. But it definitely looks a bit odd to me.'

'I think the best thing you can do is to stop looking

in the mirror, Mum – especially that one. Twenty-five-times magnification is not good for the self-esteem. I'm sure it's fine and you just need to find another interest.'

'Oh, well – if *you* didn't notice anything, maybe it's okay,' says Mum. Then she hangs up, without even remembering to say goodbye.

I'm as blind as a bat, but Mum just doesn't get that the whole purpose of your sight deteriorating as you age is so that you have no idea how truly hideous you're becoming. At least *she* wants to talk to me, though, unlike Josh.

As soon as I get home, he says he's off to Robbie's for the evening. That's the *only* thing he does say, actually, as he's still not speaking to Max or me since the incident in the underpass.

Connie more than makes up for her brother's silence, now that she doesn't have to compete for parental attention. She goes on about her new job, non-stop, for hours, while Max and I try to look as excited by the idea of flexi-time as she still seems to be, though God knows why. It's a struggle, so we're quite relieved when – eventually – she too goes out, to meet her boyfriend at the cinema.

Now for a cup of tea and, finally, some peace and quiet.

Famous last words. As soon as the door closes behind Connie, Max says, 'Talking about work . . .'

'Yes?' I say, in my MP's office voice. I don't like the sound of this already.

'I have to go abroad again – next week.'

Max busies himself in the depths of his briefcase, while I stare at him, open-mouthed. No business trips at all – ever – and then two. In a *month*? This is pushing credibility.

'What?' I say. 'Another trip? Why?'

'Business,' he says.

'But I thought the company was struggling,' I say, trying to stop my voice squeaking like Mr Meeeeurghn's. 'I'm always reading that furniture sales are down. Massively.'

'They are,' says Max. 'So, if the company wants me to go on a sales course, what choice have I got?'

Outmanoeuvred. Yet again. Why does my bullshit detector desert me the minute I get home? If I listen very carefully, though, I'm sure I can hear the sound of a faint, though horribly familiar tune.

### WEDNESDAY, 7 JULY

The quality of the letters sent to The Boss isn't getting any better, just like the quality of certain husbands' excuses for taking mysterious 'business trips'.

Today's contender for F*ckwit of the Week reads as follows:

> *Dear Mister Sincler*
> *Tony Blair kept on about wanting people to have lots of kids. I done what he wanted and me and the wife have 5, but we don't get NO HELP AT ALL.*
> *I work 16 hours a week and we have to live on benefits and tax credits but the goverment won't*

*pay for someone to take my 3 oldest kids to and from school. My wife can't do it, not with the 2 little uns at home.*

*What I want to know is what you and your party are going to do to stand up for hardworking parents now that Cameron bloke's in charge. I'm disgusted your lot told me to have all these kids. Now look at the mess I'm in.*

*Disgusted*

*Mark Betts*

*PS I'm so disgusted I've sent copys of this letter to the paper and I'm going to deliver 300 more all round the town.*

Greg and I work out what Mr Betts' total income would be – assuming minimum wage for sixteen hours a week – and it's more than mine. Quite a lot more, if you take his Housing and Council Tax Benefits into account. Now I'm *positive* that Greg's earning more than me, as he isn't half as pissed off as I am, though he *does* say some awfully politically incorrect things about the people *he's* keeping with *his* taxes.

At lunchtime, he buys a packet of five condoms and puts them into a House of Commons envelope with a compliment slip. He marks it, 'FAO Mr Betts, Father of the Nation. Try these and do us all a favour.'

The afternoon isn't very busy, but I'm so distracted by Max's business trip announcement that I get half-way home before I realise Greg and I have forgotten to remove the 'letter' to Mr Betts from the post tray. It has therefore been posted, along with the rest of the mail. Oh, shit, shit, *shit*!

I have to run all the way back to the office and stand in wait next to the postbox outside. Then I have to humiliate myself again – as if the arse photo wasn't bad enough – by *begging* the postman to give me the letter. (Actually, I have to slip him a fiver and, even then, he won't give me the damned thing until I've shown him my business card and pointed out the House of Commons crest.)

Bloody, *bloody* Greg. In fact, bloody men, full-stop.

## THURSDAY, 8 JULY

I am too depressed to even *think* about doing any work. I've just realised there are only twenty-one days left until Recess.[26] *Twenty-one!* I'm tempted to throw myself off a tall building right now. (I could even join Mr Ellis, invite The Boss and make it a media event.)

That'd probably be bad karma, though – wouldn't it? Not that Buddhists seem to worry about that much – or idiot brother Robin doesn't, anyway. Mum says he gave her a book on preparing for death for her birthday last week. I had *no* idea he'd done such a stupid thing!

No wonder she's been so obsessed with her buttocks and eyelids, and everything else in between – and, as if that wasn't bad enough, she says Robin also suggested

---

[26] Recess: Summer Recess is when constituency staff are most likely to become suicidal. This is not the obverse of Seasonal Affective Disorder, but is directly linked to the fact that Parliament takes a long break in the summer, during which time MPs tend to spend more time in their constituencies.

that he and she go to Paris this summer, so that he 'will have something to remember her by'.

I *must* try to be more sympathetic towards her in future – and kill 'caring Buddhist' Robin, as soon as I get the chance. Why are supposedly sensitive people so unbelievably crass when it comes to other people's feelings? Robin's so busy ringing his bell and saying, 'Om', he hasn't a clue anyone else exists half the time.

Even if I told him off, he still wouldn't feel any guilt about it. Not like me. I'm riddled with the stuff since I sent Johnny that stupid photo of my arse, especially as his emails have become so much more frequent ever since, along with my hiccups.

He says I'm teasing him because I still won't agree to let him see my backside in the flesh, and he's sending me messages about it so often that he can't possibly be concentrating on his job. If this keeps up, we'll probably hear about another giant oil spill soon. Then I'll feel guilty about that, too, when all those poor fish die and loads of fishermen starve.

Mind you, it *is* nice to be the centre of someone's attention for a change, instead of just a wife, mother and – worst of all – a very poor substitute for an MP.

I rather like that last phrase. It's open to a number of different interpretations, which suggests I've learned more from my years at the dull end of politics than I'd previously thought.

Robin could learn a lot, if he stopped chanting and preparing Mum for death, and started listening to me instead.

## FRIDAY, 9 JULY

Oh, for goodness' sake. I thought conspiracy theorists were supposed to be based *outside* Parliament, not be members *of* it. Now The Boss thinks the phones are bugged.

As if banning me and Greg from talking to Party staff, *and* making us attend Friday briefings separately and on alternate weeks, wasn't barking mad enough, now he's become obsessed with listening devices, too.

Why does he think anyone cares what he says or does? He's still only a backbencher, and has no hope of ever getting promoted, even if he didn't have the recently added handicap of being a member of a party that's in opposition.

Today, whenever one of the phones rings, he makes a dive to answer it himself, then takes the caller's number and insists on phoning them back on his mobile – from the archive cupboard. God knows how expensive his mobile bill will be, but I don't think the office budget is going to cope.

'Ridiculous waste of taxpayers' money,' says Greg, who doesn't seem to be having any trouble with *his* personal budget. I'm sure that's an Armani tie he's wearing, but what the *hell* is that about? I thought we were supposed to look accessible, not overdressed, for work – not that there's much choice on my budget, anyway.

Compared to Greg's sartorial splendour, I feel like a hobo – to borrow one of Josh's many offensive expressions. And I'm pretty sure that this feeling will be a hundred times worse when – I mean, *if* – I ever meet up with Johnny *International Director* Hunter.

It'd probably be better *never* to meet him. Then his memories of me could stay intact, unspoiled by any present-day reality checks. Those are thoroughly over-rated, as today's surgery only serves to prove.

First, there are several very-disabled people worrying about what's going to happen to their benefits when the rules are changed.

The Boss provides no real reassurance, as he can't resist the temptation to cast the Coalition in the most terrifying light possible – so the constituents aren't any happier by the time their appointment's over.

'Molly will accompany you down to the ground floor in the lift,' says Andrew, much to my horror. 'In case it breaks down again.'

It doesn't, thank God, but I don't know what help Andrew thinks I'd have been, if it had, seeing as I'd have been the first to lose the plot. I *hate* lifts. They make me feel trapped and panicky – just like when Max and I sometimes seem to have so little to talk about.

Anyway, by the time I've made my way back up the stairs, Andrew's already putting the fear of God into a group of public sector workers who are fretting about possible redundancies. They're accompanied by someone from their union, who talks tough and meets with The Boss' wholehearted approval. The word 'strike' crops up any number of times.

I hope my union will be just as aggressive in *my* defence if I lose my job to ensure the survival of Carlotta's. We're really pissed off with her today, since she phoned Greg to say that The Boss has asked her to write an article in his name for some publication or other, and that *she* can keep the five-hundred-pound fee!

'English isn't even her first language,' says Greg, sounding oddly like Mr Beales.

'That's not the point,' I say, because it isn't. The *real* issue is that it's me who spends my whole life writing creatively and affixing Andrew's signature to the fruits of my labours – but I am doomed to be forever in the shadows, my light firmly embedded in a bag-carrying bushel. (I can do metaphors as well as the next Spanish person, though if I'm to seriously compete with Carlotta, I probably need to grow longer legs.)

I walk home rather slowly on my short ones, to find Max proudly brandishing an airline ticket and travel itinerary.

I don't know why he's so taken with the latter, seeing as it looks just like any other itinerary – i.e. one that a reasonably competent person could have knocked up on a home computer in five minutes flat. (Ellen, for example. *She* can type.)

I make a non-committal grunt, learned from The Boss, and then Max makes a great show of writing the name of his hotel in the diary. I'm not sure what reaction this is designed to provoke, but it irritates the hell out of me – as well as making me even more suspicious. Not *all* conspiracy theories are imaginary, after all, though I'm damned if I'm going to tell Andrew that.

## SATURDAY, 10 JULY
Greg's finally taking his turn at doing supermarket surgery

today, and I'm looking forward to a very long lie-in – so, of course, he makes sure that *that* doesn't happen.

I awake to a barrage of texts in which he uses every bit of punctuation available on his mobile to denote various agonised faces. He doesn't add any actual words.

At 09:45am I give up the attempt to sleep and get out of bed.

In retrospect, this is probably a good thing as – about an hour later – Sam turns up. To stay the night, much to my surprise, though apparently not to Max's.

'Thanks for the phone call last night, mate,' Sam says, slapping Max on the back, as usual. 'Always good to get an invitation.'

Max looks puzzled, as if he has no idea what Sam's talking about, but I'm positive he *did* suggest Sam visited – probably to avoid any arguments this weekend. I stare at Max quizzically, which he pretends to be too busy cooking brunch to notice.

While we eat, Sam updates us on his love-life, or the recent lack of it. Apparently, he was 'forced to dump' the Tall Enigma, after she 'deliberately humiliated' him. 'Drank him under the table' might have been a more accurate description.

'Well, yes,' he says, when I mention it, 'she *did* drink more than me, but I wouldn't have minded if she hadn't then decided I was far too drunk to walk. I'm the only member of the team whose girlfriend's *ever* given them a fireman's lift out of the rugby club. I'll never live it down.'

Now Sam's back on the hunt for the love of his life – via

the Internet, as usual. He says that the last woman to contact him sounded perfect and so, after a series of increasingly flirtatious and innuendo-laden texts and phone calls, he arranged to meet her in a National Park somewhere in the back of beyond. (The location alone would have given *me* pause for thought, but then I'm constitutionally mistrustful. It's one of the few perks of the job.)

So, anyway, Sam says he drove up to the parking spot and saw what looked to be a very butch Park Ranger, standing near a picnic table.

'It must have been her,' he says. 'There wasn't anyone else around, so I panicked, reversed out and drove straight off again. It's a good job she didn't spot me, seeing as she'd have made a convincing prop forward.'

Now he's blocked her calls, and changed his email address. For about the fifth time this year.

Honestly, God knows what Sam expects when he *will* keep insisting that any prospective girlfriend shares his interests. I seriously doubt Kate Moss plays rugby in her leisure time.

I've just finished pointing this out, when The Boss phones me on my mobile. 'Molly,' he shouts, as if he's forgotten that phones only require a normal speaking voice. 'I'll drop off my notes from today's surgery at your house tomorrow. All right?'

'Um, why?' I say. 'No' would have been a better choice.

'So you can get on with dealing with them – straight away,' says Andrew, as if that should have been obvious.

Tomorrow is Sunday, for God's sake! There's no point mentioning that, though, so instead I try to find a subtle way to explain that Andrew's so-called notes will be worse than useless, and that Greg will have taken his own, far more coherent versions – but all to no effect. The thing about The Boss is that he never, ever, takes a hint.

In the end, I have to resort to telling him that Max and I are going out for the day tomorrow, and that it would be far too hazardous to leave the notes with Josh or Connie, as they cannot be trusted with sensitive information.

They both look at me reproachfully as I say this, but luckily don't start moaning until after I have hung up. (If I've learned one thing about handling The Boss, it's never to agree to do *anything* he claims will be a one-off, unless it's a genuine emergency – otherwise it will immediately become a regular fixture.)

'He'll still turn up tomorrow,' says Max. 'You *do* know that, don't you, Mol?'

'Yes,' I say. 'We'll just have to hide from him. Talking of hiding, where is Sam?'

'Gone to the off-licence,' says Max. 'He wants you and me to help him choose the next potential girlfriend. Says having a few drinks usually helps him narrow the field of candidates.'

That's arguable, but Sam's brief absence does give Max and I the chance to discuss what we'd have looked for in a husband or wife, if we'd ever had to advertise for one.

Max says he would have sought someone who loved cooking and travel, whereas I would have looked for a partner who enjoyed foreign-language films and reading books. Instead, Max got a travel-phobic who can't competently boil an egg, and I got a dyslexic who can't follow subtitles.

Both of us therefore question the need for a woman to share Sam's interests quite as fully as he seems to think necessary, and we feel oddly bonded by the time he returns. Then we spend the rest of the evening exchanging smug, affectionate glances – while Sam explains that all he wants is to be 'as happy as you guys are'. I don't mention Johnny Hunter, and Max doesn't mention the business trips – or his soft spot for Annoying Ellen.

By the time we've polished off three bottles of wine between the three of us, Max and I are madly in lust. By the time he and Sam have drunk another bottle, he is fast asleep. The gold stars remain firmly in the drawer.

## SUNDAY, 11 JULY

God, it's hot. And why on earth did I tell The Boss we were going out for the day?

Sam thinks I am a madwoman when I insist that we keep the curtains in the front room closed, and that Max moves the car from its usual parking spot – just in case Andrew decides to cruise by 'on the off chance'. (It has been known.)

It must be at least 95 degrees, without the windows open, but at least sitting in a darkened room means that Max and Sam can now remove their stupid sunglasses. They both claim that hangovers have nothing to do with their sensitive eyes, but there's a lot of groaning and excessive ibuprofen consumption before they're worth even *attempting* to have a conversation with.

Max probably shouldn't have driven the car round the corner, either, now I come to think of it. I bet he was still over the limit, though he says he's perfectly sober and that he's only groaning because he may have pulled his back by sleeping on the couch all night.

He groans again after he says this, louder this time – and looks at me hopefully as he does so.

I look away, as I have no sympathy whatsoever, and am still sulking about his failure to follow through on last night's brief lust-filled moment. Fancy being rejected in favour of another bottle of Australian Shiraz!

I can't get over *that*, though Max seems not to notice my bad mood. Sam does, though, or at least, I think he does – as he changes his mind about staying for another night, drinks five more cups of strong coffee, then leaves for home.

It's late afternoon by then, so I consider doing the parental phone calls, but quickly conclude that I'm still far too grumpy to avoid having an argument with one or other of them; and, anyway, we've got Connie's boyfriend coming for dinner in a couple of hours.

We've been putting this off, as Russ doesn't seem the easiest person to talk to – but Connie's getting upset by our delaying tactics now. She keeps pointing out that Josh has had Holly here for a meal on numerous occasions, whereas we haven't invited Russ at all – so there's no option but to redress the balance tonight, though none of us are really looking forward to it.

For no good reason, as things turn out. How wrong about someone can you be? The evening's miles more fun than we'd expected, though Connie may well beg to differ.

Max cooks a Thai meal, and Russ has never tried Thai food.

'It's chilli-hot,' says Max, by way of introduction. You'd think this was an innocuous comment, but the mention of chillies turns Russ from a monosyllabic introvert into a gushing fool.

For almost two hours, he tells story after story – all of them about hazardous past encounters with chillies. These were all apparently entirely self-inflicted, and carried out as tests of manhood.

Each story is identical to the last, except for the number of chillies consumed, which increases with every version. So too does the number of pints of water that had to be drunk as a result. Max and I can't even look at each other, and Connie is squirming. She already thinks we can't stand Russ.

I dread to think how long the whole thing would have gone on had Josh not completely lost the plot. He interrupts Russ firmly, saying, 'I once ate a chilli the size of my head.'

Russ looks nonplussed, and Josh continues, '*And* I had to drink thirty-seven litres of water before I could talk, or even swallow. Was wild, man – know what I mean?'

Russ nods, lost in admiration – but Connie's had enough of this now. 'It's getting late, Russ,' she says. 'I think you'd better be going, as we've all got to work in the morning.'

She glares at us behind Russ' back, as she leads him out of the dining room and towards the front door.

When she comes back, Josh says, 'Wow, Con – where've you been hiding him? I *love* Russ. *Love* him. Almost as much as he loves his chillies.' He raises his hand, in an attempt to high-five her.

'F*ck you,' says Connie, and flounces off to bed.

Not for the first time this weekend, Max and I congratulate ourselves on our extraordinary good fortune in having married each other. Imagine only having the interests of a chilli fetishist to share!

## MONDAY, 12 JULY

I arrive at the office this morning to find that The Boss has been in over the weekend and has left Saturday's surgery 'notes' on my desk. (It also looks as if he's searched all the drawers, but *that's* another story.)

I wish he'd told me he was going to do this, as at least then I wouldn't have had to spend Sunday boiling to death at home, with all the windows and curtains closed. I overheated so much I might as well have eaten one of Josh's imaginary giant chillies.

Andrew's left the notes on my desk, but I pass them straight to Greg, as it'll be his job to do the follow-up letters, seeing as he went to this week's supermarket surgery. For a change.

Greg looks at the notes, then up at me. I think incredulous may be the word. 'These notes aren't from Saturday's surgery,' he says.

'How can you tell?' I say. There hasn't been enough

time for anyone to have deciphered Andrew's handwriting yet.

'They say, "Asda" at the top,' says Greg. 'We were at f*cking *Tesco*, for God's sake.'

I can't really be bothered with Greg making a fuss about nothing, as I am ploughing through the weekend's emails, and still have the crazed answer-phone messages to tackle after that.

'Oh, wait,' he says, looking again. 'Yeah, I do recognise some of the names – but look at *these*!' He shoves a handful of A5 sheets of paper at me. All bear the House of Commons crest, and all are covered in hieroglyphics. 'What the f*ck?' says Greg, swearing even more than usual.

I can see why, once I get round to taking a look. The Boss has obviously lost his mind.

He's decided to draft the letters himself, presumably because he has forgotten our long-standing, and very necessary, agreement that only Greg or I write letters. *Never* Andrew.

When the drafts don't make him appear semi-literate, they make it obvious that he had absolutely no idea what any of the constituents were talking about. This impression is further emphasised by the fact that what he says about each constituent's case bears virtually no relation to the comprehensive notes Greg took at the time.

'Just ignore Andrew's versions, and write your own,' I say. 'It is our duty to stop him making an idiot of himself.'

I refrain from mentioning that I will still have to check

Greg's letters before they are posted. Honestly, I might as well do *everything* myself!

The Boss phones shortly afterwards to check that we've received his notes. I've no idea why he would think we hadn't, seeing as he'd left them right on top of my keyboard, but I humour him, anyway. You have to take pity on those who lack even the most basic of skills.

'Yes, thanks,' I say.

'Got the draft letters, too?' Andrew is clearly bursting with pride at his achievement. 'Cases were so straight-forward, I thought I'd help you guys out a bit.'

This is hardly an accurate reflection of the truth, but I let it pass.

'Hear about that new MP?' he continues. 'Got so pissed in the Commons bar, he couldn't manage to vote, then tried to blame it on the heat, the f*cking idiot.' The Boss can hardly contain his delight. 'Typical bloody Tory. Lightweights, all of 'em. I can manage it, no matter *how much* booze I've had.'

'Yes, Andrew,' I say, 'but you have occasionally forgotten *which way* you intended to vote. Much to the Whips' disgust.'

'Not because I was drunk!' he says. 'Those bastards change the wording of bills, and add amendments to catch you out. I can't always be expected to notice those.'

'Well, the media don't appear to have any trouble keeping up,' I say, 'and, talking of the press, I am really, really hoping that it wasn't *you* the *Daily Mail* quoted this morning, bragging about "old-timers being able to handle their drink"?'

'Anything else you need me for?' says Andrew, in a slightly less cheerful tone than before. 'No? Got to go then. My mobile will be off for a bit.'

That's him silenced, but Greg's so annoyed by the whole thing that he spends the next ten minutes ranting about his taxes funding subsidised alcohol in the House of Commons bars. After that, he photocopies the page from the *Mail* and sticks it on the wall, then gets distracted by another article it contains, which criticises the Sloane Rangers the Tories are alleged to have brought in as their Parliamentary researchers.

Greg says he can't see that Sloane Rangers are any less qualified for the job than any of The Boss' long line of researchers have been. If you collated *their* photographs, the result would look like a line-up for *Miss World*, with almost every nation represented, if not every shape of leg.

'Well, we are a multi-cultural society now,' I say, 'much to Mr Beales' disgust.'

We're supposed to be a multi-lingual one, too – though, in that case, you'd think the French in Max's itinerary would be a bit more convincing than it is. German must be Ellen's strongest suit.

## TUESDAY, 13 JULY

A builder whistled at me at lunchtime today. At least, I *think* it was at me. I looked all around and couldn't see anyone younger nearby. Now I'm just hoping he wasn't taking the piss.

It's been ages since that happened – *so* long that I can't

even remember when it last did. It's funny, isn't it? You view wolf-whistling builders with contempt when you're young and then, as soon as they stop doing it on a regular basis, you end up pathetically grateful for their attention.

I bet this one *was* taking the mickey, anyway, as I look absolutely knackered when I catch sight of myself in one of the mirrors in Primark at lunchtime, after a particularly demanding call from Miss Chambers. I must do something about this *forgotten-the-name-of-my-hotel*-induced insomnia. My face is a very funny shade of grey.

So is Max's – probably due to the weekend's excesses, and the heatwave. Oh, and now to *Josh*. Sometimes, I despair.

It's still so hot this evening that Max decides that he can't face cooking, so he goes off to get a pizza for Connie and me, and kebabs for him and Josh.

He comes back twenty minutes later, outraged. 'Where's Josh?' he shouts, dropping the bags of food in the hallway.

I'm not at all used to Max yelling, as it's uncharacteristically energetic even when we're not in the middle of a heatwave, so I just stand there, shocked into silence.

'Where *is* that little shit?' Max pushes past me and heads up the stairs, two at a time, shouting, 'Joshua, come here *now*!'

I decide I'd prefer not to know what Josh has done, so I go outside for a cigarette, but Connie refuses to join me, blaming her aversion to smoke. She loiters in the hallway instead, hoping to hear every word of Josh being given a bollocking, which he's obviously about to be.

After half an hour of incomprehensible but very loud shouting from Max, and apparent silence from Josh – during which I smoke another cigarette, unpack and serve the food, and Connie and I eat ours – Max finally re-appears, this time with Josh in tow.

Josh actually looks chastened, which is quite possibly a first.

'Do you *know* what your son did?' says Max, glaring at me as if I certainly should.

I have no idea, so I shake my head, but the use of the phrase, '*your* son' is probably an indicator that it isn't likely to be anything good.

Max continues, 'I go into the kebab shop, and the guy behind the counter reels backwards when he sees me, in shock. As if he's seen a ghost.'

'Why?' I am still none the wiser, though Josh's lips seem to be starting to twitch.

'Because he thought I was *dead*!' says Max. He stares at his kebab as if it's offended him, then pushes the plate away.

'Why the hell did he think that?' I say.

'Because *that* f\*cking comedian *told* him I was!' Max looks accusingly at Josh, who averts his head, though not in time to completely stifle a very childlike giggle.

'You did *what*?' I say to Josh, who's still trying so hard not to laugh that he's incapable of speech. He shakes his head, then Max steps in.

'He's been getting a free can of Coke with *every* kebab – for months,' he says. 'As a gesture of sympathy, for his loss.'

## WEDNESDAY, 14 JULY

Max leaves to drive to the airport before I go to work, but first he makes a great show of checking that I have the itinerary, and have noticed that he's written the name of his hotel on the calendar, as well as in the diary.

This is so annoying that I grunt, but then panic, probably due to the kebab incident. What if Max's plane crashed and the very last thing I'd said to him was, 'Humph'? (This is definitely why he and the kids get away with so much, as I'm sure they all know I'm insanely convinced that, should any of us ever part on an argument, that'll be the last time we see each other. I may well qualify as a mad constituent myself.)

So, just in case, I give Max a kiss, which he turns into a proper one. This is extremely weird, and very disturbing – because if there's one thing married people *don't* do, it's kiss as if they were in love. Even if they do still have a sex-life. It's oddly easier to shag someone while resenting them at the same time than it is to kiss them with any degree of conviction. Maybe that's why prostitutes don't kiss their clients.

It certainly puts me into a bit of tizz afterwards, which isn't helped by the walk to work. It's so hot that I nearly develop heatstroke in the process, so I'm already quite grumpy by the time I arrive – and then PMQs really doesn't help. A parliamentary question about a family living in a million-pound house in London while on benefits sets the usual suspects off on a series of virtually identical rants.

I have *no* idea how to defend a system that allows this

sort of thing to happen, so by the time I've managed to get Mr Beales off the phone, my mood is even worse – so much worse that I accidentally walk off before Joan has finished telling me about the latest fiasco with her tax credit overpayment.

I've *never* been so rude to anyone in my life – but I do wish she wouldn't lie in wait for me in the ladies' loo. It drives me mad, and it'll give *me* irritable bowel syndrome one of these days. I'll have to check if there's any of James' medication still lying around.

Talking of James, I must arrange for an intern to replace him, too – but the list The Boss has given me seems to consist solely of sixteen-year-old schoolgirls, one of whom is the daughter of the local Tory Party chairman. Has Andrew *really* not noticed this?

I phone him to enquire. 'Um, Andrew – this Fiona you've got on the interns' list—'

'Lovely girl,' says The Boss. 'Pretty as a picture, she is.'

'Well, that's all very well,' I say, 'but are you aware that she's also *George Thompson's* daughter?'

'Oh, that. Yes, of course I am.' There's no 'of course' about it, but The Boss doesn't sound at all concerned. 'The local Tories are less threat to me than those bastards in my own party. She'll be fine,' he says.

That remains to be seen, but what can you do when you've carried a horse to water and the damn thing refuses to drink?

I phone Fiona, who agrees to start next Monday. She does sound capable of an intelligent conversation, and is reasonably assertive, so at least that's promising – and if she also knows how to file, that'll be a *real* bonus.

I say this to Greg, who usually hates interns but who doesn't seem to need any persuading that this one might turn out okay.

'What's wrong with you?' I say. 'Why aren't you moaning about Fiona like you usually would about an intern?'

Greg plays dumb for a few minutes, but then admits that he's already met her – at a Council function, when she was accompanying her dad.

He starts to twitch when I ask him exactly how attractive she is.

'Well, she looks a bit like my ex-girlfriend,' he says, with what sounds like a stifled sob. I will keep on forgetting that Greg's resemblance to Patrick Bateman is only skin-deep, and that his heart has recently been broken.

Mine almost has, too – even more recently, thanks to Max and the hotel name fiasco – but *he* seems determined to compensate for that, on this trip, anyway. During the evening, he phones four times from his hotel. *Four* times, for God's sake! I miss half of every television programme I attempt to watch.

The first call is to tell me that he's arrived; the second to inform me that he's in his room, which is 'nice, but a basic single'. Call three advises me that he's going out for dinner with 'the group', and the fourth is to tell me that he's back from dinner; that the food was rubbish compared to that on the German trip; and that he's going to bed now as 'this actually seems as if it's going to be a *working* trip'.

I know I should be glad Max has remembered that I exist this time, and that he seems to want to reassure me – but talk about *methinks he doth protest too much*. Now I'm even more suspicious than I was before.

I ask Josh what he thinks, and he tells me not to be an idiot, and that while 'Dad can be a prat, he's not a *cheating* prat.'

I find that oddly comforting. I doubt Max would.

## THURSDAY, 15 JULY

I wish constituents would stop reading the *Daily Telegraph*. It just encourages them – especially Richard Bloody Levinson, who seems to have suddenly recalled that he hasn't been in touch since late last year.

This afternoon, he sends me *seventeen* emails in a row. In the first one, he wants to know why he's struggling to obtain a housing transfer, when 'these bloody people in today's *Telegraph* can get away with a million-pound house on benefits, just because they've got so many children'?

Then he reiterates his long-standing complaint about why he and his wife can't be expected to stay in their lovely two-bedroomed Council flat in East Cross, because of the stress caused by their 'uncouth neighbours'.

'We need a detached house, in the country,' he says. 'Even though there are only two of us. My wife has developed a nasty skin condition as a result of living amidst the common herd.'

Richard's other sixteen emails have no text, but contain a series of photos, all showing evidence of said nasty skin condition, on every part of the body you can imagine. And probably parts you can't – all in unrelenting close-up. Richard must have a ten-megapixel camera at least, and the results are *absolutely* repulsive.

Once I've stopped feeling sick, I email him to say that I will forward his enquiry to the Housing Department, but add, 'I regret your attachments were too large to open.' Hopefully, that'll put an end to the stream of vile skin-flicks that keep appearing in my inbox.

'I bet those are what Max is watching,' says Greg, when I mention them. 'Skin-flicks, I mean – in his hotel room, late at night. That's what men do, when they're bored.'

'Thanks,' I say. 'What do women do?'

Greg says he has no idea, which is no help at all, seeing as I have nothing to occupy me once I get home from work – not after I've cooked and eaten beans on burnt toast, and had a quick chat with Max. (He only phones once tonight, when there's hardly anything on TV to interrupt.)

Connie and Josh are both out, and there aren't any lights on in Ellen's house, so there's no point in popping in to see her, which I'm almost bored enough to do. I'm at such a loose end that, eventually, I decide I may as well give Dad a call.

'Ah, Molly,' he says. 'Glad I caught you.'

Does he *really* not know that I phoned him?

'Why?' I say.

151

'Well, I'm off tomorrow morning,' he says, as if I should have known.

'Off where?'

'Thailand.'

There is a long silence, until Dad finally steps in to fill it. 'I *told* you about it,' he says. '*Ages* ago.'

'Er, no, Dad – no, you didn't,' I say. He knows that at least as well as I do, which is probably why he doesn't bother to deny it.

'I don't even want to go,' he says, instead. 'It's my mate, y'see. He booked it, and he doesn't want to go all by himself. I can't really afford it, but I don't like to let him down.'

The trouble with Dad is that he's exactly like The Boss. He actually *believes* the stuff he says. This renders arguing with him entirely pointless, even when you can prove he's talking out of his arse, which I can't this time – annoyingly.

'Got to go,' he says. 'Haven't finished packing yet. Take care of yourself while I'm away.'

I've just opened my mouth to ask him where exactly in Thailand he's going, and how long for, when he says, '*By-ee*!' and, before I know it, all I can hear is a dialling tone.

Holy shit. I wonder if Dinah knows about this? *I'm* not telling her.

**FRIDAY, 16 JULY**

God, this is getting *so* embarrassing. I've no idea what's wrong with The Boss – let alone what (or who) is fuelling his paranoia.

Joan comes in from the Party offices to check something about his latest GC report, and Andrew refuses to even look at her, let alone acknowledge her cheery 'Good morning!'

Then he gives *me* a bollocking after she's gone, for 'consorting with the enemy'.

'What *is* wrong with you?' I say.

'Nothing,' he says. 'I've just had my eyes opened, that's all. By someone I *can* trust, for a change.'

'Who?' I say, although, 'What on earth do you mean?' might have been a better option, now I come to think of it. It doesn't make any difference, though, as Andrew's giving nothing away.

'Just an old friend,' he says. 'Not that it's any of *your* business.' Then he taps his nose, and says, 'Keep this out – and keep quiet, too. Careless talk costs lives, you know.'

Greg says we should phone the men in white coats, but I wouldn't dare, tempting though it is. I bet we wouldn't get paid if The Boss ended up in an asylum. We'll just have to try to manage him as best we can, though it's not going to be easy, now other people are starting to notice his behaviour. And to object to it.

'Don't worry, Mol,' says Greg. 'We'll work out what to do about him over lunch.'

So much for that brilliant idea. Apparently, Greg and I aren't getting any lunch, because 'lunch is now for wimps' – according to Lichford's own Michael Douglas, MP and resident nut-job, aka The Boss.

He issues this edict with great certainty, and then goes out for lunch himself, all of twenty minutes later, at which point Joan comes back to make a formal complaint about how he behaved towards her earlier.

Things don't get any better when Andrew returns from what was obviously a largely liquid lunch, just in time for this afternoon's surgery. Greg makes him eat a whole roll of extra strong mints and drink a very strong coffee, which seems to work, at least until the last appointment of the day.

Mr and Mrs Stafford have come in to complain about the inadequacies of the care home in which Mr Stafford's father now lives. The Boss keeps it together, and politely explains that we will take up their concerns with Social Services, *and* with the management of the home.

So far, so good, and I'm just pushing my chair back with a sigh of relief, and intending to show Mr and Mrs Stafford out – but they aren't going anywhere. There's more to come, as Mr Stafford launches into a diatribe about how outrageous it is that his father's house may have to be sold – to cover the costs of his place in the care home.

There follows a long pause, during which I have either a hot flush or a panic attack, and then The Boss leans forward and says, horribly slowly and with great emphasis, 'Ah, so *now* we get to what you really care about. Your *inheritance*.'

Oh, my God. It's one thing to think it, but quite another to say so, especially while breathing alcohol fumes all over a constituent. There's nothing for it but to phone Andrew's mobile from mine, under cover of the table.

As soon as it starts ringing, I say, 'There's that very

urgent call you need to take, Andrew. You'd better go and answer it.'

He leaves the room obediently, while I apologise on his behalf, explaining that I'm sure that *that* wasn't what he meant, and that he does sometimes have 'a wacky sense of humour'. The Staffords seem unconvinced, but it's the best I can do at such short notice.

When I finally return to my desk, after a sneaky ciga-rette outside, The Boss yells at me that there was *nobody* on the line, that the number was *mine*, and what the *hell* did I think I was playing at?

'Saving your bacon, as per usual,' I say.

Talk about ingratitude. I'm just considering a trip to the archive cupboard to throw a few darts at Andrew's head when I get an email from Johnny. He says he's missing me, and asks again when he's going to get to do 'wonderful things' to various parts of my anatomy.

Then he proceeds to describe those things, which, I must admit, sound pretty good, especially after the day I've had. He even sets his imaginary scenario in *my* office, rather than in his, which seems to suggest that *he* thinks I'm more than just a secretary – unlike everyone else around here.

Oh, bugger. Maybe he thinks I'm a dominatrix? That would be *typical*. I bet he'll want me to lead him around on a leash if we ever meet up – as if I don't already have to do that quite often enough with The Boss. Metaphorically speaking, of course.

**FRIDAY, 16 JULY (LATE EVENING)**
Max arrives home from France just after 10:00pm, and

155

is *awfully* affectionate, which is very disconcerting indeed. Now I can't decide if the whole German debacle was a genuine error, or if he's just over-compensating, to throw me off the scent.

Mind you, he complains that the group were only given one bottle of red and one of white at each meal – between *ten* of them – so maybe this enforced sobriety is why he was so much better behaved this time? As far as I can tell.

I must still be looking unconvinced, though, because then he says he has photos – and uploads them straight away. They're almost all of the single bed in his hotel room, except for a few showing items of furniture being made in a factory. Exciting, they're not. In fact, they're a lot *less* exciting than the things Johnny suggested doing to me earlier.

Ah, *those* things. Or, rather, *argh*, those things. And just when Max is being so nice to me, too. I am *horribly* confused.

## SATURDAY, 17 JULY

Why do I *never* learn? I spend the morning going through Connie's hair magazines in an attempt to find a photo of a haircut that will make me look less like a corpse, and eventually find a good one of Kylie, sporting a shaggy bob.

I take it with me when I go into town, and then present it to my hairdresser who, after looking me up and down without comment, puts the picture face-down on the counter and wields her scissors. I am very excited, as this may be the moment I finally recapture my youthful good looks. The ones Johnny seems to think I still possess.

An hour later, I am forced to accept that, while my hair does now resemble Kylie's, my face does not. I have therefore wasted my money, and am doomed to keep on being poleaxed with horror whenever I catch sight of myself in shop windows and unexpected mirrors.

I walk home, lacking the enthusiasm to even pick my feet up properly, and thus have three embarrassing moments of the *catch toe on paving slab, stagger, pick self up and pretend nothing happened* type.

When I walk (or limp) into the house, I find a uniformed policeman sitting on the sofa in the living room.

'What's Josh done now?' I say. It's a reflex.

'Josh?' says the policeman. 'Did you *know* the muggers?' He's addressing Connie. Oh, and Russ, the chilli boy.

'No, of course we didn't *know* them,' says Connie, glaring at me, though I am too busy freaking out to care.

'Muggers? *Muggers?* What's happened?' I say, possibly in a rather squeaky voice – but, honestly, are *all* my family destined to be regularly set upon by total madmen?

'Tell you later, Mum,' says Connie, pushing me back out into the hallway, and closing the door.

After she and Russ have finished looking through mug-shot albums, in which Connie apparently spots quite a few ex-classmates but fails to identify the perpetrators, the policeman leaves, and I finally discover what has happened.

It turns out that Connie and Russ decided to go for

157

a romantic walk at lunchtime – down the newly created 'Green Walkway', which is sited on an unused section of railway track that runs from Easemount into the centre of Lichford.

What complete idiots. (This so-called *rural idyll* might just as well be in Beirut.)

They'd just passed the first bend, taking them out of sight of the road, when they were confronted by four youths, who quickly surrounded them. (Russ says they were *men*, but Connie says they were definitely *boys*. I'm sticking with 'youths' as a democratic compromise.)

Anyway, these youths apparently just stood there at first, swaggering and looking like 'prats' (again according to Connie), or 'thugs' (according to Russ) – but then they demanded Russ empty his pockets. He complied, but only produced a couple of pounds.

At this point, Connie insists that the muggers were about to give up and move away – until Russ said, 'But *she's* got money!' and pointed at her. Russ denies this and says that Connie assaulted him with her umbrella in an unprovoked attack, which he ascribes to the stress of the moment.

Connie responds that it was the stress of having such a chicken-shit boyfriend that made her lose her temper, and ends the discussion by pointing out that, by the time she'd finished hitting Russ, the muggers had disappeared.

Russ leaves in a huff, but Josh nods in atypical approbation of his sister. 'Good one, Con. *That's* what I told you!' he says, giving her the thumbs-up.

'*What* is what you told her?' I say. I am incredulous that Connie would listen to Josh's advice, on any subject.

'Best way to avoid being mugged in the street is to behave like a mad person, Mum,' says Josh. 'You should probably try it at work.'

## SUNDAY, 18 JULY

Yesterday's acting crazy suggestion might have sounded sensible at the time but why does Josh always have to take *everything* a step too far?

Max and I decide to do a big clean-up of the house today, instead of lying around doing nothing. I am not exactly enthusiastic about the idea, but am hoping that Max's urge to carry out a late spring-clean may eventually be extended to encompass our relationship.

He volunteers to dust all the high surfaces, while I am in charge of hoovering. So far, so good – until I go to the cupboard to get the Hoover, and find that it has disappeared. Max says he has no idea where it is, and nor has Connie – apparently – though she does start to giggle when she's asked.

'*Con?*' I use my best interrogation voice, coupled with an almost Botox-worthy raised eyebrow.

'What?' She's still laughing, while I am not.

'Where is the bloody Hoover, Constance?' I say. 'Tell me now, before I start to count to ten.'

This technique hasn't worked on Josh for more than a decade, and I can't quite believe it still works on Connie – but, for some reason, it always does.

'Josh took it,' she says, as I reach number nine, and

before she bursts into another fit of hysterics. Maybe it's delayed shock from the mugging, or PTSD.

'Took it where?' I say, trying to sound less intimidating, just in case.

'*I* don't know. He just said to tell you he was popping round to Silver Hill, with some of the boys.'

I look at Max, and he looks back at me. Then we move swiftly to the door, in that wordless synchronisation that comes from years of parenting a complete lunatic.

We jog to the end of our road, and turn the corner onto Silver Hill. Half-way down, there are Josh and Robbie, accompanied by various other members of their motley crew. Josh is standing on the bottom part of our Hoover, while Robbie is pushing him along, using the handle.

Silver Hill is not a gentle rural slope, as its name would imply, but one of the steepest, and busiest roads in the whole of Lichford.

'Josh! What the *f\*ck* do you think you're doing?' Max breaks into a run, as Josh starts rolling away from him, thankfully not at any significant speed.

'Extreme hoovering,'[27] Robbie says, as Max passes him and catches up with Josh.

'Extreme *what*?' Max is almost incoherent with rage, and looks even crosser than he did about being dead. 'Give me that – *now*!' he says, yanking the Hoover away from Josh, who never, ever, knows when to keep quiet.

---

[27] Extreme hoovering is an actual sport, believe it or not. I do – now – because Josh made me look at endless video evidence on YouTube. It's still madness, though.

'It's rubbish anyway, Dad,' he says. 'The wheels are *crap*.'

Max grabs him by the ear, pushes past me, and heads back up the hill, the Hoover in one hand and Josh (effectively) in the other. Robbie and the others shuffle about looking embarrassed – as well they might.

I glare at them, then run to catch up with Max. Josh is *really* going to get it this time.

When we arrive back at the house, Connie is in a crumpled heap on the sofa, still shaking with what I initially assume is laughter, but is quickly revealed to be tears.

'What on *earth's* the matter, Con?' I sit down next to her and try to cuddle her, but she shakes me off.

'Russ . . . just . . . dumped . . . me,' she says, hiccuping between each word. 'Because I made him look a prat in front of those boys.'

'Huh,' says Josh. 'Made *himself* look a prat, if you ask me.'

'You're in no position to comment,' says Max. 'Con, I'm going to cook you a lovely dinner, to cheer you up.'

Max's food/love combination doesn't work, even though it usually would. Connie is too heartbroken to eat. I can't bear to see it, especially as Russ *was* a bit of an arsehole, anyway – but she seems to have forgotten that, and just cries all the more when I mention it.

She doesn't even laugh when Josh offers to go round to Russ' house in the middle of the night, take his boy racer car to bits, and lay all the pieces out neatly on his front lawn, though I think it's a stroke of genius.

For the rest of the evening, Connie only wants to talk to Max, as she says that he 'understands the best'. She sits next to him on the couch, and they cuddle up in front of the TV, not even speaking most of the time.

Oddly, this *does* seem to calm her, which reminds me that Max used to be able to calm me down, too, just by being there. Now he's more likely to be the one *causing* me to cry.

'It's first love,' he says later, when Connie's finally gone to bed. 'They say you never really get over it.'

Some of us do: I can't remember who mine was, though I'm sure it wasn't Johnny – whatever *he* now claims.

## MONDAY, 19 JULY

Today I have to strip naked in a multi-storey car park. Then I am hosed down by some guy dressed from head to toe in plastic. For God's sake, this is getting too much.

It all starts before Fiona, the new intern, has even arrived for her first day on the job. I am opening an envelope when white powder starts flying everywhere.

Greg and I just sit and look at each other for what seems like five minutes, then he yells, 'Start panicking!' and runs around pointlessly for a bit, while I try to work out who we should call for help. This takes a while, as it's not exactly an everyday experience.

Eventually, a police officer turns up and then the decontamination unit arrives, along with three fire engines – and two ambulances. The first step seems to be to evacuate everyone, including all those who work in the neighbouring offices, so now we're going to be even more popular with *them* than we already were after Mr Humphries kicked off.

All the officials are wearing full decontamination suits and breathing apparatus, and they set up a sort of bouncy castle-type decontamination thing in the car park. Then Greg and I (as well as the hapless police officer) are ordered to strip.

I don't even have my new underwear on, as I've been saving it, just in case I ever do go on a date with Johnny. I'm not half as embarrassed as Greg is, though. He keeps muttering, 'Bit of weight left over from Christmas,' for the benefit of any onlookers. 'I've just joined a gym.'

As if that's not humiliating enough, then we're scrubbed down with Fairy Liquid – which does nothing for my new haircut – before being told to put on white suits like those they wear in *CSI*. (Not a good look, but marginally better than the nakedness was.) After that, we're taken to hospital to be checked over properly.

Once we've seen the doctors, we're finally discharged, having been prescribed medication to take in case the powder turns out to be anthrax.

God knows when we'll get our clothes back, if we ever do. I have to go home in a plastic suit and a pair of fireman's trainers – which must be size nines at least.

'Looking good, Mol,' says Greg, now that the tension's dissipating a bit. He hasn't spoken at all since the stripping naked trauma.

'Yeah, thanks,' I say. 'Sarcasm's the lowest form of wit, you know.'

He's about to come back with a no-doubt even

less-witty rejoinder when the police call to say that the office is to stay closed until the exact nature of the powder is established, and that officers will be posted there overnight.

'Bugger,' I say, after I hang up. 'I should have asked them if they can deal with all the abusive messages we'll get from the usual suspects, while they're there. The answer-phone will have a meltdown if someone doesn't answer calls.'

'That's the least of our problems,' says Greg. 'Not when we still have to wait for Porton Down to tell us whether and when we'll die horrible deaths.'

Max takes the same view as Greg, when he hears all about it – and is *furious*. So furious that he phones The Boss at Westminster and shouts at him about how badly he's failing to protect his staff.

In response, Andrew goes on about being 'a man of the people' and 'accessibility' until, eventually, Max gets so cross that he has to do my trick of pretending that the call's been accidentally cut off. Otherwise, he says he might have resigned on my behalf, and then where would we be? (Max is not at all himself since his company started talking about redundancies.)

I'm too discomfited to do anything at all for the rest of the day, except sit at home and stew about whether I *am* going to die – and to wonder how The Boss manages to lead such a charmed life. This sort of thing *never* seems to occur when he's in the office.

If it did, maybe he'd learn his lesson and stop claiming that we exaggerate what happens, or that we do something to cause it ourselves. Until that occurs, I suppose I'd better go and check whether my life assurance covers me for acts of terrorism – especially if Max is going to lose *his* job.

## TUESDAY, 20 JULY
Bloody hell, I don't even get a lie-in this morning. I'd been hoping the office would have to stay closed all day so I could lounge around relaxing – as far as it's possible to relax while waiting to hear if you're going to die – but instead I get a call at about 9:30am, saying that I can re-open the office, as soon as I like.

The results have come back from Porton Down, and have confirmed that the powder wasn't harmful to breathe in – although it *was* potentially explosive. Apparently, we're to keep what happened to ourselves, so as not to spark a general panic.

At least we don't have to keep taking the tablets now, so that's good news, as is the fact that we're not going to die.

The bad news is that, once I get to the office, today's mail is already sitting on my desk – and I *really* don't want to open it. I've gone right off that part of my job. I consider sticking all the letters and parcels into one of the big grey plastic House of Commons envelopes and sending it to the girls in the Westminster office, so that, by the time they send it back to me, it'll at least have passed through the scanners at the House of Commons.

Then I realise that this will slow down our

turnaround time, which would be noted by that bloody WriteToThem.com[28] – so there's no way The Boss will put up with *that*. There's no option but to open the post myself.

'Be careful,' says Greg from somewhere behind me, though his voice sounds strangely muffled.

I hold each envelope out in front of me as if it is a bomb, then poke a letter-opener into one corner, before turning my back and ripping the blade through what I *think* is the top of the flap. This achieves the dubious benefit of making me feel better while I'm doing it, but irritating the hell out of me immediately afterwards – when I realise my method has a serious flaw.

I've cut through the top third of every single letter I've opened, so then I have to get Greg to stick them all back together before we can even begin to read the damned things. That's once I've persuaded him to come out of the archive cupboard, where he hid while I was opening them – 'not through cowardice, but to save the taxpayer the cost of decontaminating two of us'.

It's after he's finished with the Sellotape that the problems *really* start. So much for making sure that the public didn't know about the anthrax scare. (Max is *far* better at keeping secrets than the authorities, *or* The Boss.)

First, the new intern phones to say she's changed her mind about working here, since she heard what happened

---

[28] WriteToThem.com: Website which documents the time MPs' office staff take to respond to constituents' enquiries. It makes no allowance for traumatic incidents, or whether the enquiries are insane or not.

yesterday – so that's another one we've lost in less than a month. Even James managed longer than no days at all, so Fiona Thompson gets *nul points* for effort, and Greg says he's gone off her a bit.

'I admire courage,' he says. Presumably in other people.

Fiona doesn't want to say who told her about the bouncy castle incident, but I think we can probably guess. Andrew went to a Council jolly last night, at which Fiona's father was the host.

Anyway, after I mumble something non-specific but vaguely threatening about the Official Secrets Act, Fiona does at least promise not to tell anyone else – and then Greg phones The Boss and demands that he doesn't, either, so hopefully that's the end of the Andrew-related leaks – for today.

We're not out of the woods yet, though, as we've still got to find a way to explain to the usual suspects why we couldn't answer the phones yesterday. We can't tell them the truth, because that'd just give them ideas, and I don't *ever* want to have to go through *that* again. (Steve Ellington would get busy with the Johnson's Baby Powder and a stack of envelopes immediately.)

In the end, we decide to tell callers that there was an 'emergency in the building' then  change the subject, as fast as we can. Sometimes, the simplest solutions are the best, and this works, until late afternoon, when it's Mr Beales' turn to phone.

'You lot can't keep nothin' from me,' he says, apropos of nothing in particular.

'Excuse me?' I say. *Now* what?

'It's in the paper: "Terrorist fears spark full-scale evacuation of local office".'

*Argh*. Does he *have* to sound quite so smug about it? (I'm impressed he can read such long words, though.)

'Ah,' I say, for want of a better alternative. There follows the verbal equivalent of a particularly ungraceful fencing match, as I try to side-step Mr Beales' attempts to extract the juicy details, while he just prods deeper and deeper. He's better than a tabloid journalist when he gets going.

I'm exhausted by the time I get him off the phone, at which point Greg says that he is so traumatised by having had to expose his body to a 'bunch of gym-toned civil servants in a public place' that we are going out tonight to get drunk, in order to obliterate the memory.

This seems like a good idea, at the time. When will I *ever* learn?

## TUESDAY, 20 JULY (VERY LATE EVENING)

Greg and I decided to go straight to the pub after work, then on to The Star of India. This proved to be an exceedingly unwise decision, but now it's very late and I'm far too distraught to even *think* about what happened, let alone write about it – so it'll have to wait until I've calmed down a bit.

If I'm not arrested first. (We could have sparked an international incident, for all I know.)

## WEDNESDAY, 21 JULY

I still seem to be at liberty, but I'm also still really pissed off with Greg, though he *is* looking a bit shamefaced this morning, not to mention very hungover. I feel surprisingly alert, which I can only ascribe to the adrenalin that went flooding through my body while we were being thrown out of the restaurant last night.

Suffice it to say that we have now been banned from The Star of India, because Greg decided it would be funny to order an 'Osama Balti' and a 'Semtex Surprise'. God knows how we escaped with our lives.

Bloody Greg spent the rest of last night in a collapsed state on the couch in our living room, demanding to know how 'any ordinary, educated, hardworking family' like mine could manage without Imodium in the medicine cabinet.

Luckily, Max was finding Greg funny. I wasn't, which is why I went to bed in disgust. I *knew* we shouldn't have had all that gin before we got to the restaurant. Not on top of anthrax, anyway.

**THURSDAY, 22 JULY**
Thank God today is fairly quiet. There's the usual stuff about dog poo, violence on television, and rejected lovers wanting their exes reported for tax or benefit fraud, but the highlight is Miss Emms, who writes in to say this:

> *Dear Mr Sinclair,*
> *I am writing to you to complain about my irresponsible and inconsiderate new neighbour, who lives in the flat beneath mine. He's always smoking cannabis, and the smoke seeps into my flat and is*

*causing serious problems. The smell is so strong, it gets everywhere!*

*I have eight guinea pigs, and exposure to this drug is affecting them psychologically. I don't know where else to turn, as my Housing Officer doesn't seem to be taking any notice, and the RSPCA aren't interested either.*

*Can you please do something to help my poor, defenceless animals?*

*Yours hopefully,*

*Janice Emms (Miss)*

Greg spends an inordinate amount of time attempting to emulate a psychotic guinea pig, and then tries to persuade me to write back and ask Miss Emms for further details.

I don't want to encourage the poor woman, but Greg says he has decided to re-train as a guinea pig whisperer if The Boss ever sacks him, or fails to get re-elected, next time round. I hand him Miss Emms' letter and tell him to do whatever he thinks best.

At that moment, Johnny emails me and says, 'How are things at the heart of the UK political establishment? What are you doing right now? I want to imagine it.'

'Handling a case about a psychotic guinea pig,' I say.

It's a bit unnerving when Johnny replies with, 'Ah', though not half as unnerving as what he says next. Maybe he's been on the 'wacky baccy', as Dad would say?

**FRIDAY, 23 JULY**

I get more confused with each day that passes, and not

just by the Max and Ellen situation, either – or the one with Johnny. *Everything* is complicated.

I used to be so full of certainty – about pretty much everything, but especially political ideology. Now I'm like a rabbit in the headlights, and today's surgery makes things even worse. No wonder The Boss is losing the plot.

We haven't had much comment from constituents on one of the Tory MPs' attempts to ban the burka and the niqab – or not until now, anyway. I haven't even thought much about it myself, beyond a knee-jerk reaction that of *course* we can't.

That's until Mrs Jewson comes along.

'I want to talk about this burka thing,' she says.

'Ah,' says The Boss. His catchphrase. (And now Johnny's, too, apparently.)

Mrs Jewson glares at him, but then she carries on. 'I'm getting a bit fed up with the double standards in this country. My son wears a hoodie, like all the youngsters, and he got made to take it off in the mall yesterday. By the security guards.'

She crosses her arms, and looks at Andrew, long and hard. It's like a 'who'll blink first' schoolyard challenge.

'I see,' he says, for variation, blinking like a madman at the same time. Then he looks sideways at me, for back-up.

I keep my head down, and write 'hoodie' ten times on my notepad. I take my time while doing it.

'Well, if he can't wear a hoodie,' continues Mrs Jewson, 'then why can these women wear bloody burkas, or whatever those things are called that cover their whole faces?'

'Well, I think that's rather different,' says The Boss, looking sideways again.

'*Why* is it different?' Mrs Jewson doesn't even wait for a reply. She's really on a roll. 'Do you know *why* my son likes to keep his hood up?' she says.

'*No-o*,' says Andrew.

He's twitching a bit now, but I'm still leaving him to it. Serves him right for ignoring Joan yet again this morning.

'He's deaf! And if he doesn't keep his hood up, then all the young 'uns take the piss out of his hearing aid.'

Andrew's given up, completely. He just looks expectantly at Mrs Jewson, as do I. It's obvious she hasn't finished yet.

'So what I want to know is: say he got a teacher who wanted to wear one of these things, but he couldn't lipread her, because he couldn't see her face – whose rights would the bloody government decide were the most important then?'

I have *no* idea how to answer this question, and nor does The Boss. He looks optimistically at me once more, just in case, but in the absence of any meaningful response is left with no option but to say, 'Mrs Jewson, I'll be happy to take this up, on your behalf. Molly will let you know when we receive a reply.'

Of course, after Mrs J's left, Andrew's *furious* with me. Yet again.

'You are less and less help with every week that bloody passes,' he says.

172

'Well, I don't know *all* the answers any more,' I say. 'The same as you.'

Andrew obviously doesn't agree, as he storms off, leaving the security doors wide open.

I'm gathering up the case folders, when I'm suddenly confronted by a man wearing a full face crash helmet. He leans aggressively across the table, and nearly gives me a heart attack. A rush of something hot travels up my body, which I don't *think* is a hot flush – though who can tell? I have got *those* to look forward to, at some point.

After what seems like an hour, the man finally begins to speak. 'Getting sick of foreigners stealing all our jobs,' he says – very slowly, presumably to compensate for the muffling effect of the stupid helmet. 'There isn't a single British dentist left in the bloody NHS.'

Oh, thank God. It's only Mr Beales. I am torn between relief and fury, just like when Josh and Connie come home unexpectedly late.

'Of course there is,' I say, though I have no idea if this is true or not. (My dentist's from Denmark, I think, or Finland. Somewhere in Scandinavia, anyway.) 'But it doesn't matter where they're from, does it – as long as they're fully qualified?'

'Of course it does,' says Mr Beales, who always knows best, even if he does virtually repeat what you yourself have only just said. 'You can't understand a word foreign ones say, especially through the face masks they insist on wearing these days. My new dentist sounds like the Swedish chef from the bloody *Muppets* when he's got his on. I thought he said he was going to give me a filling, so it was a hell of a shock when he started pulling my tooth out instead.'

Probably felt like *knocking* it out, I should think. I know I do. I have no more patience this week – none at all. And I happen to *love* the Swedish chef.

'Well, if we're talking about people who are hard to understand,' I say, 'you are too, with that crash helmet obscuring your mouth.'

Then, while said mouth is still presumably hanging open in astonishment, I add: 'And while we're on the subject, I would appreciate it if you would never – *ever* – walk into this building again with your face almost totally hidden like that. It's a serious security risk.'

It's only when I get back to my desk that I realise the implications of what I've just said. And what Johnny meant last night, when he offered to take me away from 'all this'.

## SATURDAY, 24 JULY

At the risk of sounding even more like Victor Meldrew than I usually do, *I don't believe it!* The perfect end to a perfect day. Why do the rich have all the luck?

What with fretting about crash helmets and burkas, and Johnny's offer to rescue me from psychotic guinea pigs, I left it far too late to do any chores last night, so I'm tired and grumpy when I wake after only a few hours' sleep, and with all the packing still to do.

We've got absolutely *miles* to drive today.

'Why do we have to go to this stupid thing?' says

Connie, when I insist that she packs a dress. 'If David and Susie didn't mean their vows the first time round, then they shouldn't have got married at all – should they?'

I avoid answering, as Connie may well have a point. Also, if Max and I didn't have to spend all our money on a hotel room for David and Susie's renewal of their wedding vows, we could have had a mini-break or something, which might have refreshed *our* relationship.

As it is, we can't even afford to get breakfast thrown in, and Connie and Josh are furious that they'll have to share our family room. I'm not any keener on the idea than they are – seeing as *bang* goes any chance of marital relations. (That was a wholly accidental pun.)

The journey to the Midlands is awful, too. Gone are the days when we could distract the kids with nursery rhyme tapes, or by playing I-Spy. Now we have to listen to Josh's horrendous Screamo music, in an attempt to drown out the constant bickering between him and Connie. By the time we approach Malksham Priory in the late afternoon, Max and I are totally frazzled.

The forecourt looks like an episode of *Footballers' Wives*, and a press pack is crowded round a couple whose weekly dentistry bill is probably more than my yearly salary. Josh says that the groom plays for a Premiership team, and that his new bride is a 'Z-list celebrity'.

I'm feeling distinctly Z-list myself – and even more so, when we have to sneak through the glitterati, while trying to hide a Tesco carrier bag containing our breakfast supplies. 'You could at least have gone to Waitrose,' I say to Max, but he's too busy gawking at an Aston Martin that's just arrived to bother to reply.

Things don't improve when we get to our room. I've just finished stashing the milk and orange juice in the mini-bar, and hiding the boxes of cereal at the back of the wardrobe, when David phones from his and Susie's room.

'Molly,' he says. 'You've arrived at last. Good. I've booked a table for seven-thirty in the restaurant downstairs. We're all meeting there, so see you then.'

Oh, *God*. I gesture frantically at Max, who is staring lovingly out of the window at the Aston Martin and therefore doesn't notice me.

'Um, David – can I call you back in a minute?' I say. 'I just need to check on something first.'

I hang up before David can object, then drag Max away from the window and explain. To his credit, he realises the seriousness of the situation immediately, and is decisive about what we should do about it, too.

'Phone David back and tell him Connie and Josh are fussy eaters,' he says. 'Then say we've promised them a take-away, and that we'll join everyone for drinks after they've finished their meal.'

Brilliant. Or not, as the case may be. At 7.30, we're still hunting for a take-away in an unfamiliar town, miles from the rural idyll of the priory. In fact, we'd still be searching *now*, if it wasn't for one of Josh's more useful mobile phone apps, which eventually helps us to locate a pretty grotty fish and chip shop, situated in a run-down back street.

We gobble down pale, sweaty chips – with the added luxury of fishcakes for the kids – and then race back to the hotel, where Max and I try to make Primark look convincingly like Prada. I doubt it works, plus I'm sure I still smell of vinegar when we finally make it downstairs and into the restaurant.

All the other guests are already well-oiled, have wiped out four courses and are still eating pudding. There are empty wine bottles everywhere, and I have a sudden panic that, at the end of the evening, Max and I will get caught up in that nightmare scenario where the richest person in the room – who has inevitably eaten and drunk the most – decides it would be a good idea to 'split the bill', and won't remember that we haven't eaten anything at all.

Max seems oblivious to this possibility and is enjoying himself, if attracting a little too much attention from the wife of David's business partner. She looks like a horse, clad in Boden.

Admittedly, her husband is a chinless wonder, who I'd turn down, despite his millions, so I can't really blame her for fancying Max – though I think she's going too far when she tries to sit on his lap. Maybe she thinks he's a 'bit of rough'. (Not rough enough, in my opinion, as he doesn't throw her off. He just puts up with it – looking bemused, but also slightly flattered.)

I get my own back by paying close attention to a gorgeous man on my left, who resembles the Milk Tray Man but with the added benefit of conversational skills. I have no idea what he does for a living beyond 'working in the City', but I seem to be holding my end up fairly well so far.

That's until, during a lull in the general conversation, he says, in a rather carrying voice, 'Gosh, Molly. You're *so* articulate. What do you do for a living?'

Quick as a flash, David's in there. You'd swear there were undervalued shares on offer. 'She's one of those socialists, Miles,' he says. 'Never grew out of it. Takes pride in abject failure, and all that nonsense.'

I will not rise to it. I will *not*. Who needs enemies, with friends like David? Has he forgotten we used to share a flat, back in the days when he was also broke?

'Aren't you going to call me a fascist, Mol, and defend what you believe in?' he says, getting up and coming to give me a hug. 'You disappoint me, old girl. Have you lost your faith?'

Honestly, he *never* gives up.

'After the week I've had, I have no idea *what* I believe in,' I say, but he's asking for the bill now, and isn't listening. I breathe a sigh of relief – until he delivers the coup de grâce. As all the rich kids start scrabbling for their platinum cards, he says, 'Don't worry, this one's on me, guys.'

I cannot believe it. I simply *can't*. David has never picked up a tab in a restaurant in all the years I've known him – and my family ate chips in the car because we couldn't afford to join him and his other friends for dinner! I didn't even get a bloody fishcake.

David is right: my life *is* a disaster.

Max obviously thinks so too. He just keeps repeating,

'This one's on me, guys', all the way back to our room. Connie and Josh say nothing at all.

Sometimes silence can be far, far louder than words.

## SUNDAY, 25 JULY

Things don't improve this morning. Max stubs his toe, really hard, while trying to get past Josh in the queue for the bathroom and almost faints. I think he may have broken it.

There's no time to do anything about it, though, as we're almost late for the ceremony as it is. (Josh is on a go-slow because he doesn't want to wear a suit and proper shoes, and Connie's refusing point-blank to wear the dress I made her bring.) We get there just in time and hide towards the back, where it's dark – so hopefully no one can see what Josh and Connie have ended up looking like.

'It's going well, isn't it?' I say to Max, half-way through.

'Yes,' he says, 'though it's not surprising, is it? It's only five years since the last one. David and Susie can hardly be out of practice.'

'Well, I think it's surprisingly moving, *actually*,' I say. 'Maybe we should do it, too.'

Max is just about to answer, when he has to move seats to separate Connie and Josh, who've started one of those hissing and poking arguments – the kind that get out of control very quickly. You'd never think Josh was in his final year at school, and that Connie had a proper job, albeit only for the summer holidays.

She's now sitting next to me, sulking, so I have to look

past her to see Max, who's looking very attractive today and does have a firmer chin than most of the other men present. I probably would marry him again. *If* he asked.

He probably wouldn't, though. I don't think I've lived up to anyone's expectations so far – and the 'wedding breakfast' only confirms this impression. When we find our names on the seating plan outside the function room, we discover we might as well have been seated in Siberia.

We're quite obviously on the payback table. On my right is the headmaster of David's old school – the one who expelled David on the grounds that he saw every school rule 'as a deliberate infringement of his personal liberty'. On Max's left is the man who sacked David from his first job, for much the same reason.

The numbers are made up by various ex-wives and ex-husbands of the successful individuals who are seated next to the top table, along with their new trophy partners. Everyone on our table has disappointed David in some way or another, apart from the photographer, but *he* soon makes up for that.

God knows where David found him, but he must have come cheap, or should have done. He holds forth – throughout the entire meal – about his last job, which involved taking pictures of a greyhound racing stadium. This is about as interesting as you would expect.

On the odd occasion that he pauses for breath, he pokes at each course as if he has never seen food before, and doesn't trust it. Then he pounces and suddenly hurls a vast quantity of it into his mouth, which he kindly leaves open while he chews.

He eats *everything* – including a whole load of mussels which have remained closed, but which he determinedly prises open. I can't be bothered to advise him not to, as I think he'd probably stab his fork into my hand and accuse me of trying to shaft him if I did.

By the time the band arrive for the evening's entertainment, the photographer is nowhere to be seen and, as Max and I approach to say our goodbyes, we find David shouting into his mobile phone.

'What d'you mean you *think* you've got food poisoning? You ate the same as everyone else!' He pauses and then says, 'Well, if you let me down this evening, you'll be hearing from my solicitor.'

'Problems?' I ask, trying to resist giving way to schadenfreude.

'Muppet photographer says he's got food poisoning. Reckons he can't stop throwing up. So now I've got to find someone else to take decent pictures of the dancing. I'm not flying in a ten-piece band from Cuba to end up with no proper record of it.'

David's eyes are scanning the room as he speaks. Then he spots Max's camera. '*Max*, my old mate—'

'Sorry, David – I can't.' Max hides his pleasure well. 'We've just come to say goodbye. Got to head for home now.'

'Oh, that's *right*. Our Molly can't have a day off from saving the world from capitalists.'

I smile sweetly, and say, 'Don't worry. I'm sure one of your more financially astute guests will be happy to take on the job of photographer – for a fee.'

David laughs, so I forgive him. As usual. He *is* my oldest friend, after all – though I bet I'd have been much further up the table hierarchy if I'd married Johnny. *He* probably wouldn't be seen dead here, though. David's courier company is hardly global, even with a lowercase 'G'.

Anyway, it doesn't matter, does it? Not when I'm really looking forward to getting home, snuggling up to Max on the couch, and listening to him snore. I'm not cut out for a glittering social life.

## MONDAY, 26 JULY

I'm quite glad to arrive at the office today as The Boss is back in London – or, rather, I *am* glad, until I get a call from the Jobcentre saying we may start getting complaints about lack of access to their building. They've been forced to temporarily close it to the public as Mr Meeeeurghn has kicked off again and sent them into lock-down mode. Something to do with being turned down for a payment from the Social Fund.

I'd have approved his application, if I were the Jobcentre – if only to fund forged documents to get him back to his own country – especially now I know that not even the combined might of their security staff can handle him. They all look like proper gym bunnies to me.

'You'd better start bulking up,' I say to Greg. 'As soon as possible, before Mr Meeeeurghn arrives. He's bound to come here to complain.'

Greg does a couple of half-hearted push-ups, then says, 'The trouble with exercise is that it's profoundly boring. That's why I never actually *go* to the gym.'

In that case, I should probably borrow his membership – urgently. Johnny's pushing for a meeting in London during his next trip back to the UK, and I'm not at all sure my arse is as fit for inspection as he seems to think it is.

To make things worse, he suggests we meet at the London Marriott. 'Sipping cocktails there will serve as a form of therapy for you,' he says.

'How?' I say. I have no idea what he's talking about. It's Ellen who's the alcoholic.

Johnny replies that it will enable me to contemplate the House of Commons at close quarters, while pretending that I'm not just a poor relation from the constituencies, but instead someone at the heart of where the action is. (He was obviously even less impressed by the guinea pig thing than I realised.)

In case *that* isn't enough to convince me, he adds that the experience will also illustrate that capitalism is better than socialism, by reminding me of the building's previous and less glamorous incarnation as County Hall.[29] It's starting to feel like talking to David but, even so, I'm secretly thrilled by the idea – until I recall that Johnny has a wife, and kids.

Honestly, I'm turning into such a hypocrite, ranting

[29] County Hall: Home of the now-defunct GLC (Greater London Council), where The Boss' hero, Ken Livingstone, held sway. Now home to various attractions, including an aquarium (maybe as a nod to Ken's fondness for newts), and the five-star Marriott Hotel. Oh, and a Premier Inn. Maybe I should suggest that to Johnny. Let him see how the other half lives.

about Annoying Ellen's crazed, sexual-attention-seeking, and her penchant for inappropriate flirting with married men – or with Max, anyway – when, all the time, here I am, doing the same thing with someone else's husband! I'm so ashamed of myself I can't look in the mirror when I next go to the loo.

It's mostly Johnny's fault, though, as he hasn't mentioned his wife for *weeks*. I'd forgotten all about her.

I re-read his latest email and discover that he's somehow managed to describe a night at the opera, the trip there and back in his chauffeur-driven car, *and* a meal afterwards – all without ever saying, 'we'. His wife has ceased to exist – written out of his life, without a trace – which starts me fretting about whether he really *could* be a serial killer. His glasses don't have the double bar, but they *definitely* have metal frames . . .

I sit and stare at his photo while I eat my lunch. The resemblance to Vladimir Putin is unnerving (apart from the fact that Vlad doesn't wear glasses, and is older than Johnny), so am I being *doubly* hypocritical? If it's not already bad enough to be considering having an affair with a married man, am I also turned on by power, like the mutilated-dog-tails woman? It doesn't bear thinking about.

Oh, God, and *I'm* married, too. I forgot that, for a moment, somehow or other. I wonder if it's hereditary, forgetting that you're married? Dad always seemed to have trouble remembering, now I come to think of it.

Talk of the devil. *Ping* goes my computer, and there's an email from him in my inbox – from a brand-new account, and sent from Thailand. The message simply says, 'Hot'. I really hope this is referring to the weather, and not to any of his so-called 'neighbours'.

## TUESDAY, 27 JULY

Blimey, people really aren't careful enough about protecting their identities. Today, I get a call from Miss Harpenden, who tells me that hers has been stolen, and that a (metaphorical) rat is running up bills in her name, all over the place. Even worse, the police aren't doing anything about it, though Miss H doesn't manage to explain why, before she bursts into tears and hangs up on me.

I write to the chief constable, asking if he can shed some light on the situation, and then send emergency texts to Mum, Connie and Josh instructing them to shred all their old letters and bank statements, immediately. I don't think any of them will take a blind bit of notice, but *I'm* going to get rid of everything in sight.

I start by deleting all Johnny's emails, except for today's. He's still going on about meeting at the Marriott, but now he wants us to stay overnight! Even if I thought that was a good idea – which I don't – I can't afford to stay in a Premier Inn, let alone a five-star hotel at over £300 a night, especially not after what it cost to attend David and Susie's vow renewal. And, even if I *could* afford it, how would I explain the entry on the bank statement to Max, for God's sake?

Maybe having a joint account wasn't such a good idea – though I've always thought that degree of mutual trust a necessary commitment. All our friends who kept separate accounts throughout their marriages, supposedly as an insurance policy, are now divorced.

They thought I was being old-fashioned when I said a *joint* bank account was the most effective form of marital insurance. Now I suppose I'm proving my point, which is much more annoying than you'd expect.

I bet Johnny's wife won't query *his* expenditure, though – even if he hasn't killed her off. If they share a bank account, he'll just put his expenses on his business credit card instead, which probably covers the cost of hotels in every country in the world. Probably with a different woman in each of them – although Johnny insists he's never cheated on his wife before, with anybody.

It doesn't matter if I believe him, as I can't take the risk, anyway – so I email him to say that I'd *love* to meet up but can't, as there's no way to hide the hotel bill from Max.

He emails me straight back and says, 'For God's sake, woman – it's *my* treat! Yes or no?'

*Christ!* This is even worse. Does he intend to book *one* room, or two? And even if he books two, what if he's repulsive in the flesh? (There must have been something about him that persuaded me to get up to what we did behind the Science block, but I'd probably had one too many Babychams at the time.) And, if he's paying so much money for my room just because he wants to get me into bed, how easy is it going to be to say, 'Thanks, but no thanks', if I can't go through with it?

The answer's obvious. It's going to be *impossible*, and

I shall end up effectively acting like a prostitute. Only worse, because I will be cheating on my husband, and encouraging Johnny to cheat on his wife. God knows what Dinah would say about it if she knew. She's rude enough on the subject of Thai brides, even those not described as hot.

I need to go home and have a lie-down. Feel free to steal my identity while I'm gone.

## WEDNESDAY, 28 JULY

It's that hellish time of year again – Parliamentary Recess, when MPs return to their constituencies and wander around like lost souls, irritating the hell out of constituency staff and making work for no reason at all.

Also, a bored MP is even more of a pain in the arse than usual. Take this morning – The Boss has already adopted his usual Recess practice of sneaking into the office early so that, by the time Greg and I arrive, he's finished rifling through our desk drawers, *and* the fridge.

The most outrageous aspect of this – at least as far as Greg's concerned – is that Andrew has helped himself to Greg's entire secret stash of Twixes, *and* has used up all the milk.

After a very confused briefing, without the benefit of coffee, and during which Greg stares pointedly at the smear of chocolate on Andrew's chin, Andrew decides he needs to print out some emails and takes over my computer again.

Greg spots his chance and gestures for me to join him in the corridor for an emergency meeting. 'God almighty,

Mol – haven't you arranged *anything* for him to do during Recess?' he says.

'I tried,' I say. 'But Carlotta wouldn't play ball. She even made Marie-Louise *clear* space in his diary so he could spend more time in the office with us.'

'Bloody woman. Wasn't Spain winning the World Cup enough for her?' Greg is pacing up and down the corridor like a caged animal, and I am desperate for a cigarette. It's only been half an hour since my last.

'I don't know anything about the World Cup,' I say. 'I hate football.'

'What a stupid statement,' says Greg, 'but, anyway, you've got to do *something*. I can't stand this. I may have to kill him if you don't get rid of him soon.'

Greg has an unhealthy dependency on chocolate – and no imagination. Far be it from me to boast, but I do have an extraordinary ability to think creatively in an emergency.

'Go and find yesterday's local paper,' I say. 'Then search through it for mentions of organisations that are complaining about something, like lack of funding.'

'And?'

'Then phone them up, say The Boss has read about their plight, and is very interested in the valuable work they're doing in his constituency.'

'*And?*' Greg still looks unimpressed. Sometimes *he* has trouble keeping up.

'Then,' I say, 'you tell them that Andrew would very much like to come and see for himself, and could he pop over some time today?'

188

'Brilliant!' says Greg, and sneaks off into the Party office to use their phone.

Half an hour later, he comes back, gives me the thumbs-up, and says, 'Andrew, aren't you supposed to be at your meeting now?'

'What meeting?' Andrew finishes my sandwich in one very ambitious mouthful.

'The Phoenix Over-Eating Project, in Easemount,' says Greg. 'Molly, didn't you *tell* him about it?'

'God, no. I forgot,' I say. 'Greg has the details, Andrew. Shall I call you a taxi?'

'No, I can drive,' he says. 'Just put their number into my mobile, in case I get lost.'

Whether The Boss really can drive is a moot point, but who cares? Thanks to my low cunning, we're blissfully Andrew-free for the next few hours, which means I can finally get round to writing proper replies to today's letters, and Greg can spend his time arranging visits to any other local organisations that he can find.

By the end of the afternoon, Andrew is booked up for a good chunk of the rest of this week, and half of the next one too, thank God. If only I was half as good at *my* life as I am at his.

## THURSDAY, 29 JULY

Connie's done it again. I've been wondering what she was up to – she seems to have been going into work later and later each day, as well as coming home much earlier.

This evening, I ask her what she's playing at.

189

'What d'you mean, what am I playing at?' she says.

'Going into work so late, and coming home so early,' I say. 'Doesn't your boss mind that you're working so few hours?'

'*No*,' says Connie, looking at me as if I am mad. 'Why should he?'

'Well,' I say. 'You *are* contracted for thirty-seven hours a week, and you can't be working more than twenty-eight—'

'Yeah, I know, stupid!' says Connie. 'But I'm on *flexi-time*, aren't I?'

It turns out that Connie hasn't quite grasped the concept of flexible hours, which probably accounts for her earlier enthusiasm. She thinks it means you work as many hours as you like and that's okay – as long as you're honest about filling in your timesheet, so you're not being overpaid. The fact that her contract is for a *specified* number of hours per week seems to have bypassed her synapses.

I explain. Very slowly.

'Con, flexi-time doesn't mean you work *as many hours as you like*. It means you work thirty-seven hours, but at *times* to suit you!'

'Oh,' says Connie.

Max nearly wets himself when I tell him about it. Connie has a brain the size of a planet, but she must be the most literal person in the world.

I wish *I* was on flexi-time. In fact, I wish it was so flexible that it didn't involve any hours at all – until I recall that there's a recession on, and feel guilty about wishing for unemployment. I really *could* use a holiday, though.

I say so to Max as we're getting ready for bed.

'Well, book some time off, then,' he says. 'I will, too, then we can spend it together, hanging out at home, seeing as we can't afford to go anywhere.'

'I can't,' I say, though that sounds a really attractive idea now I come to think of it. 'I've nearly used up all my annual leave, don't forget.'

'Yeah – volunteering for Andrew's election campaign,' says Max, which is true. 'Though volunteering's *supposed* to be voluntary.'

## FRIDAY, 30 JULY

'Just *look* at the state of that cat,' says Josh this morning, as Charlie drags himself in through the cat flap and collapses on the kitchen floor, with all his legs sticking out at different angles.

'Even his fur looks limp,' continues Josh, prodding the unresponsive cat with his toe. 'And no bloody wonder. He spent the whole night shagging, right outside my bedroom window. You should have *heard* the noise he was making, Mum.'

'Oh, I *did*,' I say. 'I didn't sleep a wink, unlike your father. *He* slept like a log, as usual.'

I glare at Max, who laughs, then comes over and whispers in my ear. 'You should have woken me up, Mol,' he says, 'then we could have followed Charlie's lead.'

He kisses the back of my neck, then slaps my arse and walks off, leaving me standing at the sink, open-mouthed. It's a bit weird, isn't it? Using your cat's sex-life to remind you that you're supposed to be having one of your own . . .

And Max is making an effort, too, which is even weirder, what with the Charlie thing, *and* suggesting that we take some time off to spend together. Maybe he's not as bored with me as I thought – which probably removes any justification that I might have for meeting with an International Director of a Global Oil Company in a London hotel.

In fact, it *definitely* does. I shall email Johnny and turn him down, as soon as I arrive at work.


**SATURDAY, 31 JULY**
Gah. It's Annoying Ellen's birthday party tonight. I don't know why I don't just find the courage to refuse to go.

I'm probably afraid of falling out with her because I spend half my working life trying to put a stop to neighbour disputes, and I don't want to find Ellen kicking the side of *our* car in, or throwing dog poo over the garden wall. *Or* stealing my husband, for that matter.

So now I'm in a total panic about what to wear.

I do the usual *pull everything out of the wardrobe while complaining I have no clothes at all* thing, but then feel as if I've hit the jackpot when Max spots me posing in front of the mirror in a dress that could be described as body-con, had it not been from the early '80s, before that phrase was even thought of.

'You still have a great body for a woman of your age,' he says.

Wow. *Wow!* Did Max *really* just say that? I am lost in transports of joy for all of five seconds, until I realise he was being rather too specific for my liking.

Why didn't he just say, 'You look great for a woman of your age'? Or even, 'You look great'? I know why – because my body might look good, but my face obviously doesn't.

After that, I brush my hair so far forward over my eyes that Connie has to guide me on the walk round to Ellen's, and I still manage to walk into several low-hanging branches en route.

It was Max's idea to take Connie with us, in the hope that she could poach one of Ellen's toy-boys, or even one of Ellen's sons, to fill the less-than-yawning gap left by the departure of the chilli boy.

It doesn't really work, as none of Ellen's kids are there, and – after an hour or so – Connie decides that all the toy-boys are dead from the neck up, and so she won't go near any of them. I'm about to point out that Russ was hardly a rocket scientist when I get distracted by wondering where Max has gone.

Connie's sticking to me like an Elastoplast, which has freed him to wander off unsupervised – never a good thing at one of Ellen's parties. He just can't keep up with her drinking habits, or those of her friends, and he will ignore the fact that the reason *they* can each drink a whole case of beer is because of the vast quantities of coke they're shoving up their noses at the same time.

By the time I manage to spot him, it looks as if he's already had several beers and a whole bottle of wine, and now he's found a second bottle that he's carrying around with him as he moves from one group of people to another. He's having no trouble fitting in with any of them – unlike me. I seem to be the only married woman here.

All the other women are divorced, highly vocal about their sex-starved status – *huh!* – and wearing very shiny tops to match their very shiny foreheads. What *is* it with women of my age? They seem to have a uniform for parties, which basically involves jeans, paired with strappy tops that reveal far too much low-slung cleavage. I bet all that beaded decoration was stitched on by starving children in sweatshops, too.

I feel like a visitor from another planet in my black dress, an alien invisible to everyone except Connie – and this feeling isn't helped by the fact that, every time I look over at Max, one or other of the shiny women is staring into his eyes and giving a very good impression of hanging onto his every word.

They don't seem half so interested in talking to me or Connie, so we end up sitting in the garden for most of the evening – where I smoke fit to bust and Connie nags me about my filthy habit. That's when she's not going on about her amazement at the behaviour of some of Ellen's friends – who turn out to be teachers at Josh's school.

No *wonder* Josh is like he is. They're probably the ones who taught him to play cards for money in the first place, seeing as they've just suggested we play a round of poker. I'm bored enough to play Snap! by then, though, so – after checking we're not talking about *strip* poker – I persuade Connie we should both join in.

It's only after we've sat down at the long dining table that I realise that Max is seated at the other end, next to Ellen. If her incessant giggling and irritating amount of energy is anything to go by, she's obviously just been upstairs for another snort.

Max isn't displaying any energy at all and looks totally obliterated by alcohol. I get up from the table and make him a coffee, which he refuses in no uncertain terms – so there's nothing for it but to retire back to my seat, and to scowl at him as he accepts a large shot of frozen vodka from the tallest of the toy-boys. He downs it in one, looks at me triumphantly, then starts to slip sideways on his chair.

I'm just considering whether I should ride to his rescue when I realise that he's slipping *towards* Ellen, while wearing a beatific smile. Then, as if in slow-motion, he moves in towards her neck, upon which he plants a long, slow kiss. Suddenly, the room falls quiet, and I feel as if I have been paralysed.

'What the *hell* are you doing, Dad?' says Connie, breaking the spell. She stands and goes to pull Max off his chair, pushing past Ellen, who's still laughing.

I'm so angry and humiliated that I can't move, until Connie gestures at me to come and help her – but even with our combined efforts we still can't get Max to his feet, so we have to draft in help, in the shape of two of the toy-boys. They hoist Max up, then half-carry, half-drag him back to our house.

Connie walks behind them carrying Max's jacket, while I storm ahead wielding my keys as if they were weapons. In the hallway, Max shakes off the toy-boys, lurches into the living room, and falls onto the sofa, laughing like a lunatic. Connie throws a blanket over him, and then looks at me in disbelief. I have no words, which is most unusual.

I *have* made a decision, though. As soon as Connie's gone to bed, I'm going to email Johnny and tell him that I've changed my mind. Marriott County Hall, here I come.

# CHAPTER FOUR

# August

(Which doesn't rhyme with anything,
either – except for 'lust' or 'dust'.)

**SUNDAY, 1 AUGUST**

Argh. I feel like shit, and seem to have entirely lost my sense of humour. *And* my appetite.

When Max finally wakes up, he staggers into the kitchen and cooks an enormous fry-up, which seems to remove any trace of a hangover. There is no justice. I can't face eating *a thing*.

I'm still feeling sick when the doorbell rings. It is Alex, Ellen's toy-boy-in-chief, who says he wants his jacket back. Apparently, Connie picked his up by mistake during our hasty escape from the party last night.

He sounds less than happy to have discovered that he is now the not-so-proud possessor of Max's Primark jacket, while there's a crumpled Armani version down the side of our sofa. They don't look any different to me,

197

though I don't say so, as provoking Alex is probably a bad idea. I've got a feeling Ellen met him at kick-boxing or something equally violent, and he already seems quite cross enough by the time he throws the jacket onto the back seat of his car and slams the door.

He's still revving the engine like a maniac when Max comes into the hallway to see where I've got to. He seems oblivious to the narrowly averted toy-boy danger and is calmly eating a left-over sausage.

'What's up, Mol?" he says. 'Why are you in such a mood with me?'

'I should have thought you'd *know* what is bloody well up,' I say, throwing his jacket at the coat stand, and missing by a mile.

'I haven't got a clue.' Max does seem genuinely perplexed, unless he's been taking acting lessons from Josh. 'What have I done? Or, rather, what's my jacket done?'

'Well, let me see – how can I sum it up for you?' I say.

I am so angry that I can barely think, so I buy time by throwing the jacket at the coat stand again, equally unsuccessfully.

'Oh, yes – that's right,' I say, eventually. 'You moved in on Ellen in front of everyone – including me. *And* your daughter.'

'I did *what*?'

I'm pretty sure Max thinks I'm joking, though God knows why. My expression ought to rule *that* impression out.

'And then you kissed her. On the neck.'

'I didn't!' Max starts laughing now, which is a very bad move.

'Er, yes – you did, Dad, and it's not funny,' says Connie, who looks almost as annoyed as me. She picks Max's jacket off the floor, and throws it at him. *She* doesn't miss.

'Good God,' says Max, disentangling himself as Connie and I stalk off and both go back to bed.

I stay there for the whole of the afternoon, trying to work out whether I'm entitled to be as angry with Max as I am, given that he was so drunk that he can't even remember what he did, but I just can't seem to reach a decision and stick to it.

I do get up again in the evening, to check my email, but there's nothing from Johnny in reply to the message I sent him last night about meeting up. I forgot – he's travelling around Eastern Europe again this weekend, and did warn me he might be unavailable for much of the time. Something to do with patchy mobile phone coverage in Uzbekistan, I think he said.

My inbox isn't completely empty, though. Dad is back from Thailand and has sent me an email, snappily titled, 'Thai adventure'. I open it. There is no text at all, just six photos. I open the first one, expecting beaches, or mountains. There's scenery, all right – but it isn't of the landscape variety. It's of a young Thai woman in a bar.

The next picture is of the same girl, next to a swimming pool. There's no sign of Dad until the third picture, where he appears – showing more man-boob than should be allowed *anywhere* in the world.

In picture number four, the Thai girl is draped around Dad's neck, like a fresh-faced boa constrictor. By picture six, she is sitting on a bed in a hotel room, wearing nothing but a bathrobe.

*For God's sake!* I'm incredulous.

I have to tell someone, but I am still not speaking to Max, so I call upstairs to Connie, who's now spent almost the whole day lurking in her bedroom, out of the reach of parental strife.

'Con, you won't *believe* what Grandad has just sent me!' I yell.

'I bloody well will,' says Connie, coming back downstairs at last. 'Didn't you notice he copied me in on the email, too?' She makes a vomiting noise. 'I'm *mortified*.'

'What?' says Josh, from behind me, much to my surprise. (I'd thought he was out with Holly – but he must have been staying out of harm's way too.)

I show him the photos and he starts to laugh.

'What are you laughing at?' I say. 'There's nothing funny about sending your daughter something like this.'

'You know what Grandad's like, Mum,' Josh says. 'He's just *trying* to wind you up.'

'He's succeeding,' I say. 'It must be the day for it.'

I turn back to the computer and start typing. Then, before I know it, I press *send*. Now an email saying only 'Come back, Gary Glitter – all is forgiven' is winging its way to my father's inbox.

I'm going to have an early night. I think it's best.

## MONDAY, 2 AUGUST

God, the nutters are out in force today, or on the phone, anyway. All the usual suspects call first thing – I think they store up their bile over the weekend and are bursting to vent it at someone by the time Monday morning rolls around.

Miss Chambers is in full flood about her neighbours, who she still thinks are stealing her electricity. Now she claims they've rigged up some sort of Heath-Robinson-style construction between her attic and theirs, and she wants me to get the police to take her seriously. This would be impossible, as the woman is clearly barking mad.

Talking of the less-than-sane, Mr Beales is next on the phone. 'Bloody speed cameras,' he says, without preamble.

'Oh, yes?' I say. I'm bored already.

'I've been done for speeding!' he says.

'And *were* you?' I say, while staring out of the window and wondering what the hell I am doing with my life. 'Speeding, I mean?'

'Well, yeah – but I wouldn't have been *done* for it. Not if a bloody policeman hadn't been hiding in a bush!'

Oh, for God's sake. I have absolutely no patience with people who complain about being caught speeding. As far as I'm concerned, it's simple – if you don't want to be caught, then just don't do it.

'I should pay the fine and have done with it, if I was you,' I say. 'Now, was that all?'

'No – of course it isn't *all*,' says Mr Beales, somewhat predictably. 'The policeman wasn't wearing his luminous jacket!'

'What's *that* got to do with it?' I say, without really caring about the answer, though I'm certainly not expecting the one that I get:

'Well, I wouldn't have *hit* him if I'd seen him, would I?'

That's not the only thing I don't see coming today. At lunchtime, Johnny replies to the email I sent him after Max's stunt at Ellen's party. He's only gone and booked us rooms (plural) at the Marriott County Hall, for the week after next! *Oh, my God.*

Our dirty mid-week 'weekend' suddenly seems a horribly real prospect, and I want to change my mind, until I recall Max moving in on Annoying Ellen's neck like a predatory, if semi-conscious, slug. Then I reply, saying, 'Send details, and see you then.'

I still can't decide where Max's offence rates on the scale of marital infidelity, though. How much does something count when you're so drunk that you probably don't know what your own name is, let alone whether you're married or not?

Talking of names, and not knowing them, the landline is ringing when I open the front door to let myself into the house this evening. Josh is ignoring it, and Connie and Max are still not home. Connie's got a lot of flexitime hours to make up, but Max is probably just avoiding me.

I sigh, then pick up the phone.

'Are you Bonjour Freight Shippers?' says someone whose voice I don't recognise at all.

'Um, no—'

'Well, *this* was the number I got from 1471.[30] I checked the last caller after I got your answer-phone message, as your man forgot to leave his number.'

'Er, sorry – who is speaking, please?' I say. I still have no idea.

'Mr O'Nyons,' says the man.

He pronounces it exactly as you would expect: Oh – Nye – Ons. I have never heard of him.

'Well, I'm sorry,' I say, 'but I have no idea what you are talking about. There must be some mistake.'

'No,' says Mr O'Nyons, speaking very slowly, as if I am a halfwit. 'The man who left the message said that you had a large shipment of onions that you'd been asked to deliver to me, and that you wanted to confirm my address.'

Oh. Oh, *Christ*. Onions. O'Nyons. *Bloody* hell.

'I'm very sorry, but I have never heard of Bonjour Freight Shippers, and I can only assume that there must have been an error at the exchange,' I say, after an over-long pause. 'Now, if you'll excuse me, I have a family emergency to attend to.'

I put the phone down, take a deep breath, and go upstairs. Josh is lying on his bed, laughing his head off.

'*You* are grounded,' I say. 'For the next ten years. And don't you *dare* touch that phone again while I am at work.'

'You've got to admit it was funny, Mum,' says Josh.

[30] 1471: UK telephone number to phone in order to identify the last person to call you. Mum uses it a lot, as the voicemail revolution has apparently passed her by.

203

'*O'Nyons!* What a muppet. I did mean to put 141 in first, though.'

I don't reply. I am married to a Botox-Queen-snogger, I have Gary Glitter as a father *and* I am raising a juvenile delinquent. I see nothing whatsoever to laugh about.

## TUESDAY, 3 AUGUST

This evening, Dad replies to the email I sent him on Sunday by saying, 'Women never understand.'

My reply is equally terse: 'Women understand only too well.'

Now I'll have to wait and see what his next move is.

It doesn't take long to find out. Dinah phones less than half an hour later. 'Why have you upset Dad?' she says. 'There was no need for that.'

'What d'you mean?' I say. 'What's wrong with you? You're usually the first to go nuts about the way he behaves. Remember the Peyronie's thing?'

'I know – that *was* disgusting – but calling him Gary Glitter, for no reason?' she says. 'Bit strong, wasn't it?'

Ah. I think I know what's happened now. 'Dinah, has Dad actually sent you his holiday photos?' I say.

'No,' she says. 'Why?'

'You'll see. Just check your email in a few minutes, when all will become *crystal-clear*.'

I forward Dad's pictures to her as soon as she hangs up and, thirty seconds later, she sends me a text. It just says, 'Holy shit!'

The sweet sound of vindication.

## WEDNESDAY, 4 AUGUST

I'm telling Greg about Dinah's reaction to Dad's photos, when I get a call from the policeman who's dealing with Miss Harpenden's stolen identity.

'Can we have an off-the-record conversation, Molly?' he says. 'I *can* call you Molly, can't I?'

'Um, yes,' I say. 'To both questions, I suppose.'

Another outing for the good old dual-purpose answer – though I probably should have chosen a version that contained the word 'no'. I'd have been *much* better off not knowing what the officer tells me next.

'Well, Molly,' he says, 'there's a reason we don't seem to be doing anything to help Miss Harpenden, though there *is* a lot of work going on behind the scenes. To put it bluntly, we suspect that her long-term boyfriend's the one committing the identity fraud, and we don't yet know if she's in on it, too. So we need more time . . . to find out.'

'Oh, my God,' I say, once I've got over the shock of Miss Harpenden having a boyfriend, let alone a long-term one. (Greg's always been *convinced* that she's lonely and a lesbian.) 'I'm sure the poor woman has no idea – what am I going to tell her if she phones?'

'Just try to fob her off, until our investigations are complete,' says the policeman. 'In the meantime, it'd be best to pretend you know nothing at all.'

Oh, *brilliant*. That'd be no problem for The Boss, but a) he often *does* know nothing, and b) he's far better at lying than I am. I'm absolutely *hopeless* at it. And, anyway, I'm sure Miss Harpenden hasn't got a clue that it might be her boyfriend who's stolen her identity, or she wouldn't have reported it in the first place, would she?

What a piece of work *he* must be, if he isn't being unjustly accused. I can't get over it.

'It's hard to believe that anyone could do that to a loved one, isn't it?' I say to Max, later, as he's cooking dinner.

'I don't know,' he says. 'I was concentrating on chopping these onions, sorry. *What* can't you believe someone could do to a loved one?'

'Make them think that you're entirely innocent, when you're not,' I say. '*And* let them jump to all the wrong conclusions as a result. Imagine being cruel enough to do *that* to someone you've spent years living with!'

'Ow,' says Max, as he tips the onions into the wok too fast, and splashes hot oil all over his hand.

Third-degree burns seem a bit of a drastic way to change the subject, and I can't imagine why Max would need to, anyway. Unless he thought we were talking about Ellen, not Miss Harpenden, of course. I can't think *why* he would.

## WEDNESDAY, 4 AUGUST (THE MIDDLE OF THE NIGHT)

Dinah's insomnia's getting out of hand. So is mine, seeing as I keep forgetting to turn the sound off on my mobile when I go to bed.

I've just got off to sleep (difficult enough while trying to work out if Max burned his hand on purpose or not), when *ping!* goes my phone, to tell me that I've got an email. Dinah has sent me the same article about the man who killed all those people as she did before, the bloody idiot.

I'm about to delete it without reading it when I spot that this email has a different subject line to the previous one. It says, 'Check the photo, Molly – see if you can spot the difference.'

The picture is of the man's Thai girlfriend, who is alleged to have used a false name, and to have conned him out of thousands of pounds, before dumping him for someone else. She looks exactly like the girl pictured sitting on what was presumably Dad's hotel bed – while virtually naked.

Dinah's only other comment is :o, which I imagine my expression closely resembles. Is *nothing* ever as it seems?

Max may say my job's made me too cynical but, after today's goings-on, I'm obviously *far* from cynical enough.

## THURSDAY, 5 AUGUST

As part of his mission to collect every disaffected non-constituent within a 300-mile radius and add them to our workload, now The Boss has brought Igor back into the fold.

He looks astonished when Greg and I bang our heads on our desks simultaneously when he says, 'Our friend Mr Popov may pop in, in a minute.' (Try saying *that* after a couple of vodkas. The Boss obviously found it a struggle.)

'Oh, God,' says Greg, 'Not bloody Igor again?'

Igor Popov is a madman, who looks exactly like Alexei

207

Sayle in *The Young Ones*. He's convinced he's being persecuted by the Russian Mafia, even though he claims only to have been a bin man when he lived in Moscow. (I don't think *bin man* is a euphemism for *hit man* in Russia, though I suppose it could be. I'll ask Johnny when I get a chance.)

Igor's definitely not a spy, though, as he's far too big and flamboyant for that. He's also a shameless flatterer, which is probably why Andrew can't resist him. (*He* could use a healthy dose of my cynicism, when it comes to hearing good things about himself.)

Anyway, Igor breezes into the office shortly afterwards, and promptly falls to his knees in front of The Boss – whom he clasps around the thighs while muttering various overblown expressions of gratitude. Then he stands up and sings us a Russian song about brotherly love and comradeship. That's what he says it's about, anyway. He could be singing a shopping list for all we know.

The Boss sits there smirking, with his feet up on *my* desk, lapping up the adoration – while Greg pretends to be throwing up.

'This is *nauseating*,' he says, as he grabs his jacket and heads for the door. 'Thank God it's finally closing time. I need to leave immediately, to avoid being overcome by the urge to beat Igor to death. I'm far more of a danger to him than the bloody Mafia.'

I do my best to verify the truth of *that* assessment (after waiting until Andrew and Igor have also left the building), by sending Johnny an email, asking whether the Russian Mafia are really as bad as Igor claims they are.

I also tell him that I'm now an unwilling police collaborator, and that I'm feeling terrible about being forced to stonewall Miss Harpenden earlier this afternoon. I'm hoping for some Igor-style shameless flattery in response, to make me feel better about myself, but nothing ever goes to plan.

Johnny's reply snaps back, within seconds: 'Those of us who live and work in Russia do *not* discuss the M-word. Not here, or anywhere.'

*Ouf.* That's put me in my place, which is not much fun. I've never known Johnny to behave like an International Director of a Global Oil Company before.

'Presumably you don't discuss the Spanish Inquisition, either?' I say, in an attempt to raise a laugh – which fails. Johnny doesn't find the *Monty Python* reference funny, in the slightest.

'This is not a joking matter,' he says, so I tell him about Miss Harpenden, instead – even more to his disgust.

'For God's sake, woman,' he says. 'Do stop talking about your job. We're supposed to be having an affair. Can't we behave as if we are, for once?'

'Okay,' I say, which is a very bad move, as now I seem to have had virtual sex – by accident.

Being compliant obviously buggers your judgement, though it *was* rather nice, and at least I didn't feel as if I needed to put a bag over my head in order to participate – so I'm quite exhilarated as I lock up and start walking home. I even do a skip or two when no one's looking.

By half-way there, I'm dragging my feet, and in a total

panic. Where in the scale of marital infidelities would *my* misdemeanour rank? Higher or lower than kissing a real, albeit cosmetically-enhanced person, in front of your wife and daughter? More or less forgivable than that?

## FRIDAY, 6 AUGUST

Well, if my faith in men hadn't already taken a nosedive this week, Miss Harpenden's boyfriend has sent it plummeting *to the depths*. As soon as I arrive at the office, I get a call telling me that he has just been arrested, because 'the evidence against him has become overwhelming'.

Poor Miss H had already left for work by the time that the police arrived, so she doesn't even know about the arrest yet – though I suppose *that* will ultimately pale into insignificance in the face of everything else she'll discover that she also didn't know.

Maybe I should find out what's *really* going on between Max and Ellen – as long as Max doesn't make a similar effort to find out what's going on with me.

Apparently, *that's* obvious. According to some people, I might as well have a neon sign affixed to my head.

'You have sex last night, Mol?' says Greg at lunchtime, as he downs two cans of Red Bull in preparation for this afternoon's surgery. 'You look different, and you've got a bit of colour in your cheeks.'

'Yes,' I say. 'Green. From deceit-induced nausea, and anxiety in case Miss Harpenden calls to ask why I didn't tell her what was happening. I can't *wait* for the office to close tonight.'

'The day's misery doesn't end there,' says Greg. 'Not

for you, anyway. Have you forgotten it's that stupid fundraising thing tonight?'

Oh, no. I *had* forgotten. I am the unluckiest woman in the world (apart from Miss Harpenden). As if every weekday during Recess isn't already bad enough, I've got the highly dubious pleasure of The Boss' company to look forward to this evening as well.

One of the senior Party activists has organised an event to raise funds, and an ex-Minister is going to attend, to rally the troops. Of course, as soon as he found this out, The Boss lifted his ban on Greg and I mixing with Party staff – temporarily – and insisted that we *had* to go.

'Bring your partners, too,' he said. 'Labour's the party of hardworking *families*, don't forget.'

Greg was infuriated by Andrew's insensitivity. He *still* hasn't got over his girlfriend.

'Has that idiot forgotten that he's not the only single person in this cruel world?' he said, before making an excuse about being unable to attend, and claiming he had to give his mother a lift to the all-night Tesco's on the outskirts of town.

When The Boss objected, Greg said, 'Mum's too busy working hard to go shopping during the day, and she's given up her car, in an attempt to reduce her carbon footprint.'

'Well, good for her,' said The Boss, after a short pause, presumably to recall Labour's manifesto. 'But you and Max had better come, then, Molly – and that's an order. It's listed as "any other duties" in your contract.'

It probably is, too – so, at 7:00pm sharp, Max and I

arrive at the venue, and immediately want to run away again when we're met by the man in charge. He's a notorious loony with delusions of grandeur, and an inexplicable desire to impress The Boss – which is all the evidence you need to prove the loony part, as far as I'm concerned.

We can't escape, though, as we're made to sit at the front, and to look adoringly at the ex-Minister as he gives his speech (just in case any press photographers are here). Then we have to endure the 'entertainment' part, which takes the form of a completely random dance performance given by the loony's rather unattractive teenage daughters. (It's like watching the dance of the elephants in *Fantasia*, only far less graceful and with much more thudding.)

'I can't see what political or fundraising value *this* will have,' I whisper to Max, as the thudding reaches its crescendo.

'Perhaps we were supposed to pay to make it stop,' he says.

Someone must have done, as the girls file off-stage shortly afterwards, and the loony comes on in their place to announce that the buffet is open. I have a very nasty moment when he says that he has employed the entire staff of a local Indian restaurant to cook and serve the food, but – thank God – they're not from The Star of India.

There's plenty of champagne, too – which seems to be *de rigueur* at Party social events these days, though I absolutely *hate* the stuff. It guarantees a hangover even before you've managed to go to sleep, as I often remind The Boss.

As usual, *he* ignores my warnings, though I notice that Max is sticking resolutely to soft drinks tonight.

It might have been better if he wasn't.

'*Max*,' says Andrew, as he lurches towards us, after being cold-shouldered by Joan. 'Good to see you. And isn't our Molly looking *great* tonight?'

'Um, yes,' says Max.

Try harder, I can't help thinking, but then The Boss continues: 'She's looking *so* good this last few weeks, she must be having an affair! What d'you reckon?'

Max must assume this is a politician's rhetorical question, unless he isn't even listening, because he doesn't answer, just helps himself to another samosa.

I glare at Andrew, who takes a huge swig of champagne, looks me up and down – several times – and then continues, 'I'd keep a *very* close eye on her, Max, if I were you. Know what I mean?'

Then, with a wink worthy of Mr Beales, or Ellen, he staggers off to annoy someone else.

Oh, my God. Is Andrew reading my emails during his early morning snooping sessions, or can you *really* tell by looking at me? I feel even sicker now, than I did before.

## SATURDAY, 7 AUGUST

It's at weekends that I realise that, even though I spend every working day sorting out other people's problems, I'm completely *useless* at dealing with my own.

I still have no idea what's going on with Max and me. If *anything's* going on, that is.

I think he might have been up for earning a gold star last night, though God knows whether that was due to The Boss' intervention or not. He was definitely making an effort when we got home from the fundraising thing. He put the kettle on to make a coffee, then started cuddling me, while making oddly appreciative noises.

All I really wanted to do was to go to bed and forget about Andrew's very disconcerting comments by falling asleep, but I tried my best to go along with it, anyway. I was doing quite well, too, until Max's hug turned into a kiss on my neck, and I had a flashback of him moving in on Annoying Ellen's. Then *that* was totally the end of *that*.

Within minutes, we were having an all-out slanging match – the kind where Max pretends not to understand what he did to annoy me, and I get crosser and crosser as a result. Especially when he falls back on his favourite old chestnut. The one reserved for the long-term married: 'Well, if you don't trust me after all these years, then I – just – don't – know.'

He did that infuriating thing of shaking his head in mock-despair at the same time. That's always a red rag to a bull. Or to me, anyway.

After I've listed every time that I've had to give Max the benefit of the doubt during our marriage, and enumerated every single occasion on which he has humiliated me, he then says, right on cue: 'You're like a f*cking elephant, Molly, you really are. You never forget *a bloody thing*.'

I *hate* the weary way he says it.

'Well, maybe if *your* recall wasn't so buggered,' I say, 'you wouldn't keep repeating the same things over and over again, then acting surprised when I object.'

I've climbed up onto the kitchen counter by now, and am sitting cross-legged, settling in for the long haul. Max must have noticed this familiar manoeuvre, as he just slams the kettle down, turns away and walks off down the hallway. Now it's time for his other standard set of lines: 'I'm going to bed. There's no talking to you when you're in this mood. You're so *bloody unreasonable.*'

There you have it. I am *so unreasonable.* And just when I was thinking that *he* was the one who'd kissed someone else in front of me.

## SUNDAY, 8 AUGUST

Max stays well out of my way today, which is probably a good thing as I have quite enough to deal with, what with that idiot son of mine. Or of his.

I'm going to have to block outgoing calls on our home phone again. It's a pain in the arse: last time I did it, Max and I both promptly forgot what the code was and ended up at least as inconvenienced as Josh. But needs must, where the devil drives. The devil Max and I so kindly produced, to stop Connie being an only child.

She doesn't seem particularly grateful for her parents' generosity this afternoon, when she's trying to make arrangements to do something with her best friend tonight. She comes stomping into the living room, and says, 'Mum, can you please get Josh off the phone?'

'Well, I'm sure he won't be long,' I say.

I'm still endeavouring to be more reasonable and less prone to criticism, since the things I said to Max on Friday night.

'He's been on it for hours already,' says Connie. '*Do* something, Mum. *Now!*'

'Well, use your mobile, if it's so urgent,' I say. I really can't be bothered to get off the sofa and trek upstairs to where Josh must be using the extension. I'm too tired after Max snored all last night.

'I'm out of credit. Please, Mum. You're always telling Josh to keep the bills down, anyway.'

Given my aversion to hypocrisy, I'd better be seen to make *some* effort, I suppose.

I walk into the hall and shout upstairs in the vague hope that I will be heard over the hideous sound of Screamo emanating from Josh's room, along with shouts of laughter from him, Robbie and God knows how many of the other boys. It's like Grand Central Station in our house these days, sometimes including the sitting-down-and-weeping part.

'Josh? Josh!' No answer. Bloody hell. '*Josh!*' (This last attempt is worthy of Miss Chambers.)

'What?' says Josh, as if he's only just heard me calling him.

'Get off the phone,' I say. 'Your sister needs to use it, now.'

'Okay, Mum. In a sec.'

Sorted, so I return to the important business of doing nothing. I'm just reaching that attractive pre-snooze drooling state, when Connie comes back into the room, picks up the phone, then slams it down and glares at me.

'He's *still* on the bloody thing!'

Honestly, Josh would try the patience of a saint. I am *not* going upstairs, so I just pick up the phone instead. Someone is speaking, but it isn't Josh. It sounds more like Robbie to me. I have no idea what makes me listen in, instead of saying something straight away.

'So, sir, as I was explaining,' Robbie says. 'With it being National Book Week, Bonjour Books will donate a pound to a charity of your choice for every minute that you listen to one of our authors reading from one of their best-selling works of fiction.'

'Sounds a good idea,' says the man at the other end of the phone, so Robbie continues: 'Today, we have Joshua O'Nyon-Quavers reading from his book, *Strange Things On The Shore*. I will pass you over to him now. Take it away, Joshua, when you're ready.'

I'm transfixed by curiosity – so, instead of yelling, I carry on listening. I am a very bad mother indeed.

'Chapter One. As I walked slowly along the seashore, the shells crunching under my feet like Pringles, the air was filled with the crisp tang of salt and vinegar. I watched, as sunbathers the colour of Doritos stretched their limbs on stripy towels, and their children played with Hula Hoops—'

Josh pauses, to chomp loudly on something crunchy, and then continues – in much the same vein as before. He sounds exactly like Robert Webb.

The story continues for ages, until the branded snack

metaphors become so excessive that I finally get a grip. I replace the handset, then sprint upstairs. Once there, I march into Josh's room, clamber across various skinny-jean-clad teenage legs, and reach over to unplug the extension.

Robbie and the others start giggling, while Josh misses the point, as usual: 'But, *Mum*!' he says. 'I *remembered* to put 141 in before I dialled this time! What's your problem?'

I'll tell you what my problem is: this is what my inadequate parenting skills have achieved – a son whose notion of an excuse for his behaviour is that he did everything he could to avoid being caught. I wonder who he gets *that* from?

## MONDAY, 9 AUGUST

The Boss has opened all the mail by the time I get into work this morning, so trying to work out what he's done with it proves a bit challenging, to say the least. The office looks as if it has been rented out to a playgroup over the weekend, and envelopes are strewn everywhere – though there's no sign of the letters they originally contained.

Greg finally finds most of them shoved behind the cushions of the couch in the Oprah room, along with a gold earring of questionable origin. Andrew claims not to have seen *that* before, but he does pocket it after giving it a cursory look, much to Greg's disgust.

'Molly, why the bloody hell did you give him the earring?' he says. 'Are you a total idiot?'

'He took it from me, when I asked if he knew whose it was,' I say.

'You should have held onto it, and just let him look at it from a distance!'

I am already confused and it's only 9.30 in the morning. I wonder if it's my age?

'Why?' I say.

'It belongs in the staff insurance folder,' says Greg. 'As should have been blindingly obvious, even to you.'

'Why?' I say. Again. 'We don't even know *whose* it is, or do we?'

'Well, no, we don't – but if Andrew doesn't *want* us to know, then that earring could come in very useful indeed. Maybe he's got a secret lover!' Greg laughs as if that idea's ridiculous, but not quickly enough to stop me having a couple of very nasty palpitations. God knows what he'll say next. I could still be wearing that 'Molly's having an affair' sign by accident for all I know.

I decide to borrow some Rescue Remedy from Joan and, by the time I return, there's an email from Johnny in my inbox. The subject line says, 'State of emergency'.

I assume that's ironic, until I open the message and begin to read. It's deadly serious – Moscow's on fire! Well, not Moscow itself, but it's surrounded by wildfires and blanketed in a thick, choking smog. The conditions are so bad that Johnny says it's unsafe for his family to remain there any longer, so *they're* flying back to the UK tomorrow. They'll stay at his wife's parents' house in

219

Dublin, until the fires have been brought under control. He intends to stay put, though – just like Putin.

I'm quite impressed by this courage in the face of danger, as well as relieved. Johnny *can't* be a murderer, if his wife still exists. Although, now I know that she does, I feel worse than I did when I thought she was dead. Here I am, planning to do to her what Annoying Ellen would do to me, given half a chance. *If* Ellen hasn't done it already.

It serves me right that Johnny's obviously going to cancel our date.

'It's okay,' I type, without reading any further. 'I understand why you're cancelling, and I think you're right.'

I hit *send*, but have only just started making notes on a case file when Johnny's reply arrives.

'Read the whole thing, you silly woman.'

Oh.

Johnny's decided that, when he comes to the UK next week – to see me – it would now be awkward for him not to stay with his in-laws while he's there. But he can 'get away with a stopover in London for one night' before travelling onwards to Ireland, 'subject to a few minor alterations to the schedule'.

Then he goes on to explain that he'll be 'pressed for time' due to the early flight he'll have to catch to Dublin the next morning, so he's cancelled our booking at the Marriott County Hall and booked us into a hotel near Heathrow instead. He doesn't even ask me if *I* think this is okay, or acknowledge that it'll make the journey a damn sight longer and more inconvenient from my point of view. His resemblance to Putin's increasing by the minute. *And* to The Boss.

He probably thinks I'm going to stand in the arrivals lounge, holding a placard saying, 'Johnny Hunter's Bit On The Side', and then offer to carry his bags when he turns up. As far as he's concerned, I have nothing better to do than to cater for his every whim – so now I'm *very* cross indeed.

I don't *think* I let this show in my reply, though – I'm still exercising caution with regard to emails, since the Gary Glitter incident.

My fourth draft reads:

> *Johnny*
> *Whereas I have a fairly convincing reason to be seen hanging around near the House of Commons, I have no excuse at all to be waiting for someone at bloody Heathrow.*
> *The Boss doesn't take holidays, so I couldn't even claim I was meeting him. And with my luck, there'd be some sort of terrorist incident, I'd be taken hostage – no doubt involving being grabbed by the neck – and then my picture would suddenly pop up on the news coverage, while Max was watching. Then he'd want to know what the hell I was up to, if I ever escaped.*
> *I don't think I can make it. Sorry.*
> *Mx*

I resist the temptation to add a flying rat to the list of hypothetical occurrences, in honour of Miss Harpenden.

## TUESDAY, 10 AUGUST

I must be wearing another one of those signs that are visible to others but not to me – this one saying, 'Molly is miserable now she's not meeting Johnny' – as everyone seems to have agreed that I need cheering up. How to achieve it is where the consensus breaks down.

While we're getting dressed this morning, Max suggests that he meets me in town, straight after work. Seeing my expression, he says, 'What?' – as if he made that sort of suggestion on a regular basis.

'I'm just surprised, that's all,' I say. 'What brought *that* on?'

'Thought it might cheer you up. Where shall we meet?'

'Well, it'd better be somewhere where I won't feel an idiot, sitting by myself waiting for you to turn up,' I say.

Max looks wounded. 'I *always* turn up,' he says.

'Eventually.'

Oh, honestly. I never know when to accept an olive branch when it's offered (not that I concede Max's point about resembling an elephant). Anyway, I apologise, and then we arrange to meet at Caffè Nero. Again. You can't say we lack imagination.

It's a date, though, isn't it, wherever it is? I'm quite chuffed, not that Greg is convinced about that. He says I still look as miserable as sin when I arrive at work, which must have something to do with the effect of gravity on my mouth. I don't know what his excuse is for *his* expression.

He looks even more like the Infected than I do today – and, after he's attended this morning's 'briefing' with

Andrew (which is even briefer than usual), he comes back rolling his eyes, sits down at his desk with an exaggerated sigh and buries his head in his hands.

Then The Boss bounces in, like an ageing Tigger on speed. God knows why he's suddenly so cheerful – unless he's bi-polar now? (Greg says it's Stephen Fry's fault that *that's* becoming such a popular diagnosis.)

'What are you so excited about, Andrew?' I say. 'Have you finally worked out that no one in the Party's out to get you?'

'Don't be daft,' he says. 'They all are. You'd realise it, too, if you weren't so idiotically trusting of people. Never mind that, though – did Greg tell you about my idea?'

'Not yet,' I say. 'What have you gone and thought of now?'

'Something to boost office morale.' Andrew's self-satisfaction is almost tangible. He puts his shoulders back and struts into the kitchen, like President Putin heading back to the Kremlin. 'Can't say I'm not sensitive to my staff's needs,' he says.

Greg and I are still lost for words when Andrew asks his next question. 'Anyone want a coffee?' he says. 'I'll make them myself.'

'Is *that* his plan?' I ask Greg. 'Making us coffee?'

'No,' says Greg. 'Worse than that. Much, much worse.'

He's about to explain, when there's a crashing noise, some swearing, and then The Boss sticks his head back round the kitchen door. 'Where the hell are all the cups and spoons?' he says. 'Can't find a thing in here.'

The cups and spoons are where they always are, first

223

thing in the morning: in the sink, waiting for me to wash them up. The drawer, however, isn't in its usual place. It's in the middle of the floor.

'What happened to the drawer?' I say, going to the rescue, as usual.

'Must've pulled it out too far, trying to find a spoon.' The Boss steps round it, looks at his watch, then says, 'Oh, I'm late for the Silverhill Remembering Project. Better go.'

When I've finished washing up, rebuilding the kitchen cabinet and making the coffees, Greg has recovered enough to tell me what Andrew's great motivational plan is. Let's just say it's unlikely to work.

He's decided to invite the girls from the London office to come here on Friday, so that we can all have lunch together. He says this will also give Carlotta and Marie-Louise the chance to 'see and appreciate' what we do here in the boring old provinces.

When I call her to make the arrangements, Carlotta doesn't sound any more enthusiastic about it than we are. By the time she's given me a list of her dietary requirements, together with far too much information about Marie-Louise's allergies, I can't think of one single restaurant that will fit the bill. Maybe Caffè Nero will be the default option, yet again.

I'm quite excited about meeting Max there, which is odd, as it's hardly the Marriott, or even Heathrow.

Before I leave work, I freshen my make-up, and squirt Rive Gauche around with gay abandon, while Greg mutters about the office smelling like a tart's boudoir.

I'm already ten minutes late by the time I get to the cafe, but there's no sign of Max anywhere.

By the time forty-five minutes have passed, I'm almost the *only* customer left – and I've drunk so much coffee that I've given myself palpitations, yet again. I keep checking my mobile, under cover of the table, in case anyone thinks I've been stood up, but there's nothing from Max. No texts, no missed calls, no answer-phone messages. Nothing – or 'ничего' in Russian. (I'm learning a few phrases, just in case.)

A full hour after we arranged to meet, I give up, pay the annoyingly sympathetic waitress, and start to walk home. Then my mobile rings.

'I'm *really* sorry,' says Max. 'I had an emergency.'
'Did you?' I say. 'What sort of emergency, exactly?'

'The drivers missed a customer's coffee table off this week's delivery round. So I had to take it there myself, after work.'

'Ah,' I say. 'Well, that *is* an emergency. Undoubtedly. Unlike the eviction case I nearly killed myself trying to finish, so that I could meet *you* on time.'

Then I hang up, turn my phone off, and walk the rest of the way home. I can't say I feel noticeably more cheerful, but maybe Connie or Josh can think of something to improve my mood.

They can't do any worse than the f*ckwits who've already tried.

**WEDNESDAY, 11 AUGUST**
Greg's still on a mission today. He says things have been

225

much too miserable around here since Recess began and that we need to try something far more effective than yesterday's disastrous attempts at raising morale. Especially *my* morale, as now he says I have a face like a wet weekend, which he rates as even less attractive than my 'Infected' one.

He suggests a session of *Writing Honest Letters* at lunchtime, if we can get rid of The Boss for a while. This seems more likely to cheer me up than anything else that's been tried, including Johnny's series of grovelling emails apologising for being 'crass and thoughtless', so I agree.

'On condition we shred the letters immediately after we've read them out loud,' I say. 'That postman has no sense of humour, and he said bribery won't work a second time.'

'Fair enough,' says Greg. 'If he wants to lose a nice little earner. Now for Mr Beales and his sister-in-law's "unfair treatment".'

He starts typing without hesitation.

*Dear Mr Beales,*

*Thank you for your letter regarding your sister-in-law being 'forced' to lose five stone before her gastric band can be fitted. Whilst I take your point that the only reason that she wanted the operation was to lose weight, surely she has now proved she can achieve this, without the need for surgery?*

*I realise this may seem a radical suggestion, but why doesn't she just forget about the operation altogether and stick to her diet instead? It's obviously working and, were she to continue, the funds that would otherwise be spent on surgery for her could be used to help someone else. (Preferably someone whose illness was not caused by spending too much money on Cornish pasties.)*

*I do hope you will take my suggestion in the spirit in which it was intended. I may even propose it to the Department of Health.*

*Yours sincerely,*

*Andrew Sinclair, MP for Lichford East*

Greg hits *print*, sits back in his chair and smiles at me.

'Ooh, contentious,' I say. 'Especially the bit about the pasties.'

'That's the *best* part,' says Greg. 'Now your turn. Who are you going to choose?'

So much choice, so little time. I opt for Mrs Backhouse, in a panic.

*Dear Mrs Backhouse,*

*Thank you for your letter regarding your housing situation. It was kind of you to write, but you really didn't need to bother as, to all intents and purposes, your letter was identical to the last ten that you have sent me, not to mention that it merely reiterated what you have said during the half-dozen constituency surgery appointments that you have already attended since the most recent general election.*

*As I have repeatedly explained to you – and*

*indeed to Mr Backhouse, though I am never quite sure if he is listening – I am unable to force Lichford Council to re-house you and your family, whilst Mr Backhouse refuses to agree to the move.*

*Furthermore, as Mr Backhouse is the only tenant named on the tenancy agreement, not to mention your husband, and your children's father, the Council cannot approve your* exchanging *the property either, without his permission.*

*I am enclosing a leaflet which gives information about the services offered by our local branch of Relate, and I also enclose a list of solicitors who specialise in divorce, should you decide to take more drastic measures. Might I also request that, should you attend any more surgery appointments, you consider bringing your own box of tissues with you.*

*Yours sincerely,*

*Andrew Sinclair, MP for Lichford East*

*Working hard for hardworking families, as well as those who appear wholly unable to communicate with each other*

Talk about therapeutic.

'I feel like a new man,' says Greg. 'Energised, and ready to carry on this futile struggle. I might even be able to conjure up some enthusiasm if I try.'

I raise my eyebrows at him.

'Well, all right,' he says. 'Until Andrew gets back from his meeting at the Agoraphobics Group, anyway.'

I'm expecting trouble on *that* front. Imagine if you'd

been locked in your home for ten years and had only just found the courage to venture out – then the first person you ran into was The Boss!

## THURSDAY, 12 AUGUST

This evening, there's a minor miracle, when I actually manage to leave the office on time – which is a good job, as I'm supposed to be cooking dinner when I get home. Max must have lost the will to live since the Caffè Nero debacle if he's considering eating something I've prepared, but he's got an important meeting after work. Or so he claims.

I'm standing in the kitchen stirring a rather lumpy-looking sauce, intended for macaroni cheese, when I realise I haven't spoken to Mum for days.

Never try to do two things at once when one of them involves cooking, that's all I can say. By the time I've spent half an hour listening to Mum telling me about an article she read about the negative health effects of dairy foods, the sauce is looking even more dubious than it did before.

'What's up, Mum?' says Josh. 'You look even more of a stress-head than usual.'

When I've explained that I have been listening to Nanny's latest health scare warning – and that my concentration is therefore shot – Josh takes one look at the macaroni cheese, declares it 'catastrophic, as predicted' and suggests we watch *Channel 4 News* instead.

'We can have a mother and son bonding session while discussing world events,' he says. 'That'll make you feel better, won't it? You're always saying me and Con should spend more time with you, and take more interest in your job.'

I am, but I'm not sure it's my job to find a solution to the budget deficit, which is all that seems to be making the news tonight. I don't need to, though. Josh has got *that* sorted.

'Mum,' he says, 'are we still an empire, or something?'

Sometimes I despair of comprehensive education. What sort of question is that for someone who's got GCSEs, and is expecting three A-levels in less than a week?

'Well, not exactly, Josh,' I say. 'Though there *is* the Commonwealth. *And* the Crown Territories. And—'

'Never mind the detail, Mum. All I want to know is: do we *own* any other countries?'

Never mind the detail? Who does Josh think he is – an MP, for God's sake? I make allowances, though, on the grounds that A-levels in Photography, Resistant Materials and Film Studies probably don't help much with situations such as this.

'Um, yes, I suppose we do,' I say. 'In a manner of speaking. Why?'

'Problem solved, then,' says Josh. 'We should just phone China and say, "Hey, China – do you want to buy Australia?" I bet they'd *jump* at the chance.'

**FRIDAY, 13 AUGUST**

Carlotta and Marie-Louise arrive mid-morning, to see Greg and me 'in action' – while they take it easy, according to The Boss.

'Go and get them from the station in your car,' he says to Greg, who scowls and says, 'It's only a five-minute walk.'

'I don't care,' says Andrew. 'Give your colleagues a proper welcome.'

Greg had been hoping the girls would get lost and we could lose an hour or so of their company while we 'tried' to find them. He'd even sent them a slightly inaccurate, hand-drawn map.

'I'd have bought one of those traffic-light air-fresheners if I'd known I was going to have to give them a lift,' he says, as he crawls under his desk in an attempt to find his car keys. 'Bet they'll be expecting one, here in the smelly old provinces.'

I say that I doubt they will, but am proved wrong, for once. When Greg gets back, he tells me that, when he showed the girls into the building, they passed Joan in the corridor. Greg says Carlotta looked Joan up and down, then sniffed, as if at a very bad smell.

Poor old Joan. She's one of us, not that The Boss agrees with that assessment. When Carlotta says, 'We just met Jean or whatever her name was', he grunts and looks disgusted. That man couldn't tell who was on his side if his life depended on it.

'Joan,' I say. 'Not *Jean*. A valued member of the Labour Party team.'

Then I get my own back by suggesting it might be 'a useful learning experience' for the girls to sit in on today's surgery.

'Damn good idea, Molly,' says The Boss, much to my satisfaction, if not to theirs.

231

They look a bit shell-shocked afterwards, and so does The Boss. Maybe that's why they all drink so much over lunch, and are legless by the time they stagger back to the office for a quick coffee.

I like them a whole lot better that way – especially when it makes them lower their guards. Marie-Louise admits that they'd been counting the days *until* this Recess, because Andrew 'has been so paranoid recently'.

'*Why* is he paranoid, though?' I say. 'Greg and I can't work it out.'

'He said something about an old friend he could trust telling him some – how'd you call it? – home truths,' says Carlotta, while Marie-Louise gives an expressive Gallic shrug.

'*Cherchez la femme*,'[31] she says. 'That's what we say in France, when a man is acting out of character.'

Greg asks for a translation, then nods and mentions the earring we found the other day – but neither Carlotta nor Marie-Louise has any idea who its owner might be. Greg describes it to them in minute detail, anyway, and they agree to keep an eye out for any women visiting The Boss at the House of Commons wearing only one earring that matches its description.

'She'll probably have a white stick, too, if she's having a thing with Andrew,' says Greg. 'Just *look* at the state of his hair.'

---

[31] Cherchez la femme: Literally, 'Look for the woman' in French. Difficult to know which woman, though, when so many of them seem to find Andrew irresistible. Somewhat inexplicably, unless painted-on hair is a fetish now.

When Carlotta makes a Berlusconi[32] joke in response, our bonding is complete – and, appropriately enough, it's kisses all round when the taxi arrives to take the girls back to the station. I think The Boss misunderstands the protocol, though, as he goes for everyone's lips, except for Greg's. We all wipe our mouths ostentatiously, while going 'Psshaw'.

Greg refers to Andrew as 'Silvio' for the rest of the afternoon, much to Andrew's irritation. Finally, he says he needs a lie-down and is going to leave early, 'just this once'.

'He's not as daft as he looks, though, is he?' says Greg to me, while waving Andrew an enthusiastic goodbye. 'He's succeeded in raising office morale rather nicely.'

'Yes,' I say. 'Just not in the way that he intended. Now we're all united by despair.'

## SATURDAY, 14 AUGUST
Idiot brother Robin rang me last night, and asked me to check on Mum's sanity.

'It's getting more like a bloody nursing home round there every time I go,' he said. 'What the f*ck are all those tables about?'

He's referring to the type of small table just big enough to hold a single cup and saucer – and when I arrive at

---

[32] 30 Berlusconi: Silvio Berlusconi, ex-Prime Minister of Italy (on several occasions), with what has been described as a 'waxing and waning hairline', which may or may not owe its appearance to the use of a coloured spray to fill in gaps. Also known as The Boss' 'guru of style' by Greg.

the house, I discover he's right: Mum *has* bought even more of them. They're everywhere, their legs sticking out so far they're an accident waiting to happen. I tip two of them over, on my way to join Ted in the sitting room.

I've only just righted those when Mum comes in, bearing tea. She places our cups on three more tables, one for each of us. I try to move mine nearer to my chair, catch its leg in the rug, and tip this one over too.

When I've cleaned up the spilt tea, we're finally ready for 'a nice chat', as Mum puts it. Ted promptly falls asleep, which I wish I could, too. 'A nice chat' is code for Mum asking me how Dad is. I do wish she wouldn't. What's the right answer supposed to be? *Fine*, or *totally miserable since you and he divorced*?

The latter would be a bit unconvincing, wouldn't it, since the whole Gary Glitter thing? Best to carry on keeping *that* stuffed firmly under my metaphorical hat.

'Another oatcake, Molly, dear?' says Mum. 'Plenty left, and they're dairy-free. Oh, and I hear your father's gone to Thailand again.'

'What? He's only just come back,' I say, before I can stop myself. How does Mum even know he's been to Thailand *once*? Did I tell her by mistake, or did Connie do it, the total dingbat?

I'm so distracted that I drop half of the oatcake I've been dunking into my tea, so I stir it in and try to swallow the result. Anything to buy some thinking time. I *have* to get to the bottom of this.

'How did you know about that, Mum?' I say, having failed to think of anything remotely subtle. 'And what d'you mean, he's *back* in Thailand? He can't possibly be.'

Mum looks flustered, as well she might. 'Oh, I must have just got the wrong end of the stick, dear,' she says. 'I thought someone mentioned he'd gone recently, but maybe it was a while ago now. I do get terribly confused these days.'

Pah. Confused, my arse. Mum's as sharp as a tack, despite the table mania – but, before I can point out that there's nothing wrong with her memory, she changes the subject, almost as adroitly as Max does whenever I mention Annoying Ellen. Or Germany.

'And how's dear Josh?' she says. 'Do you think he's done okay in his exams?'

'Only if they're giving A-levels away with packs of playing cards,' I say.

Mum says she's sure I'm wrong, and I'm pretty sure I am, too – though not about Josh's prospects. There's something about the certainty with which she said, 'Your dad's back in Thailand', that makes me think there's much more to this than meets the eye. There usually is, where men are concerned.

## SUNDAY, 15 AUGUST

Dinah phones first thing, waking me from a nightmare in which The Boss is trying to kiss me repeatedly while whirling me round the office to the accompaniment of a crazed Russian band. All its members look like Igor, and keep referring to me as 'a jewel of womanhood beyond compare'.

235

That last part's surprisingly enjoyable, so my heart sinks when I pick up my mobile, and see Dinah's face filling the screen.

'Do you know where Dad is, Molly?' she says.

'Um, no,' I say. 'I phoned him last night, but got the answer-phone.'

'God, that bloody thing.' Dinah drags on what probably isn't her first cigarette of the day, and continues, 'I wish he'd take Stepmother Mark III's name off the message, don't you? It's at least two years out of date.'

'Well, yes, but Dinah, you just woke me up. And anyway, she's only Stepmother Mark II to you. Can I make a cuppa, then phone you back?'

By this, I mean *Can I make three cups of tea, have a couple of cigarettes and brace myself to talk to you?* – but Dinah's unstoppable once she starts.

'Shut up, Molly!' she says. 'Just listen, I'll only be a minute. Are you *sure* Dad hasn't gone away somewhere?'

The sinking feeling's getting worse, but I'm still trying to ignore it. 'Yes, well – no,' I say, remembering that I don't like telling lies. 'But where would he go, if he has?' (Don't mention Thailand. *Don't* mention Thailand.) 'Why do you think he's gone somewhere, anyway?'

'Because,' says Dinah, before pausing for effect, 'one of my mates just phoned me, and asked why Dad's car has been parked outside the railway station for the last few days.'

'Ah,' I say.

'D'you think he's dead?' says Dinah, who always seems

to think that everyone we're related to has kicked the bucket. I've no idea why, unless it's wishful thinking.

'Don't be daft, Di,' I say. 'We'd have heard.'

'We're always the last to know anything about that man,' says Dinah. 'Tell you what: you ask everyone on *your* mum's side of the family, and I'll ask on *my* mum's side, and then we'll try his neighbours, if all else fails.'

'Okay, speak to you later,' I say, then – under my breath – *unless I can think of a really good excuse not to.*

I make a cup of tea, and sit mulling over what to do next. No point asking Mum, and idiot brother Robin won't have a clue, as Dad's not *his* dad, luckily for him. I shall just do nothing. That's usually the best option where Dad's concerned: wait and see.

It's a remarkably efficient option, too. Connie and Josh have just got up, and are locked into their first argument of the day – about Josh flicking through the TV channels and saying, 'Con – look! Look, look, *look*!' every few minutes, while Connie is trying to read her emails.

She loses her temper and walks out of the room, taking her laptop with her. 'Mum,' she yells, as she stamps upstairs, 'tell that moron Josh I don't give a flying f*ck about watching *Dirty Sanchez*, stupid *Cribs* or *Pimp My* bloody *Ride,* and get him to leave – me – alone!'

Less than a minute later, she comes running back downstairs, slams her laptop onto my knees – sending the Sunday paper flying everywhere – and says, 'Mum! *Mum!* Look! *Look!*'

'Pack it in, Connie,' I say. 'It isn't funny when *Josh* does it, as you well know.'

'Just *look*,' she says, pointing at the screen. 'An email from Grandad.'

'What?'

'He's back in Thailand!' Connie's eyes look fit to pop out.

'He's *what*?' I say. Oh, my God. 'Why did he email you, and not me?'

'You'd better read it,' Connie says.

Now I really wish I hadn't.

> *Dear Connie*
> *It's your Grandad here. I'm back in Thailand. I haven't told your mother as, when I told her about my last trip, she called me Gary Glitter, and I'm in no mood for sarcasm. I'll send you a post-card and see you when I get home. It's still very hot.*
>
> *Love from Grandad*

It's only been two weeks since Dad arrived back, for goodness' sake! I need a cigarette – or two – before I have to impart this information to Dinah, and deal with the consequences.

I've only just lit the first one when my phone starts to ring and Dinah's face appears on the screen. It looks quite scary in that photo.

'Dad's only gone back to bloody Thailand already,' she shrieks, when I answer, reluctantly. 'Can you believe it? Mum told me. She said he'd asked her not to tell me as I wouldn't approve. Damn right I don't.'

She pauses for breath, then goes on: 'Fancy not telling your daughters! The man is *unbelievable*.'

'I know,' I say. 'He's just emailed Connie. Apparently he's upset I called him Gary Glitter.'

'You were a model of restraint,' says Dinah. 'Compared to what I'm going to call him when he gets back.'

I just hope it *is* when, and not *if*. Dad's always been partial to the heat.

## MONDAY, 16 AUGUST

I'm typing a message to Dad this morning, warning him that Dinah's email account has been hacked by someone with Tourette's, and so he should ignore anything she might send, when Igor walks into the office.

He wants The Boss to help him get a job, and he's clearly willing to flatter anyone and everyone in order to achieve his aim.

'Ah, the beautiful Molly,' he says, 'bringing joy to men's spirits, like the sun. And like my lovely wife, Natalia, back in Moscow, who I miss so *ve-ery* much. May God keep her safe – from these *terrible* fires, as well as the Mafia.'

Greg rolls his eyes at the mention of the M-word, but I'm starting to like Igor a whole lot better than I used to. First he compares me to a jewel, and now to the sun! *And* he's devoted to his wife – as all men should be, including the one who's married to me.

I say as much to Greg, but then recall that Igor didn't *actually* call me a jewel, except in a dream – which makes me feel a bit stupid, until I realise that Greg wasn't listening, anyway. He's too busy admiring the bribes, I mean *gifts*, that Igor has brought with him, to add weight to his charm offensive. Three bottles of Slivovitz and a fedora hat the same as his own.

The Boss is vocal in his thanks for the alcohol but seems less sure about the hat. He sneaks it onto my desk, behind a pile of filing, when Igor suggests they go and have 'breakfast-lunch' together.

I wait until Andrew thinks he's got away with it and is about to go out of the door, then run after him and say, 'Don't forget your lovely new hat!'

'Oh, don't worry, Molly,' he says, glaring at me. 'I'll come back and get it later.'

Then he tries to walk on, but Igor's having none of it. He takes the hat from my hand, crams it onto Andrew's head and says, '*There*, my friend. Now we look like the brothers we are – in our hearts.'

'You look more like the Chuckle Brothers to me,' says Greg.

**TUESDAY, 17 AUGUST**
Oh, my God. The Boss should never be allowed on a phone unsupervised.

I pop out to buy a sandwich at lunchtime and come back to find him cosily ensconced behind my desk, talking on the phone. He's looking a bit flustered and red in the face, but when I raise my eyebrows in enquiry, he waves me away and says into the receiver, 'Well, I really don't know *what* to say.'

Whole sentences instead of '*Ah*'s' mean that Andrew

is way out of his depth, so I kick his feet off the desk and pass him a note saying, 'Who is it?'

He mouths back, 'Mrs Saunders.'

God all-bloody-mighty. The last thing that poor woman needs is a conversation with The Boss, particularly not when he's under the weather after a breakfast-lunch with Igor that apparently ended up turning into a dinner-supper as well. Liberally fuelled by Slivovitz.

I watch, paralysed with indecision, as Andrew says, 'So he didn't manage it this time, then?'

Oh dear. Harry Saunders must have made another suicide attempt. That's the fourth this year. And he is *not* one of our numerous half-hearted attention-seekers. Harry is deadly serious, if that's not an absolutely terrible pun. We're not talking taking a few tablets then phoning for an ambulance, which is Mr Ellis' usual ploy. In Harry's case, we're talking throwing himself off walkways, trying to set fire to himself, and other horrors. He's only twenty-one, and his poor parents are beside themselves with powerlessness and fear. The Boss is absolutely the wrong man for this job.

I try to pull the phone away from him but he swings the chair round so that his back's to me, and then says, all too clearly: 'You do realise, don't you, that Harry's so determined that – ultimately – he *will* succeed?'

*Enough*. More than.

I run into Greg's office, where the main 'switchboard' is situated, over-ride Andrew's call and cut it off. Then I crawl under Greg's desk and unplug the phone altogether. I seem to spend half my life unplugging phones.

'Hello. Hello? Molly – something's happened to the phone!' Andrew shouts, from my office.

'And to this one,' I say. 'I'll have to report it to BT.'

'But I was in the middle of an important conversation and—'

'*I* can handle that, Andrew – on my mobile. Mrs Saunders, wasn't it? I'm calling her now. There's a sandwich for you in that carrier bag.'

It's *my* bloody sandwich, actually, but that's a small price to pay. I sincerely hope he chokes on it.

It takes me ages to calm poor Mrs Saunders. How can someone as apparently well-meaning as The Boss be so incredibly crass? How the hell can he lack the imagination to understand what she must be going through? I can't even bear to contemplate how I would feel if it were Connie or Josh. God forbid, touch wood, and anything else that can be done to ward off such a terrible situation.

'Imagine being an event planner, or a play specialist – or any job that didn't involve dealing with people who are suffering and in distress,' I say to Johnny in an email, later on.

'What – suffering from lost *joie de vivre*?' he replies. 'Like me?'

Honestly, even when people are healthy, rich and successful, it doesn't seem to make them happy, does it? Johnny's been as miserable as sin ever since I said I wouldn't meet him at Heathrow.

He sends me a total of five emails this afternoon. In the fourth one, he says he feels like he did before we 'met' again via Facebook – 'old, jaded, and as if the spark is missing' from his life. Ironic, seeing as he's still in Moscow, where sparks are probably the last thing anyone needs.

I do know what he means, though. My fire seems to have gone out again since I decided not to meet him, and to try to damp the situation down. Life has slid seamlessly back into its rut, which is just as rut-like as it was before – not that *that* makes any difference. I still can't think of a good reason to be at Heathrow by myself, so I tell Johnny there's nothing I can do about it.

His fifth email arrives just before I leave the office. It says, 'Right, woman – I can't stand this any longer. If you can't get to me, I shall come to you.'

Good God. An International Director of a Global Oil Company, willing to cross half the world to the dot on the map that is Lichford, just to see *me*? Well, willing to cross most of Europe, anyway. That's still pretty impressive, even if it's not quite as far as a trip from Dorset to Pattaya.

I shall buy a copy of *Glamour* magazine on my way home. Sod *Woman and Home*. Maybe glamour's not as irrelevant to my life as I've always thought.

### WEDNESDAY, 18 AUGUST

I am going to starve if I keep buying sandwiches for lunch. I never get to eat the damned things, as The Boss always does, either without my knowledge, or as part of an emergency diversionary tactic.

Today's no different, as Mr Beales phones at lunchtime

'for a chat about the European Union'. By the time I've got him off the phone, Andrew's eaten both my lunch, and Greg's.

'Nice one, Mol,' says Greg, when he arrives back from a meeting at Easemount parish council. 'You were supposed to be keeping an eye on him. He hasn't even wiped the crumbs off his beard, again.'

He accepts my apology surprisingly quickly, though. 'Oh, well,' he says. 'Suppose it wouldn't do me any harm to lose a bit of weight.'

That's exactly what Max says when he arrives home tonight, and mentions that he's thinking of joining a gym. So much for the sit-ups falling by the wayside.

'Ellen says that you have much more energy when you do regular exercise,' he says.

Energy for *what*? I don't like the sound of that – at all – so I suppose now I'm going to have to get fit, too. Maybe Max and I could bond over a new-found shared interest in exercise, buy matching gym wear, and post pictures of ourselves on Facebook, looking manically happy while doing extreme sports, not including hoovering.

Inspired by this prospect, I decide to experiment with the exercise ball Connie bought for Max a few years ago but, when I finally find it hidden in the cupboard under the stairs, it's gone completely flat and, by the time I've pumped it back up, I'm exhausted. Then, when I try to sit on it, I promptly roll off backwards and end up stuck between the ball and the wall, while Max tries not to laugh. He fails.

'Stop laughing and help me,' I say. 'I can't get any purchase with my feet. This bloody ball keeps moving around.'

'Can't,' he says, 'I'm on the phone. Oh, hi, Sam. How are you, mate?'

Oh, *hell*. I could be here all night if I can't get a grip – which is not something that's easy to do while stuck on top of a giant purple ball. It won't stay in one place long enough for me to gain any equilibrium, and I'm still wriggling around ineffectually when Josh comes into the room.

After he's done his share of laughing and pointing, he finally comes to the rescue and pulls me to my feet. I'm quite touched by this, until he says, 'Mum, aren't you too old to be starting an exercise programme without seeing your doctor first?'

'No,' I say, though now I'm not so sure. Knowing my luck, I'll break a hip next time I fall off, or tear all my stomach muscles simultaneously. Once I can actually *find* the buggers.

It's probably safer to do some research first – so I get my laptop and join Max on the sofa, which has the added advantage of allowing me to eavesdrop on his conversation with Sam.

'What?' he says. 'You want *Molly* to do it? Are you sure that's wise? You know how truthful she is.'

I feel a bit bad about that, partly because I'm not quite sure it's one hundred per cent accurate any more, not since Johnny made an appearance, anyway, but mainly because of Max's obviously negative view of telling the truth. *Everyone* should try it, once in a while – especially husbands, and nymphomaniacs.

I glare at Max, but he just waves at me dismissively, and continues: 'And are you *sure* you want to keep going with this online dating thing? You know you're a loony magnet. Mol and I watched that programme about it on Channel 4 last night, and those women scared the *shit* out of me.'

Max is telling the truth about *that*, anyway. He went white when the women using the websites started talking about how they cyber-stalk their dates, and even paler when one of them – a woman who blogs about her dating experiences – said that she was 'immediately' suspicious of her new boyfriend because he 'had sixteen female friends on Facebook'.

Max kept repeating, 'Only *sixteen*?', and Josh just sat there muttering at the blogger: 'Yes, well, *you* can't get a long-term relationship out of this – can you? Seeing as it's your *job* to write about internet dating. You'd make yourself unemployed.'

Josh is such a cynic; I can't think *who* he gets it from. I was quite enjoying the whole bunny-boiling thing, myself, as I figured it might make Max far more grateful for what he's got: i.e. *me*. I don't think he made the connection, though, so then I had to point it out to him – which somewhat diluted its effectiveness.

'Well,' he said. '*Those* women were probably on a site called *mentally-disturbed-dating dot com* – but I'm sure they're not typical of *all* single women.'

(I didn't like how positive Max seemed to be about

*that* at the time, and I *still* don't like it. It sounded far too much like the voice of experience.)

I'm just about to ask him what he meant when he hangs up the phone and announces that he's promised that I'll write Sam's profile for the latest dating site he's decided to join. And that I'll have it finished *this* evening, before I go to bed.

'Oh, for God's sake,' I say. 'Why have I got to do it *tonight*? What's the urgency?'

'Sam says he hasn't had sex in ages,' says Max. 'Not for weeks, if not for months.'

'Perhaps he's finally ready for marriage, then,' I say.

If Josh hadn't got me off the exercise ball when he did, I'm pretty sure Max would have left me there all night.

## THURSDAY, 19 AUGUST

This year's A-level results come out today. Josh has been up all night worrying, and he looks very twitchy when I see him before I go to work.

It seems to have just occurred to him that Robbie and the others may have been being economical with the truth when they said that they weren't doing *any* work for their exams, as apparently they didn't sound half as worried as he was when he spoke to them last night, after rescuing me from the exercise ball. (I *kept* telling him they were talking rubbish, and that *of course* they were studying at least some of the time, but no one ever listens to me.)

Connie's got no sympathy for Josh, as he always called

her a teacher's pet when she was at school, but he looks so anxious that he starts to make me fret, too – so I make him promise he'll phone me at work as soon as he gets the results. He nods, but doesn't say a word, which is even more unnerving.

I'm still fretting about him when I get to work, and my concentration's totally shot, so badly that The Boss notices and asks me why. When I tell him that I'm worried that Josh may not have done very well in his A-levels, he's quite reassuring, though Greg *really* isn't.

He says that Josh is going to end up as a NEET,[33] who will still be living off me and Max when he's thirty. Considering that Greg's almost thirty himself, and still lives with *his* mother, I'm not sure what he's trying to prove, so I answer the phone to avoid the need to respond.

It's Miss Chambers, who almost breaks the sound barrier.

'British Gas,' she screams. 'I sent you a copy of the bill – what have you done about that overcharge?'

'If you stop shouting at me, I'll be able to tell you,' I say.

'I'm not shouting,' she says, shouting.

I wait for the irony of that to sink in, then try again. 'Right, then,' I say. 'If you've finished shouting now, look at your copy of the bill. That £13.48 that you said was an overcharge?'

[33] Neet: Not in Education, Employment or Training, i.e. a total write-off. (According to Greg. Oh, and Connie.)

'It *is* an overcharge. How many times do I bloody well have to tell you people?'

The volume's increasing again, for God's sake. I take a deep breath, then say, 'It is *not* an overcharge. It is a *credit*.'

'What do you mean?' she says, going up another few decibels.

'They've given you some money *back*,' I say. 'That's why it says "credit" on the bill. Okay?'

'Well, why the *hell* didn't they say so?' she shrieks, before slamming the phone down on me.

What do they teach these people in school, when they can't even tell a credit from a debit? If I ever get time, I'm going to learn voodoo, and then spend every evening sticking pins into effigies of that stupid woman.

I tell Greg about my plan.

'Good idea, but she obviously hasn't finished yet,' he says, as the phone starts to ring again.

'Yes?' I say, cautiously, holding the phone well away from my ear.

'Hurrm.'

'I'm sorry, what did you say?' Is this Miss Chambers' idea of a joke? First full volume, then garbled whispering?

'Mum.' It's Josh. A very quiet Josh. Oh, *hell*.

'How did you do, darling?' My voice is so optimistically bright and brittle, it even manages to annoy me. Josh doesn't seem to notice, though.

'Crap,' he says.

'What do you mean, *crap*?' I say. 'It can't be that bad, can it?'

'Well, I got a D in Film Studies,' he says, as if that is meaningless – which it could be, for all I know. What exactly *is* Film Studies, when it's at home? Now's probably not the time to find out, judging by Josh's tone of voice.

'Oh, well,' I say, 'that's not a terribly important subject, is it? How did you do in the other two?'

'U's in both,' says Josh. ''Bye, Mum. I'm sorry.'

Oh, my God. One D and two ungradeds. I may not understand the current education system very well, but I'm pretty sure that ungradeds must be *fails*. I try phoning Josh back, but he doesn't answer, so I try a few more times, then give up and resort to texting Robbie: 'Hi Robbie – is Josh with you? And how did you do in your A-levels?' I say.

Robbie's reply comes straight back: 'Hello, Mrs B. Josh went home – said he wasn't feeling well, so I think Holly went with him. I got two As and a C :-)'

I have no idea what I am going to say to Josh when I see him. It's not that I think university's a guarantee of success – I'm living proof *that's* not the case – but there are no jobs for under-twenty-fives at the moment, and no one's going to be offering them apprenticeships either. Greg suggests Josh could become a stand-up comedian, which is no help at all.

After work, I walk very, very slowly all the way home, and when I finally get there am tempted to turn around and head straight off in the opposite direction – anything rather than go inside. But Connie's obviously been on the look-out and opens the front door before I can make my escape. She is absolutely *beaming*.

'Mum, Josh failed almost everything,' she says. '*What* a muppet!'

If there were exams in sibling rivalry, both my kids would have doctorates. Now I have to find a way to convince Josh that there's more to life than academic success – without making Connie feel I don't value hers. Sometimes parenting's much closer to the practice of politics than is generally appreciated.

**FRIDAY, 20 AUGUST**

I get a brief email from Johnny first thing, via his BlackBerry. He says he's at his in-laws' now, so can't message me as much as usual, but that he has a solution to Josh's under-achievement: bring back grammar schools.

'It worked for us,' he says.

'Some of us,' I say, meaning him. He's got a point, though. He definitely wouldn't have got where he is today if he'd gone to Josh's school.

'You're turning into a Tory,' he says, when I tell him I'm inclined to agree with him.

I can't be. I just need a holiday, then I'll be fine – and better able to deal with surgeries, too. God, today's is aggravating, though it starts out okay. First up is Paul Taylor, who I rather like. He's been divorced for a few years now, ever since his ex-wife ran off with a fitted kitchen salesman, and he's desperate to see his daughter Ava more regularly.

I admire Paul's latest photo of her, while he tells us that his latest attempt to get the courts to enforce his right to access has failed.

'My ex complied for a few weeks this time,' he says, 'but then she started messing me about again. I haven't seen Ava for the last three months, though obviously I'm still paying maintenance for her. I don't want her to go without.'

I wish I could say the same for Mike Templar, who comes into surgery next, accompanied by his second wife, Penny. Mike ran off with her, leaving his first wife and three young children without, it seems, a second thought. Maybe he liked her day-glo tan and WAG-inspired sense of style.

I don't know why they've bothered to come to see The Boss, though, seeing as Penny already phones me every week without fail – always to complain about the amount of money Mike's supposed to pay to support his children.

She's looking oddly smug today, and the reason for that soon becomes clear: she is pregnant.

'So now the CSA[34] will *have* to agree to reduce the amount Mike has to pay that grasping bitch,' she says. 'Won't they?'

I count to ten in my head, then say, 'Well, they do have a formula they work to, which takes account of the number of children a parent's responsible for.'

'Damn the formula, that'll hardly reduce it at all,' says Penny. 'We need a much bigger slice taken off. We'll have to move, fit out a nursery, and we need a holiday, too.'

I count to ten again, while trying to send Andrew a

[34] CSA: Child Support Agency, responsible for gathering money owed as maintenance (or alimony). Even less effective than certain MPs, according to some constituents. Too effective, according to others.

thought-message that he should join in any time he likes, preferably right this minute. He's never been any good at telepathy, though.

'Well,' I say, after the silence goes on for just a little too long, 'I'm sure your husband wants to be sure that *all* his children are well cared for, doesn't he?'

I look at Mike Templar, urging him to say the right thing, but he wimps out and starts fiddling with his shirt cuffs, as if his life depended on them.

'You lot need to explain to the CSA that his *new* family is the most important thing,' Penny says, slapping her hand on the table for emphasis. 'That bloody woman needs to get a job. I mean, *I* won't be able to work once my little 'un is born.'

I am counting to ten for the third time, this time *very* slowly. It doesn't work – I still want to punch her. God knows how I manage not to. It hasn't even occurred to her how she'll feel if Mike trades her in next, and she becomes the one relying on his payments to feed and clothe *her* child. Affairs are so messy, aren't they? Oh. Oh, *God*. I may be having one.

## SATURDAY, 21 AUGUST

Holly's been here for the last two nights, in an apparently fruitless effort to cheer Josh up – so, as soon as she finally goes home today, Max and I decide it's time for the 'what next' conversation: the one you have with sons who've just failed almost all their A-levels. It takes far less time than we anticipate.

Josh says he is *not* going back to school to do re-sits,

and nor is he going to do them at the local further education college.

'It's not as if I even *want* to go to university,' he says. 'I'm not cut out for academic crap, I have no patience with stupid teachers and, anyway, you and Dad can't afford it. Plus I don't want all that debt.'

Connie is infuriated, and keeps saying, 'Crap? *Crap?*' while I try to reassure Josh that, however broke Max and I might be, we'd still find a way to help him out somehow, just as we do for Connie.

Max keeps completely quiet throughout the whole discussion and, all of a sudden, it feels like the girls against the boys, or the university-educated against those of the University-of-Life school of thought.

It's not as if I'm in favour of everyone going to university anyway, despite what Max and Josh may think, so I suggest to Josh that he could learn a trade skill instead.

'Greg says you might enjoy it, and it'd probably be more lucrative than getting a poor degree in a made-up subject,' I say. '*And* he says you wouldn't have to spend years trying to pay off your loans while delivering pizzas for a living either.'

'Great,' says Josh. 'So that's all Greg thinks I'm capable of, academically, is it? A degree in a made-up subject?'

I've just managed to negotiate my way out of that one (by telling Josh that academic study is not the be-all and end-all, and that we'll support him in whatever he decides to do), when Connie goes ballistic and reminds me that she still has another two years at university to go. It's like walking on eggshells around here – or across the San Andreas fault.

In the end, the whole conversation becomes impossible to continue while both kids are in the same room. I'm wriggling like a fish on a line, so it's a relief when Josh goes upstairs to indulge in some Xbox violence – probably involving the virtual murders of a posse of sisters or university students – while Connie stays downstairs with Max and me, looking through details of houses to rent.

She starts her *Year in Industry* internship soon, so time's getting short for her to sign the contract on somewhere to live.

'Mum,' she says. 'Do you think I'm wasting my time with all this study, then?'

'No, of course I don't, Con,' I say. 'I'm very proud of you.'

'So why is it right for me, but a waste of time for Josh?' she says. 'It's not as if he's stupid – even though he *is* a tosser. He scored two points higher than me on the *Big Intelligence Test*, on TV.'

'Well, Con – I don't know,' I say. I've had enough. 'Max, *you* explain it.'

There's no reply. Max has dozed off. Sleeping while family fault lines open up in every direction is obviously a skill they need to teach at university.

### SUNDAY, 22 AUGUST

Max and I go into town, more for a wander than to shop, as we are broke until payday. We leave Connie and

Josh at home, arguing desultorily about whether university is a waste of time.

Max says maybe we should try to arrange something for next weekend, and suggests we ask David and Susie if we can borrow their holiday cottage. Just the two of us.

I've no idea what brought this on, but I'm thrilled – especially as it's entirely Max's idea, and not the result of furious hinting. And, if anything is likely to result in sex, this is it. Being fifty miles away from the kids would mean there'd be no chance of being interrupted by one of them wanting us to referee a stupid argument.

'Phone David now,' I say. '*Quick*, before you change your mind!'

'Why would I change my mind?' says Max.

'Oh, I don't know,' I say. 'But something always crops up, and then we end up doing nothing.'

Max gives me a hug and picks up his phone.

David and Susie must be otherwise engaged, as Max's call goes straight to answer-phone. He's about to hang up but, after some nudging from me, he leaves a message first, asking if we can borrow the house. Hooray! I'm so happy that I'm almost bouncing along as we start to make our way back home.

When we come out on the other side of the underpass, thankfully uninterrupted by bad skateboarding, Max's phone starts to ring. Surely it can't be David calling back already?

'You what?' says Max. There is a barely discernible note of panic in his voice. 'He's done *what*?'

I stick my head up close to his, and can just make out Connie's voice – which is pitched rather higher than usual.

'Well, don't move him,' says Max. 'We're almost home.' He breaks into a run, and I follow suit – but he's too fast for me. By the time I walk into the house, he's examining Josh, who is lying on the floor, half inside the living room and half in the hallway. He looks distinctly green and is unusually quiet. So is a rather twitchy Connie.

'What happened, Con?' says Max.

'He was getting really stroppy about students, so I told him to piss off and leave me alone,' says Connie.

'And?' Max raises his eyebrows and looks hard at her.

'Well, he wouldn't,' she says. 'He just kept bugging me.'

'You *thumped* me,' says Josh. (Thank God for that – at least he's capable of speech.)

'Not hard! And, anyway, it was your bloody fault what happened.'

Connie's chin is sticking out – as it always does when she feels under attack. She's about to continue when Max interrupts. 'Look,' he says, 'never mind that. Josh's arm is blue – so we need to take him to A&E. I'll go and get the car.'

As he heads for the door, I say, 'What d'you think is wrong with him?'

'I think he could have broken his arm,' says Max, 'and the bone might be cutting into his blood supply.'

'Oh, Christ,' I say, sitting down on the stairs, without having intended to.

'Get his coat and a blanket, and I'll bring the car

257

round,' says Max. 'And you can stay here while I take him to the hospital. You'll just wind him up if you come, you look so worried.'

Gah. I deal with stressful situations every day of the week – so why does my husband think I'm useless in a family emergency?

'I'm coming,' I say. 'Connie, you can prepare dinner while we're gone. I'll phone you when we know what's going on.'

I'm not sure, but I could swear Connie says, 'Serves him right', as Max and I help Josh to the car.

We wait for hours in A&E, as usual. Josh perks up a bit while he's waiting, as all the nurses seem to recognise him, but he won't tell us any more about what happened to his arm. He just sits there muttering, 'Connie's *so* f\*cking unbelievably annoying.'

When a doctor finally arrives, he orders an x-ray, but not before he has asked Josh to explain exactly how 'this latest accident' came to happen.

Max and I look at Josh expectantly. He says nothing, just hangs his head.

'Go on, tell him,' says Max. 'We're all waiting to hear this one.'

'Well, it's my sister, you see,' Josh says to the doctor. 'She's just really – *really* – annoying. I mean *really* annoying.'

'I see,' says the doctor. 'And?'

'She wanted me to go away, so she thumped me.'

'What – hard enough to break your arm?' says the doctor. 'What is she, some sort of prize-fighter?'

258

'No-o,' says Josh. 'She's a wimp. I tried to kick her back . . .'

'Ah,' says Max. 'What sort of kick, exactly?'

'Well, a roundhouse kick, of course,' says Josh, the family's self-appointed ninja.

'So why are you here in A&E with a possibly broken arm, when you were the one who kicked your sister?' says the doctor.

'I missed,' says Josh.

I'll give the doctor his due, he doesn't laugh out loud, though I'm pretty sure he sniggers a bit.

It's really late when we finally get home, and Josh's arm is in a sling to support it. It's not broken after all, but very badly bruised. The doctor says that the injury's probably temporarily damaged some of the nerves and that blood vessels have been affected, hence the attractive blue colour of the skin.

Connie gives Josh a big hug, which makes him wince, and then she says, 'How did you tell them you did it, bro?'

'Told 'em I bloody well kicked you,' says Josh.

'*And* that you missed, and fell *onto your own arm*?' says Connie. She's enjoying this far too much, but then so are Max and I.

'I suppose so,' says Josh. 'Now can you get me a drink? You're going to have to wait on me until my arm's better. I'll phone you on my mobile whenever I need you.'

That wipes the smile off Connie's face pretty effectively. And mine, once it occurs to me that we can't possibly leave these two alone while we have a dirty weekend.

They'd probably murder each other – through incompetence, if nothing else.

## MONDAY, 23 AUGUST

God, Josh is getting on everyone's nerves, with his endless requests for waitress service. Holly got fed up with it less than an hour after she arrived this evening, so she promptly went home again, and Connie's at the end of her tether.

She comes stomping into the kitchen while I'm chatting to Max, who's busy preparing dinner.

'If that incompetent ninja asks me for any more "urgent deliveries of snacks for the disabled", I'm going to kill him,' she says. 'And I'll do it properly this time. He hasn't stopped ringing my mobile for *hours*.'

'You shouldn't talk about me like that,' shouts Josh, from the sitting room, where he seems to be having no trouble adapting to the need to use his left hand to change channels on the TV. 'I have super-sensitive hearing, you know, *and* super-sensitive feelings too, since the trauma of the injury you caused.'

'Good,' says Connie, even louder. 'So did you get the bit where I called you *an incompetent ninja*? I'll repeat it, in case you didn't.'

She does, several times, whereupon Josh appears in the kitchen, looking as if he's about to risk another roundhouse kick.

'Calm down, Josh,' I say, stepping between him and Connie. 'Remember – sticks and stones may break your bones, but words can never hurt you.'

Josh looks disgusted, as well he might. That platitude never works, as I am forced to admit when he says it back to me, later, after Dad calls *me* incompetent, in an email. *Totally* unprovoked!

## TUESDAY, 24 AUGUST

I'm still stewing about Dad's comment this morning, when he sends me a half-arsed apology for losing his temper with me last night, which he blames on a touch of heatstroke.

Then he reiterates his argument that we should chat on Skype in future, not just while he's in Thailand but also once he gets home again. He says it would be much be cheaper for him to call everyone that way, seeing as he's now retired and 'on a fixed income'.

I mention it to Dinah when she calls just before lunch-time, to see if she thinks it's a good idea, but she says that Dad could make much more significant savings by cutting out the trips to Thailand.

'I wish I'd thought of that,' I say. 'Especially when he called me an "IT-incompetent" when he couldn't understand the instructions I gave him for linking his Facebook account to Skype.'

'You? IT-incompetent?' says Dinah, before pausing to sneeze then blow her nose loud enough to almost burst my eardrum. 'Has Dad forgotten that you're the idiot who taught him to use a computer in the first place?'

'Yes,' I say. 'Clearly, he has.'

I can't be bothered to discuss it, as I'm too busy reading an email from the Parliamentary IT help-desk man, asking what happened to The Boss yesterday, in the middle of a telephone conversation they were having.

'I was just explaining to Mr Sinclair about how remote access to the intranet works,' he says, 'when he suddenly seemed to lose interest and stop listening.'

The same thing's happening to me, now Dinah's getting into her stride.

'Well, I *haven't* forgotten that it was your fault, Molly,' she says, 'and just look at the result! You can't say I didn't warn you, either.'

'Well, at least Dad still wants to talk to us while he's in Thailand, and see our faces,' I say. 'It's nice to know he retains *some* affection for his daughters, isn't it?'

I'm pretty sure Dinah snorts with laughter at that, though she claims it's just another sneeze.

'Don't be daft,' she says. 'Even you must be able to see why Dad really wants Skype – for when he gets back, seeing as there's a language barrier between him and the Thai bride. Apart from *body* language, that is.'

It takes ages to get over the horrible image *that* conjures up, as it keeps popping into my field of vision when I'm least expecting it. I'm a bit worried that the optician will be able to see it, too, when I go for my eye test at lunch-time, but luckily she doesn't mention it.

My eyesight's apparently even worse than last time it was tested though, but then I knew that already, given my recent inability to see any eyelashes at all in my mirror. The optician gives me the usual lecture about working on a computer all day being very hard on the eyes, and the need to take regular breaks.

'Tell me something I don't know,' I say. Famous last words.

'Well, you won't know this,' she says. 'You need to make an appointment to see your GP. Look at this picture.'

'Yuck,' I say. 'What *is* that? It looks like one of those Lennart Nilsson photos of a foetus in the womb.'

'Put your glasses back on,' says the optician. 'Now look again.'

It turns out that the photograph is of the inside of my eye, and shows signs that there may be a problem with my blood pressure. Absolutely *marvellous*.

I tell Max about it when I get home from work, in the misguided belief he may provide some reassurance.

'Bloody hell,' he says. 'What a coincidence.'

'What d'you mean?' I say.

'Well, I just ran into Bob from round the corner when I was parking the car – you know, the one whose house backs onto Ellen's?'

'Ye-es,' I say, trying not to wonder why Max always parks the car as near to a nymphomaniac's as he can. 'What about him?'

'His wife dropped dead last week. Had a stroke. Undiagnosed high blood pressure – *and* she was only the same age as us.'

'Great,' I say. 'Thanks for that.'

No prizes for guessing in which direction my blood pressure is currently heading. I bet my eyeballs will soon go *pop*.

## WEDNESDAY, 25 AUGUST

*Men*. I've had just about enough of them today.

First The Boss infuriates me, when I ask him if he is going to Joan's summer barbecue.

'No, I am bloody well *not* going,' he says. 'And neither are *you*.'

'What?' I say. 'What on earth are you talking about? We *always* go to Joan's for August bank holiday. The constituency activists expect us to.'

'They're all out to get me, and I've told you before, I do *not* like you socialising with any of them. If you knew where your loyalties lay, you wouldn't even *want* to go.'

I do a double-take to see if Andrew is joking. He doesn't seem to be, if his heightened colour is anything to go by. I dread to think what the insides of his eyes look like.

'Oh, for goodness' sake, Andrew – get a grip,' I say. 'The Party staff are the people with a vested interest in *supporting* you. They are not spies, no matter how many John le Carré novels you may have read.'

Andrew says nothing to that and just glares at me – so I keep going. (I've always had a problem knowing when it's time to stop flogging a completely dead horse, as well as watering an unthirsty one.)

'If you keep on like this, you'll *make* them your enemies,' I say. 'And I don't want to encourage your paranoia, or make my working life any more difficult than it has to be, so *I* am going to the barbecue. And if you had any sense, you'd come too – and thank everyone there for all their hard work on your behalf.'

Nothing. No response. Not to me, anyway. The Boss turns his back, and looks at Greg.

'I think I'll do the morning briefing with you today, Gregory,' he says. 'Even though it isn't your turn.'

Andrew's disapproval is funny for the first couple of hours, but it wears pretty thin when he doesn't speak to me for the rest of the day. He doesn't even refer to me in that 'tell Molly something' way he usually falls back on, whenever he's in a mood. He just behaves as if he can't see me at all.

To make things even worse, he doesn't respond when I take a call for him and try to pass the phone over, not until Greg says, 'Andrew, Molly has a call for you.' Then he rips the phone out of my hand, and perches on my desk with his back to me, so I have to sit looking at the back of his arse until he has finished blathering.

I wish he'd go and sit in the Oprah room instead. At least then I could put his calls through to the extension next to the sofa, and could get on with something useful myself – without having to look at his backside. Even *that* has a sulky expression.

I'm so fed up with his rear end by the time that I leave work that I'm actually looking forward to drinks at Max's boss' house tonight. At least there'll be people there who *are* talking to me. And it'll do me and Max good to escape from the realm of the incompetent ninja, too.

It does, at first, and both Max and I are enjoying ourselves, when the conversation turns to the subject of cock-ups while travelling abroad. Colin (Max's boss) tells a couple of (rather tedious) stories about trains he's missed, and someone else bangs on about the 'trauma' of being stuck in Spain on an extended holiday during the volcanic ash situation. Then Colin says, 'And what about Max's classic stunt in Germany? That was a good one, wasn't it?'

'Oh God, no one wants to hear about *that* again,' says Max.

I assume that Colin's referring to Max's alleged inability to recall the name of his hotel – which would be bad enough – but he isn't. It turns out that Max had another little problem while he was on his business trip. One that I haven't heard anything about, until now.

The full story becomes clear only in stages, not that Max appears to want it to.

'Fancy getting so pissed you didn't even hear us banging on the door of your room,' says Colin. 'Even though the fire alarm was going off.'

I look at Max, who avoids looking back, so I turn to Colin, one eyebrow raised. 'When was this?' I say, very clearly and slowly.

'Oh, it was on the first night, the really heavy-drinking one,' says Colin. 'The one where we went on those racing simulators, and then we hit the pear schnapps a bit too hard. Max had to go to bed *very* early.'

'And then he slept through a fire alarm?' I say. 'Seriously?'

'Yes,' says Colin, grinning at Max, who shakes his head and rolls his eyes. 'We thought he must have had a woman in his room.'

Everyone laughs, as if this would have been really, *really* funny – except for me.

'Ah,' I say. I can't think of anything else.

I think everyone's realised that this is not going well by now, so then there's a mad flurry of *trying to change the subject-itis*, while I make an effort to pull myself together. I think I do quite a good job, too – until we get into the cab to head for home.

Then it's as if the subject had never been changed at all.

'What the hell's the matter with *you*?' says Max. 'You've been in a mood all night.' He always works on the principle that attack is the best form of defence. It never succeeds.

'What do *you* think's wrong with me?' I say.

'I don't know.' Max looks at me with a puzzled expression. 'Is it something to do with that hotel room thing?'

'What – the hotel room that you may have had another woman in?' My voice is rising. 'In a hotel whose name you conveniently couldn't recall? Why on earth would I be upset about *that*?'

'Oh, for goodness' sake,' says Max.

Then he stops speaking to me, and goes straight to bed as soon as we get home. He positions himself so close to the edge of the mattress that he almost falls off it, whenever he turns over during the night. I notice because I stay awake fretting for most of it.

Two men in a mood with me in just one day – not even counting the usual suspects. Looks as if the rest of the week may be somewhat lacking in conversation.

## THURSDAY, 26 AUGUST

Max still isn't speaking to me this morning, though I'm not entirely sure how he's managed to cast *me* in the wrong. I stick my tongue out at him as he leaves the house and am rewarded with a reproving glance from Connie and an outrageous 'How juvenile' comment from Josh.

I somehow resist the temptation to explain exactly *why* the frosty atmosphere is entirely down to Max and stomp off to work instead, where I am greeted by Greg, who informs me that he is definitely on a diet.

Apparently he came to this decision while he was watching *How to Look Good Naked* last night – which he has re-titled *Help Me, Gok – I've Eaten Too Much*.

He starts doing press-ups while I make the coffee, but has to give up as soon as The Boss arrives.

Andrew greets Greg and ignores me completely, even though I say hello to him twice. There are plenty of other people who *do* want to speak to me, though, including a complete nutcase who says he's the ruler of the Channel Islands. He wants to be recognised as such by the British Government, so I put him through to The Boss as a small act of revenge.

This enables me to concentrate on reading Johnny's latest email. He's back in Moscow now, but wants me to recommend a hotel in Lichford for the Thursday after next. In the meantime, he wants more photos of my arse, and of 'any other parts of my anatomy that may also be of interest'.

I can't think of *any* parts of me that would look good naked, but I'll have to try – especially as it's just occurred to me that, if Johnny simply wanted to get laid, or to have some variety in his sex-life, he must have a *world* of opportunity.

After all, he's away from home more often than not, stays alone in luxury hotels, and earns a fortune. He could afford some seriously high-class call girls, and I bet there are loads of ambitious female staff who wouldn't be averse to his attentions, either. Just look at the inexplicable effect even the Boss' rather pathetic semblance of power has on almost every female that *he* encounters – though admittedly those don't include his staff.

Now I'm more confused than ever. If Johnny *could* have his pick of women, probably all much younger and more attractive than me, then why on earth does he want to fly half-way across a continent – to see me? It's a mystery.

### FRIDAY, 27 AUGUST
Gah. Only one more week of Recess to go, thank God – though a week's going to feel like a year if The Boss keeps me in Coventry for much longer. Metaphorically speaking, of course. The real Coventry must be a whole lot more fun than Lichford is at the moment – at work, *and* at home.

Max is still only communicating in monosyllables. He even wrote me a note to tell me that David called to say

269

we can't borrow his holiday cottage this weekend, because he and Susie are using it themselves.

It's probably a good job, as they're more likely to have fun in it than Max and I would be, given how things are between us. We've never really been into arguing-and-making-up sex, which is a pity, since we seem to be arguing most of the time. Maybe I should suggest we give it a go?

I ring Max at lunchtime to see what he thinks of my idea but he doesn't answer his phone, so I eat my lunch at my desk, quickly, before The Boss can swipe it. Then Greg asks me to cover a meeting with some of the local councillors, as he doesn't feel he's up to it – despite apparently having taken over my role as Andrew's randomly-designated *Goldenballs*. 'It's a tricky situation we'll be dealing with,' says Greg. 'And tact is not always my forte, you know.'

It's not Andrew's, either. He glares at me when I tell Greg that I'll do it, but he doesn't actually forbid me to attend. Unfortunately, as things turn out.

The meeting's been requested by Jimmy Barton, Leader of Lichford Council, who is complaining that The Boss is poaching cases that local councillors should be dealing with. He brings several councillors with him to back him up.

Things get off to a bad start, as Andrew's first response is that, if councillors did their jobs properly, then constituents wouldn't approach their MPs in the first place. This goes down about as well as you'd expect. Then he makes things even worse.

'The whole problem is that, since all these corruption

scandals in local politics, we can't attract any decent candidates to stand for election,' he says.

I don't know if The Boss doesn't notice the expression on the newly elected councillors' faces, or whether he doesn't care – but he looks set to carry on like this for the rest of the meeting if someone doesn't do something to stop him. I guess that someone will have to be me.

'I'm sure what Andrew *means* is that perhaps we need to have better communication between this office and you guys,' I say. 'And that maybe there's a training issue for *new* councillors, too?'

'Rubbish,' says Andrew, in a loud voice.

Jimmy Barton looks at him, then back at me. I think it takes a moment to work out that *I* am the target of that hostile statement – but then his expression softens, and he takes the olive branch I've offered him.

'Well, Molly, girl,' he says. 'There might be a grain of truth in that. What d'you suggest we do?'

I'm so relieved to have averted any further conflict that I launch into a series of suggestions about what Greg and I could offer new councillors to help them find ways to manage their case loads. The councillors join in, and it's all going really well until the discussion is interrupted by a snore. A really loud, stagy snore.

All heads turn to look at Andrew, who is sitting slumped in the corner of the sofa, wide-awake, and staring at me.

'I think that's enough, Molly,' he says. 'We don't want to bore Jimmy and the others to death, do we, now?'

I am *not* going to let him make me cry. I *am* not. I never have, and I never will.

I excuse myself and leave the room. As I pass Greg, he tries to stop me to find out what's wrong, but I just shake my head and keep on going. When I get outside, I stand around for a while, smoking and ordering myself to get a grip so I don't give Andrew the satisfaction of knowing that he's managed to upset me.

On the second cigarette, I finally start to calm down – but then there are noises in the lobby, and someone pushes open the main door a few feet from where I'm standing. *Shit.* They must all be leaving. And they're going to walk right past me, when they do.

I move towards the door, but then I hear something.

'Wasn't that awful?' says a familiar voice.

'God, yes,' says another. 'That poor woman. He made her look a complete idiot. I'm bloody glad *I* don't have to work for him.'

There's nothing for it, but to face them anyway. I'll have to do it some time, after all.

I take hold of the door and say, 'Excuse me' to Jimmy, who looks startled, but then moves out of my way. The other councillors turn towards me, and smile rather too sympathetically – like those hushed-voice types who always annoy me so much when I encounter them at meetings of the Mental Health Trust.

'Good to talk to you all,' I say, as I walk away. 'Look forward to seeing you at Joan's barbecue.'

Then I go back to work. It is a very good thing that The Boss is still not speaking to me, as *I* am now not speaking to *him*.

I bet this isn't how International Directors of Global

Oil Companies treat their staff – and *they* probably speak to their wives, as well. Thursday week can't come soon enough.

**SATURDAY, 28 AUGUST**
Connie and the other interns have found a house and are moving in this weekend – so it's back to testosterone hell for me. Once she's gone, I shall again be the only woman in the house. No doubt this will cause a dramatic increase in facial hair, and I shall soon be fairground material.

In the meantime, Max and I have been nominated to 'help' Connie with the move, so now we're *having* to talk to each other, like it or not.

Josh has escaped being drafted in, partly due to his arm injury – the one that he's still milking for all it's worth – and partly because he's gone off to the coast with the boys, to stay at the beach house belonging to Robbie's parents.

I had no idea they were so well off. Imagine owning a beach house, for goodness' sake! Maybe Max and I could have arranged to borrow *that*. Then we could have gone there this weekend, instead of running around like maniacs, trying to fit what seems to be enough stuff to equip three houses into one smallish car.

Connie must be the world's most useless packer, too. She persuaded Max to pick up loads of boxes from the supermarket yesterday, but God knows why he bothered – she only seems to have used about ten of them, into which she's packed the most random selection of stuff

I've ever seen. There's half a ton of make-up loosely scattered inside saucepans and bowls, and her pot plants have been nestled inside her jumpers. There's soil *everywhere*.

If she'd taken her time, she might have made a better job of it, but she seemed incapable of any activity while *Big Brother* was on, and didn't even start packing until about 11:00pm last night. The result is that the bulk of her belongings are in bags. Not bin bags – which would have been embarrassing enough – but carrier bags. *Hundreds* of the damned things. And Connie is even worse at unloading than she is at packing.

When we get to the new house she stands next to the car, 'directing' us – until Max notices, and suggests she might like to join in when she's ready. She scowls as if this is unfair, so I start counting how many trips Max and I make to and from the house – but give up fairly quickly when I run out of energy. Why is it always impossible to park anywhere near a student house on moving-in day? (Well, actually, I *know* the answer to this – it's because no student can ever get it together to obtain a parking permit in time for their poor parents to be able to use it – once they're been conned into helping their child move in. Or *Connied*, in this particular instance.)

*Our* precious little con-merchant carries only two carrier bags on each of the very few trips she makes. I have seen far more dynamic slugs. Then she takes a bag of food into the kitchen, and that's the last we see of her – though we're so busy that we don't miss her for about an hour, at which point we find her sitting at the kitchen table with the other interns, all having a really good chat.

It's almost 8:00pm by now – and the car is *still* full of stuff.

When I mention this, Connie says that she and the others think it would be nice to go for a drink 'to get to know each other'. She asks Max to lock up when we've finished unloading, and to post her keys through the door.

A brief hug and a kiss, and off she goes – before I've even started weeping. (I cry whenever we take Connie back, but she always stays resolutely dry-eyed. You'd think she'd at least *pretend* to be a bit sad, but she never does. She's just ecstatic to escape from life with Josh; I suppose it's not all *that* surprising.)

This *is* a nice house, though. I'm almost tempted to suggest Max leaves me here for a few days, but he might agree too readily – and, anyway, I shall be needed at home, to prevent Josh from turning Connie's bedroom into a gym.

I overheard him and Robbie discussing *that* idea the other night. They were planning on calling it 'Bonjour Better Body' and charging admission. Josh said he'd already persuaded Greg to sign up.

## SUNDAY, 29 AUGUST

Max and I are knackered when we finally get back from Connie's. No sooner has Max said, 'I am never moving Connie again', than he falls asleep – though not for long.

The phone rings at 4:00am. It's Robbie's dad, John,

who needs Max to join him in a rescue mission. Honestly, you couldn't make it up.

It turns out that the much-hyped 'beach house' is a hut – where staying overnight is prohibited. Upon his return, Max explains what happened.

Apparently, Robbie, Josh and the others dug an enormous fire pit, which then got a bit out of control and eventually caught the attention of the guy who supervises the beach, as well as the car park.

'This guy said he went to investigate and found all eight boys stacked up, one on top of the other,' says Max. 'In a *tiny* hut, fast asleep. He said he might have missed them, if their feet hadn't all been sticking out of the door.'

The boys were ordered to leave, immediately, but were all too drunk to drive, hence the calls to the parental emergency service. The one from which you never get the option to resign.

Josh seems to have sobered up a bit by the time Max brings him home, although his relief at being rescued appears to be based solely on having escaped from Robbie's snoring, which he says prevented him from getting any sleep.

'Join the bloody club,' says Max.

'Well, it's not my fault,' says Josh. 'I was still awake when the supervisor arrived, but I was stuck under Jim and Robbie, and couldn't wriggle out. Otherwise, I'd have slept on the beach. Robbie's snoring's almost as bad as yours.'

'I'd shut up about my snoring, if I were you,' says Max. 'I'm not really in the mood.'

'Sorry, Dad – I'm just tired. It's been a stressful night.'

'Stressful? I think you ought to count your lucky stars I got rid of the supervisor before sunrise,' says Max. 'If he'd seen that giant sand phallus you lot built, you'd have been in even more trouble than you were already.'

Josh chokes with laughter, then yawns, and sets me off too.

'So how big *was* this beach house?' I ask Max. 'I mean hut?'

'About six foot by six foot,' he says. 'For Christ's sake. Those boys all need their heads testing.'

'Being so cramped made my broken arm a bit sore,' says Josh – who never knows when to stop.

'It's not broken,' says Max. 'Or not *yet*, it isn't. But it could be arranged if you ever pull any more stunts like this. I'm going back to bed.'

That sounds like a damned good idea to me so I follow suit – but we seem doomed not to get any sleep this weekend. As soon as we've both snuggled back down – temporarily united by despair at being the parents of an idiot – my mobile starts to beep. I can't ignore it, not now that Connie's no longer at home. It could be her: cue instant panic. *Now* what's happened?

I blunder around looking for my glasses. It's such a pain not being able to read texts without them. When I can finally see, I realise the text is from Dinah, not Connie – *oh, the relief* – although that's only momentary.

Dinah's message says, 'Oh. My. God. Guess what the Thai bride's name is?'

'What is it *now*?' says Max, his voice muffled by the pillow he's pulled over his head.

'Dinah,' I say. 'She wants us to guess the name of the Thai bride.'

'Yung-Fuk,' says Max, from the depths.

I text this suggestion to Dinah. 'It's a good guess, but it's not right,' she replies. 'Was that one of Max's? Try again.'

Who *does* she think she is? Roy Walker? 'Dinah, I can't be bothered to play *Catchphrase*. It's the middle of the night. Just *tell* me what the Thai bride's called!'

'Porn!' is her reply. 'Though you probably don't spell it exactly like that.'

Christ almighty. I'm in the middle of telling Max, when he lets out an enormous snore. I've had quite enough of *that* this week. In fact, I've had quite enough of this week, full stop.

## MONDAY, 30 AUGUST

Oh, good grief. The world's gone mad, or rather, Andrew has.

Today is Joan's famous Bank Holiday Labour Party Barbecue – the one Andrew banned me and Greg from attending – so, of course, we fully intend to go.

Max comes too, as moral support, as I'm not looking forward to seeing all the local councillors again after Friday's events, but I can't wriggle out of going now. I've already promised Joan I will.

Her Party barbecue's a tradition and, anyway, I like her and most of the Party staff, so I'm not going to let any of them down. They're the ones who rescue me and Greg whenever a constituent goes berserk, too – so Andrew's disapproval is a small price to pay to ensure continuing protection.

By the time Max and I arrive, it's stopped raining, which seems a good omen and compensates for the embarrassment of being late. It's my fault we are, because I kept changing my mind about what to wear. These events are always a sartorial challenge as there's no accepted dress code whatsoever, not least because Lichford Labour Party has a class divide wider than Mr Franklin's arse.

On the sunny side of Joan's garden, there's a conclave of most of the town and county councillors, together with those middle-class activists whose names crop up on every committee, from the Lichford Preservation Society to the Mental Health Trust. They're all school governors, too, and have fingers – or rather relatives – in every local pie. Jimmy Barton is there with his wife, Peggy, and he smiles at me as I walk past.

On the other side, in the shade, sit the Party members who live on Lichford's Council estates, or who are union reps, and who are therefore deemed to have their finger on the pulse of the core vote. Far fewer members of this group have managed to become councillors and, although those who *have* interact slightly more comfortably with the elite squad than do the rest, you can still sense the mutual distrust. And probably dislike.

Over the last few years, a third group's been on the rise. These are the young, university-educated Party activists who stand by the drinks table, as their legs don't tire as easily as everyone else's.

They have an understanding of demographics and voting intentions that puts the rest of us to shame, and which form their only topic of conversation. I'm not sure how much real-life experience they bring to their policy analyses, but there's no doubt their voices are becoming more influential – and their overt personal ambition scares the hell out of The Boss.

Despite knowing everyone, Greg and I usually spend these events on the periphery of any group we try to join – probably because we're equally distrusted by all of them. Half think we're snobs because we work for the MP, and the other half that we're idiots who know nothing about politics at all. Poor old Max is treated as being even more irrelevant than Greg or I.

'Molly! Max! Over here!'

It's Greg, who is sitting in no-man's land in the middle of the garden, with some of the regional Party staff, who I really like. Max and I join them and, after everyone's eaten what probably represents Iceland's entire stock of frozen beefburgers – consumed with varying degrees of enthusiasm – it's time to play a game of cricket. Not poncy cricket, but Labour Party cricket, which normally turns into rounders pretty quickly.

'Shame Andrew's not here yet,' says Jimmy Barton. 'What with him being a cricket pro and all.'

He goes in to bat, leaving Greg and I trying to work out whether his tone was ironic or not.

'Hmm,' says Greg, which is a useful alternative to, 'Ah.' Then, 'Holy shit!'

'What?' I say. 'Have you been stung? There *are* a lot of wasps around—'

'Ssh,' says Greg, gesturing madly towards the hedge separating Joan's garden from the street. 'Look over there. Not *now*, you idiot! In a minute, and don't let anyone else see what you're looking at.'

I wait a few seconds and then look again towards the hedge – but I can't see anything. I've forgotten to bring my distance glasses.

'It's Andrew,' says Greg. 'Hiding behind the hedge. What the *hell's* he up to now?'

'Spying,' I suppose,' says Max, giving me a meaningful look. 'He doesn't trust anyone, even when they're innocent. Must be part of the job description, when you work in politics.'

I ignore him, and swig most of my glass of wine, while Greg tries to make his way closer to the hedge, unseen by all the other guests. This seems to involve first diving into a large rhododendron bush, then crawling out on its far side on his stomach and wriggling his way across the lawn.

Everyone is watching him by the time he stands up again, and peers over the top of the hedge.

'Ah,' says Andrew, popping up on the other side. 'Hello, Gregory, um, everyone. Forgot Joan lived here. I'm just doing a bit of canvassing.'

'Come in, Andrew,' says Joan, saving his bacon. 'You *were* invited, you know.'

I'm not sure how many people notice that he isn't carrying any leaflets when he comes through the gate. Or spot the woman who's walking away, with her back to us.

'Who's that?' says Greg, in a very breathy hiss. The commando-style crawling has really taken it out of him.

'God knows,' I say. 'I can't see her face. Why?'

'She was crouching down with Andrew behind the hedge when I caught them by surprise.'

'Ask him,' I say – but Andrew's already moving away, making a beeline for the county councillors and the rest of the elite squad. *Kissy, kissy, kissy.* It's horrible to watch. He's still oblivious to the kissing-on-the-cheek protocol, too, though no one seems to object today.

Why *do* women like The Boss so much? They all start giggling, and pay him rapt attention while he holds forth about the merits of the personal touch when canvassing. Jimmy Barton seems less than pleased to see him, though, which is rather gratifying after Friday's events.

'Come on, Andrew – we're in the middle of a game of cricket,' he says. 'You're just in time to show us the old semi-pro in action!'

After Andrew is out for a duck, I'm sure I spot Jimmy smiling to himself. Greg revisits the rhododendron, to hide *his* expression. And the sound of hysterical laughter.

## TUESDAY, 31 AUGUST
It's incredible what you find lurking on the peripheries of people's gardens when you're least expecting it. And I am not going to feel guilty about Johnny *any more*.

That should put an end to all the hiccups I've been having.

Tonight, Max is about to take the rubbish out, ready for tomorrow's refuse collection, when – amazingly – Josh decides to be helpful and offers to do it instead. It *is* late and Max *does* look tired, but even so, I'm not used to Josh being considerate. Maybe he's turned over a new leaf at last?

'No, don't worry, Josh, I'll do it,' says Max, looking a gift horse squarely in the mouth.

'Max,' I say. 'Are you mad? Josh – *Josh* – is offering to do a household task – *voluntarily* – and you are turning him down?'

'Well, he'll probably fall over something in the dark,' says Max. 'And what with his arm, and everything . . .'

Josh is as contrary as the usual suspects. If you refuse him anything, even something he doesn't want, it immediately becomes irresistible. He grabs the bin bag from Max's hand and heads out of the back door. Max looks really annoyed for a minute and almost goes out after him, but then he just sits down heavily on the couch and starts doing a Sudoku puzzle instead.

Josh is gone for what seems like ages and, just as I'm about to go out looking for him, I hear the back door slam, and his footsteps along the hallway. He's shouting, 'Dad. *Dad*!'

'What?' says Max, as Josh comes into the room.

'Now I see why you wanted to take the bins out yourself. *Bloody hell!*'

Max is suddenly very red in the face. 'I don't know what you're talking about,' he says.

'You bloody well do,' says Josh.

'Well, I *definitely* don't,' I say. 'So could someone please enlighten me?'

'Come with me,' says Josh, and drags me outside, along the garden path and out of the back gate. It's pretty dark, and I can't see where I'm treading, so I get a bit unnerved.

'What am I looking out for, Josh?' I say. 'I can't see a thing.'

'Sshh!' says Josh. 'Now look up.'

'Oh, my God,' I say. 'Is that what I think it is? Or rather, *who* I think it is?'

'Ellen?' says Josh. 'Yeah. I saw her face when she first put the light on. Before she hid it behind the curtains.'

'But she's naked,' I say. 'And why's she pressed against the glass?'

'Oh, I think the answer to that is obvious,' says Josh.

If there were any eggs left after today's Yorkshire puddings, I'd throw them at that bloody woman's window. What the *hell* does she think she's doing? And is this (presumably regular) floor show only for Max's benefit, or is it aimed at *any* of the neighbours who might be putting out their rubbish?

'Max! How often has that f*cking woman done this?'

I may be yelling a little too loudly, as Ellen jerks backwards and shuts her curtains properly. I have startled her, unless she's just achieved what she set out to do.

'Hush,' says Max. 'Come inside. You're making a spectacle of yourself.'

'*I* am making a spectacle of myself? *I* am? What about *that* bloody lunatic?'

God, I'm angry. I wouldn't mind so much if Ellen didn't always pretend that she is *my* friend when I see her alone, and that she only likes Max because he's my husband. I'm so angry that I accidentally burst into tears – until I remember my rule about not giving people who upset you the satisfaction, and get a grip instead.

'Okay, tell me the whole story,' I say to Max. 'How long has she been doing this, and how many times?'

'No more than four or five,' he says. 'That I've noticed, anyway.'

'Oh, I think you'd notice. How did it start?' I am beginning to feel icily calm.

'One night I was taking out the rubbish and I smacked the bin bag into the gate, so it made a noise. Then something caught my eye, and I saw Ellen naked at the window. I think she was trying to fasten it.'

'Oh really? Did she dive out of the way once she spotted you?'

'Well, no – now you come to mention it.' Max sounds genuinely surprised. 'But I looked away really fast anyway, because I was worried she'd think *I'd* been spying on *her.*'

I take a deep breath, think again about my no-crying rule, then say, 'Okay. So when were you going to tell me about it – if ever?'

'I kept hoping it'd stop. And the longer it went on, the more impossible it got to tell you, as I thought you'd flip out and go round and smash her door down or something.'

'Dad, she's been playing you,' says Josh. 'You are an idiot. You should've said.'

It comes to something when teenagers are smarter than their parents, doesn't it? But *playing* – or playing *with*?

# CHAPTER FIVE

# September

(Season of mists and mellow fruitfulness, allegedly.
Or of agitated fruit-loops, in Lichford's case.)

**WEDNESDAY, 1 SEPTEMBER**

Greg answers the phone first thing, then lets out a '*Whoop!*' when he hangs up: The Boss is taking two days off – probably to avoid having to tell us what the hell he was up to behind Joan's hedge.

We still have no idea of the identity of the woman who was lurking next to him, unless she was related to Ellen. They do share an ability to pop up in very unexpected places. (The one with Andrew did have clothes on, though – and, anyway, I'm trying not to think about Max and Ellen any more. Or Johnny, for that matter. My sanity's at stake.)

'Wonderful news about The Boss, isn't it, Mol?' says Greg, after he's imparted it. 'I shall do some sit-ups immediately, to celebrate.'

I even attempt a few. Well, one – but it's a start.

Greg and I are so elated that we zoom through this morning's work, and – even better – our sandwiches are still safely in the fridge when lunchtime arrives, so then we turn on the answer-phone and go and eat them in the park.

It's one of those gorgeous bright but chilly September days, of the kind that I always associate with new starts and the beginning of the academic year, so I'm quite sad that Josh has decided to forego the university experience. He's due to sign on for the first time this afternoon, though, so maybe the Jobcentre can find him a job with possibilities. There must be *something* he can do, with all that imagination. Preferably something safe – and lucrative.

I spend the rest of lunchtime envisaging myself as the mother of a famous inventor which, coupled with The Boss' absence, proves so cheering that by the time that we return to work I've almost forgotten about naked nymphomaniacs, and whether they entitle me to have an affair. My glass seems more than half-full for once, which is more than confirmed by the first two calls that come in once I switch the answer-phone off.

Each one is about a young woman who has recently been diagnosed with cancer. Two *different* young women, and *two* sets of terrible news.

One of them has only just got married, and has a six-week-old baby. She's been found to have a malignant tumour of the brain. The other – also aged twenty-five – has breast cancer, and is due to have a full mastectomy tomorrow. There's a family history of the disease, so the hospital isn't wasting any time.

Both girls live in completely unsuitable accommodation and their families want to know if there is anything we can do to get them moved, as soon as possible. Imagine trying to cope with the effects of chemotherapy when you live in a bedsit and have to share a bathroom with five virtual strangers – or trying to keep your wounds clean when everything in your flat is covered in black mould.

I don't *want* to imagine it, but that's what these girls are dealing with in real life, so Greg will have to handle all the phone calls from now on while I prioritise their cases. It's a precaution, in case Miss Chambers calls. If I have to listen to her going on about one of her conspiracy theories today, I may snap and start screaming at *her* for once.

'Good point,' says Greg. 'Though I'd quite enjoy seeing that, if not hearing it. But don't worry, I'll do the phones, even if La Chambers calls. I've got some earplugs in my drawer. You just concentrate on what you need to do.'

That's the only way to cope with the stuff we sometimes hear in this job – you can't waste your time mouthing sympathetic platitudes, or getting emotional. You just have to do whatever you can, as fast as you can, to try to make a difference, however small. If you allowed yourself to dwell on the full horror of what happens to some people, you'd go completely round the bend. Not that that's any excuse for The Boss behaving like a lunatic.

It's no excuse for wallowing in self-pity, either, not when your own problems only involve neighbours with a penchant for nakedness, *and* your husband. I need to get – *and keep* – a sense of proportion.

'I'm going to suggest The Boss introduces a Private Member's Bill,' I say to Greg, after some serious thought about how best to achieve my aim. 'We need a government agency to send daily texts or emails to those of us who don't have major problems, saying, "Don't forget – things could be a whole lot worse. Now stop moaning."'

'Are you mad?' says Greg. 'You just referred to "a government agency" and a form of technology, in the same sentence.'

'Ah,' I say. 'Yes. Good point.'

Some idiot would be bound to program the system to send 'cheer-up' messages to those suffering from terminal diseases – like those Council Tax departments that keep sending bills to people who've been dead for years. Only even more incompetent.

Josh seems to share Greg's and my opinion of government agencies, if his view of the Jobcentre is anything to go by. When I ask how his visit there went, he starts ranting like Mr Meeeeurghn.

'Why don't they *tell* you not to join the queue in the entrance to the building the first time you sign on?' he yells. 'Standing there like a muppet made me late, and then I got into trouble when I finally went to the right desk, even though I'd been early when I first arrived.'

'In trouble?' I say. 'What sort of trouble?'

'The woman said she was showing me a yellow card.'

'What?' I find this hard to believe. 'Did she *actually* say that, or are you exaggerating?'

'Yes, she did,' says Josh, becoming more irritated by the second. 'I *never* exaggerate, unlike you. And would it really kill the staff to call people by their full names when it's time for their appointments?'

'What do you mean?' I say. Now I'm completely lost.

'When it's your turn to sign on, they only call you by your *surname*,' Josh says, pulling an incredulous face. 'She was worse than Mr Thumb. She just shouted, "Bennett!" over and over again. Totally dehumanising.'

I am amazed that my son knows that word, let alone uses it in normal conversation. Maybe I am not such a bad mother after all.

'I am never signing on again,' says Josh. 'My self-respect is more important than my income.'

'Spoken like someone whose parents pay his living expenses,' says Max, injuring Josh's pride still further. 'I bet it's a deliberate policy, to deter people from making claims. And, if it works as well as it seems to have done on you, it'll be more effective in reducing the budget deficit than selling Australia to the Chinese.'

'Much sneakier, though,' says Josh. 'And how did you know about my idea to sell Australia, anyway?'

I wish I *hadn't* told Max about it now, if all he's going to do is make fun of it. It seemed quite a good idea to me, and Josh's self-esteem has already taken a battering today.

'Have one of your father's Ferrero Rochers, Josh,' I say, much to Max's disgust. 'That'll cheer you up.'

291

'I won't need to sign on again, anyway,' says Josh, taking three. 'I shall have a job by the end of next week. Probably.'

He must have compensated for the yellow card somehow, as he says the Alex Ferguson woman has 'pre-selected' him to apply for a job at the local cinema.

'I told you Film Studies would come in handy,' he says. '*And* the job's full-time, too, so I'll soon be moving out, if I get it. Can you help me write a CV, please, Mum?'

'Yes,' I say, envisaging Max and I being able to have rampant sex all over the house – if Josh ever does leave home, and Max doesn't run off with Ellen before that happens. 'We'll put one together as soon as we've finished eating dinner.'

Easier said than done, that's all I can say. Honestly, what chance do school-leavers have of finding work in this economic climate, when listing their skills and experience barely fills half a side of A4? It would have been even less than that if Josh had chosen to study subjects with shorter names.

'We could try to make your hobbies sound as if they demonstrate some transferable skills, I suppose,' I say, in desperation – thinking mainly of Bonjour Freight Shippers and its subsidiary company, Bonjour Books.

'Good idea,' says Josh. 'Don't forget "National Skateboarding Champion".'

**THURSDAY, 2 SEPTEMBER**
Oh, *God* – I'm meeting Johnny in a week's time and I still can't remember any important details about him,

such as how tall he is, or whether he was wearing platform shoes at that bloody fifth-form disco we went to. How many Babychams *did* I drink that night?

None of this occurs to me until Johnny sends me an email to thank me for the photos he requested: the ones showing unspecified parts of my anatomy.

'I wasn't exactly expecting pictures of your foot, elbow and knee,' he says. 'Though they were all undoubtedly fascinating.'

Then he asks whether the sandal I am wearing in the foot photo is a 'dancing shoe' and says that he and his wife went to a ball at the British Embassy last night.

'It wasn't anything like dancing with you,' he says. '*That's* been a private fantasy for years, together with what happened next.'

I'm a bit embarrassed by all this flattery, and become so flustered that I end up telling him that Max and I always avoid dancing together, as other people mock us because of the difference in our heights.

Johnny's reply comes back with indecent haste: 'How tall *is* Max, by the way?'

He doesn't usually ask anything at all about Max, and I don't volunteer anything either. Call it a warped sense of propriety. I don't suppose someone's height really qualifies as sensitive personal information, though, so I reply: 'Six foot two.'

'Bloody hell, woman,' Johnny says, then, '*Shit*.'

'What's the matter?' I say.

'I don't know how I'm going to live up to that.'

I'm amazed. Is this *really* Johnny talking? Go-getting

Johnny Hunter, International Director of a Global Oil Company, who spends half his life ordering me to 'keep up' with him? It can't be. And how tall is he, anyway? Or – more importantly – *how short*?

I bet he's going to turn out to be just like The Boss, with a raging case of small man's syndrome. Then, while Max is swanning about with Ellen, who's all shiny and James Blunty, and tall enough to see over other people's heads in a crowd, I'll be blundering about in the undergrowth with a version of Napoleon.

It's odd how I always end up comparing Johnny to dictators, too. Must be because I'm surrounded by the buggers, both the male *and* female kind. I'm on my way home from work, and am nearly there, when I get a text from Dinah, Baroness of Bossiness.

'Molly,' she says. 'Prepare yourself for a shock. I've had bad news.'

*Now* what's Dad done? This sounds like something better discussed by phone, so I try to call her as soon as I've opened the front door and waved hello to Max, but she doesn't answer. Instead, she sends another text, before I've even replied to the first one: 'I don't want to talk about it.'

Now I'm really worried, *and* quite cross, so I text back: 'What the hell has happened, Di?'

There is a lull, and then three texts arrive in quick succession. In them, Dinah spells out her distress at being 'diagnosed with a serious illness' when she saw her GP this morning. This all sounds horribly familiar, after yesterday, and those poor girls with cancer.

'God, I'm sorry, sis,' I say, which sounds pathetically inadequate. 'What did the doctor say it was?'

Back comes Dinah's reply: 'HPD.'

What the hell *is* HPD? I didn't even know Dinah was feeling ill.

'Di,' I say, 'I'm sorry, I've never *heard* of HPD. What does it mean?'

'Histrionic Personality Disorder,' she replies.

Max thinks I'm choking, and starts trying to do the Heimlich manoeuvre on me, until I fight him off. It's a struggle, what with him being both tall and strong – but I know his weak spot: he's ticklish.

'What the hell's the matter with you?' he says, having backed off to a safe distance first. 'Why are you laughing like that? Are you hysterical, or something?'

'Probably,' I say. 'Dinah's just been diagnosed with Histrionic Personality Disorder.'

Max stares at me, then also starts to laugh. 'Drama Queen-itis, you mean,' he says. 'How did it take Di's doctor so long to work that one out? Your whole family has far too much imagination – including *you*.'

I don't like the look he gives me when he says this, so I ignore him and watch *Channel 4 News* instead – or pretend to, anyway. I'm a bit worried, in case he's right.

What if I've imagined that Johnny's of normal height? Or, worse, what if I've imagined the Max and Ellen thing, and have no reason to be involved with Johnny, whether he's tall *or* short? Or – *even worse* – what if I *haven't* imagined the Max and Ellen thing, but I *have* imagined Johnny isn't a dwarf?

I get into such a state that I decide to distract myself by stalking what the kids have been up to, via Facebook, but there's no sign of activity by either of them in my timeline. The only person who's done anything today is Dinah, who's just updated her status. It now reads, 'Dinah is finding it very hard to cope with her diagnosis of HPD.'

I resist the temptation to leave a comment. Some of us are still trying to keep a sense of proportion – no matter *what* the provocation.

## FRIDAY, 3 SEPTEMBER

The Boss is back from his two-day holiday, which is bad news, especially as he's still not speaking to me, and refuses to tell even *Goldenballs Greg* what he was up to at Joan's barbecue. However, it's the last day of Recess, which is very, *very* good.

To add to my joy, Josh phones at lunchtime to tell me that he's got an interview at the cinema on Monday – so all my worrying about his unemployability was for nothing.

I shall cook tonight, in celebration. Something special.

I'm looking forward to it but by the time I get home after spending a fortune on Taste the Difference ready meals, for safety's sake, it's already quite late, and Josh is running around like a lunatic getting ready to go out.

'I thought you were staying in tonight,' I say.

'Nah,' he says. 'Don't be daft, Mum. I'm not a tragic oldie with no social life like you and Dad. I'm taking Holly out. She's got a 2 for 1 voucher for Pizza Express and I've got a discount code for the cinema, so first we're going to recce what working there would be like, while we watch a film, and then we're going for a meal. If you're lucky, I'll bring you a dough ball home.'

I don't even have time to express my gratitude for that, as then Josh goes out, leaving his geriatric parents to their usual exciting Friday night, during which Max has several glasses of wine, and I have one – in a misguided attempt to set an example. Then I sit and contemplate the side of Max's head while he snores on the sofa.

This goes on until just before 11:00pm, when his mobile starts to ring. He continues to sleep while I try to work out how to answer the damned thing – but, finally, I manage it.

'Mum,' says Josh. 'Where's Dad?'

'Asleep,' I say. 'Why? Are you okay? You sound peculiar.'

'No, I'm not,' he says. 'Okay, I mean. Can you get Dad to come and pick me up from Pizza Express? Holly's gone off in a huff, I haven't got any money left, and I can't walk properly.'

'Why? Now what's happened?' I say, trying to wake Max at the same time by prodding him with my foot. Unsuccessfully.

'I think I've dislocated my knee again. Smacked it on the table when I got up, and it's agony. Just like when that skateboard ramp collapsed under me last year.'

'Oh, for God's sake, Josh. Okay – but Dad won't be able to come. He's had too much wine to drive,' I say. 'Stay put until I get there.'

Honestly, we might as well get a season ticket for

A&E, and it's going to be like a war zone in there at this time on a Friday night. That'll teach me to view a quiet night in as boring.

I fish the keys out of Max's pocket, grab my coat and bag and power walk to the car – but it isn't there. I run up and down our road a few times, then check the side streets in case Max has had to park further afield than usual, but there's still no sign of it anywhere. Bloody, bloody *hell*.

There's nothing for it but to go back home.

'Max. *Max!* Wake up! The car's been stolen and I need to get Josh to A&E,' I say, dialling for a cab.

He finally starts to stir when I phone Josh to warn him that I'll have to pick him up in a taxi because the car is missing. By the time I've finished explaining that, the cab's outside.

'Max – you'll have to phone the police and report the theft,' I say. 'I've got to go.'

'Um,' he says. 'Yes, um.'

'Yes, um, what? Hurry up – the meter's running!'

'Well, the car hasn't exactly been stolen,' he says. He won't meet my eyes when I ask what he means, so I repeat the question, rather louder this time. He's still staring very hard at the floor when he answers: 'I may have lent it to someone for the weekend.'

'Who?' I say, as the taxi driver beeps his horn for about the hundredth time.

'Ellen,' he says.

I slam the door so hard on my way out, it's a miracle I don't shatter the glass.

## SATURDAY, 4 SEPTEMBER

I am knackered after last night's stint in casualty, though I'd really like some of their zero tolerance posters for use in the office. We could exclude at least a quarter of our constituents if we implemented those.

Tolerance is definitely close to zero at home today, though I'm not sure who's the grumpiest: me or Josh. He's worried that Holly's going to finish with him if he doesn't stop being so accident-prone, and is disgusted that he has to wear a brace to support his kneecap, particularly as it won't fit under his skinny jeans.

'I don't know what you're moaning about,' I say. 'Wearing them was probably what *caused* your kneecap to dislocate. They're *ridiculously* tight.'

'Don't be stupid, Mum,' he says. 'They're probably *better* than a brace – seeing as they cover the whole of my leg.'

'Well, if you don't do as the doctor told you and it dislocates again, you'll have to *hop* back to the hospital. I can't afford any more taxi trips this month.'

Max looks very uncomfortable when I say this, but he still hasn't volunteered how Ellen happens to have been lent our car without me even knowing about it. He always leaves it to me to broach contentious subjects.

When I do, it turns out that her car has broken down and that Max offered to lend her ours so that she could visit her mother for the weekend.

'But why didn't you consult me first?' I say. 'It is *our* car, after all. And I am your wife – or I *was*, the last time I looked.'

'There wasn't time,' he says. 'Ellen was supposed to get to a family party by 8:00pm, and didn't realise her car was buggered until nearly 5:30pm. You weren't even home, so I couldn't ask you if you minded.'

'Ever heard of Alexander Graham Bell?' I say. 'He came up with an answer to that.'

Max glares at me, before going on the offensive. 'I knew you'd be awkward about it if I asked you, anyway,' he says. 'I was just trying to be neighbourly.'

'I'd only have been awkward if our *neighbour* had been naked when she asked you,' I say. 'As she so often seems to be. And being *husbandly* would make a change.'

Josh says, '*Ooh!*' which doesn't help at all, so I stomp off into the living room, and turn on the TV. Sod my rule about never watching it in the daytime, to avoid brain death: I'd quite like to stop thinking for a bit. Max follows me into the room, though, and makes himself comfortable on the sofa, as if preparing to continue the conversation. Some people just can't take a hint.

When I press *play* on an old recording of an episode of Swedish *Wallander*, he gets up and walks out again.

'Bloody subtitles,' he says.

Now *he* knows how it feels to have no idea what is going on, for once.

## SUNDAY, 5 SEPTEMBER

I am knackered. I know I've said it before but, honestly, snoring really should be grounds for divorce. I finally drag myself out of bed, mid-morning, but can't be bothered to get dressed.

So at lunchtime I'm still sitting around in one of Connie's old nighties – attractively topped off with Max's dressing gown – when the doorbell rings. There's the sound of muffled conversation for a while, and then Max invites Ellen to come in, the idiot.

I glare at him, while she produces a gift-wrapped plant pot and hands it to me. 'This is for you, Molly,' she says. 'To thank you for the loan of the car.'

I'm not exactly sure what comes out of my mouth next, but it's something along the lines of, 'Humph.'

Gracious is obviously my middle name where nympho-maniac neighbours are concerned, and I don't like cactuses anyway. They never flower, just sit there promising much and delivering *very little*. A bit like certain MPs I could name.

My lack of enthusiasm must be obvious, because then Ellen says, 'Max says you weren't very happy about him lending it to me – but it was all my fault. You mustn't blame him, you *really* mustn't.'

She pats Max on the arm at the same time, and it's all I can do not to swat her hand away. And what gives her the right to tell me not to be cross with my own husband? He deserves it. Probably.

'Humph,' I say, again, while Max looks at Ellen apol-ogetically and then shrugs, as if powerless to control a lunatic.

I don't know why he thinks 'Humph' is so embar-rassing. It seems pretty restrained to me, and I'd say a lot worse than that if I had any definitive proof that he's sleeping with Ellen. The trouble is, I don't, so I try to pull myself together, which is challenging in an outfit like this.

'Coffee?' I say, in a way that suggests the right answer is, 'No.'

'No, thanks,' says Ellen, on cue for once. 'I need to do some food shopping. I've got nothing in the house to eat.'

Then she gives the car keys back to Max, apologises again to me, and takes her leave.

Max goes to show her out while I unwrap the cactus and put it on the table, and then I start to feel a bit guilty for being so rude to her, even though it really is a *rubbish* plant. What if she *isn't* up to anything with Max?

I should probably apologise to her, just in case.

'God, Molly, did you have to be like that to Ellen?' says Max, coming back into the room and throwing the car keys onto the table. 'There was no need for it.'

Now I'm definitely *not* going to say I'm sorry.

'Yes, I did,' I say. 'And I hate cactuses, anyway.'

'But this one's been cultivated to remove its prickles,' says Max, as if it would be very good news, were the same thing to be done to me.

## MONDAY, 6 SEPTEMBER

It's Josh's interview at the cinema today so, soon, I may be the mother of a paid-up member of the working class.

Then he can fund his own taxis but, in the meantime, I have to pay for another one as he can't possibly get there on foot, and neither Max nor I can get the time off work to drive him there. He's still hobbling like

Hopalong Cassidy, even with the dubious bracing effect of those stupid jeans.

'It'll be worth the money, if he gets the job,' I say to Max. 'And, anyway, we should reward him for getting an interview on the back of his first-ever application. That's a hell of an achievement in itself.'

I'm not quite so convinced of that when, afterwards, Josh tells me that the Jobcentre sent *eighty* candidates along to the cinema. Pre-selected, my arse.

Anyway, they were split into two groups, and then set some of the most ridiculous tasks that even *I* can imagine (and The Boss is *really* good at thinking of *those*). Josh says that, first, they were given an exercise in recalling and repeating everything the previous ten people had said, and then each candidate had to name their favourite film.

'What did you choose?' I say to Josh, expecting something horrifically violent and full of swearing.

'*Mrs Doubtfire*,' he says. 'I think that made me stand out from the crowd.'

Next, they were each paired up with another applicant to act out dialogue from various film scripts, before being asked the *pièce de résistance*: 'If you were a fruit, which one would you be?'

'I *definitely* nailed it on that one,' says Josh. 'Everyone else chose a vegetable.'

He finds out some time in the next two days if he's been successful. It'll be *very* worrying if he hasn't.

Max and I are still laughing about the fruit and vegetable thing when I open my laptop to email Connie about it – only to discover that I've got a message from Dad. The text is brief, as usual: 'I'm sending you these photos so you will understand why I had to come back to Thailand.'

I think we already know the reason for that, actually – even without the clue afforded by the Thai bride's name.

Oh, *bloody hell*. There are three picture attachments, and I really, *really* don't want to open those. God knows what they contain. Probably gynaecological shots. I make Josh open them instead, while I stand behind him peering through my fingers at the screen. (I know it's irresponsible – it's in the genes.)

'Mum, what are you on about?' Josh says. 'There are no naked women in these pictures, at all.'

Does he have to sound *so* disappointed? I give him a warning look, then realise that he's right.

Photo number one is of Dad, who appears to have grown a very dodgy-looking moustache and is kitted out in what must surely be a set of new clothes. He looks exactly like a pub landlord, circa 1975. He's wearing grey slip-on shoes, and what on earth is *that* around his neck?

'God,' says Josh. 'Where the *hell* did he get those horrible shoes?'

'Same place he got the medallion, I should think,' says Max, who's also come to have a look.

Photo number two is of a group of unidentified old Thai people, and number three shows four young Thai children. All are fully dressed, and there is no sign of the Thai bride at all.

'Who *are* these people?' I ask Josh.

'Probably Grandad's new family,' he says. 'The ones he's keeping with your inheritance. Either that or he's got amnesia and thinks he's Thai himself. Maybe you should ask him what sort of fruit *he* is, when you get the chance.'

'I don't need to,' I say. 'The answer to *that* would obviously be cake.'

## TUESDAY, 7 SEPTEMBER

God, talk about cock-ups. It turns out that Marie-Louise hasn't booked me and The Boss into a hotel for the Party conference yet, and now she's struggling to find us rooms anywhere in Manchester.

She claims she thought that *I* was doing it – as if I haven't had enough to do during Recess, while she and Carlotta have been taking holidays and swanning around Westminster as if they owned the place.

'I'm not going,' she says, 'so why should *I* book the rooms?'

'Because *you* are Andrew's Diary Secretary,' I say. 'And I have been otherwise occupied, managing *him*. That's considerably more difficult.'

I'm not sure, but I think Marie-Louise says something abusive in French in reply, so I try to recall the phrase Dad learned from a Breton fisherman, and which he always shouts at motorists when they drive too slowly, but it's hopeless. I *can't* remember it. My brain's still in a post-Recess fug.

I suppose I could email Dad and ask him, but he's

probably busy learning the Thai for 'Bring me my slip-pers'[35] now, anyway, and will have abandoned any interest in French. There must be another way to deal with Marie-Louise, if I put my mind to it.

When I have found a copy of her contract and faxed it through to her, we finally reach agreement on whose job it is to make The Boss' hotel arrangements. Hers, of course. I think I manage to hide my satisfaction fairly well, though Greg accuses me of 'sounding smug without saying a single word', which he describes as 'an enviable skill'.

At lunchtime, Max phones to tell me that he's just spoken to David and has mentioned that I don't quite seem myself. I don't know what makes Max think that he's *himself*, but avoid saying so.

'David says we can have the cottage for the weekend after this,' he says. 'So we can spend some quality time together, and *you* can calm down a bit. He also said to remind you that, if you weren't so averse to capitalism, you could get a job that paid well enough to buy your own place in the country.'

Ha, ha, ha. David could be a comedian, if he was *ever* capable of being funny. Anyway, maybe Josh will become a cinema owner, over the course of a stellar career in the film industry, and then he'll be able to keep me in the style to which I'd like to become accustomed.

Or maybe not. He phones mid-afternoon to tell me

---

[35] The Thai for 'bring me my slippers' is, according to Google Translate, 'นำรองเท้าแตะของฉันฉัน' or, read phonetically: 'Nả rxngthêā tæa k hxng c hạn c hạn.'

that he got the job. I'm thrilled, but he doesn't sound very pleased at all.

'What's the matter, Josh?' I say. 'You don't sound as chuffed as I thought you'd be.'

'Well, I'm a bit pissed off, actually, Mum,' he says. 'You know how they said it was a full-time job?'

'Yes. I thought that's what you wanted?'

It's certainly what he *needs,* if he's to stand any chance of keeping me in luxury in my old age.

'Well, it sounds as if *that* was a bit of a con,' Josh says. 'They only give you a four-hour contract.'

'What?' I can't believe it. 'Four hours – at minimum wage? How are you supposed to support yourself on that?'

'I don't know,' says Josh. 'Holly's not impressed. She says now it'll be ages before I move out.'

She's got a point. At this rate, Max will beat him to it – seeing as *he'll* only be moving next door.

**WEDNESDAY, 8 SEPTEMBER**
I am a nervous wreck – *and* an idiot. I have just worked out that, as I haven't told anyone about my plan to meet up with Johnny tomorrow, he could kidnap and murder me, without anyone even suspecting him.

This is very stupid behaviour indeed – the sort of thing I'd expect from a teenager let loose on the net for the first time, not from someone responsible like me. Supposedly.

'Can you open today's mail?' I say to Greg. 'I've got something urgent to sort out. It shouldn't take a minute.'

It doesn't. It takes *hours* before I come up with a plan: to write a letter addressed, 'To whom it may concern, in the event of my disappearance and/or death'. It will detail who I am meeting and where – and will be secreted in the top drawer of my desk. The only one with a working lock.

This plan is aborted before I've even written the note, for a number of compelling reasons.

Firstly, I'm *sure* The Boss has a duplicate key to the drawer – seeing as there were definitely more packets of Fruit Pastilles in there before the start of Recess, and *I* haven't eaten them – and it'd be just my luck if he decided to snoop around when he gets back from London tomorrow night, before I can retrieve the note on Friday morning. *If* I'm still alive by then.

Then Andrew would be bound to tell Max that I'm having an affair – if only to prove that he *can* be right about something, occasionally. (*Occasionally* being the operative word.) So I'd have survived a potentially murderous encounter, only for my marriage to fall apart.

Secondly, if Andrew *doesn't* have a key, then no one will find the note anyway, or not until it's far too late to do me any good. Back to the bloody drawing board.

Another hour passes before I come up with Plan B, which is much more straightforward than its predecessor. Tell someone I can trust. This rules out ninety-nine per cent of the people I know, and the remaining one per cent all think Max is wonderful, and would be absolutely horrified by what I'm up to. I'm pretty horrified myself.

I can't think of a Plan C, so I resort to staring

hopelessly into the middle distance and eating a whole packet of sweets instead. When my eyes regain focus, there is the answer, staring me in the face. Or, rather, doing sit-ups in the doorway between our offices.

'Greg,' I say. 'I need to tell you something. In confidence.'

'Not now, you fool,' he says. 'Can't you see I am *working out*?'

Oh, *honestly*. I'll change my mind about telling him in a minute if he doesn't hurry up.

'This is much more important than that,' I say. 'It could be a matter of life and death.'

'If I don't lose this bloody flab, it'll be my love-life that's dead. Stop distracting me.'

Greg does another few sit-ups, if raising your head, but not your body, counts, while I try to work out how to get his full attention. It's not easy, given how focused he seems.

'Love-life's sort of what I want to talk about,' I say, eventually. 'Getting one, I mean.'

'Well, why didn't you say so?' Greg says, rolling over sideways and sitting up. 'I'm all ears, so fire away.'

Oh *God*, now I've gone and done it. There's no choice but to spill the beans.

After I've told him (almost) the whole story, Greg's appalled, but also fascinated. I don't think he's ever thought of *me* as someone with a love-life – and certainly not one involving an International Director of a Global Oil Company. Now he doesn't know *what* to think.

'Are you *sure* about this, Mol?' he says. 'Max is *so*

nice – but, God, this Johnny must be rich. Has he got any daughters who are single and fancy-free?'

'One,' I say. 'She's about five years old, so you're out of luck.'

'True,' says Greg. 'Though you'd better not mention her to Mr Beales. Just in case.'

## THURSDAY, 9 SEPTEMBER (DAYTIME)

Greg and I spend all morning and half of the afternoon arguing about the finer details of Plan C, in between dealing with the usual suspects. Finally, we reach agreement: I am to text Greg as soon as I meet up with Johnny, *and* if we change location, and *again* when I get home. Which has to be before 1:00am or Greg will declare a state of emergency, phone the police, and report me missing.

I don't want to think about what will happen after *that*. There's no turning back now, anyway – not now that Johnny's already in the UK.

'Arrived Heathrow, and boarding train,' he says, in a text. 'Can't wait to see ALL of you.'

As I'm reading the message, my mobile rings. I'm so startled that I nearly drop it, and I'm even more flustered when I see that the caller is Max. Bloody *hell*. For one panic-stricken moment, I think that he may be able to read Johnny's text, simply because it's still on the screen when his call comes in. I am *really* losing the plot.

'What time are you going to this Law Society thing tonight?' he says. He must be driving, as I can hear the car engine in the background.

'What?' Oh, yes – my cover story. I am such a *useless* liar.

'Seven-thirty. Why?' I say, after a pause.

'I'll be back sooner than I thought from this customer's house, so I'll be home in time to give you a lift,' says Max. 'Which hotel is it that you're going to?'

Oh, good God. My mind goes blank for a minute. I can't think of a single hotel apart from the real one, and I can't tell Max the name of *that*. Then I recall the Marriott County Hall.

'The Marriott,' I say. 'You know.' (I hope he does, as I'm not entirely sure Lichford even *has* a Marriott, now I come to think of it.)

'Oh, right,' says Max. 'That's a bit of a long way out. You'd better be ready by seven, then. See you when you get home. 'Bye, darling.'

Shit, shit, shit, shit, shit, shit, *shit*. Where *is* the bloody Marriott? I ask Greg, who starts to laugh. It turns out that it isn't even in Lichford, but is miles out in the sticks somewhere. I'd need to take out a mortgage to afford a taxi back into town, and I'd be horribly late even if I did.

'What's it worth?' says Greg, after I've explained my dilemma.

'What?' I say. I can't think straight.

'What's it worth, to save your arse?' he says. 'Obviously, I'll have to pick you up at the Marriott in the Gregmobile, as soon as Max has dropped you off there, then drive you back to the right hotel, just in time to meet the Baron of Oil.'

Sometimes that boy is a genius – even if he does take advantage of other people's difficulties. Now I have signed my life away for the next two months. Greg says I have to deal with every campaign postcard and lobbying email, single-handedly – plus I have to make coffee whenever he likes.

'Without swearing at me,' he says, as we shake on the deal.

This date had better be worth all the discomfort it's causing, that's all I can say. I'd cancel the damn thing if Johnny wasn't almost here. It's not as if I can take a last-minute raincheck, though, is it? Not when he's come all the way from Moscow, just to see me. God knows why – I look like hell.

It's going to take a lot more than Connie's abandoned make-up samples to hide the guilt and stress that's written all over my face. As well as today's crop of new wrinkles.

## THURSDAY, 9 SEPTEMBER
## (VERY LATE EVENING)

What a total shambles. It seems that I am *much* better at affairs of state (at an admittedly wholly unimportant level) than I am at affairs of the heart.

When Max drops me off at the Marriott – which really *is* miles out of Lichford – Greg is waiting for me in the lobby, hiding behind a parlour palm. So far, so good. He bundles me straight into the Gregmobile and heads back into town as fast as he can.

Considering what a terrible driver Greg is, this is not as frightening as it could have been, although there is one very hairy moment when we almost catch up with Max, who is waiting at a set of traffic lights. I don't think he notices us but it's unnerving, all the same.

To avoid any repetitions, we then have to pootle along at about 20mph for the rest of the journey, which makes me late for the meeting with Johnny.

I rush into the hotel, looking very windswept and even more harassed, and am so busy trying to smooth my hair out that I walk straight into someone waiting at the reception desk.

'Ex*cuse* me,' he says, in a very snooty way, then, 'Molly?'

'Johnny?'

God, he looks *exactly* like Putin. Same build, probably the same height – considerably shorter than Max, though thankfully not a midget like me. He even has the same air of authority, initially, but this doesn't last, when he fails to get the hotel to sort out the error they've made with his booking.

He's been given a single room instead of the luxury double he'd booked – probably because he normally has someone like me to arrange his hotel accommodation, and is incapable of doing it himself. Let's hope the similarity with The Boss ends there.

Things improve slightly when we sit down at our table, even though we're still being very polite and formal. It feels more like an interview than a date so far – and you'd never guess we've had virtual sex! I completely forget we have at first, and am quite embarrassed when I do remember.

It doesn't help that Johnny keeps staring at me, which makes me feel really, *really* self-conscious, though I don't *think* he can see my incipient beard. Luckily, the lights are dim.

'Molly,' he says, after I've spent ten minutes asking him about his rail journey, and apologising for the state of Network Rail, 'you are *not* the Transport Secretary. You have much, much better legs – even better than I remembered. Now, for God's sake, calm down, and have a drink.'

I have three G&Ts in quick succession, which seem to do the trick, as I relax a bit. Then we eat and everything gets better and better. For a while at least.

We're just two people, talking: about life, our hopes, how we feel about the choices we've made since we were last together. No one mentions kids, or bills, what's for dinner, or the mystery of where all their socks have gone. And *no one* needs to go to A&E. I haven't felt this way in years: like a woman, not a function – or a paramedic.

By the time we've finished dessert, it's already quite late. Johnny leans back in his chair and looks at me for a moment, half-smiling. Then he says, 'So, now what, Molly? Do we go to my room? No pressure, if you don't want to – but I know *I* do.'

No pressure, my arse. Half a continent travelled, the vagaries of Heathrow and British Rail negotiated, a hotel cock-up and an à la carte dinner paid for using Johnny's platinum credit card. I could hardly say no, even if I wanted to. And I don't *think* I want to, anyway – though I'm not sure whether my shivering is due to excitement, nerves or the omission of my thermal underwear in honour of the occasion.

'Okay,' I say, after what seems a very long pause.

Johnny takes my hand as we walk along the corridor. It's the first time we've touched, and it feels more intimate than you'd think possible for such a small gesture. Then he opens the door to his room, flicks off the overhead light that the cleaner must have left on, and leads me inside.

Oh, God, God, *God*. Past the point of no return.

'So here we are,' he says. 'At last. I've waited a very long time for this.' He pulls me towards him and leans forward to kiss me.

'Ouch,' I say.

My hair has caught in the hinge of his glasses.

Untangling it seems to take ages and, once we've managed it, Johnny puts his glasses down on the chest of drawers. This is a relief, as I'm sure I look a whole lot better without them. Then he moves in for another attempt at a kiss, misjudges the distance and head butts me.

'Ow!' I say, or rather, yell.

He steps back, catches his foot on something, and promptly falls over the corner of the bed.

There's a hell of a crash and I start to laugh. Uncontrollably. It's a nervous thing: I *always* laugh when someone falls over – though I stop when I switch the light back on and see the bloody gash on Johnny's forehead and his deeply unamused expression. He must have hit the edge of the bedside table when he fell.

315

So, just when I should have been turning into a femme fatale, I have to do a Florence Nightingale instead: cleaning the wound and searching in my bag for a plaster, while Johnny lies on the bed with a terrible squint.

It's not a good look, but I try not to judge him for that. I doubt he can focus on anything without his glasses, judging by how thick the lenses are. I can't see *a thing* when I try them on in a misguided attempt to lighten the mood. No wonder he thinks he fancies me: to him, I'm in soft-focus, all the time.

'There's no need for that,' he says, as I try to shine my key-ring torch into his eyes to check for concussion. 'Come here. We haven't got all night, though I wish we had.'

He shuffles over on the bed so that I can lie down beside him. Then he takes me in his arms – it's a good job I'm so small, as the bed is absolutely *tiny*. He starts stroking my shoulder and kissing my neck, and then his mobile rings.

'I'd better get this,' he says, after replacing his glasses to peer at the screen. 'Sorry – I've got no choice.'

Half an hour later, he's still talking, though God knows what about. His side of the conversation seems restricted to questions about degrees of fever, and the number and location of someone's spots. It must be another Global Oil Company disaster. What have they done *now*? Poisoned a water supply, or something?

I am dying for a cigarette so I mime that I am going outside onto the balcony, but Johnny waves at me to wait. Then he says into the receiver, 'Hang on a moment

316

– room service is here.' He covers the phone with his hand and says, 'Molly, I'm *really* sorry this is taking so long. It sounds as if my youngest's gone down with chicken pox.'

Youngest? Youngest what? Oh, *Christ*. Youngest *child*. Johnny's on the phone to his wife. His *wife*. And what the *hell* do I think I'm doing, when *my* husband is at home managing our lunatic son and waiting for me to come back? I deserve to be hung, drawn and quartered for this – or, at the very least, shot.

I find my shoes and my bag, blow Johnny a kiss and walk out, before he can even hang up the phone.

When I reach the lobby, I spot a taxi that's just dropped someone off at the hotel, so I dive into the back of it and arrive home before the *Newsnight* credits have finished playing. Max is asleep on the sofa and hasn't heard me come in, so I tiptoe upstairs and take a shower, as fast as I can. I feel *so* grubby – even though I've already had chicken pox.

Not that I was likely to catch anything else, given that there was no exchange of bodily fluids of any kind. There wasn't any nudity, either – so I could have worn my thermals, after all.

**FRIDAY, 10 SEPTEMBER**
I wake to mad beeping from my mobile. A barrage of texts, all from Johnny.

'Good morning.'

'I'm so sorry about last night.'

'I can't stop thinking about you.'

'When can we meet again?'

'I'm on the train. And wishing I wasn't.'

Max looks a bit curious, so I tell him the texts are all from Orange.

'Bastards,' he says. Orange's relentless marketing is a sore point with Max. He always claims that they send him so many text messages that they obscure the very few that I send him – which is why he never replies to those. *That's* the sore point with me – though, to be honest, it's probably a good job he rarely uses his phone, otherwise it might have been him calling me last night, instead of Johnny's wife calling him – at exactly the wrong moment.

Unless it was exactly the *right* moment, to stop me in my tracks . . .

Five more minutes and *anything* could have happened, though further injuries seem a more likely outcome than sex, on the basis of what had gone before. God knows why Johnny wants a repeat performance of *that*.

I'm not at all sure that I do. As it is I can barely look at Max when I leave for work.

'What the hell happened to you?' Greg says as I walk into the office fifteen minutes later.

'Oh, shit,' I say. 'I forgot to text you.' Then I realise the significance of what he's just said. 'Oh, *hell*! Did you report me missing to the police?'

'Um, no,' says Greg. He fidgets a bit, and then says, 'Want a coffee?'

He's obviously forgotten that that's *my* job for the next two months, to repay him for the lift to Johnny's hotel last night. I'm about to say so, when I realise why I'm off the hook.

'*Why* didn't you phone them?' I say. 'Weren't you worried about me?'

'Well, I would have been,' says Greg. 'But, after I went for a run, I fell asleep in front of the TV and didn't wake up again until eight am. This exercise thing really tires you out.'

'Oh, for God's sake,' I say. 'I could have been dead, for all you knew.'

'Don't be daft, Mol. If you can cope with the nutters we get here, you can definitely handle an oil baron by yourself. So how *is* the man from Moscow, anyway? A success in the bedroom as well as the boardroom?'

'What man from Moscow?' says The Boss. 'And *what* did you say about success?' He has a snakelike ability to creep up on you. It's quite repulsive.

'Igor,' says Greg, winking at me. 'And I was being ironic. Substitute "failure" for "success".'

How does Greg do it? How does he *know*?

## SATURDAY, 11 SEPTEMBER

I am obviously not cut out to have an affair, so I am going to be much nicer to Max and see if I can win him back from whatever – or *whoever* – it is I need to win him back from. And I'm going to ignore Johnny's attempts to persuade me that it's pointless to try. He's just being cynical, or opportunistic, or both.

I shall help Max with the gardening today and see if we can bond over a love of nature.

'I can manage by myself, Mol,' he says, 'if you'd rather do something else.'

'I wouldn't,' I say. 'Now how can I help? Nan always said green fingers were hereditary, and she was a *brilliant* gardener.'

After I have fallen over a trowel, cut through the tap-root of my favourite clematis and dug up a stack of freesia bulbs by accident, Max suggests I get a deck chair and 'sit down and enjoy the autumn sunshine, out of harm's way'.

Out of Ellen's way might have been safer. No sooner have I made myself comfortable than she appears, hanging a pile of washing on the line. Why has she only got *matching* sets of underwear?

'Still smoking, then, Molly?' she says when she spots me over the back wall. (Why *do* people think it's necessary to state the bleeding obvious?)

'Um, yes,' I say. I almost add, 'D'you want to make something of it?' but decide that would make me sound like Steve Ellington, so I don't. I remain a master of restraint. I'd say *mistress* but, in the presence of Ellen, this would provoke uncomfortable thoughts.

'You really should give up,' says Ellen. 'It's a filthy habit.'

I have no idea why some people's filthy habits are deemed disgusting, while certain other people's are considered worth bragging about and doing in public – mentioning no names beginning with *E* – so I light another cigarette from the butt of the previous one, just to show Ellen who's the boss.

The effectiveness of this is somewhat undermined by

an immediate coughing fit, but I think I manage to disguise it by pretending that I have choked.

While Max pats me on the back, a little too hard, Ellen turns her attention to him.

'You should give up, too, Max,' she says. 'Nicotine's linked to erectile dysfunction, you know.'

Max stops patting my back, but doesn't seem to know how to respond to that, so I do it for him. Unasked.

'Not a problem Max is familiar with,' I say, before realising what an idiot I am. Even if Ellen doesn't already know the truth of that statement – *argh* – now she'll *definitely* want to check it out.

'God's sake, Mol,' says Max, disappearing into the shed and closing the door with a bang.

'Anyway,' says Ellen, after a pause. 'I suppose I'd better get on with this.'

'Yes,' I say. 'So should I.'

The trouble is, I'm not exactly sure what 'this' is, in my case. Or in hers.

## SUNDAY, 12 SEPTEMBER

Max is in a horrible mood, and seems to be getting through an entire packet of extra-strong mints every five seconds. He's trying to super-glue the root of the clematis back together, but his concentration isn't up to its usual standard.

'What's the matter with you?' I say, after he's spent the last five minutes swearing about having stuck two of his fingers together. 'And why do you keep eating so many mints?'

'I'm giving up smoking,' he says, peeling his fingers apart.

'What?' I say. 'Why?'

'Why?' says Max. 'Don't be silly, Mol. Everyone knows it's not good for you. And it's like having social leprosy these days.'

'Well, not when *both* of us smoke, it isn't,' I say. 'And we never go anywhere socially, anyway. Or are you thinking of getting up close and personal with someone else? Someone who *doesn't* smoke?'

Max sighs, then pops another mint into his mouth. 'Oh, for God's sake,' he says while he chews. 'I want to give up before I enter my next decade. Just like you said *you* were going to. I'm a bit more determined than you are, that's all.'

Talk about unfairness. Has Max forgotten the provocation I was subjected to on *my* birthday?

'Well, that wasn't my fault,' I say. 'What with Ellen and her very public search for a big you-know-what at my party, and The Boss going on about Gordon Brown, it's no wonder I forgot I was supposed to be giving up.'

'Excuses, excuses,' says Max.

There is nothing as annoying as a reformed smoker, except for the people who attempt to reform them.

I'm trying very hard not to jump to conclusions and lose my temper, though – so I'm quite glad to see the back of Max, when he agrees to give Josh a lift to Holly's straight after lunch.

Less than two minutes later, Josh comes pelting back in through the door, leaving it open.

'Mum, have you seen the cat?' he says, his voice almost drowned out by the sound of Max shouting, 'Charlie! *Charlie!*', outside.

'No,' I say. 'He's probably still out shagging. There seem to be about ten females on heat around here at the moment.' (Not to mention the noisy human kind.)

'No, he *isn't*,' says Josh. 'He was asleep in the wheel arch of the car again, when Dad and I got into it just now.'

'Then you know where he is already. So why are you asking me?'

'Well, I told Dad Charlie was sleeping there—'

'And?' I say. I don't like the sound of this, or of Max's increasingly frantic tone. He's still calling for the cat.

'And Dad said not to worry – that Charlie'd move as soon as the engine started. Only he didn't. Or not fast enough, anyway.'

*Marvellous.* So now Max is a nicotine-deprived cat murderer. I'm just waiting for the Facebook hate page to be created when Josh explains that, although there was a big bump, Charlie then ran off somewhere, yowling and looking very cross.

'So he's not dead yet,' says Josh. 'But we've got to find him and take him to the vet as fast as we can.'

Honestly, I'm sure some people have *restful* weekends.

We search for hours, but there's no sign of Charlie anywhere. Josh is distraught and keeps telling us that cats always go somewhere off the beaten track to die. This is not particularly helpful in the circumstances.

When it gets dark, we have no choice but to admit

defeat and go indoors. Max looks devastated, and Josh even more so.

We're all in the kitchen, sitting in silence, not knowing what to do next, when there's a bang at the back door. The cat flap flies upwards and Charlie comes barrelling through it, shakes his fur, then swaggers off into the hallway.

Max grabs the cat basket, scoops Charlie into it, and then we pile into the car and race to the vet's.

'You may have been right that we should have bought pet insurance,' says Max on the way back home. 'Especially as I feel like killing the bloody cat properly, after that. Sixty-five quid, and there's *nothing* wrong with him!'

'He's obviously better than Josh at ninja rolls,' I say.

Max doesn't laugh. Giving up smoking *obliterates* your sense of humour.

## MONDAY, 13 SEPTEMBER

'Good news,' says Dinah when she rings me at work first thing this morning. 'Dad says he's bored.'

'That's not good news, you idiot,' I say. 'It's *always* bad – *and* dangerous, you know that. And, anyway, how can he be bored? He's still in Thailand with the Porn Queen for another two weeks.'

'Well, that's where you're wrong, Molly,' says Dinah. 'As usual. He's coming back early, so which one of us is the idiot now?'

I ignore that, as I'm more interested in finding out what's going on. Di says that Dad emailed her last night, said that he was 'bored with lying around in the sun, even though the company is lovely', and 'fed up with scorpions the size of lobsters lying in wait for him in the toilet' – so he's decided to fly back early. Tonight.

'I've got to go and collect him from Heathrow tomorrow,' says Dinah. 'He reckons he'll be too tired to get the train.'

'Your dad's obviously got it out of his system,' says Max when I tell him later. He makes it sound as if having something to get out of your system is the norm.

Connie's pleased about it, anyway. 'I only ever wanted a cuddly grandad,' she says, during tonight's phone call. 'Not a pervy one with a girlfriend called Porn.'

Then she bursts into tears.

'Talking of funny names,' she says, 'I *hate* my new job. I wish I hadn't applied for this internship now.'

'Why?' I say.

Doesn't Connie realise what an honour it was to be selected? There aren't many internships as prestigious as this, nor as well-paid. She could be stuck at the cinema with Josh, for four hours a week.

'A trained monkey could do what I'm doing,' says Connie, sounding oddly like her brother for once. 'Or a robot. And my boss is *awful*.'

'Oh, well – join the club on that one,' I say. Now she sounds *just* like me.

'Mum! He's *much* worse than Andrew,' says Connie, who barely knows The Boss at all. 'He talks to the male interns all the time, but he only speaks to me when he has no choice.'

325

Talk about déjà vu. My maternal sympathy finally kicks in, only a little later than it should have done. (I've been trying to stick to my 'if it isn't cancer, then shut up about it' rule until now.)

'Oh, Connie,' I say. 'You poor thing. I know all about bosses who behave like that. Give it another week, and then speak to yours about it if it doesn't improve.'

'I would, Mum,' she says. 'But I can't pronounce his name properly. I can't call him Dr Snuffleopagus, can I?'

## TUESDAY, 14 SEPTEMBER

I'm in the kitchen at work, making coffee and mulling over how to respond to Johnny's latest series of emails – all still trying to persuade me to change my mind about a second meeting – when the phone begins to ring.

'Ah, Mr Beales,' says Greg. 'No, I'm sorry. *Still* no progress on ensuring that speeding tickets become null and void if the policemen who issue them get themselves run over while doing so. As I think Molly may have already told you, we are not wholly optimistic of success on this particular issue.'

I stick my head around the doorframe and pull a face, but Greg's not paying any attention to me. He appears to be reading *The London Review of Books* at the same time as listening to Mr Beales.

'Yes, well,' he says. 'I think you may have a somewhat dystopian view of society, if you'll forgive me saying so.' There's a pause, and then he says, very slowly: 'Dys-*to*-pian.'

Then he hangs up and starts leafing through a copy

of *New Scientist*, while I search for a safe place to put his coffee down on his desk. It seems to be covered with piles of new magazines and journals, though I can't see a copy of *Hello!* magazine anywhere.

'Did you just say "dystopian" to Mr Beales?' I say.

'Yes,' says Greg. 'I am attempting to raise the calibre of conversation around here. Given the inexplicable omission of my name from the list of the UK's top three hundred intellectuals.'

'Oh,' I say – which I don't think lives up to Greg's expectations. He raises his eyebrows, and waits for me to try again. 'A laudable aim. Though what did Mr Beales reply?'

'He asked why The Boss can't employ someone who speaks proper English,' says Greg. 'I am bloodied, but unbowed.'

I wish I could say the same for Dinah. She's absolutely *traumatised*.

'God-all-bloody-mighty,' she says when she phones tonight to confirm that Dad's now safely back at home. 'I've never been so embarrassed in my life.'

Apparently, Dad lost his wallet somewhere in the airport, and someone else found it and handed it in.

'What's so bad about that?' I say. 'I think it's reassuring that not everyone in this country is dishonest.'

I brush aside what this might say about me or Johnny, or Max and Ellen. I'm getting *much* better at brushing aside. And, anyway, Max and I are going to be back on track, as soon as we've had our romantic weekend in the country.

'I'm not telling you anything else about it,' says Dinah, her voice rising to a squawk. 'It was *bloody* awful, and I can't cope with re-living the trauma. Not with my mental health problem. You'll just have to phone Dad and ask him yourself.'

I'm not sure I want to, but Dad saves me the bother. He phones as soon as Dinah's hung up.

'I'm back,' he says, as if that's cause for celebration. I suppose it is, really, if he's back for good, and hasn't brought a new stepmother with him – but I don't want to bolster his ego too much.

'So I hear,' I say. 'What happened at the airport? Dinah sounds a bit upset about it.'

'Oh, that's just that stupid HDP thing she's got,' says Dad, 'or whatever it's called. Making a mountain out of a molehill, if you ask me. It was bloody funny, actually.'

Dad's sense of humour isn't everyone's, so this isn't particularly reassuring, though the story seems innocuous enough at first. He and Dinah were running around the arrivals lounge looking for his wallet when there was an announcement on the tannoy system asking for the owner of a lost wallet to return to Customs.

When Dad and Dinah did so, the woman behind the desk asked Dad his name and then asked him what was in the wallet. Dad says he listed everything he could remember but the woman said he'd forgotten something. Then she waved a packet of blue tablets at him and asked him what they were.

'Oh, God,' I say. 'Tell me they weren't Viagra, *please*?'

''Course they were,' says Dad. 'Trying to embarrass me, wasn't she?'

'I assume it didn't work,' I say – in the voice of experience.

'No,' says Dad. 'No one embarrasses your father, as you know. I suggested we could go behind the screen and test them, if she wanted to be sure what they were. She didn't seem too keen on that.'

Now I wish he'd stayed in Thailand, and I bet I'm not the only one.

## WEDNESDAY, 15 SEPTEMBER

Huh, so much for Max's much-vaunted self-discipline. It's at least as poor as mine.

I'm sitting in the garden after work today – smoking, of course, but then *I'm* not the one who's giving up – when Josh comes outside to complain about how few hours he's been allocated by the cinema this week. He goes into such a long rant about it that, eventually, I ask him to go back inside and leave me alone, just for a while. Is ten minutes' peace and quiet *too* much to ask?

'I only came out here to calm down after work,' I say.

'No, you didn't,' says Josh. 'You're a filthy addict, unlike Dad. If he can give up smoking – *just like that* – then I don't see why you won't even *try*.'

'Unlike your father, I have a genuinely stressful job,' I say. 'And maybe I'm not motivated by the same rewards.'

I don't mention who the rewards are most likely to come from, and Josh isn't listening, anyway. That's *so typical*.

'Look at that,' he says, pointing towards the side of the shed. 'Something's on fire.'

He's right. There are clouds of white smoke billowing around from the back of the shed wall and drifting across the garden.

'Dad. *Dad!*'

Honestly, I don't know why the kids always assume Max is the only person who can deal with an emergency. He doesn't even know the *meaning* of the word, not to mention that I am the designated fire officer at work. (There's no need for everyone to keep pointing out that I can't lift the extinguisher by myself.)

'Yes?' comes Max's voice – from the other side of the shed.

'What are you doing? Are you okay?' says Josh. 'Don't try to put the fire out yourself – get out of there!'

'Don't be daft,' says Max. 'I'm just feeding the rabbit, and cleaning the hutch. Nothing at all to worry about.'

'But there's smoke coming from the back of the shed.' Josh is getting very worried now, and is heading towards it.

'No, that's just dust from the hay,' says Max. 'Stay put. I'll be with you in a minute.'

He's too late. Josh moves faster than you think (except on a skateboard), even with a dislocated knee and skinny jeans.

'Oh, for God's sake, Dad,' he says, in a tone of deep disgust. 'Mum, he's smoking a bloody cigarette. Right next to the poor old rabbit. Dust from the hay, my arse.'

'Oh, honestly, Max,' says Ellen, over the garden wall. 'And when you'd been doing so well, too.'

I *do* wish Ellen would stop appearing from nowhere, even when she's fully clothed – although I'm quite enjoying watching Max blustering and claiming it is 'just a lapse'. At least, I am, until I remember that he is *my* husband and yet I'm not the one he's been trying to please.

I don't say anything about that, though. Some of us are capable of *genuine* self-discipline.

## THURSDAY, 16 SEPTEMBER

I've just got off the phone to the Council's housing department – about the girls with cancer, who I'm *still* trying to get re-housed – when it starts to ring again. It's Mr Meeeeurghn, who's managed to get himself a Council flat, somehow or other, but who now says that one of his new neighbours is picking on him.

I don't get the neighbour's name, as Mr M's so wound up that he's making even less sense than usual. And that's *really* saying something.

'Woman mad crazy,' he says, without apparent irony.

When I enquire further, he says that she lives in the flat above his, and that she stares at him and sniffs every time he passes her in the lobby. She also bangs on the floor whenever he has a cigarette. She sounds a bit like Ellen, but thank God Mr Meeeeurghn's new flat isn't anywhere near our house. We'd have to move immediately, if it was.

'You write and tell her,' he yells. 'Tell her *now*!'

'Tell her what?' I say. I want to go home already. And it's only 10:30am.

'You tell her stop sniffing me and be nice, because I am refugee,' he says.

I wish I had even a tiny proportion of the vast influence that Mr Meeeeurghn believes me to possess. If I had, I'd have given one of the girls with cancer his flat but, as I don't, I have to spend ages trying to convince him that it is up to *him* to improve his relationship with his neighbour. All by himself.

He loses his temper and slams the phone down on me. I can't say it bothers me overmuch.

Greg sighs when I tell him what Mr Meeeeurghn wanted this time, then says, '*He's* on the list for our next DIY CRB check.'

I say that I don't think we need to go and spy on Mr Meeeeurghn to know that he's as mad as a box of frogs – not since the letter from the Home Office and the Primark incident – but I suppose we *could* check out whether his neighbour looks to be a reasonable person or not, just in case Mr M is telling the truth for once.

The sniffing did sound a bit peculiar and you do have to *try* to keep an open mind, after all. Even though that's sometimes an extremely tall order.

I do a bit of sniffing of Max when he gets home from work, until he asks me what the hell I'm playing at and tells me to stop. He smells smoky, which ought to be repulsive, but is actually *very* reassuring.

He looks at me as if I am as demented as Mr

Meeeeurghn when I say, 'Oh, good, you've been smoking again.'

I don't say that, as far as I'm concerned, anything that he does to annoy Ellen is fine by me, though I am a bit worried that we only seem to be bonding over smoking. Have we *really* grown that far apart?

Johnny says that he and his wife have, but maybe that's the fault of his clumsiness. I wonder if that's linked to being crap in bed? Max is awfully dexterous – which isn't necessarily an advantage, now I come to think of it. It could facilitate juggling more than one thing at a time, by which I mean, 'women'.

## FRIDAY, 17 SEPTEMBER

As if last night's dream about Max juggling three naked Ellens and a partially clothed Miss Chambers wasn't quite traumatic enough, now I have seen inside someone's head. Not telepathically, by virtue of *The Twilight Zone* theme, but *literally*!

If I'd *wanted* to be a brain surgeon, I'd have made far more effort to pass Biology when I was at school, instead of only concentrating during sex education. (And a fat lot of good *that* did me, anyway.)

It's all Mr Lawson's fault. He's never been to surgery before, so this is the first time I've ever met him. I hope it's the last, as well.

'I want to talk to you about mental health,' he says, as he sits down and removes his jacket.

'Ah,' says The Boss. 'And what about mental health, exactly?'

'The professionals' unwillingness to use tried-and-tested methods to alleviate people's misery.'

This sounds interesting. Maybe there's something in it for me? I could occasionally do with some cheering up, so I stop doodling and pay attention.

'Did you have anything specific in mind?' I ask.

This proves to be absolutely the *worst* thing I could have said. Mr Lawson smiles – a bit like a crocodile, slowly and with definite menace – then he pulls off his hat, leans forward so that his head is almost touching my notepad, and says, 'This!'

'What?' I say. I can only see greying hair and a smattering of dandruff.

'*This*,' he says again, parting his hair to reveal what looks like a hole, but cannot be.

Now Andrew's the one who's interested, while I have lost all desire to find out *anything* more, thank you very much indeed.

'Is that a *hole*?' he says. 'In your *head*?'

Mr Lawson nods, which makes me flinch – *Christ*, bits of his brain will probably fly out and spatter me if he doesn't stop doing that. This is *horrible*.

'Have you had brain surgery, then?' says Andrew.

Can't he tell Mr Lawson to put his bloody hat back on, instead of *encouraging* him? And stop asking questions which could lead to more nodding? I am starting to feel faint – just like the time when I was forced to dissect a cow's eyeball in class. (The damned thing definitely jumped when I cut through the optic nerve, no matter what Miss Rosen claimed at the time. It nearly gave me a heart attack.)

'Yes, I have had surgery – in a manner of speaking,' says Mr Lawson. 'Ever heard of trepanning?'

'Good God,' says The Boss, who obviously has. 'Are you serious?'

'Absolutely,' says Mr Lawson. 'Can't recommend it highly enough.'

So now I am supposed to write a letter to the Secretary of State for Health, asking why the NHS doesn't offer trepanning to those suffering from mental health conditions. The world is going *mad* – which is not a recommendation for Mr Lawson's idiotic solution.

Greg says he'll save me the bother of writing to the Department of Health and will ask his doctor about trepanning this evening when he attends his 'emergency appointment'.

'What emergency?' I say. He looks perfectly all right to me – and *his* skull is intact.

'I think I may have an ulcer,' he says, in a portentous tone. 'Bound to have, doing this job. I had a terrible pain in my side when I arrived at work.'

'That was a stitch,' I say. This keep-fit thing is getting out of hand, or Greg's 'sporting injuries' are, anyway. He only jogged from the bus stop to the office this morning.

'Exactly,' he says, when I point that out. 'Which is why I need the alarming symptoms it caused investigated – as soon as possible. Most men don't take their health seriously enough.'

Then he buggers off, leaving me to do the surgery letters and finish all the other casework as well. Sometimes I think I'm sadly lacking in the assertiveness stakes.

Max is over-compensating for my shortcomings by being far *too* assertive when I get home, almost two hours later. He's done almost all the packing already, and informs me that we are *not* taking the laptop with us, as we are going to 'spend quality time together, without distractions'.

He even wants me to leave my mobile behind but, although I agree, I've no intention of doing so – not when I am leaving an incompetent ninja at home, with a sex-pest for a neighbour.

I write Josh a very long list enumerating the dire consequences that will arise should he be unwise enough to consider anything as stupid as a house party in our absence, and ask Mum to drop in daily to check that the house is still standing, and that the cat and the rabbit have been fed. *And* that Josh is still in one piece. She agrees, though she says that it's probably 'unrealistic to expect that Josh won't have one or two little accidents'.

I try to ignore that less-than-reassuring statement, as now it's bedtime, and tomorrow Max and I are off for our romantic weekend. At least, I *hope* it's going to be romantic. I could use some of that, to cheer me up, and it'd be a lot less painful than having a hole drilled in my head.

### SATURDAY, 18 SEPTEMBER

Mum rings in the morning, to ask Max if he can come round and pad out her sofa so that the cushions won't make her buttock hurt so much.

'Did you ask her if she's tried taking anti-inflammatories

for that?' I say. 'And has she forgotten we're supposed to be going away today?'

'Yes, I did ask her,' says Max. 'And no, she hasn't forgotten. She says she doesn't take drugs, and that it should only take a minute.'

It doesn't, so I have deal with everything at home while Max adds layer after layer of foam to Mum's cushions, and then ends up taking it all out again when she declares the result 'too padded for comfort'.

My time is mainly spent trying to make Josh pay attention while I read out the long list of safety instructions I wrote last night, while he tries to shoot everything in sight on a particularly violent video game. Of the kind that Steve Ellington probably plays every day of the week.

Dad phones to complain about Dinah, Dinah phones to complain about Dad, and Connie phones to complain about Dr Snuffleopagus. It's almost lunchtime before Max and I manage to leave.

He gives me a quick kiss as I do up my seatbelt, then turns away to start the engine. I pull him back, and kiss him again, properly. You may as well start how you mean to go on.

'Did you leave your phone at home?' he says, as we pull out of our street then turn left onto the main road, heading for freedom and romance.

'Yes,' I say. It's what's known as a tiny white lie in the trade.

Max believes me, and is furious that he ordered me to do such a stupid thing when we break down half an hour later.

'I forgive you for lying to me,' he says, as he phones the AA, after I've confessed and passed him my mobile. 'Though don't make a habit of it.'

I feel a bit nauseous after that, though I suppose it could be motion sickness. That is, once we're finally in motion again – the repair takes ages, and it's already late afternoon by the time we arrive at David and Susie's holiday cottage.

'I wonder if they've left us a welcome hamper,' I say. 'From Fortnum and Mason, or somewhere like that. You never know your luck.'

You do, really. There's no hamper, but David *has* left Max a list of a few 'odd jobs' he can do, 'if he has any time to spare, and in lieu of rent'. We're only going to be here overnight!

By the time Max has worked through three-quarters of the things on the list, I'm wishing I'd ignored his ban on bringing the laptop, as well as the phone. I've never been so bored in my life, and I really ought to check that Josh hasn't invited all of Lichford's under-twenties to a house party via one of those Facebook public invitation things. I text Connie and ask her to check.

She texts back, and says that Josh's status says, 'If you're reading this, Connie – *you craven spy* – then tell Mum I'm not an idiot, Holly's here keeping an eye on me, and no, I'm not having a party'.

I just hope none of *those* are white lies, big or small.

'I'm going to start cooking dinner,' says Max. 'Put your feet up and relax.'

I do try, but David's sofa could really use some extra

padding and, anyway, Max has forgotten to pack any books – *typical* dyslexic behaviour – so then I root around the cottage trying to find something to read. Now I'm wondering if David and Susie are dyslexic as well.

There are no books worth reading *at all*, only Sharon Osbourne's autobiography and numerous books on motivational management techniques, full of idiotic homilies like 'Always abide by the three Cs: never Criticise, never Complain, and never something-else-beginning-with-C.' (I lapsed into a coma before I got to that bit. Maybe that's what the third 'C' was for.)

When I return to consciousness it's pouring with rain and really chilly for September. The nearest pub is a four-mile walk, so Max suggests that we stay in.

'We'll eat dinner, watch a bit of TV and then we can have an early night,' he says.

There's something about the way he says the last bit that makes me think a gold star may be on the cards.

This seems less likely when the TV doesn't work and Max gets so annoyed that he insists on climbing onto the roof and fiddling about with the aerial for hours, while I stay down below, first running inside to check if there's a picture, and then back outside to report that there isn't. Repeatedly.

'We may as well go to bed, then,' says Max, eventually, with a somewhat less than flattering degree of enthusiasm.

He tries to make up for it once we get into bed and snuggle up for warmth. ('Fix the central heating' was also on David's list, but even Max thought *that* a bit ambitious.)

'Put the light back on, Mol,' he says. 'I want to see you. You know I still think you're gorgeous.'

Put the light on? Oh, my God. Now I need a bag to put over my head. And, as if that wasn't bad enough, being in bed with someone who can't see me properly sounds *horribly* familiar.

'Hic,' I say. Then, 'Hic, hic, hic, HIC.'

'Oh, shit,' says Max. 'That's you out of action for tonight.'

Why do I *always* get hiccups when I'm stressed, or in the wrong? And *why* do they take so long to stop?

## SUNDAY, 19 SEPTEMBER

I was up half the night trying every technique under the sun to put an end to my bloody hiccups, but the damn things just would *not* stop. In the end, after nearly asphyxiating myself several times – during prolonged periods of holding my breath while swallowing like a maniac – I had to admit defeat and get out of bed.

'Go and try your dad's remedy,' said Max, trying unsuccessfully to hide how fed up he obviously was. 'That usually works when all else fails.'

That's true, but nothing Dad recommends is *ever* dignified. His hiccup cure involves drinking a large glass of water, upside down. Well, not exactly upside down, but it feels like it, when you get it wrong, and all the water goes up your nose or down your front. Or both.

By the time it did work and my hiccups had finally stopped, I was soaking wet and Max was fast asleep. I was wide-awake, so now I know more about Ozzy

Osbourne than I ever wanted to. God knows why Sharon didn't walk out on him if the stories she tells are true – unless he's very, very good in bed. That's a bit hard to imagine, but I suppose he couldn't possibly be more of a wipe-out than me.

Max doesn't give up easily, though. Sharon would be proud of him. When I wake up this morning, he brings me breakfast in bed, and he's put one of David's prize roses on the tray!

'Eat,' he says. 'Slowly, so you don't get your hiccups back.'

Then he runs me a deep bath, sloshes in a load of Susie's bubble bath, and then sits on the loo talking to me, while I try to find a pose that will make me look as attractive as possible. I'm not sure if that's what does it, or the food, but all of sudden I'm in agony.

'Ow,' I say. 'Ow, ow, *ow*.'

'What?' says Max, as I writhe about in the bath, splashing water all over the floor. 'What's the matter, Mol?'

'Stomach cramp,' I say, before I begin to hiccup again.

'So much for a romantic weekend,' says Max as we drive back home, once all my symptoms have finally disappeared. 'Maybe we've just lost the knack.'

There's something terribly hopeless about the way he says it, and I have to bite my lip, hard, in order not to cry.

At least the house is still standing when we arrive home, so things *could* be worse. I'm apprehensive when Max opens the front door, but there doesn't seem to be

341

much mess when we get inside. Well, that's not strictly true – everything looks incredibly messy – but as that's the norm, we can't blame Josh. For once.

He announces that he's just finished doing all the washing up (though it seems to be Holly whose hands are still wet), and he's even put the rubbish out already – or rather, he claims he has, until Robbie informs me that Josh bribed *him* to do it.

'Bribed you, how?' I say.

I forgot to leave Josh any money for emergencies, and I doubt the proceeds of his four hours at the cinema would constitute much of a bribe.

'He told me I might catch a glimpse of your naked neighbour, if I did,' says Robbie. 'But he lied.'

'Ellen must be saving herself for Dad,' says Josh.

Max really doesn't need to look so pleased about *that*. I'd be surprised if Ellen was immune to hiccups.

## MONDAY, 20 SEPTEMBER

Now even the houseplants are mocking my sex-life. This morning, I'm making a cup of tea when I notice that all the leaves of the basil plant in the kitchen have grown faces, and *all* of them are laughing at me.

I think I'm going completely round the bend, until Max spots them too and starts to laugh. It turns out that a bored Josh has had an artistic moment with the leaves and a biro. Is he on drugs? I must find that 'Talk to Frank' leaflet and see if I can spot any more of the giveaway signs.

'I'm really sorry about the weekend,' I say to Max,

before we both leave for work. 'Maybe you could come to conference with me? I could smuggle you into my room, and sneak away from Andrew to meet you in our secret love-nest every few hours or so.'

'Good idea,' says Max. 'As long as you don't get any more hiccups. There'd be nothing secret about *those*.'

He gives me a hug, and seems to have forgiven me, so I try to ignore how pleased he seemed about Ellen's naked floorshow being reserved for his eyes alone. A few nights in Manchester and we'll have recaptured all the sexual chemistry that led to Connie – and to Josh.

The thought of another Josh puts me off the idea a bit, but I'm still determined to go ahead with my plan. Until I get to work, that is.

As soon as I arrive, Greg pulls me back out into the corridor and says, 'Mol, The Boss is *definitely* up to something. I just don't know what it is.'

'Why?' I say, checking my desk drawers to see what's gone missing over the weekend. (The rest of the Fruit Pastilles and, weirdly, a packet of Period Pain Relief.)

'He says he's going to conference by himself,' says Greg, searching for his missing Twix, and failing to find it. 'Says he doesn't need a minder.'

'He's delusional,' I say. 'He's never been known to get himself to a meeting on time yet. Or not one he was *supposed* to be at anyway.'

'Well, *you* tell him,' says Greg. 'I've already tried. He says he's meeting someone there who can help him out if necessary.'

I have no idea who *that* could be, and Andrew refuses

to tell me, when I phone him to discuss it. He also refuses to budge.

'I'll be fine,' he says, 'and I don't want you there, anyway, Molly. I'm not convinced you're on my side, seeing as you *will* keep disobeying my clear instructions not to talk to Party staff.'

There follows a protracted argument, during which I win points by reminding Andrew of the various near-disasters that I managed to avert when I accompanied him to conference last year; then lose them all again when he accuses me of implying that he's an idiot, and says that Greg can go with him this year instead of me.

Now I just have to find a way to tell Max that I've botched our secret love-nest plan. Hic. *Hic.* Oh, bloody hell.

### TUESDAY, 21 SEPTEMBER

I know Greg admits that tact isn't his forte but honestly – talk about rubbing salt into my (self-inflicted) wound.

He appears insanely cheerful when I arrive at the office, and is wearing the ridiculous hat Andrew got from Igor, to which he has attached a piece of A5 paper bearing the House of Commons Crest. On it he's written – in *huge* black letters – 'Guess who's off to conference!'

That reaction's *such* a mark of inexperience. If Greg had ever been to conference before, he'd know it's nothing to get excited about – not unless you have a plan to turn it into a secret love-nest, which I don't think he does. The jogging hasn't succeeded in attracting *any* girlfriends yet, and his stupid hat's not going to help.

'You do realise your room will be shitty, even though

344

you're the new *Goldenballs*, don't you?' I say to him. 'And that Andrew will describe it as "perfectly functional", however bad it is – which is probably *very* bad? Marie-Louise said it was the only one she could get in the same hotel as his, and that it isn't used at all outside conference season.'

'I don't care,' says Greg. 'I won't be there much. I'll be in a *lady's* room. There's sex on tap at conference. That's what Tony from Regional says.'

'Well, *I've* never had any of it, if it is,' I say.

I'm not likely to get any now, either, am I? Not now that Max and I can't go. Life's a bitch and then you die, as Dinah always says, when drunk. Sometimes when she's sober, too.

Greg remains so over-excited that he can't concentrate on anything all day. He just keeps skipping around the office, singing, 'I'm off to conference and gonna get laid, hurrah, hurrah!' to the tune of 'The Animals Went in Two by Two'. It's like being incarcerated with someone with a very bad case of ADHD.

'Don't be offensive,' he says, when I mention the similarity. 'My mother is a *fabulous* woman.'

'What's that got to do with it?' I say.

'The alternative name for ADHD is "Bad Parenting Syndrome",' says Greg, in a manner that leaves no room for doubt.

As a result, I decide I'd better be the one to phone Mrs Engleby back. She wants the authorities to do more to sort out her son, who's already on Ritalin even though he's only six.

During our conversation, she swears compulsively, and with perfect enunciation, but the rest of her conversation is virtually unintelligible, partly because she pauses every few seconds to shout highly inventive threats at someone, in a very loud voice. Presumably her son, though I suppose she *could* be aiming them at me.

By the time she's finished, I feel like running around and kicking things, too, and I can't concentrate at all, unlike Johnny, who's becoming *hyper*-focused. He spends the afternoon trying to persuade me to meet him again next month, and says he's willing to repeat the journey to Lichford, too – as long as I take charge of his hotel booking this time.

'So I don't end up with another crummy single room,' he says. 'There'll be fewer hazards in a less confined space.'

True, but when is he going to realise that I am *not* his PA? Maybe he'd like me to remember his wedding anniversary, and send flowers to his wife, while I'm arranging a location in which to have sex with him. Or *not* to have sex, if the shambles last time is anything to go by.

Anyway, I'm not at all sure that I want to carry on with this affair, if an affair is what it is. I shall take a trip to Ann Summers instead and buy something that Max will find impossible to resist. Along with some gripe water, for hiccup prevention.

## WEDNESDAY, 22 SEPTEMBER

I have never felt such an idiot in my life. And I am *never* going to Ann Summers again. What on earth are you supposed to *do* with some of that stuff?

It's all Greg's fault. His conference song's becoming really tedious now, so when he asks me to go to the pub at lunchtime, 'to wash away the sound of Mr Meeeeurghn's malodorous voice', I refuse. Greg's singing is way more annoying than Mr Meeeeurghn's screech.

'I can't,' I say. 'I've got to go shopping.' I don't say for what.

I'm not too sure myself, but I need to do *something* to get things back on the right track with Max, and to stop these bloody hiccups. I get them every time Johnny sends me an email now.

I've never been in Ann Summers before. I know Ellen has, because she says it's 'crap compared to Sinsins', wherever *that* is. I couldn't find it on the Lichford retail map.

Anyway, I stand outside the shop for a while, plucking up courage, and then dive in through the door when no one's looking. I have a near-miss with a rotating display and have to stand still again for a moment to calm myself down. Then I start to look around.

Everything's made of *luminous* plastic, like those horrible toys the kids used to insist on putting on their Christmas lists. I always ignored them and got something wooden and tasteful from the Early Learning Centre instead, but I'm not sure what the Brio equivalent of a sex toy is.

There's tons of stuff for sale, too. So much that I get quite dizzy trying to take it all in. No wonder psychologists say we're becoming stressed by having too much choice, not to mention a shortage of clear instructions.

Don't get me wrong – not everything is a complete mystery. I'm not *totally* stupid, and anyway some of the things are self-explanatory, but I've no idea what others are for. *Or* where they're supposed to go. I used to have my finger on the pulse!

Might as well face up to it: I'll have to ask someone for assistance. Maybe I can pretend to be foreign, and say I'm having trouble reading the labels.

'*Bonjour*,' I say, as I approach the counter. '*Je m'appelle Marie-Louise. Pouvez-vous m'aider, s'il vous plaît?*'[36]

'Why you talkin' like that, love?' says an all-too-familiar and excessively loud voice. 'You're Mr Sinclair's secretary, aren't you? Mrs Bennett?'

Oh, *Jesus* Christ. It's Mr Beales. Oh, and *Mrs* Beales, too. How lovely. Their Ann Summers bags are full to bursting.

I have no idea what to do next, except run away – so that's *exactly* what I do.

## THURSDAY, 23 SEPTEMBER

I'm still getting over yesterday's trauma when Josh ruins another shopping trip. Honestly, my son poses a serious danger to the general public. Or at least to certain people's mental health – including mine. God knows what Holly sees in him.

Max and I decide to do this week's food shop straight after work – at the Asda near the cinema, instead of our

---

[36] Bonjour. Je m'appelle Marie-Louise. Pouvez-vous m'aider, s'il vous plaît?: Hello, my name is Marie-Louise. Could you help me, please? (She asked for that.)

local branch of Sainsbury's. I have decided that going further afield will lessen my chances of being spotted and harassed by constituents, and save me having to wear a disguise. Now I wish we hadn't bothered.

'We'll pick Josh up once he finishes work, and then shop together as a family,' says Max. 'Then no one can argue about what we have for dinner.'

This sounds reasonable, but the trouble starts when Josh doesn't finish work on time and, then, when he does finally get into the car, he claims that he's far too exhausted to traipse round a supermarket.

'It's tiring, standing around for four-and-a-half hours, bored out of your head,' he says. 'And with people being rude to you.'

Apart from the fact that I'm full-time and sit down to work, after today I know exactly how he feels, and I can't face doing the shopping either. It's quite snuggly here in the car, with the seat reclined – and peaceful, too.

'I suppose I'll have to go in by myself, then,' says Max. 'While you two lazy buggers stay in the car and lounge about.'

I feel a bit guilty, but still very snuggly – until Josh suddenly opens the car door and lets in a gust of cold air.

'Shut the door, Josh. It's freezing,' I say, then, 'Where do *you* think you're going?'

'Ssh,' he says, then rushes over to the photo booth machine that's situated just outside the shop.

I watch as he fumbles around in the slot where the photos come out, before he comes running back to the car, yanks the door open and throws himself headlong onto the back seat.

'Got it,' he says. 'He can't outwit *me* by changing his schedule.'

Before I can ask *what* he's got, or who he's talking about, I see a man pull back the curtain of the booth and step out onto the pavement. He goes to the slot and removes what is presumably a set of photos, looks down at them, then jerks his head up and starts scanning the car park. He doesn't look very happy at all.

'Who is that man, and what's he doing, Josh?' I say.

'Shut up, Mum, and tell me when he's gone.' Josh seems to be fumbling about and trying to put something into his wallet.

'What have you got there?' I say, at the same time as I make a grab for it. Call it maternal instinct, but I *know* when Josh is up to something.

I turn on the interior light, to find myself looking at a photograph of a man. The same man that I can see out of the car window. It's a single photograph, not the usual set of four, and has two very neatly torn edges.

'Josh,' I say. 'What *is* this? Why have you got a photograph of that man over there?'

'He's the photo booth repair man,' says Josh. 'I just really like his funny face.'

'Why?' I say. The man doesn't look like a bundle of laughs to me. In fact, he looks very grumpy indeed.

Josh explains that he and his new work colleagues are regulars at Asda, where they buy their snacks after work. (Josh says only idiots pay cinema prices for food.) Then

350

they hang around in the car park outside, eating and gossiping, and watching the man who services the photo booth. *This* man.

'He comes quite often,' says Josh. 'I suspect he thinks there's a major problem with the workings of the booth.'

'Why are you giggling, Josh?' I say. I can't see anything amusing about a man who's just trying to do his job, against all odds. I know exactly how he feels.

'I'm *trying* to tell you,' says Josh, who's still laughing, 'if you'll just shut up for a minute. He gets into the photo booth, starts fiddling around with the machinery, and then he takes some photos of himself.'

Josh pauses while he sits up cautiously, peers out of the window, then ducks down again, very fast. The man is still standing where he was five minutes ago, still looking around him for something or other. He still doesn't look very funny, either.

Josh wriggles around on the back seat, trying to find somewhere to put his legs, and kicks me with the foot of his dodgy one.

'Ow,' I say. 'That hurt. Stop fidgeting, and sit up sensibly. You shouldn't be bending your damaged knee like that.'

'Can't sit up,' says Josh. 'Sorry, Mum. I might be seen, but there's no room to lie properly flat in here. Anyway, where was I? Oh, yes. So, then he carries on working inside the booth for a while – with the curtain still drawn across the front. When he's finished, he comes out, and picks up his photos, to check whether they've printed out okay.'

351

'And your involvement in this is . . .?' I say, though now I'm not sure that I want to know.

'Well, as soon as the photos come out, one of us rushes over, and grabs them out of the machine,' says Josh. 'While the man's still inside the booth.'

'You take his photos?' I say, appalled. 'That's *theft*, you know.'

'Not *all* of them,' says Josh. 'We just tear one off, and then we put the others back into the slot. Really confuses him.'

'Give me your wallet,' I say. '*Now*, or you're grounded. *Hand it over!*'

'Killjoy,' says Josh, glaring at me, as he does as he's told.

'Joshua,' I say, looking inside it in disbelief. 'There are twelve *different* photos in here. How long has this been going on?'

'A few weeks,' says Josh. 'Ever since I started work. He's getting crosser every time it happens.'

I don't blame the poor guy. I am, quite clearly, the parent of a juvenile delinquent.

## FRIDAY, 24 SEPTEMBER

The Boss graciously allows me to do surgery with him today, as Greg is otherwise engaged in frantically trying to make last-minute changes to Andrew's schedule for the Party conference, for which Marie-Louise has now abdicated *all* responsibility. You'd swear she knew I'd implicated her in the Ann Summers incident.

'Greg will need to know where Andrew is supposed

352

to be when he's in Manchester, more than I will,' she says, when I phone her to ask why she's not handling the conference diary. 'And I hear *he* is going instead of you, this year – *c'est vrai?*'

'Yes,' I say, 'it *is* true. Greg is the new *Goldenballs* – but you should still have warned him not to let The Boss make any entries into the diary himself, for God's sake. Now Andrew's double-booked all over the place.'

I'm pretty sure Marie-Louise stifles a laugh when she says, '*Mon Dieu!*'

Greg's language skills are limited to saying, '*Shit!*' and '*F\*ck's sake!*' for most of the day, as he tries to re-schedule all the appointments that Andrew claims to have already 'arranged'. The stress seems to have made him forget all about his attempt to expand the nation's vocabulary.

'The Boss probably caused all this confusion on purpose, so that he can lose me once we get there,' he says. 'Seeing as he didn't want a minder interfering with his plans.'

'Maybe we could fit him with a GPS tracker,' I say. 'Perhaps Officer Sexy could help with that?'

'Too late now,' says Greg, 'I'll just have to stay on duty twenty-four hours a day. It's going to be *hell*.'

His mock-despair is totally unconvincing, as he's still really over-excited about conference, and I'm tired of it now. Especially as he's cost me and Max our chance of a hotel room *à deux*.

'It's not going to be *that* much fun at conference, Greg,' I say, in another mean-spirited effort to rain on his parade (which is where that stupid hat he's still wearing looks as if it belongs).

Greg disagrees, and then says that he's decided to stay teetotal throughout so that he can keep his wits about him. I assume that this is because he wants to stand the best possible chance of keeping up a politically correct facade, but he says that's *not* the reason.

'I don't want to put the ladies off, by getting in a state,' he says. 'Not while I am in such great physical shape, thanks to my programme of exercise.'

Then he jogs off to the bus stop, and I walk home, in the opposite direction.

I'm quite out of breath when I get there, as I tried a quick bit of jogging en route, just in case it does help your sex-life, so now I'd better put my feet up for the next hour or so, and phone Connie for an update on Dr Snuffleopagus.

I need to take much better care of myself, seeing as I have such a stressful job – especially as I've just remembered that I've forgotten to make an appointment with the GP about my blood pressure, which I'm positive isn't going *down*.

Josh's is probably even higher than mine, though – and his face is green when he finally comes in from work, close to midnight.

'Good God,' I say. 'What on earth's the matter, Josh? You look *terrible*.'

'I *feel* terrible,' he says. 'You won't believe what I found, when I was on clearing tonight.'

'Clearing?' I say. It must be a technical cinematography term.

'Cleaning up after all the punters have left,' says Josh. 'I picked up a large Coke cup from under one of the seats and – oh – my – God.'

'What's so bad about a Coke cup?' I say. 'Am I missing something?'

'I wished *I'd* missed the bloody thing,' says Josh. 'There was a *huge* poo inside it.' He adds that, when he told his manager about it, she didn't even seem surprised.

'She just told me to get rid of it,' he says. 'Behaved as if it was perfectly normal, so God knows how often the same thing's going to happen.'

I get up from the sofa to give him a sympathetic hug, but he shakes me off and says, ''Night, Mum. I'm going to bed, as soon as I've had a shower. Probably using bleach or something. Don't tell Holly about this, will you? She's bound to dump me if she finds out I'm handling faeces for a living.'

Max wakes up at that point, so I tell him instead. He is less than sympathetic. 'Bet they didn't warn Josh about *that* in Film Studies,' he says.

I am going to write to the manager of the cinema and suggest that they allocate customers' names and addresses to specific seats, like airlines do. Then, if customers leave *anything* behind when they leave, the cinema staff can post it back to them.

Greg would probably offer to hand-deliver it, now I come to think of it. He *is* an expert in the field.

**SATURDAY, 25 SEPTEMBER**
Sam's here for the weekend again. Well, he's here in

person, but I'm not at all sure where his head is. Somewhere in the Isle of Skye, I think – home to his latest conquest, courtesy of the internet dating site.

Her name is Shona, and she has six children. *Six* – imagine that! Six boys who could all turn out like Josh. It doesn't bear thinking about.

'I didn't know you even *liked* kids,' I say.

'Depends if I like their mothers or not,' says Sam. He spends the afternoon making us look at all the photos that Shona has sent him, on his laptop. I can't see them properly though, as I'm standing at completely the wrong angle to the screen, probably because Max has elbowed me out of the way.

He's only supposed to be faking interest out of politeness, but then I catch a glimpse of Shona and realise why he's paying such close attention. I wouldn't have thought you could buy underwear like that in the wilds of Scotland. They must have a branch of Ann Summers on Skye.

'I'll be seeing *that* in the flesh next week,' says Sam, with what can only be described as a leer.

'Huh,' I say. 'Not if she's got six children, you won't.' Does he know nothing about teenagers at all?

'It's the week they're at their dad's,' says Sam. 'So we all know what that means, don't we? We can have sex all over the house, if we like.'

I scowl in envy, at the same time as Max decides to go and make a coffee. He's got a *very* thoughtful expression on his face, though God knows what he's thinking *about*.

While he crashes cups and spoons around – rather more noisily than is necessary – I wonder how long Sam thinks that a love affair with someone who lives on Skye is going to last. About the same time as a 'relationship' with someone who lives in Russia, I should imagine – despite Johnny's claim that distance makes the heart grow fonder. (*That's* certainly not why Igor's so desperate to get permission for his wife to join him in the UK. He's just worried about what she gets up to in Moscow now that he's not there to keep an eye on her.)

Anyway, there must be a nice girl closer to home who would suit Sam just as well as Shona – and if we leave 'nice' out of the equation, I have the perfect solution.

'Well, if you don't mind kids part-time, Sam,' I say, 'why don't you ask Ellen out on a date? Lichford's a hell of a lot nearer to where you live than the Isle of Skye.'

Such a cunning plan, devised on the spur of the moment – and which would kill two birds with one perfectly rounded stone. I am *such* a creative thinker when under pressure. Some of the time.

'I don't *like* Ellen,' says Sam, unhelpfully.

'Bugger,' I say, at the same time as Max says, 'Why on earth not?'

The answer to that question should be obvious, as far as I'm concerned.

'You said she makes a lot of noise during sex,' says Sam. 'I can't be doing with all that. Whatever would my lodgers think?'

'Same as me, probably,' I say. 'That she protests too much.'

'Are you questioning my sexual capabilities?' says Sam, missing the point as only someone with a penis can.

Now he sounds just like Dad, who – coincidentally – phones very shortly afterwards.

'I'm knackered,' he says, by way of introduction. 'Dinah's been here all day, getting in my way. I'm *trying* to do some DIY.'

'What?' I say. 'Why?'

'Why what?' says Dad.

I don't blame him. My syntax has gone to pot, following the abject failure of the Sam and Ellen project.

'Why *both*, I suppose,' I say. 'Why was Dinah there, and why are you doing DIY?'

'Dinah was snooping,' says Dad, 'and I'm doing DIY because the house is looking tatty. I've spent too much time abroad this last few months. Need to get back on top of things.'

There's a lewd joke there, but Dad would usually be the one to make it. Oddly, he doesn't.

'Anyway,' he says. 'Enough about me. How are *you*?'

'Fed up,' I say, once I've got over the shock of being asked. 'I don't know why.'

'You need a holiday,' says Dad. 'And some excitement in your life. I feel twenty years younger these days.'

'Ah,' I say, thinking of all the fun Dad would normally have had with *that* comment, too. He's not his usual self at all.

Maybe he had a revelation while he was away, and realised he needed to give his life a bigger purpose? Perhaps he's going to volunteer for Oxfam, or become a goodwill ambassador with the United Nations, doing his bit to increase understanding between people from different cultures?

'So,' I say, 'are you planning on going back to Thailand, then, if you reckon it does you so much good? Or have you got something else in mind? You did say you were bored, last time you went.'

'I was,' says Dad. 'Everyone there speaks bloody pidgin.'

## SUNDAY, 26 SEPTEMBER

Honestly, I might just as well have gone to conference. Greg's been on the phone all day about one thing or another. He's still texting me now, completely distraught, even though I keep replying that I am asleep.

'I am going to have man-boobs the size of a house again,' he says. 'And I will *never* get another girlfriend.'

I give in. There is quite obviously no point in aiming for an early night. 'Why?' I say. Or text, to be more accurate.

'Third meal I've had to eat in the last four hours,' Greg replies.

It turns out that one of Andrew's diary cock-ups involved accepting invitations to three separate dinners, all scheduled for this evening. One buffet and two sit-down meals.

'Even The Boss is full,' says Greg. 'Never thought I'd see the day. He could live off all the food he's got stuck in his beard for the next week, too. Answer the phone, I'm going to ring you.'

*God*. I do as I'm told. It's not as if there's anything better to do, I suppose. I should have tried much harder when I was in Ann Summers.

'He didn't remember about the third meal until we were half-way through the second one,' Greg says, as soon as I answer the phone. 'I feel sick.'

'You sound sober, though,' I say. 'Congratulations. I didn't think you'd manage this teetotal thing.'

'There's no room in my stomach for anything other than all this bloody food,' says Greg. 'And anyway, Andrew's drunk enough for both of us. *And* he's left his mobile somewhere – so if he wanders off, I'll *never* find him.'

'Well, don't feel obliged to look too hard if that happens,' I say. 'How's it going apart from that?'

'I haven't got off with *any* women yet,' says Greg. 'It's a dead loss. Andrew keeps getting in there first. Why *do* they like him so much?'

'Raw sensuality,' I say, to which Greg makes a retching noise that sounds alarmingly realistic. Then the line goes dead.

Much like my sex-life, as Max is now asleep.


## MONDAY, 27 SEPTEMBER

I miss Greg. It's weird not having anyone with whom to share the horrors of the day, though it sounds as if he's got his own nightmares to contend with.

When he phones mid-morning, he says, 'Any idea where Andrew is?'

'No,' I say. 'You're the one minding him. In Manchester. Why don't *you* know where he is?'

'Well, I was supposed to meet him in the hotel lobby, and he hasn't turned up. *And* he's not answering his phone.'

'Oh, so he found *that* then, did he?' I say.

'I found it, not him,' says Greg. 'But as soon as I'd given it back to him, he said he had to go outside to make a call, and then I lost him. F*ck knows where he's got to.'

'Well, he's bound to turn up,' I say. 'Like the proverbial bad penny.'

'Yeah, but what on earth's he going to get up to in the meantime?' says Greg. 'The man can hardly dress himself.'

'What?' I say. I know Andrew's not renowned for his sartorial splendour, but nakedness? Who does he think he is – Annoying Ellen?

'I had to do up half his shirt buttons before we left for all those dinners last night,' says Greg. 'And re-tie his tie. I felt like bloody Jeeves.'

'Well, have you tried his room?' I say. Sometimes people do overlook the obvious.

'He's not answering the door, even if he *is* in there,' says Greg, reminding me of something I'd prefer to forget. 'Phone me if you hear from him. I'm going to search the secure zone now.'

I don't hear anything further until mid-afternoon, when Greg texts: 'Found him. Who is Vicky?'

Bloody hell. There's a blast from the past. Vicky was an intern once, back in the days when I was still relatively beard-free and Greg was probably still at school. She was useless at casework, but an expert in schmoozing The Boss. All that manic hair-flicking used to make me feel quite murderous.

I text Greg back: 'Ex-intern. Why?'

He doesn't reply, and now he's stopped answering his damned phone as well. So I spend the rest of the afternoon bursting with curiosity, while trying to fend off all the constituents who are phoning up to discuss Red Ed,[37] and whether we're going to have another Winter of Discontent. None of it does my blood pressure any good at all.

Things don't improve when I get home, as now Max seems to have gone AWOL too. There's no sign of him for hours, and he's not answering his phone either. I've envisaged every possible disaster that could have befallen him by the time he finally turns up, at about 9:00pm.

'How was your day?' he says, as if he hasn't arrived home three hours later than usual.

'Never mind that,' I say. 'Where have you been? I was really starting to worry.'

I don't mention that, in between imagining various hideous fatal accidents, I have also been envisaging Max having rampant and no doubt unnecessarily noisy sex with Ellen, in a secret location somewhere, probably while a fire alarm was going off. I'm not sure which scenario was the worst.

---

[37] Red Ed: Ed Miliband, now leader of the Labour Party, after stabbing his brother in the back according to Greg, or striking a blow for socialism according to The Boss. Also known as Gromit by Mum, who tends to get him and Wallace muddled up.

'I was at a customer's,' he says. 'I had no signal, sorry, Mol.'

'What – at a customer's until *now*?' I say. Max usually finishes work before I do.

'It was Mrs Bloom again,' he says. 'This time she couldn't get her electric chair to work.'

'Well, couldn't it have waited until tomorrow?' I say. 'You won't get paid for this.'

Good grief, now I'm going all jobsworth. Before you know it, I'll be working to rule and picketing the office, while the union stands behind me, albeit only in spirit. I can't think what's got into me – and obviously, nor can Max.

## TUESDAY, 28 SEPTEMBER

Blimey. Sounds as if things aren't going well at conference. Well, not for Greg, anyway. (David Miliband might say the same, but that's another story.)

I'm not used to Greg sounding insecure but, just before I leave work, he phones to say that he thinks he's been rendered surplus to requirements by Vicky. God knows what's going on.

'I don't mind not having to do The Boss' buttons up any more, Mol, but she's getting on my bloody nerves, marching about carrying all his papers, and making me walk two steps behind,' he says.

I don't like the sound of this at all. 'Well, how did he meet up with her?' I say.

'No idea. It must've been the night that he disappeared. When I finally found him the next day, she was already in tow. There's something familiar about her – but I just can't work out why. I'm sure we've never met before.'

'You can't have done,' I say. 'She's well before your time.'

'Well, I don't know what's familiar then,' says Greg. 'But something is, and it's horrible anyway. *She's* horrible, to be exact. I feel like a member of the First Wives' Club. Redundancy can only be a step away.'

I hope he's wrong, as that's a very unnerving thought, but Vicky's bound to have a hidden agenda of some sort. She always did. That's why she got such a good job, as a lobbyist, which I thought she still had. But if she *has*, then why is she wasting time with Andrew? You could lobby him all day, and he'd still forget how you wanted him to vote.

I'm so distracted by wondering why Vicky's made a reappearance now, and what it might mean, that I almost walk straight into Ellen on my way home. She's heading in the opposite direction, into town.

'Molly,' she says. 'How are you? Long time no see.'

I consider saying, 'Not long enough' but, before I can pluck up the courage, she continues, 'Max was late home last night, wasn't he? Wonder what *he'd* been up to?' Then she winks, says, 'By-ee!' and carries on walking.

Now Greg's not the only one who feels as if he's a wife who's about to be traded in.

## WEDNESDAY, 29 SEPTEMBER

Honestly, sex is like buses, isn't it? You wait for months for a smidgin of it, and then – all of a sudden – it's coming at you from every angle under the sun. (The bus analogy could have been better, but my brain is toast.)

At lunchtime today, I'm still wondering what Ellen meant by what she said last night, when Johnny sends me an email, catching me by surprise.

'I am ordering you to have virtual sex with me,' he says. 'Right this minute.'

It's a very different approach to his real-life one, and much more effective, surprisingly. I had no idea I was so unquestioningly obedient. It's a rather worrying startle response.

Johnny's not happy with things staying in the realm of fantasy, though, and so he spends the whole of the virtual post-coital period going on and on about when we're going to meet up next.

'You said "No commitment" at the beginning of all this,' I say. 'So what happened to that?'

'Yes, well,' he says. 'I know I did. I wasn't expecting you to sneak your way under my radar like you have.'

If I have, I don't know how, as I certainly haven't been trying to – and the comparison with a guided missile isn't particularly flattering.

'We could be like the couple in that old film,' continues Johnny, unaware that he's given offence. 'The one where they meet up once a year for twenty-five years, always at the same hotel. *Same Time Next Year*, I think it was called.'

'Well, then, that means we shouldn't meet up again until *next* year,' I say. 'Seeing as we've already had this year's rendezvous.'

'That doesn't count,' says Johnny. 'We stayed fully clothed throughout, in case you've forgotten.'

Imagine having to re-live *that* twenty-four more times! I don't think I want to, so I tell Johnny that the fire alarm has just gone off and that I need to take charge of the evacuation myself.

'I am the designated fire officer,' I say, to which Johnny sends back one of those annoying emoticons. The one that denotes an incredulous face.

I ignore him for the rest of the afternoon, and am feeling horribly guilty about the virtual sex by the time that I get home. That is until Max says he's not speaking to me after my reaction to the Mrs Bloom business, and claims to have no idea what Ellen was winking at. Then I don't feel guilty at all.

'Right,' says Josh. 'I've had enough of this parental not-speaking business. Let's all watch *X Factor* on catch-up together. Then you two can bond over your astonishment at the sheer number of delusional people in the UK. Always works for me and Holly, whenever she's in a mood with me.'

He presses *play*, while I give him a funny look, in case the delusional reference was directed at me. Then Dinah phones.

'It gets worse,' she says.

'What does?'

I have no idea what she's on about, although it probably doesn't matter much. That contestant is *obviously* a usual suspect. I can always tell the nutters before they open their mouths.

'P-ns nm,' says Dinah, or something like that.

Max has just announced that Louis Walsh would put a potato through to the judges' houses, if it was the only Irish thing available.

'What did you say, Di?' I say. 'I couldn't hear you. Max was talking.'

'Well, tell him to be quiet,' she says, slurping what could be tea, but is probably wine. 'This is important. Porn's name, or *names*. As in the plural.'

I forget to answer. Well, I don't, really – but with Dinah you never know if a pause indicates your turn to speak, or whether she's just stopping to breathe in, or light a fag.

'Wake *up*, Molly! Didn't you hear what I said?'

'Um, yes,' I say. 'Double-barrelled. Porn.'

This creates a thoroughly unpleasant image of Mr and Mrs Beales in the act, accompanied by the paraphernalia they bought in Ann Summers.

'Yes, *Porn*,' says Dinah. 'And, *yes*, double-barrelled. Guess what her *other* name is, though? I overheard Dad telling his neighbour, when I visited.'

'I don't know, Dinah,' I say. 'Why do I always have to *guess*? Can't you just tell me, for once?'

I might as well give up watching this whole series of *X Factor*. I missed it last week too, due to David and Susie's stupid aerial.

'Well, you've spoiled it now,' says Dinah. 'But I might as well tell you, anyway. It's Poon!'

'Now you're really making it up,' I say. 'Don't be ridiculous. *Poon?* As in Poon-*Tang?*'

Josh looks up and makes a shocked face. Sometimes I'm sure he thinks I know nothing, and that he is the product of an immaculate conception.

'*Yes*, as in Poon-Tang,' says Dinah, accompanied by the sound of more wine being poured into a glass. '*Porn-Poon. That's* our father's girlfriend's name. And I am not telling you anything else, as you are obviously not listening. Phone me when you can be bothered to give this the attention it deserves.'

Seems to me that I've already given this whole sex thing *plenty* of attention today, but apparently not.

'I'm off to work now,' says Josh, after *X Factor* has finished. 'I'm on the stupidly late shift tonight. Expect more stories about poos in cups when I get home.'

Max doesn't say goodbye, as he's already fallen asleep on the sofa. (Louis Walsh always has that effect.) I may as well catch up with some of the other programmes that I've missed this week: the latest episode of *Wallander* for a start. I know it's subtitled, but I'm *trying* to learn some Swedish while I watch, though that's impossible when Max's snoring is so loud. I glare at him for a while, but daren't yell at him to stop in case that ruins the effect of the *X Factor* bonding experience.

Then I remember Connie's latest scientific tip for the best way to wake someone up.

'If you use this technique, Mum,' she said, 'Dad will return to consciousness so gradually that he won't realise you did anything to him, and he'll think he woke up naturally.'

Presumably this *would* be the case, if I removed my

368

finger from Max's ear quickly enough – but it gets stuck.

'Wha' the hell?' he says, batting my hand away. 'What *are* you doing?'

I don't want to tell him, in case he gets annoyed, so I try to convert the ear-poking into an ear-tickling manoeuvre, motivated by nothing more sinister than affection. I forget that Max's ears are erogenous zones, until my 'caress' is reciprocated with uncharacteristic enthusiasm, and one thing leads to another.

So now I've accidentally had sex with two people, in one day. And I feel riddled with guilt about both. I may as well change *my* name to Porn-Poon, if I'm going to behave like this.

**THURSDAY, 30 SEPTEMBER**

Endorphins are funny things. I'm in a really good mood this morning as I stick a gold star into the diary, watched by Max, who suggests we don't leave it quite so long before we earn another.

Then he gets a text from Sam, who's still away on his sex trip to Skye. It says, 'Incompatible in bed and nothing to talk about. Supposed to be here another two days. Help me, for the love of God!'

Max looks vaguely disappointed. I think he quite fancied Shona, too.

'What shall I tell him to do?' he asks. 'I've got no idea what to suggest.'

'I don't know,' I say. 'He's your friend, and anyway, he always ignores my advice. I *told* him to start reading the women's profiles instead of just looking at their pictures.'

'True,' says Max. 'You did. But you're the one who works for a politician. You *must* be able to think of a cunning excuse to get him out of this.'

'No time,' I say. 'I'm late for work. 'Bye! Give Sam my love.'

Max looks a bit panic-stricken, but I'm sure he'll manage to think of something, which is what I need to do, fast, to help Mr Warner. He's waiting outside the office when I arrive at work.

'You've got to get TV Licensing off my back,' he says. 'They've been persecuting me for years. Won't accept I haven't got a television set.'

Then he goes on to say that he can't sleep at night because he's so sure that they're going to raid his flat.

'You should see all the threatening letters I've had,' he says. 'Once, they even posted a sign on the bus shelter at the end of my road, saying that one household in the street didn't have a TV licence. Everyone *knew* it was me.'

When I tell him not to worry, and that I'm sure I can sort the situation out quite easily, he looks at me as if I am mad.

'How do you prove a negative?' he says, which I have a feeling someone else has said to me fairly recently. I can't remember who it was, though, so I stop trying after a minute or so. It's bound to come back to me when I'm least expecting it. Most things do, whether you want them to or not, sometimes accompanied by hiccuping.

I still haven't remembered by the time I start walking home from work – which is when my brain usually relaxes and starts to process things – so my recall's taking rather longer than usual today. Maybe it's because I'm concentrating on sucking my stomach in while I walk, to make up for not having done any exercises since the purple ball fiasco.

If I power walk everywhere, while breathing in, then I shall be super-fit by the time Max and I earn our next gold star – hopefully very soon, since we've remembered marital sex doesn't *have* to be a chore.

Now I have a big smile on my face, after recalling last night's events – until I turn into our street and nearly get run over by an idiot in a little red convertible, the type that Max always calls a 'hairdresser's car'.

I shout something vaguely abusive, and am in the process of holding up two fingers when the car pulls in and parks just beyond our house. Oops. And *double* oops – the driver's door swings open and Ellen gets out, showing far more thigh than necessary.

I peer towards her in an attempt to spot cellulite, and have just been rewarded by the sight of a dark dimply patch when the passenger door opens and Max almost falls out onto the pavement.

'Holy shit,' I say, as Ellen spots me and shouts, 'Molly! Hi! Look what I picked up on my way home.'

She does one of those infuriating giggles, then says, 'Your husband! So I thought I'd give him a cheap thrill and take him for a spin in my hot new car. What d'you think? Isn't she a babe?'

Gah. *Ga-a-ah*. And why do supposedly adult women feel the need to use words like 'hot' and 'babe'?

'I wouldn't know,' I say, immediately sounding like a repressed introvert who never has sex. And who definitely has no sense of humour. 'I don't know many hot babes with whom to make a useful comparison.'

'Oh, you *are* funny, Molly,' says Ellen. 'You always make me laugh.'

I don't ask whether she normally laughs with me, or *at* me. I'm too busy glaring at Max, who looks awfully red in the face and is very windswept. He really needs to wear his glasses more often, as he obviously hasn't spotted *my* expression.

'God, that was fun,' he says, walking towards me. ''Bye, Ellen, and thanks for the ride. Really blew my cobwebs away.'

I rather thought *I'd* done that, last night.

'Any time,' says Ellen. 'We can make it a regular date.'

I've turned my back by now, so no one can see the face I'm pulling. It's a close approximation of Munch's 'The Scream'.

'Great, isn't she, Mol?' says Max, oblivious to the end. 'I'd love to get my hands on one like that.'

I have no idea if we're talking about the car, or Ellen – and *now* I remember who said you can't prove a negative. Max did – maybe because he didn't think I could prove the opposite. I'm going to have to try, if I want to retain what little remains of my mind.

# CHAPTER SIX

# October

(I can't think of a rhyme for this, or a line of poetry.
I wish I'd never started the whole thing now.)

**FRIDAY, 1 OCTOBER**
Unlike me, The Boss and Greg are both in amazingly good moods this morning, albeit for very different reasons.

'God, I'm glad to be back,' says Greg. 'I'm even pleased to see *your* face, Mol.'

'*Marvellous* conference,' says The Boss. '*Marvellous* company. And now we have the right man as our leader, *The Fightback* can begin in earnest. Red Ed, *he's* our man.'

Greg pulls a Wallace face, while I ask the burning question: 'So, Andrew,' I say. 'Greg tells me Vicky was with you at conference. How did *that* come about?'

'Synchronicity,' says The Boss, also pulling a face. The one he uses to suggest that he's innocent of whatever you suspect him of.

Then he goes off to his meeting, while Greg continues to expound on the joys of being back at work.

'I felt so useless at conference,' he says, 'with that awful woman taking care of everything. Must be how Andrew feels, when there's never anything meaningful for him to do.'

An hour later, Greg demands that he be allowed to take an early lunch. He says that it is an emergency as, if he does not escape this madhouse, he will be forced to resign, with immediate effect.

'Why?' I say.

I've been at least as polite to him as usual, and I didn't even swear when he ordered me to make him another cup of coffee, or point out that being *Goldenballs* was going to his head.

'Mr Franklin's just phoned,' he says. 'From the seaside. He took his fatmobile there on the train.'

'And?' I say.

I can't see what's so surprising about that. Mr F takes his fatmobile everywhere – *because he's fat*. That's the whole point, plus I am too busy to bother with this. I am trying to decipher an invitation from the Brazilian ambassador, and flowery handwriting is hard to read.

Greg sighs, as if there is no hope for dingbats like me. 'He's run out of petrol, for f*ck's sake,' he says. 'Half-way down the bloody pier. And now he wants *me* to rescue him.'

'Ah,' I say. 'Did you say you would?'

'No,' says Greg. 'If I'd been there, I'd have pushed

him off the end, but as that's not an option, I told him to phone the AA instead. And if I don't get out of here for a bit, I'll be needing the *other* AA.' He puts his coat on, and heads for the door. 'So much for a renewed sense of purpose,' he says, as he stamps off down the corridor.

'Gregory here?' says Andrew, when he returns from wherever it is that he's been for the two hours since his meeting ended. Food must have been involved, as there's a large stain on his tie that definitely wasn't there this morning.

'No,' I say. 'He was called away on a rescue mission.'

'Pah. You'll have to do surgery with me, then,' says Andrew, his good mood evaporating before my eyes.

He's no happier when he realises that none of the usual suspects have made an appointment for today – though that's a miracle in itself. Even I don't recognise any of the people in the waiting room, for once.

Most of them want to talk about the government's NHS and welfare reforms, which is not quite as easy for The Boss to handle as signing a shotgun licence for a madman. As a result, Andrew looks quite relieved when Miss Ventnor decides to buck the trend: she's got a thing about light pollution.

'City dwellers are being deprived of the pleasure to be had from seeing the stars,' she says. To The Boss, as she doesn't seem to have noticed me. Maybe she only sees properly in the dark.

'I agree,' says Andrew. 'It's a *terrible* shame. There's nothing like a starry sky.'

He's been looking a bit starry-eyed himself, since he got back. I do hope it isn't the Vicky effect.

It may just be due to Miss Ventnor, who's rather pretty, and also quite poetic, especially on the subject of what birds and animals suffer as a result of becoming confused between day and night. Andrew's nodding his head so much in agreement, I'm sure I can hear vertebrae cracking.

The mutual love-in takes so long that – by the time The Boss has agreed to join the Campaign Against Light Pollution, and I have shown Miss Ventnor out and ushered in Mrs Jackson to take her place – we're running *really* late. The Boss doesn't seem worried, though. Mrs J's even more attractive than her predecessor.

'I'm sure you didn't agree with that Tory MP's comments about degrees of rape, did you, Mr Sinclair?' she says.

'No, indeed I didn't,' says Andrew, right on cue. '*Wholly* irresponsible.'

'Well, then,' says Mrs J. 'What are you going to do to protect the women of Lichford – and to stop the Council's plans to turn the streetlights off?'

'If you'll just excuse me,' I say, standing up. 'I have an urgent call to make. You'll be able to manage this one without me, won't you, Andrew?'

I don't wait for an answer, as I beat my retreat.

The Boss is furious when he finds me hiding in the Labour Party office, telling Joan what's just happened. He's even crosser when he hands me back the surgery notes I left behind, the ones with 'synchronicity' written all over them.

## SATURDAY, 2 OCTOBER

Bloody, bloody Christmas. Why does it have to start so early? And as for that stupid Hallowe'en . . .

The florist I pass on my way into town has pumpkins piled up in the window, but they're all swathed in Christmas tree lights.

It's obviously the same story where Dinah lives, so she makes a pre-emptive strike.

'Now Gary Glitter's bored with Thailand,' she says, 'are you going to have him over for Christmas?'

'What?' I say. 'No, I'm *not*. It's not my turn. I did it last year. Why can't he come to you this time?'

'He's too annoying.'

I don't know why Dinah thinks that means that *I* should put up with him twice in a row, but she claims she's a special case.

'Dad likes *your* kids,' she says, 'but he *hates* Jake. He even calls him *Damian*, to his face.'

'Damian?' I say. I've never heard Dad call Jake anything other than 'that disturbing child'.

'From *The Omen*,' Dinah says, as I hear her lighter click. 'Dad thinks it's funny, but I don't appreciate him looking through Jake's hair every five minutes, saying that he's trying to find the number 666.'

I laugh, and she hangs up on me.

I feel quite well-disposed towards *my* kids after that, so I try to call Connie but she doesn't answer. There's no point even *trying* to contact Josh, as he's at work. There's only one way to see my offspring's lovable faces, and that's by looking at their photo albums on Facebook.

'What are you doing, Mol?' says Max, when he looks over my shoulder. 'Stalking our kids? It's probably not necessary.'

'I know it isn't,' I say. 'I am *not* stalking them. I am admiring them. Like some people admire mid-life crisis-style sports cars, and their drivers.'

Max looks up at the ceiling and sighs, but doesn't say anything at all. He doesn't need to, seeing as he's already managed to make me anxious. What does he mean by '*probably* not necessary'?

I check Connie's page first, as she's the one who's furthest away, but she appears to be doing nothing more sinister than playing on *Farmville* most of the time, so I don't need to worry about her. Unless that's not the *only* thing that she's doing in a virtual reality environment.

She could be up to *anything* online, with strange men from Eastern bloc countries, now I come to think of it. Which I wish I hadn't, as now I've started to hiccup again. I breathe in and hold my nose while Max brings me a glass of water.

'I don't know why the hell you keep getting hiccups so often these days,' he says, 'or why you've got such a thing about Ellen. She's just a nice friendly neighbour of ours.'

I pretend I haven't heard him and, once the hiccups have finally subsided, I open Josh's Facebook page. He hardly ever updates his status, but he's posted a few photos of Holly – looking unusually grumpy – and a video, since the last time I snooped. Its title is *24 Minutes, Episode One*, which sounds innocuous enough so I press *play*.

I don't know who is doing the filming, but the video opens with Josh and Robbie in Robbie's car driving towards Sainsbury's (so at least the Asda photo booth repair man seems to be off the hook). The next shot is of the boys unloading something very large into a space in the middle of the car park, which is full of shoppers. A number of them glance over at the boys, who are struggling with metal poles and what seems to be a padded, long, black thing.

Josh is giggling like a maniac – I'd know that laugh *anywhere* even though he's not currently in shot – but I still have no idea what he and Robbie are up to, until . . . Oh, *Christ*. I can't believe my eyes. Josh's weights bench is now fully assembled, and situated smack bang in the middle of the car park.

Josh is lying on it, lifting weights, while Robbie is his personal trainer, convincingly attired in a black and orange shell-suit and wielding a stop-watch. Both boys appear oblivious to the incredulous stares of passers-by, and the whole thing seems to go on for hours.

I can barely watch by the time a very unamused security guard approaches, and the film stops dead.

Max replays the clip several times, without comment, while I wonder what numbers I'd find on Josh's scalp. *If* I ever dared to look.

## SUNDAY, 3 OCTOBER

Josh says that he and Robbie have set up a film company, and are making a series of episodes of *24 Minutes* in order to convince Holly that Josh won't always have to spend his days (and nights) picking up poos in cups to earn a living. (Apparently, Robbie spilled the beans about *that*, and now Holly's embarrassed to tell people what her boyfriend's job involves.)

'I am going to become the Jack Bauer of Lichford East,' says Josh, 'and then Holly'll be *proud* of me, instead of ashamed. As long as I can prove I haven't got nits.'

'Why does she think you have?' I say, trying to ignore the fact that my head started itching, just at the thought.

'Last time she came to the cinema she saw a little kid scratching like mad,' says Josh. 'Just after I'd served him some popcorn. I'm sure I haven't caught them, but can you double-check, please, Mum?'

I inspect his scalp three times, but there are no nits at all, nor any numbers, as far as I can see. I wonder if you can get nits in *facial* hair? Not that I'll need to worry about that, not once I've had a chance to use my brilliant new eBay purchase, the one that arrived in yesterday's post . . .

It's a springy wand thing, called a *Tweeze-ease* or something, and it works on the same principle as threading, apparently. It also has lurid pink plastic handles, and therefore looks as if would be quite at home on the shelves of Ann Summers.

I wait for Max to doze off after lunch, and then get started.

An hour later, my face is as bald as a baby's bottom, which – surprisingly – proves not to be an entirely good thing. I don't think your face is supposed to be *completely* hairless.

It feels very odd indeed, and I definitely shouldn't have tried to use the wand between my eyebrows. Now I look astonished, probably at the fact that one eyebrow is only half as long as the other. *And* I seem to be developing blotches all over the place.

I slap on some aloe vera, in the hope that this will calm the eruption down.

So much for optimism. When Max wakes up, he opens his eyes and looks straight at me, then blinks several times, before opening them again, much wider this time.

'What the hell's the matter with your face, Mol?' he says, eventually. 'Have you got chicken pox or something?'

I don't reply. Luckily for Max, the phone is ringing.

'Some people are so bloody insensitive,' says Dad, apropos a greeting.

'Yes, they *are*,' I say, looking at Max, though Dad's usually the worst offender. 'What makes you say that now, though?'

'I went to see my next-door neighbours a few days ago – to get away from Dinah for a bit – and I told them all about Porn-Poon while I was there.'

'Ah,' I say. So Dinah *was* right about the double-barrelled bit. 'What did they say that was so upsetting, then?'

'Nothing, while I was there,' says Dad. 'But I've just found out that, afterwards, they told the landlord of my local that I was a dirty old man. Bloody *outrageous* thing to say.'

'Ah,' I say, again, after a fruitless search for a politically correct yet honest response.

'Can't you say anything except, "Ah"?' says Dad. 'Anyone would think *you* were a politician yourself.'

I count to ten, then try again. 'Well, what were they referring to?' I say. Disingenuousness is often grossly under-rated. It's a key skill when you work for an MP.

'God knows,' says Dad. 'I only said that everyone looks the same age in the dark.'

'I hear you're going to Dinah's for Christmas,' I say. 'So that'll probably cheer you up.'

Sometimes, you just have to save yourself.

**MONDAY, 4 OCTOBER**

The first thing Greg says to me this morning is, 'What's the matter with your face? Did you catch chicken pox from the Baron of Oil?'

After seeing my expression, it's also the last thing he says to me until lunchtime, when The Boss phones with some news: Marie-Louise is off sick.

'You'll just have to do my London diary until I sort something out,' he says.

'Why can't Carlotta do the diary?' I ask. 'She's *in* London. That does help, you know – with your *London* diary.'

'She's too busy,' says The Boss.

I seriously doubt *that*. Greg's convinced that Carlotta still takes a siesta every day – probably something to do with her cultural heritage. But I let it go, as I'm more concerned with what's wrong with Marie-Louise. I really hope it isn't chicken pox.

'It's Norovirus,' says Andrew, 'and anyway, it shouldn't take long to find a replacement. I have *a plan*.'

I don't like the sound of this. Andrew's plans always tend to involve shooting himself firmly in both feet. Or shooting me in *my* feet, actually. Also, he sounds even more smug than usual, so that's definitely a worrying sign.

When I phone her to ask, Carlotta claims to have no idea what Andrew's plan might be – though she does blame him for the Norovirus.

'That man *never* washes his hands,' she says. 'Not even when he visits hospitals.'

Then she faxes me through the most urgent appointment letters, and forwards all the emails relating to the diary. There are *millions* of those.

'There's *loads* of other stuff, too,' she says, 'but I'll send all that through to you in this evening's post.'

This promise does not improve my mood. In fact, I am so cross that I spend five minutes swearing while kicking the filing cabinet. Then I have to spend another fifteen minutes trying to get the bottom drawer to open.

Greg starts laughing, so I try to wither him with a look. It doesn't work, even though my face resembles the Infected more than usual.

'Trying to add repairwoman to your job description, now?' he says.

'Shut up, Greg,' I say. 'It's not funny, and I haven't got time for this! Not with all the diary stuff to do.'

'Cheer up, Mol,' says Greg. 'Think of all the fun you can have, sending The Boss to the wrong locations.'

I'd quite like to send the usual suspects to the wrong locations. In far-flung destinations, and with one-way tickets. Miss Chambers rings just before we close, to complain that the man who owns the local post office is refusing to serve her any more.

'Why?' I say.

'Because he didn't like me calling him a Paki,' she says. 'Do something about it. I don't know what this country's coming to.'

'Nor do I,' I say.

I envy that man his self-respect.

## TUESDAY, 5 OCTOBER

I *knew* I was right to be worried about The Boss' plan to deal with the absence of Marie-Louise.

When I arrive at work this morning – ten minutes late, due to phoning NHS Direct to check whether you *can* catch chicken pox twice – Greg is looking very stressed.

'What's up?' I say. 'You look as if you've seen a ghost.'

He puts a finger to his lips and mouths, 'Sssh!'

'Huh?' It's Tuesday, so The Boss can't be here. Carlotta will be suffering *that* joy today.

'In your office,' Greg says, or rather, whispers. Then he pulls an extraordinary face that is no help at all and makes some very peculiar gestures with his hands. He'd be absolutely *useless* at charades.

I give up on him, and open the door.

Bloody *hell*. Even with Greg's half-arsed warning, I am really not expecting *this*. Someone is sitting in my chair, and flicking through the pages of my day book. It's like

384

finding a brunette Goldilocks in your bed. One who's never read the Data Protection Act.

'Can I *help* you?' I say, in my best frosty voice.

The woman starts, then turns to face me. 'Molly,' she says. 'I see nothing changes here – except you!'

'*How* have I changed?' I say, before I can stop myself.

'Oh, nothing. Just age, you know – it'll happen to us all. Eventually. And what are those strange blotches on your face?'

'Nice to see you, too, Vicky,' I say, through gritted teeth. 'And what are *you* doing here?'

'I'm your replacement diary secretary,' she says. 'Didn't Andy tell you I was coming?'

*There* it is, the bloody hair flick. Vicky's right – some things *never* change. Unfortunately. And what's with the 'Andy' business? I doubt The Boss has ever been called Andy before, not even by his mum. He hasn't got the face for nicknames.

'Oh, Andrew probably overlooked it,' says Greg, coming up behind me, and jabbing me in the ribs. 'Minor details were never his thing.'

'Oh, I hardly think he sees *me* as a minor detail,' says Vicky. 'Now where shall I sit? Here?'

'No,' I say.

'Yes,' says Greg. 'We've got to go downstairs and meet with that constituent, Molly – so it doesn't matter where Vicky sits at the moment – *does it?*'

He hustles me out of the office so fast that I don't even have time to ask, 'What constituent?'

There isn't one, and we spend the next hour locked

in the surgery room, trying to find out what the hell is going on. Greg phones The Boss repeatedly, but he's probably hiding from the Whips again and isn't answering his mobile or his pager.

I phone Carlotta to see what she knows about the situation. The answer to that is nothing, or *nada*. She is as stunned as we are, but Spanish, don't forget.

'Wha-at?' she says. 'A replacement? For Marie-Louise?'

'Apparently,' I say. 'Though I can't see why. We haven't got any money in the staffing budget to cover a temp. Get Andrew to call me when he turns up, please.'

'Oh, I *will*,' says Carlotta, who sounds unusually determined. She obviously remembers Vicky all too well.

While I wait for Andrew to make contact, I reclaim my desk, but at a price: Vicky settles herself in the Oprah room instead, where she kicks off her shoes. God knows how she can afford those: don't red soles denote Louboutins? Then she reclines on the sofa, as if waiting for someone to peel her a grape, while making notes – though she doesn't say what about. Probably how many wrinkles I've gained since the last time she saw me.

It's late afternoon by the time The Boss finally bothers to phone. 'You wanted to speak to me?' he says. 'I'm in a rush, so make it snappy.'

'Um, yes. Andrew, about Vicky—'

'Great to have her back, isn't it? She's a breath of fresh air, and loyal with it, not like some of you.'

'Back?' I say. 'But Marie-Louise is only off sick. She won't be away for more than a few days.'

'Oh, well, we'll see about that,' says Andrew. 'You just

look after Vic, and get her anything she needs. Now can you put her on? I want to welcome her back into the fold.'

I put the call through to the Oprah room, then Greg and I both put our ears against the door. All we can hear is giggling and the occasional, 'Oh, *Andy*!'

Maybe we're going down with Norovirus too, since it's all we can do not to start throwing up.

## WEDNESDAY, 6 OCTOBER

I'm sure Max thinks I'm contagious. He hasn't given me a kiss for days, not even a peck on the cheek when I get home from work. Anyone would think he knew I'd been indirectly exposed to chicken pox – and how.

*That's* a very uncomfortable thought, so I concentrate on hot babes, naked bin routines and German wine in an attempt to feel less guilty again. It works a treat, if how depressed it makes me is anything to go by.

Vicky has that effect on me, too, though at least she likes to take extremely long lunches, which comes in very useful today. She's just left the office when there's a buzz on the intercom. A delivery.

I send Greg to collect it, because I am busy – mainly because Vicky still hasn't done any diary work at all, as far as anyone can tell.

'I thought you said you *didn't* shag Johnny?' Greg says, coming back into the office.

'I didn't,' I say. 'He nearly knocked himself out, and then his wife called to say his daughter had chicken pox, remember?'

387

'Oh, yes,' says Greg. 'Are you *sure* that's not what's wrong with your face? I haven't had it, you know.'

'Ha, bloody ha,' I say. 'Johnny didn't even kiss me properly – and, anyway, why are you asking me about him now? It's been ages since he and I met up, and I'm still not sure if I want to repeat the experience.'

'Because of these,' says Greg, reaching behind him into the lobby and producing three vast bouquets of deep red roses.

He dumps them on my desk, and then continues, 'The card says, "Enough of the delaying tactics – when do we do it again? Johnny. Kiss. Kiss. Kiss. Kiss. Kiss."'

'You opened *my* card, and read it, without even asking me?' I am *outraged*, though even more astonished. Johnny – sending flowers, to me?

'Well, yes, I did take the liberty of having a little peek,' says Greg. 'To protect you, of course. You can't be too careful, Molly – these bad boys might have been sprayed with anything.' He looks me up and down, as if he's never seen me before, then says, 'You must have done *something* pretty spectacular to get him to send all these.'

'I don't think I did,' I say, 'but I'm certainly going to need a pretty spectacular excuse to explain them to Max.'

Or I *would* need one, if I was going to keep them – which I obviously can't. But, oh, they are *so* beautiful, and they even have a scent, not like most shop-bought flowers these days.

I decide to drape them around my office – just for a little while – while I try to persuade Greg to drive them

388

over to the Easemount hospice, but then the intercom goes again. There, I *knew* it. The deliveryman is going to say there was some mistake, and the flowers were meant for a totally different Molly Bennett.

Sent from a totally different Johnny Hunter. Ah. Hmm. That would mean that *both* our names were wrong. Is that likely? I'm still trying to decide, when – oh, *Christ*! – Max walks in behind Greg, who is rolling his eyes in a silent (and grossly ineffectual) plea for mercy.

'Couldn't stop him,' he mouths.

'Bloody hell,' says Max. He looks at me, then at Greg, then back at me. 'Who are this lot for?'

'The Boss,' says Greg, at the same time as I say, 'Joan.'

Joan? *Joan?* Have I lost my mind? If there's anyone less likely than me to be deluged with floral tributes, it's Joan. Even if she'd just dropped dead.

'Joan Collins,' I say. 'From The Boss. They've been delivered to our office by mistake. Should have gone to the London one, so that he could give them to her in person. Some gala do.'

Greg's nodding so hard that he's going to give himself a brain injury if he's not careful.

'Bit over-the-top, aren't they?' says Max. 'I've always thought red roses a bit naff, myself. You had your lunch yet, Mol? I've got a free half-hour, so I thought I'd surprise you.'

'Oh, you *have*,' says Greg.

I glare at him, but Max doesn't seem to have heard. He takes down my coat from the hook and hands it to me.

'Come on, then, let's go to Caffè Nero and I'll buy you a panini,' he says. 'I know how to treat a woman.'

'Indeed you do,' says Greg.

I fix him with a glare and run my finger across my throat, before I turn and follow Max down the corridor towards the stairs. God *knows* what my blood pressure's doing now.

## THURSDAY, 7 OCTOBER

I think I'm coming down with something. I keep sneezing and my temperature's going up and down like a yo-yo. Maybe it's an allergy to roses, or to Vicky?

She's still swanning around on those impossible heels, and referring to The Boss as *Andy* to everyone, including Joan. *She's* lying in wait for me, when I walk into the loo. As usual.

'Molly,' she says, 'what is that *awful* woman doing back here? I thought we'd seen the last of her.'

'I don't exactly know,' I say. 'She was at conference, and then she turned up here. To help out with the diary while Marie-Louise is off sick. Oh, and before I forget, I've got some roses for you in my office, if you pop by later on. They're from The Boss, in recognition of your fantastic work in helping him get re-elected.'

Joan gives me a funny look, but doesn't argue. I just hope she doesn't thank Andrew for them next time she sees him. That could get *really* complicated. Especially as Greg made up an entirely different and even more ludicrous story to explain the flowers to Vicky, when she asked him where they came from.

'I think she thought they were for her,' says Greg. 'From her *lover man*, Andy Sinclair. The one who seems to think that *she's Goldenballs* now. I really enjoyed telling her they weren't, even though I probably made that a bit too obvious.'

I don't care if he did, and none of this stupid subterfuge would have been necessary anyway if the bloody hospice hadn't refused to accept donated flowers, even when I assured them that mine were definitely not contaminated. So much for my good deed for the day.

'You can have the second bunch for your mum,' I say to Greg. 'But I am *not* giving the third one to Vicky, though God knows what I *am* going to do with it.'

'Take it home with you,' says Greg. 'Max seemed to swallow the Joan Collins story – hook, line and sinker.'

'Hmm,' I say. 'Unless he just didn't care.'

Greg doesn't answer that. He's wearing his mulling-things-over face. (This morning I told him about the kiss on the neck and the putting-out-the-bins routine. He already knew about the car, and Germany. He said the last two things were circumstantial, but hasn't reached a verdict on the others yet.)

When Joan comes to collect her flowers, she is almost as overwhelmed as I was when they first arrived. 'I've never had such a beautiful bouquet,' she says, burying her nose into one of the blooms. 'Not even on my wedding day. I love red roses – they're *so* romantic.'

'Aren't they?' says Greg. 'Just what I was telling Molly. A symbol of true love and appreciation. *And* of a man with a fat wallet, of course.'

As if on cue, Johnny sends me an email. 'Did you like the flowers?' he says. 'And were you surprised when they arrived?'

'Astonished,' I say, which is the best word that I can think of to convey shock, elation and panic, at the same time.

Johnny seems to find it appropriate, anyway. 'Good,' he says. 'Thought I'd make sure you were thinking about me while I was out of contact yesterday.'

'Well,' I say. ' You certainly managed *that*.' He doesn't need to know that what I was *mainly* thinking about was how to hide the fact that the flowers came from him – and were meant for me.

They *were* quite romantic, though, weren't they? I feel like a new woman, the sort that men send flowers to, in abundance. Or I *would* feel like a new woman, if it weren't for whatever is wrong with me. What *are* the first symptoms of chicken pox?

'Sneezing and a fever,' says Johnny, when I ask. 'And blotches, of course. Now can we talk about something more interesting, like whether you've been missing me?'

'Um, yes,' I say, giving the dual-purpose answer its first outing of the day.

'I've thought about you all the time over the last week,' he says. 'Especially when I was alone in my hotel room last night.'

'Did I have a red nose and a stinking cold at the time?' I say.

'I don't know,' replies Johnny. 'I wasn't envisaging your face very much.'

So much for romance. I must be *delusional*. No wonder Max doesn't care what I get up to, if even my so-called lover can't bear to picture my face.

I take the third bouquet of roses home with me, to make up for my lack of self-esteem. 'The Boss told me I might as well keep some of them, as they wouldn't get to Joan Collins on time,' I say to Max, crossing my fingers inside my coat pockets, as insurance.

'Didn't you say that Andrew wanted you to send them on to London by courier yesterday?' Max's eyebrow is doing that quizzical thing that he normally reserves for Josh's wilder explanations.

'Um, yes,' I say. 'He *did*, but then he changed his mind when I told him what it would cost.'

'Hmm,' says Max, 'I shouldn't think the cost of delivery's much of a factor, not when you can afford to send tons of roses like those.'

Thank God the doorbell rings at exactly the right moment, for once in its life. It's like a miracle, even if it is going to involve a request from a nymphomaniac to borrow a corkscrew. I've got a horrible feeling Max doesn't believe the Joan Collins story in its entirety, though I can't imagine why.

He goes to answer the door while I peer out of the window to check who's outside. There are two men, both dressed in dark suits. Maybe this isn't such good news, after all. They're either debt collectors, or Josh has been up to something again.

I walk into the hallway and stand behind Max, for moral support. I probably owe him that.

'Hi,' says one of the men. 'We're here to share a message for all faiths—'

Ah, Mormons. That explains the suits – *and* the haircuts.

'Not interested, thanks,' says Max, 'We're in the middle of something important here.'

He's already trying to close the door, which really isn't like him at all. Max will always listen politely to chuggers,[38] way past the point at which I've already lost the will to live and have started tugging at his sleeve.

'Hang on,' says the man. 'Is there anyone else who *would* be interested?'

He must have spotted me. Maybe he thinks *I* need saving? Oh, God, maybe I do. I told two or three lies a few minutes ago, in quick succession. I've never done that before, on my own behalf.

'Anyone who'd be *interested*?' says Max. 'No. Not on *this* planet, there isn't.'

'*I'm* on this planet,' says the man, who obviously doesn't know when to take a hint.

'Are you?' says Max, and shuts the door. I've never heard him be so rude to anyone in my life. I hope we're both not damned for this!

'Max,' I say, in desperation, 'why not give the roses to Mrs Bloom? I bet she doesn't get flowers very often.'

He smiles for the first time this evening, as he agrees,

---

[38] Chuggers: Charity muggers, according to Josh, and especially to Connie, who is always being conned into setting up direct debits to give them more money than she can afford. Probably our fault for choosing her name.

so it seems a small price to pay to avoid hellfire and damnation. And Mrs Bloom probably *should* be given flowers, with a name like that. If that really *is* her name.

## FRIDAY, 8 OCTOBER

Max seems a bit more cheerful this morning, and goes off carrying the bunch of roses for Mrs Bloom. I cry a little inside as I wave them goodbye.

Then it's off to work, and this week's surgery. This one's all about men, and bad behaviour.

First Mr Beales turns up, bearing photos of the policeman who gave him his speeding ticket. 'See?' he says. 'He's not wearing his luminous jacket *again*.'

'Ah,' says Andrew. 'Yes, I do see.' He passes the pictures to me.

'He's also not wearing his uniform,' I say. 'And is that a *pub* garden he's sitting in?'

'Might've been. Can't remember now.' Mr Beales shuffles about a bit as he says this – always a dead giveaway that he knows that he's in the wrong.

'Well,' I say, 'was the policeman even *on duty* when you photographed him? I don't think they're required to wear high-vis clothing in their leisure time, you know.'

'Molly does have a point there,' says Andrew. 'Good photos, though.'

'Well, the policeman has most of his head,' I say. 'Which is always a bonus. Though I do think Mr Beales should check the anti-stalking legislation, don't you?'

'Hmm,' says Andrew, while Mr Beales glares at me

through his paedophile glasses. I *will* keep forgetting about his shotgun licence. And that dog.

Thank God, it's Angie Osman next. She's much nicer than Mr Beales, and I haven't seen her since early May, when she brought me a box of Turkish Delight for sorting out her husband Mehmet's indefinite leave to remain.

This case was a small triumph, as Mehmet's application was originally refused and their wedding treated as a marriage of convenience – just because Angie's a bit older than Mehmet. That rarely happens when male pensioners marry twenty-five-year-old bar girls from Pattaya, like Porn-Poon. Thank God Dad came to his senses, just in time.

Maybe it's a sign – of a new beginning – and now all the men in my life are going to start behaving much better than they have been recently. The Boss will calm down, stop being so paranoid, and get rid of Vicky; Josh will become a responsible adult, stay away from supermarket car parks, and move out; and then Max will lose interest in James Blunt, fall back in love with me, and we can all live happily ever after, like Angie and Mehmet.

Sometimes, positive thinking is all you need. There are probably three Cs for that.

I'm so busy living out my Mills & Boon-style fantasy that I miss the first thing Angie says. 'Sorry,' I say. 'I didn't hear you. What did you say?'

Angie doesn't reply. She's looking down at her lap, and tearing a tissue into tiny pieces in her hands.

'Are you okay?' I ask, at which she promptly bursts into floods of tears.

Andrew looks horribly uncomfortable, but does produce some whole (cleanish) tissues from one of his pockets, while I try to calm Angie down. Finally, she's capable of speech.

'Mehmet's left me,' she says, in between sporadic sobs – and some hiccups, too. She nearly sets mine off again.

Even though she's clearly beside herself with misery, both Andrew and I are completely unprepared for what she says next, once the crying finally subsides: 'So I want you to do something about him. Urgently.'

'Have you tried Relate?' I say, as it's not as if anyone can kidnap Mehmet and drag him back.

'No, that's no good,' says Angie. 'He's been having an affair with my next-door neighbour almost since the moment he arrived in the UK. *And* he tried to make me think I was mad for being suspicious, when he kept on claiming he was working late. So now I want you to write to the Border Agency and get his leave to remain revoked. That'll teach the bastard to play me for a fool.'

So much for thinking positive – and happy endings. I must be mad.

### SATURDAY, 9 OCTOBER

'You know Angie Osman?' I say to Max, this morning, as soon as I wake up. 'The one you met when we went to the International Club that time?'

'What?' says Max. 'I'm *trying* to sleep.'

I'm not surprised, given the time he got in last night, but this can't wait. 'Angie,' I say, again. 'Osman. *You* know. Well, anyway, her husband, Mehmet—'

'Oh, you mean "The Visa",' says Max, interrupting me, while keeping his eyes firmly closed.

'What?' I say. 'What do you mean, "The Visa"?'

Max finally gives up trying to go back to sleep and looks at me, bleary-eyed. 'That's what *everyone* calls Mehmet,' he says. 'Behind Angie's back. I thought you knew.'

'I did *not* know,' I say. 'And the bastard's been having an affair with the next-door neighbour, also behind Angie's back. *And* telling her she's mad to accuse him of doing it!'

'Well, that's sad,' says Max, 'but why are *you* so upset about it? You only know them through work, don't you?'

I'm just about to tell him *why* I'm so upset, when the landline begins to ring. Max groans, but jumps out of bed as fast as he can, to go and answer it. I mutter, 'Saved by the bell' under my breath, as he rushes down the stairs.

Five minutes later, he reappears, looking very concerned.

'What now?' I say.

'It's your mum,' he says. 'No, don't panic – she's all right. She's just had a fall. Over a table leg, I should imagine.'

'Oh, my God,' I say. 'Those bloody tables. And just when Ted's away, too, and she's all on her own. Is she in casualty?' I'm sick of that hospital, thanks to Josh.

'At home, with the paramedic. It was him who called, so I told him you'll get round there as soon as you can. I'll take you in the car, then I can go and do the food shopping afterwards.'

'But we were just about to have a conversation,' I say. 'An important one. A *very* important one.'

'Were we?' says Max, almost convincingly. 'Well, if your mum's okay later on, let's go and have a meal somewhere nice this evening. I can afford it, as Mrs Bloom gave me a tip last night. Oh, and she said to thank you for the flowers, too.'

I don't have time to ask what Max *did* to earn a tip from 'Mrs Bloom'; I'm too busy getting dressed and trying to find the arnica. I don't care what the LibDems say about homeopathy, this stuff works. Josh has proved *that* on numerous occasions.

But bloody *hell*. Talk about bad timing. I know it's selfish but, honestly, did Mum have to fall over one of those damned tables just when I was getting ready to force Max to tell me what's really going on with Ellen? Now I'll have to wait until tonight.

'Has anyone told Robin about Mum?' I say, suddenly remembering my idiot brother. Max shakes his head, so I start dialling the number as we head for the car.

'Ah, Mol,' says Robin, the albino Isaac Hayes of Buddhists. 'How's it hangin', dude? All cool with you?'

'Yes, I mean, no. Rob – Mum's had a fall. I'm on my way there now. Are you coming over?'

'Oh, no,' says Robin. 'You're the expert at family stuff. I'm sure you've got it covered – and I've got some mates coming round later on. Usual Saturday night game of poker.'

I don't say anything to that, as I don't trust myself, so he continues: 'I'll leave it in your capable hands then, shall I?'

'Sounds like I don't have a choice,' I say, before I hang up on him. Practise compassion daily, my arse – Rob only lives five minutes away.

Talking of arses, God knows what Mum's been playing at. When I walk in, she's sitting on the sofa, wrapped in a blanket and looking very pale. The paramedic has a word with me and then starts bustling around, packing away his emergency kit. Then Mum starts mouthing something.

I have no idea what she's trying to say, so I move closer, and she whispers in my ear. 'Pants.'

'I know it is, Mum,' I say. 'But the paramedic says you're fine, if a bit shaken up. You just need someone to keep an eye on you for the next twenty-four hours or so.'

'No,' she says, looking very agitated. 'Not that sort of pants, I mean *pants*. I need you to get me some. I'm not wearing any under my skirt.'

Good God. Now my mother's going commando? What the *hell* is going on? First Mr Beales and his Ann Summers habit, and now this. It's all too much.

I search through Mum's underwear drawer and bring her the largest pair of knickers I can find. *I* know what's age-appropriate, even if she doesn't.

After she's wriggled into the pants under cover of the blanket, and claimed to have tripped over the hem of her skirt, and not a table leg, Mum tells me that the reason she was walking around without knickers is due to her sore buttock, and the effect of seams on tender skin.

'If you say so,' I say, as the doorbell rings.

It's Robin, all smiles and bonhomie. Maybe he did some emergency chanting, or divination, and the Buddha revealed that it might be a good idea to turn up and earn some karma points. He sits down next to Mum and takes her hand, smiling devotedly. Then he orders a cup of lapsang souchong from the waitress, i.e. me, and suggests I make Mum some scrambled egg.

'We need to look after her, Molly,' he says. 'She's had a nasty shock.'

'Yes,' I say. 'Are you going to keep an eye on her for a while, then? Max and I were supposed to be going out tonight, for once. I could come back and relieve you, after we've had our meal.'

'Sorry, Mol,' says Robin, standing up and reaching for his coat. 'No can do.'

Then he kisses Mum on the cheek and says, 'Gotta run, Ma. People to see, places to go – you know how it is. I'm sure Mol will stay overnight. She's the expert, what with having kids and all.'

It's a good job he leaves immediately afterwards, or the frenzied fratricide of a Buddhist with a penchant for bling would have been *all over* tomorrow's papers.

**SUNDAY, 10 OCTOBER**

I've never had such a terrible night's sleep in my life. I hate staying at other people's houses, anyway, but why are old people so attached to sheets and blankets? The damn things are accidents waiting to happen, along with table legs.

I was wide-awake for hours after I'd put Mum to bed,

wondering what Max was getting up to while I was away, and then – when I did finally fall asleep – I had a nightmare in which I was being made to wear a straitjacket by a bunch of immigration officials, who looked like much less cuddly versions of Igor. They wanted to know where Max had absconded to and who our next-door neighbour was.

Then I thought I heard Mum calling and, when I went to climb out of bed to go to her, I got horribly tangled up in the sheet and ended up falling onto the floor.

Mum heard the crash and came to see whether *I* was okay, so our roles got a bit muddled, to say the least. By the time I'd put *her* back to bed it was already light, so I didn't bother trying to sleep again. I texted Max instead.

'I miss you,' I said, but he didn't reply. Maybe he was still asleep?

Anyway, now it's lunchtime, and I've just made Mum more scrambled egg, as she says it's just what you feel like eating when you're poorly.

'Good thing Robin reminded me about it,' she says.

'Humph,' I say, as my mobile rings. It's Robin. Talk of the devil. Or the *Mara*, if we're speaking Buddhist.

'Just checking in, Mol,' he says. 'Before I go off to the seaside for the day. How's Ma?'

'I'll put her on,' I say, passing Mum the phone. I stand behind her while she chats, making frantic 'V' signs at Robin, until I realise she can see my reflection in the window. She's a bit off with me after that. It's a relief when Ted arrives back from his fishing trip in the early evening and offers to give me a lift straight home.

When I arrive, the house is in darkness and I realise I've left my keys on the kitchen counter at Mum's. I knock on the door for ages, just in case, but no one answers and so eventually I walk round to the back alleyway. Maybe Max has left the gate open, if he put the bins out earlier.

He *has* locked the gate, but that doesn't matter. Not compared to what he's doing, right this minute: sitting at Ellen's kitchen table. I can see him clearly, over the wall.

I phone his mobile. Now let's see where he *says* he is.

'Mol,' he says, when he answers. 'Where are you? Are you ready for me to come and pick you up?'

'No,' I say. 'Where are you?' I hold my breath. Now I wish I hadn't asked. I'd take it back, if I could.

'I'm at Ellen's,' he says. 'She wanted me to re-light her boiler. So I'm just having a quick cup of coffee before going back home.'

*Argh.* Can he *see* me? How does he *do* that?

'I'm outside,' I say, after a moment's pause to collect my thoughts. 'At the back. Can you come and let me in? I've left my keys at Mum's.'

'Well, why on earth didn't you say so?' says Max, wrong-footing me, as usual.

## MONDAY, 11 OCTOBER

Is it possible to have PMT *every* day of the month? I'm starting to wonder – unless it's Vicky's constant hair-flicking that's causing me to be so grumpy, as well as Max always managing to come up smelling of roses, even when I think I've caught him out at last.

Today I manage to fall out with both him *and* Johnny. Talk about narrowing one's options.

Max announces that he's going to be late home again tonight, while we're in the middle of breakfast. Mrs Bloom has 'asked a favour' and he is going to fix a new bolt and security chain to her front door after work.

'But what on earth has that got to do with your job?' I say. 'You sell sofas and stuff, not door furniture.'

'I know,' says Max. 'But it's not a bad idea to keep your best customers happy in a recession. And it won't take me *that* long, anyway.'

I can't think of anything to say to this that wouldn't involve sounding as if I'm lacking in age concern, so I don't bother. I rely on some passive-aggressive huffing and glaring instead. It's only 7.30 in the morning, and the best I can do.

Not that my restraint has the desired effect. Max raises an eyebrow and says, 'PMT?'

Gah. Why do men *always* think that women's irritation is due solely to their menstrual cycle, and not to whether it's justifiable or not? I'm sure I read an article once – probably in one of Mum's cuttings – that said that, although women may be slightly more irritable in the days immediately before their period, they are still *less* irritable at that point than men are *all the time*.

I remind Max of this, and of the fact that there is no such thing as *Post-Menstrual* Tension, which is what my mood would be due to, if I *was* in a mood. Which I'm not – unlike him.

When I say that we'd need a much more regular

sex-life than the one we have to give him *any* chance of judging where I am in my menstrual cycle at any given point, *he's* the one who gets irritable. He's stopped talking to me entirely by the time that I leave for work.

'I'm not irritable, am I?' I say to Greg, who replies, 'Well, maybe a bit.'

So would he be, if he'd had to spend all morning watching Vicky rolling her eyes and tutting at everything *he* said, instead of going to a nice little meeting at the CAB.

I *definitely* should have tried much harder to get a job in Primark. I bet they don't allow their temps to speak to people the way Vicky does to me. But then they probably operate a normal hierarchy, too – not one based on whether their boss likes them best that day or not.

*Goldenballs Vicky* is winning that particular contest hands down at the moment and, as she's really only answerable to *Andy*, I've got no choice but to put up with her until Marie-Louise is well enough to come back to work.

I can't wait for *that* to happen – hopefully by the end of this week, or so Marie-Louise says anyway. It's the first thing I ask her about when she phones shortly after lunch to give me an update.

It's also the *only* thing I ask, as – after I hear her answer – I accidentally disconnect the phone, by punching the air over-enthusiastically with the hand that's holding the receiver, while saying, 'Thank *God* for that!'

I wish The Boss would invest in some better phones. The cord pulls clean out of the back of ours if you make any sudden movements while holding them. I've just finished plugging mine back in when it starts to ring again, but this time it's Johnny calling – from Russia.

'What on earth are you doing, calling me on the office phone?' I say. Very quietly. There are ears under all Vicky's hair. Waggly ones.

'What?' says Johnny. 'Speak up, woman. There's no point in me phoning to hear your voice if you're going to whisper.'

Oh, bloody hell. How does he expect me to have a conversation with him while Vicky is listening in? I decide that, if it's only my *voice* that he wants to hear, then it won't matter what I actually *say*, so I can pretend I'm talking to a constituent.

'Ah,' I say. 'So you're not happy with what Iain Duncan Smith has said about people needing to travel further to find work, if necessary?' (It's the best I can do, off the top of my head.)

'What? What are you talking about? Of course I'm happy with it – I travel an entire bloody continent in my job, you idiot,' says Johnny.

Now his tone resembles a grumpy constituent's rather too convincingly for my liking. Not to mention that his job is hardly typical of those I was referring to. I bite my lip, then plough ahead.

'Well, I see your point,' I say. 'Spending large amounts of money on travelling to work is all very well, if you have a full-time job. But all those poor people who are on zero- or four-hour contracts, or who are sent home

406

early when they're not needed, are indeed in a wholly different position to you. I commend your sensitivity to the predicaments of others.'

'Molly, what the *hell* are you talking about?' says Johnny. 'How is this supposed to be seductive?'

Honestly, sometimes even International Directors of Global Oil Companies are *very* slow to catch on. Vicky's still earwigging, though – so I'll have to adopt a two-pronged approach.

I start typing an email to Johnny, while still talking to him on the phone. 'I will be happy to raise this with the Minister for Work and Pensions,' I say. 'I'll send you a copy of my letter, and we'll take it from there.' At the same time, I hit *send*, and my email saying: 'Johnny, get OFF the phone!' is on its way.

'For God's sake,' says Johnny. 'Oh, hold on. Ah. I see. Well, I'm sorry to interrupt your *vital* work.' Then he hangs up.

Was that tone of voice *really* necessary? I send another email: 'There's no need to be sarcastic.'

Johnny's reply comes straight back: 'PMT?'

Is there *any* point in having an almost-lover who's just as annoying as your husband? I can't see that there is, myself.

## TUESDAY, 12 OCTOBER

Everyone's in such a good mood today! Well, everyone apart from the constituents. It's unnerving.

In the morning, Max gives me a cuddle and apologises for his comment about PMT. 'I was just being immature,' he says, as he gives me an exaggerated kiss on the cheek, which is finally blotch-free.

'Humph,' I say. (I am not being an elephant, just playing hard-to-get.)

'Well, I *am* your toy-boy, after all,' he says.

A six-month age gap and you never hear the last of it. Which reminds me, I really must start planning Max's surprise birthday party – which is bound to be better than mine, if only because I don't intend to tell him about it in advance.

Unlike him, I understand the concept of surprises – and one of *his* will be finding out that I haven't invited Annoying Ellen. *If* I can get away with excluding her, though I'm not quite sure how I'm going to make *that* look like an oversight. She'll be round at the first sniff of alcohol.

Talking of alcohol, I arrive at work to find that good old Igor has dropped off a bottle of vodka to warm us all up, now that the weather's getting much colder. Greg has already tested it for purity, or so he says.

'Can't be too careful, Mol. You are lucky I am prepared to risk my life, as your official taster. Usually only *important* people have those.'

'I don't *need* a taster,' I say. 'Or not where Igor's concerned, anyway. He wouldn't give us anything that might harm *me*, seeing as he says I remind him of his wife.'

'How do you know that's a good thing?' says Greg, as he pours another shot, 'to be on the safe side.'

Then he tells me that Vicky has gone to London to

meet up with The Boss, so I pour myself a large shot, too. *That* news is worth a sizeable celebration. A whole day free from eye-rolling, hair-flicking and supercilious comments about how unkindly life is treating my face! It feels as if it's *my* birthday, without the disadvantage of having become another year older.

The vodka even helps to dull the volume of Miss Chambers' voice, when she phones to say that the police have stolen a teapot that she inherited from her mother, during a visit to investigate her latest allegation: that her neighbours have started running a brothel.

Greg offers me a refill as soon as he hears Miss C's distinctive shriek echoing around the office, but I refuse, just in case the alcohol affects my judgement – or my reaction time. (Crucial to picking the right moment at which to get cut off, by accident.)

'Commendable abstinence, Molly,' says Greg. 'Not that it did me any good at conference. I'd have stood a better chance of getting laid if I'd been legless the whole time, like The Boss.'

He's almost convinced me that there's a direct link between how much you drink and how often you have sex, when Johnny sends a series of emails, which make me very glad that I'm still sober.

He says that he's sorry for his PMT comment, but that he's 'losing patience' with me.

When I ask why, he says that I am 'teasing' him.

Me? A tease? I wouldn't have the faintest idea where to start – as the Ann Summers debacle showed only too clearly – but Johnny insists that this is *exactly* what I am doing, by refusing to commit to another meeting.

'Well, I'm not sure,' I say, then hesitate. Maybe it's time to bite the bullet. 'All right, then,' I continue. 'The truth is that I can't help thinking that maybe we should both make a bit more effort to salvage our marriages, before we start planning to meet again. Don't you?'

'No,' says Johnny. 'I don't. It's not supposed to be a *job*, being married – and is it really worth it, if you have to *work* at it?'

Of course it's a job. And I bet his kids would think it was worth it, even if he doesn't. Is he on another planet, hanging out with Max's Mormon friends, or something?

I don't put it quite as bluntly as that in my next email, but it might have been better if I had. At least then he might have understood what I meant. Instead, his reply sends me on a frantic search for the vodka bottle: 'Molly,' he says. 'It's not as if you can help who you fall in love with, is it?'

I take several large swigs of vodka before I respond. 'That's what Dad said about the Thai bride, too,' I say. 'But really, it was just sex, and now he's tired of her.'

There's such a long pause at Johnny's end that I'm just considering whether to stop waiting for an answer and go home, when his reply finally pops into my inbox.

'I was only joking around,' he says. 'Sex, that's all I want from you. You obviously know me too well to be fooled.'

I'm not sure whether the last statement is a test – or a fact. And I have *no* idea which I want it to be.

## WEDNESDAY, 13 OCTOBER

God, these nightmares are getting worse. I had two last night, both of them *insane*.

In the first one, Max and Johnny were playing poker against each other. Whichever one lost, won me, as the booby prize.

In the second, they were each captaining a team on *Call My Bluff*, trying to persuade the other side that they weren't in love with me. All the other members of the teams looked like Kim Jong-il.

'Or Kim il-Loon,' says Greg, when I tell him about the dreams. 'Did they both have groupies like demented baton-twirlers waiting outside the studio?'

'Yes,' I say. 'How did you know? They all looked like mini-Ellens to me.'

'Telepathy,' says Greg. 'So do you think Johnny *is* in love with you – or was he joking, like he said?'

I don't really want to think about it, not when I still don't know whether Max would be pleased to win me in a game, or not. Or whether *I'd* want him to win, or lose.

'I don't know, Greg,' I say. 'I'll just have to try to work it out from what he says next, I suppose. Why's it so cold in here? I'm freezing, even though I'm wearing a ridiculous number of layers. And where's all Igor's warming vodka gone?'

Greg pretends that he didn't hear the last question, but says that he thinks the boiler's playing up. Then he tries to push me over.

'What the hell are you doing?' I say.

411

'I wanted to see if you wobbled, but didn't fall down,' says Greg, 'given your resemblance to a Weeble.'

I mention this somewhat unflattering comparison to Johnny, who asks me to send him a photo, as evidence. Greg takes one immediately.

'Then Johnny will see that I am a man who can be relied on to give him the unvarnished truth,' he says. 'Which could be *very* useful to an International Director of a Global Oil Company.'

Even *he's* started capitalising Johnny's job title now. It's rather worrying. I do wish I could tell Vicky about Johnny, though. It'd be nice to impress her, just for once.

'Gosh, Molly,' she says, when she arrives for work, three hours late. 'You're looking even rougher than usual today. And where on earth is that awful jumper from? Primark, or some other godforsaken place?'

I don't answer. I don't trust myself and, anyway, Johnny's just responded to my Weeble photo.

'Wow. You look great,' he says. 'I'd be really proud to walk into a room with a woman who looked like that on my arm.'

'Are you taking the piss?' I say. 'I am already having a very bad day, so it's inadvisable.'

'No,' he says. 'For Christ's sake, woman, can't you ever take a compliment? "Thank you" is the appropriate response.'

Whatever must Johnny's wife look like, if he thinks *I* look good? I apologise anyway, and blame my grumpiness on the fact that I spent the night being the reluctant prize in a terrifying fight between two teams of North

Koreans. (I don't say that he and Max were their captains.)

'Also, I'm freezing to death,' I say.

'North Koreans?' says Johnny. 'What the hell are you talking about? And have you forgotten that I live in *Russia*? Generally considered to be somewhat chillier than the UK, by *qualified* meteorologists.'

You can put a woman down, but you can't keep her there. Not when you don't know what you're talking about. After a referral to the BBC's *World Weather View*, Johnny is forced to admit that it's colder in the UK today than it is in Moscow, although he's quick to point out that it's much worse there in the depths of winter.

'Minus 10 is common,' he says.

'Good job I don't live with you then,' I say. 'How on earth does your wife manage?'

'Oh, she has a mink coat,' he says.

The phones start ringing again then, and Vicky keeps coming up behind me and looking over my shoulder at my screen, so I don't manage to send my anti-fur response until after the office has closed and she and Greg have left the building. Johnny is completely unimpressed by it anyway.

'Yes, yes, nasty fur coats,' he says. 'Sometimes, Molly, you are so predictable, but just wait until you've tried a winter here without one. You'll do a Naomi Campbell within a day.'

He obviously means, 'You *would*', and not, 'You will'. Imagine it, though.

No more Molly Bennett, overlooked wife and

under-rated MP's caseworker. Hello, Molly Hunter, wife of an adoring (if bossy) Baron of Oil. I could spend my life dancing at embassy parties and swanning around Moscow in designer clothes.

Including a fur coat – which, even if I didn't object to it on moral grounds, would make me look exactly like a bloody Ewok.

## THURSDAY, 14 OCTOBER

I'm losing touch with reality now, thanks to these demented dreams. I spent last night playing Lara to Johnny's *Doctor Zhivago*.

Sometimes Johnny resembled Omar Sharif, but then he kept turning back into President Putin whenever I was least expecting it. I secretly preferred Omar-Johnny, who was a hell of a lot more romantic than Putin-Johnny, as well as being better-looking. (Putin-Johnny kept ordering me to keep up, as I trudged interminably through the snow.)

The best bit by far was being Julie Christie. She *really* knows how to wear a fur coat without so much as a hint of Ewok.

The dream was so convincing that, when I wake up, I still think I'm Julie – until I look in the mirror. Then I'm distraught to find that it's not her face that looks back at me, but mine, incipient beard and all. Now I *wish* the subject of Ewoks had never come up.

If I do manage to grow fur all over my body, though, at least I'll be better adapted for cold weather. The office was chilly enough yesterday, but when Greg and I arrive

414

today, we discover that the boiler's completely given up the ghost.

We have to keep our coats on all morning while I try to find a gas engineer with a free appointment before next July – unsuccessfully. Vicky says that she will 'work' from home, as a result. Apparently, she can't risk low temperatures, due to her chilblains.

'Think she's confusing *those* with bunions,' says Greg. 'Caused by those stupid bloody shoes.'

'She says *they're* a political statement,' I say. 'Due to their red soles.'

'I wish they were *all* red,' says Greg. 'Then she could click her heels, trot off down the Yellow Brick Road, and re-join the Wicked Witch of the East. When *is* she going to bugger off? Marie-Louise is back at work on Monday.'

Vicky doesn't seem to have any intention of going anywhere. Now she says she's working on something 'highly confidential' for The Boss, which is 'really going to shake things up around here'.

I have no idea what her secret mission is, but it seems to involve making notes of anything anybody says about Andrew in her presence. Joan says Vicky even follows *her* when she goes to the loo, which I think ought to teach Joan a salutary lesson, though I rise above saying so.

It's even colder in both the toilets than it is in the rest of the building, and Greg says his 'Private Member's Bill' may drop off if I don't do something to get the boiler fixed by the end of the day.

'Can't you ask Max to have a look at it?' he says,

wrapping himself up in a layer of the local paper. He's positioned the front page photo of Andrew's face right over his nether regions. At the back.

'Well, I don't know,' I say. 'He's still not very happy with me for comparing him to Mehmet Osman.'

'But he wouldn't want you to freeze to death, though, would he?' says Greg. 'Or me. He's fond of *me*.'

'He *tolerates* you,' I say. 'Because your Imodium obsession amuses him.'

Greg pulls a wounded face, then tries again. 'But you told me he fixed *Ellen's* boiler,' he says. 'The other day.'

'Re-lit it,' I say. 'Not fixed it. Not the same thing at all.'

Not when one's a repair, but the other could all too easily be a euphemism. *That's* only just occurred to me.

**FRIDAY, 15 OCTOBER**

I don't know what Vicky's doing for The Boss, but it can't all be bad, even if Joan did think she saw them standing rather too close to each other in the car park this morning.

Anyway, not only has Andrew managed to fix the boiler by 'jiggling something that looked a bit loose', but he also seems to have got his mojo back. I'd forgotten how likable he can be, sometimes. Unlike people with leylandii trees.

Greg and The Boss have just gone off to do today's surgery, when I get a call from a Mr Parker. He's elderly, immensely polite, and in tears because his wife is dying. At home, in bed, and in the pitch dark.

416

This isn't because their electricity has been cut off, or because she is blind, but because their neighbour's monster tree has now grown so large that it blocks all light from reaching the Parkers' house.

Mr P wants his wife to be able to see the sun on the rare occasions that it shines, but the absentee neighbour refuses to respond to letters, and the Council have said there's nothing they can do to help. I promise to see what I can do, and Mr Parker thanks me profusely before ringing off.

Once he does, I look up the regulations governing leylandii only to discover that they don't apply to single trees, no matter how large they are. Then, for some reason, I start to cry, so I kick the desk and put my head in my hands.

The picture Mr Parker has painted of his sick wife, stuck in her bed and with no view from her window, is almost viscerally clear in my mind's eye.

Then The Boss walks in and surprises me. 'What's up, Molly?' he says. 'You okay? Are you *crying*?'

Bloody hell. This is the first time he's spoken to me properly for weeks. Or maybe even months.

'No,' I say. 'I'm not crying. A constituent's situation just got to me a bit, that's all. I'll be fine, in a minute.'

'If you say so,' says Andrew, patting me on the shoulder. 'Tell me about it, anyway.'

So I do. He genuinely seems to want to know, for once.

'Ring Mr Parker back,' he says, as soon as I've finished telling him what the problem is. 'And ask if I can go and visit him and his wife this afternoon.'

'Are you sure?' I say. 'You've only just finished surgery and your diary's been manic for the last few weeks. You're looking a bit knackered, too.'

'I'm not knackered, I'm just old – but not that bloody old,' says Andrew. 'And, anyway, this is what my job is *supposed* to involve. Helping people.'

So, just after lunch, off he goes to see Mr and Mrs Parker, while Greg and I look at each other in disbelief. (Vicky says nothing, and just looks disapproving, but we take no notice of her. We're far too happy to care what she thinks.)

'Christ,' says Greg.

'I know,' I say. 'This is more like it.'

Two hours later, Andrew phones. 'Know anyone with a big saw, Molly?' he says.

He sounds very emotional, and nearly starts me off again.

'Not sure,' I say. 'Max might have one. Why?'

'Never seen anything like this f*cking tree.'

So it really is *that* bad. I look at the view out of the window, and try to imagine what it would be like to be able to see nothing at all.

'How was Mrs Parker?' I say.

'She looked tiny in that bed,' says Andrew. 'I had to put the damned light on to see her properly.'

There's a long pause, while both of us process what he's just said. Then Andrew clears his throat and says, 'I'm thinking about becoming an amateur tree surgeon. Want to come and help?'

'Yes,' I say.

Part of me's hoping he's deadly serious. The other part – the one that has to deal with the consequences of his actions – really isn't.

## SATURDAY, 16 OCTOBER

God, Greg and I shouldn't have gone out drinking last night to celebrate The Boss' redemption. I've got a terrible hangover, and Dinah's phone call doesn't help.

'I am ringing to tell you that I am *never* speaking to you again,' she says. 'Fancy telling Dad he was coming to mine for Christmas! What the *hell* got into you?'

I can't tell her what Dad said to his neighbours to make me do it, or she'll be even crosser than she is already, so I claim that I disassociated for a moment, due to stress.

'You understand the funny things *that* can make you do, Di,' I say. 'What with your HPD and all.'

'I suppose you're right, for once,' she says. 'Seeing as I understand stress *better than anyone*. But don't think you're getting off the hook *that* easily. You'll have to have him for the next two Christmases, to compensate.'

That thought really doesn't help my headache, or the nausea, so I take a huge swig of coffee and almost choke on it.

'He might be in Thailand by then anyway,' I say, once I am finally able to speak again. 'We don't know he's gone off the idea permanently.'

'Oh, he *has*,' says Dinah, who didn't even ask if I was okay while I was choking to death. 'Definitely. He's sounding more settled every time I speak to him. It's not

419

just the DIY – he's having a new kitchen and bathroom fitted, and he's even taken up fishing now.'

I don't believe the last bit, until Dinah orders me to check my email. She's sent me Dad's latest set of photographs – all of fish.

'See?' she says. 'And that proves there's no point in me running the book on what's going to happen with the Thai bride any more, either. No one put a stake on *nothing*, so I'll give you all your money back.'

I hope she's not running another book on what's likely to happen to me and Max. I wouldn't have a clue what to bet on *that*. Especially after what happens next.

I've just gone out into the garden to get some fresh air, when Ellen appears. She's obviously one of those morning people.

'Dee dah, dee dah dah,' she says – or rather hums – very loudly, while hanging out even more sets of sexy underwear.

I wince, both at the volume, and the sight. Presumably audibly, as Ellen spots me after that.

'Hi, Molly,' she says. 'Isn't it a *lovely* morning? Makes you feel like singing, doesn't it?'

'Not so as I've noticed,' I say, before I remember that I don't *know* she's having an affair with Max, so I do still have to try to be polite. 'But then I've got a hangover, so don't let me stop you enjoying it. Carry on.'

Politeness is a curse, as she takes me at my word. 'Dee, dah, dee dee dah; dee, dah, dee dee dah,' she sings, wiggling about as if on a podium, surrounded by spectacular knickers and bras. 'Don't you just love Take That? Especially in their Robbie Williams days?'

'Not especially,' I say, 'though what are you singing? It sounds familiar.'

'"Relight My Fire",' says Ellen. 'Ooh, which reminds me, can you thank Max for getting my boiler lit? It hasn't gone out again since he sorted it. Used to do it all the time before.'

I know I mocked synchronicity the other day, but I may have to eat my words. *That* was no coincidence.

'Want to pop round for another coffee, Molly?' says Ellen, who has stopped humming at last. 'Now you've spilled the one you're holding?'

'No, thanks,' I say. 'I've got to go and organise Max's birthday party.'

As I turn away and start to walk back towards the house, I don't even realise what I've done.

'Oh, I'll look forward to *that*,' says Ellen. 'See you there!'

*Bloody brilliant, Molly.* Well done in the not-inviting-Ellen stakes. I think it's time to tackle Max.

He's only just got up, and seems in a fairly good mood, so I take a couple of deep breaths, then say, 'Max, I need to talk to you about something important.'

'Hmm?' he says, turning the TV on.

I turn it off again, which makes him look slightly less good-humoured.

'Talk,' I say. 'You know, that thing we used to do occasionally. Along with having sex.'

'Oh, you're having that sort of day, are you?' he says.

'Is it the result of your gin-fest with Greg last night? If so, maybe having a conversation now isn't such a good idea.'

Max sips his coffee and stares at the blank screen. He must be able to see something that I can't, given how hard he seems to be concentrating. I stand in front of it and take a deep breath.

'I want to know – um, well, I *think* I want to know – er, yes, I want to know *what is going on with Ellen*.'

There, I've said it. Now I feel even sicker.

'How would I know?' says Max. 'I haven't seen her for days. Why?'

Could he make this any more difficult? I run my fingers through my hair and then regret it. You should probably look your best when questioning your husband about his other woman.

'That's not what I meant,' I say. 'I want to know what's going on between you and Ellen. I know there's *something*. She's outside in the garden, prancing around and singing about when you re-lit her boiler.'

Max starts laughing, and I glare at him until he stops. It takes a lot longer than when I do it to Josh.

'You're serious?' he says. 'Oh, for God's sake, Mol. If you don't know me better than that after all these years, what hope is there? Now can you please turn the TV back on? I want to watch the motor racing.'

There's so much I want to say, but for some reason I can't find the words, so I press *on* and go for a cigarette instead.

It's a good job I'm not Kim il-Loon. I could cheerfully lob a ballistic missile at the sofa right this minute.

## SUNDAY, 17 OCTOBER

I have another try at talking to Max this afternoon, while Josh is still out at work.

'So, this Mrs Bloom,' I say. 'The one who keeps making you come home so late—'

'Yes?' says Max. 'What about her?'

'Well, are you sure her name really *is* Mrs Bloom? Not Mr Blunt, by any chance?'

I give Max one of those tell-me-the-truth-or-else looks that work so well on Connie, on the rare occasions she's tempted to lie. He looks back at me, with a bewildered expression.

'What are you talking about?' he says. 'That sounds like something out of Cluedo to me. I haven't even *got* a customer called Mr Blunt.'

Oh, honestly. Does *everyone* in this family have to be so literal all the time? I count to ten in my head, then try again.

'I didn't say he was necessarily a customer,' I say. 'Or that *she* was, actually.'

'Far too cryptic for me, Mol,' says Max, patting his pockets down until he finds the keys to the car. 'Got to rush, said I'd give Josh a lift home from work, seeing as it's so cold. I'll see you when I get back.'

Gah. I wonder what someone else would think about the way Max is behaving if I told them about it? Maybe

I should find out, so I call Greg, who doesn't answer. It'll have to be David then.

*He's* about as much help as a hole in the head, or less – if you believe what Mr Lawson claims. So much for best friends, that's all I can say.

When I've finally finished describing all the weird Ellen-related incidents there have been over the last six months, mine just says, 'Well, I know you've wasted your potential, Mol, but I never had you down as *stupid*.'

'What d'you mean, David?' I say, trying not to over-react, and only just managing it.

'It's bloody obvious what's going on,' he says, exhaling noisily. 'You'd be the *first* to say so, if it was happening to someone else.'

I bet he's smoking one of those stupid Cuban cigars he bought for his show-off renewal of vows. For a moment, I hope he chokes on it, until I recall that I did ask him to give me his honest opinion. He's just got the wrong end of the stick, that's all.

'But I haven't got any proof,' I say. 'And Max always goes beyond the call of duty to help people. *You* know that.'

'Humph,' says David, pretty ungratefully if you ask me, after all the repairs Max has done for him over the years. 'There's helping, and then there's *helping*, if you see what I mean. If I were you, I'd come here for a visit while you decide what to do. Might help Max realise what he stands to lose.'

I say I'll think about it, but I won't really. Leave the

field clear for Ellen and more re-ignition of her boiler? That would *definitely* make me stupid.

Oh, and here come Max and Josh, back already. They're both shivering and stamping their feet up and down on the doormat.

'It's snowing, Mum,' says Josh. 'Look out of the window! It's like Russia out there.'

'It is,' I say, staring outside. 'Pretty, isn't it?'

No wonder Igor gets so homesick – even I'm starting to see how a fur coat could have *some* appeal.

## MONDAY, 18 OCTOBER

I've got a funny feeling I really may have PMT today, though I'd rather die than admit it to Max or Johnny.

I spend all morning bursting into tears at inopportune moments, not that there's ever an *opportune* time to indulge in that. Not unless you're about to be booted out of an X *Factor* judge's house.

Greg thinks I've gone off my rocker, and starts another campaign to cheer Molly up. He even donates a Twix to the cause. It doesn't work, and just makes me weepier instead. Unexpected kindness always has that effect.

'What on earth's the matter?' he says, when I hand half of it back to him. 'It must be *terrible* if a Twix won't sort it out.'

'Nothing,' I say. 'I'm fine.' Big fat tears roll down my face at the same time, though at least the crying isn't the noisy hiccuping kind. That would be even worse.

'Well,' says Greg, 'unless you've got some bizarre eye infection, you're telling me porky pies. You look a mess.

425

And move that invitation from the Mayor out of the way – you're dripping on it.'

He passes me a tissue from one of those little travel packs that his mum supplies. I'm sure she thinks he's still a Boy Scout.

'You should be singing from the rooftops today,' he continues. 'Seeing as Marie-Louise is back at work. Which means we've seen the last of you-know-who.'

So much for *that*. No sooner has Greg finished speaking than Vicky comes swanning in and gives me a funny look, which stops me crying immediately.

She's in a *very* chatty mood. I much prefer it when she isn't.

'Molly,' she says. 'You need to buy a better-quality mascara. Yours is all over your face.'

She tuts as I scrub it off, using another of Greg's mum's tissues, and then she moves her attention to the rest of me.

'Look at the state of your nails, too,' she says. 'Why on earth don't you grow them – or get yourself some false ones, if you can't?'

'Because I like to be able to pick things up properly,' I say. 'And I can't see the point in long nails anyway.'

Vicky looks down at hers, and wiggles her fingers to show those weird squared-off ends to their full cringe-making effect. 'There's *always* a point to being well-groomed,' she says. 'Men appreciate it, even if you don't.'

I can't believe this is true of *all* men, whatever she says. The Boss' grooming habits make me look like a beauty salon regular but, as I am trying not to rise to provocation, I don't point this out. You should never let people like Vicky know they've rattled you. It's better to be cool, yet polite, and to change the subject to something more neutral. In theory.

In practice, as soon as I open my mouth, Freud sneaks in and takes control: 'So, Vicky,' I say. 'How much longer are you staying with us? Marie-Louise is back now, you know.'

'Yes,' says Greg, rather too heartily, from the depths of the archive cupboard, where he spends a lot of time whenever Vicky is around. 'When *are* you leaving? Is it soon?'

He really should try to sound less keen for Vicky to go. If there's one thing she enjoys – other than inspecting people's nails – it's frustrating the desires of others. (That's as far as I can tell. Joan thinks The Boss may take a different view.)

'Well,' says Vicky. 'I am a bit disappointed Marie-Louise is back so soon, but I spoke to Andy last night, and he's persuaded me to stay on as an intern, until he can sort something else out.'

'Oh,' I say. 'Sort something else out, like what? There's no budget to pay another member of staff, you know.'

'No, there isn't,' says Greg, sticking his head out of the cupboard, but almost at ceiling height, which is most unnerving. 'So what exactly is he going to sort out for *you*?'

Vicky's about to reply when Greg's bloody foot chooses that moment to slip off the shelf that it's balancing on, causing him to drop like a stone. It serves him right, but

I wish he hadn't let go of the boxes containing *Adams–Edmonds* in the process.

By the time I've finished putting all the files back together, and Greg has found an old ice-pop in the freezer compartment and applied it to his twisted ankle, Vicky's had a change of heart.

'Thinking about it, it's probably not my place to tell you what Andy has planned,' she says. 'I'm sure it was meant to be a private chat between the two of us.'

'I'd kill her if I could just stand up,' says Greg, in the paper aeroplane note he sends winging onto my desk. 'I bet she's after one of *our* jobs now. Probably yours, seeing as – technically – you're in charge of me. *And* you're a *senior* caseworker, not just a bog-standard one. Vicky strikes me as a meaningless status kind of girl.'

He's right, so now I shall have to add my job to the list of things I need to save, along with my sanity and my marriage. Now I'm crying again – so, of course, Johnny chooses exactly that moment to call me on my mobile.

'What's the matter?' he says. 'You sound really sad.'

'I don't know,' I say, caught unawares, and rushing into the corridor to get away from Vicky. 'I think I just miss romance a bit. You know, someone who has eyes for no one else, and who *really* loves you. Like Robert Redford and Barbra Streisand, or Dr Zhivago and Lara What's-her-name.'

'Well, *Dr Zhivago* wasn't set in Russia by accident,' says Johnny. 'It's a lot more romantic here than in the UK. That's why, if romance is what you want, I'm your best bet. I've been here so long, I've practically gone native.'

I'm sure you shouldn't be so surprised when the person you're supposed to be having an affair with starts talking about romance.

'Oh,' I say, while I try to think of something better as a follow-up. 'But you don't make your life in Russia sound as if it's any more romantic than mine. You're always moaning about how dull it is.'

'That's because *my* Lara is in bloody Lichford,' he says. 'And won't travel to Heathrow to reach me, let alone over the Urals in the snow. Or even let me come to visit her again.'

I'm such a sucker for snow, and feeling guilty. Now I've only gone and agreed to meet Johnny again, just before the end of this month. *And* my hiccups are back, with a vengeance. I bet Lara never suffered from those.

## TUESDAY, 19 OCTOBER

Greg has replaced The Boss' photograph on the dartboard with one he covertly took of Vicky. He's just landed three darts in a row between her perfectly drawn-on eyebrows, when she finally turns up, at about 10:00am.

'There's a man on a mobility scooter stuck in the corridor, outside the lift,' she says as Greg rips her photo down, screws it up and throws it towards the bin. He misses and hits Vicky's foot instead.

'He's enormously fat, and wearing the most vulgar shirt I've ever seen,' she continues, bending down to pick the missile up.

Greg and I look at each other, then both say, 'Mr Franklin.'

'I don't know *who* he is,' says Vicky, throwing the paper into *my* bin, thankfully still in a ball. 'But someone needs to go and rescue him. He's already knocked over the weeping fig.'

'So why didn't *you* help him?' says Greg. 'While you were in the vicinity?'

'He looked really grumpy,' says Vicky. 'And he was smelly, too.'

God knows why anyone who objects to grumpy constituents would want to work for an MP in the first place, but Vicky obviously doesn't see it as a hazard of the job – which is how Greg and I find ourselves trying to manoeuvre a forty-stone man and his fatmobile, in a confined space, by ourselves.

Mr Franklin is no more help than Vicky, and adds insult to injury by refusing to tell us how he managed to get through the ground-floor security doors and into the lift without anyone having noticed him, especially while wearing an XXXL Hawaiian shirt. Then he demands answers to questions about Coalition policies while we struggle to turn him around.

After he's covered bankers' bonuses and VAT, he starts on the NHS. It'll be the Ambulance Service next, probably after Greg and I have to be carted off by paramedics when we've collapsed in the corridor from exhaustion.

'What are these reforms going to mean for my wife's hip operation?' he says. 'Though maybe they'll be an improvement, seeing as your lot did nothing to speed things up.'

'Oh, I don't think that's true,' says Greg, jerking the scooter rather viciously.

'Ow,' I say, as Mr Franklin's shopping bag falls off the handlebar and lands squarely on my foot. It hurts a lot more than a screwed-up ball of paper would.

'Watch out, you idiots!' says Mr F. 'My HobNobs'll be nothing but crumbs by the time you two have finished.'

'I'd like to crush his *other* HobNobs,' says Greg, under his breath.

He looks cross enough to do so, too – so I have to step in before things get completely out of hand.

'Well, has your wife been back to see her GP?' I say. 'She needs to tell him if her hip has got worse. When a GP refers a patient, it's usually what they say in their letter to the hospital that decides how urgently the patient's seen by a consultant.'

'I hope you're not just passing the buck,' says Mr Franklin. 'I know what you buggers are like.'

I assure him that what I've said is true, while Greg makes various rude gestures behind his back. If there's one thing Greg hates, it's when MPs' staff are accused of lying when they're not.

'Was that everything you wanted to talk about then, Mr F?' he says, as, with a burst of energy borne of sheer desperation, we finally manage to turn the scooter around so that it's facing the lift. Greg doesn't wait for Mr Franklin to answer before he says, 'Yes? Oh, good. 'Bye, then.'

431

He gives the back of Mr F's seat a congratulatory slap, while I press the button to summon the lift. Then we both leg it down the corridor as fast as we're capable of moving – which isn't very fast at all, as we're both completely knackered, and one of us is gasping for breath. I *must* give up bloody smoking.

We've almost made it to the door of the office when the lift goes *ping*, and we hear a plaintive voice: 'Hang on, you two – what do I do when I get to the ground floor? You meeting me there in case I get stuck again?'

Greg stops in his tracks, turns to face Mr F, then says, 'Oh, no – don't worry. There'll be a nice girl with long dark hair coming down in a minute. Just tell her we said that she'd been sent to help you. She's much stronger than she looks.'

I raise my eyebrows, but Greg just taps his nose and winks. Then, as soon as we walk back into the office, he rushes over to his desk and hides all of today's newspapers in the bottom drawer.

'Where the hell have the papers got to?' he says, rather louder than necessary.

Vicky and I both shrug, at which point Greg blames the disappearance on someone from the Party offices, and asks Vicky to go and buy some more.

'It's an emergency, so if you could do it straight away, that'd be great,' he says, as he puts a ten-pound note into her hand. 'A constituent said there was a big piece about Andrew in one of them, but I'm not sure which.'

'Ooh, lovely,' says Vicky, for whom the word gullible

occasionally seems to have been invented. 'Maybe there'll even be a photograph!'

'Stranger things have happened,' says Greg, as Vicky heads for the stairs and her date with destiny.

She doesn't come back for a very long time and, when she does, the look on her face suggests that this is yet another of Greg's good ideas that I'm going to regret having gone along with. Especially when she discovers that there isn't even a single quote from The Boss in any of today's editions.

Greg and I decide that now might be a good time to go for lunch.

'You shouldn't wind her up so much,' I say, as we walk back from the pub. 'Not when The Boss is behaving more normally since she got here.'

'Huh,' says Greg. 'I don't know why you're defending her. She never has so much as a good word to say for *you*.'

It turns out that he's right. When I get back to my desk, the screwed-up photo of Vicky is no longer screwed-up, but flattened out, and lying on the sofa in the Oprah room. There's no sign of Vicky, so I go to the Labour Party office to check if she's there.

'She's gone home, I think,' says Joan. 'And good riddance, too – you need to watch your back with that one, Molly. She's gunning for you. You should have heard what she said to Andrew about you on the phone.'

'Well, tell me then,' I say, after waiting what feels like ten minutes for Joan to continue without a prompt.

'She said, "If you want me to stay, Andy, then you can

forget about me being an intern. You can't pay someone as useless as Molly and expect someone like me to work for free."'

'Oh,' I say. 'Oh, dear. Could you hear what Andrew said?'

'No,' says Joan. 'But he must have asked her what she meant, because she said, "I mean incompetent, Andy. And yes, I'll *prove* it. Just you wait and see."'

When I tell Greg, he says he'll own up to the dartboard photo, and the Franklin stunt, but that might just make things worse. If Vicky got *his* job, then I'd have to work with *her*. Or, more likely, *for* her, seeing as her metaphorical balls are growing ever more golden by the second.

## WEDNESDAY, 20 OCTOBER

While we're all eating breakfast this morning, Josh orders Max to take me out for dinner tonight.

'You two don't spend enough time doing nice things together,' he says. 'And I don't want to risk becoming a child from a broken home. Just look at the mess it's made of Aunty Dinah—'

I'm pretty sure he's about to mention me, as well as Dinah, but he doesn't get a chance to complete his sentence. Max tells him that we can't afford to go anywhere for a coffee, let alone an evening meal.

'We've had barely any customers in the shop at all for weeks and weeks,' he says. 'So there'll be hardly any commission to add to my salary this month. If this keeps up, I'll be lucky to have a job at all. Your mother will be the only breadwinner in the family.'

'I win *some* bread,' says Josh. 'Though admittedly only

four hours' worth a week, as Holly never ceases to point out. Mine really *is* a shitty job.'

'Well, hang onto it,' I say. 'Apparently, Vicky's trying to lose me mine, so yours may be the only thing standing between us and penury.'

'Christ, Mol,' says Max. 'We can't afford for you to lose your job, too. Can't you just be a bit nicer to her?'

I agree to try, but he wouldn't ask me that if he'd ever *met* the woman.

'Tell her she's welcome to your job,' says Johnny, when I tell him about it later on.

Very easy for *him* to say. There's probably much more demand for International Directors of Global Oil Companies than there is for caseworkers, these days. Especially for those used to managing Labour MPs. Half of *them* have lost their seats.

'Well, work for a Tory MP, then,' says Johnny, as if that solves all my problems. 'They probably get a better class of complaint.'

Greg thinks he's right, but I'm not so sure. It'd be safer to just hang onto the job I've got, though I'm not quite sure how. Every time I speak to a constituent today, Vicky listens in, while writing things down in that notebook of hers. Then she puts it back into her briefcase and locks it, looking smug.

It's a relief when lunchtime arrives and I can go and eat my sandwich in the park. Greg says he'll stay behind with Vicky and try to 'suck up to her so nauseatingly' that she'll do anything to escape from him. Including refusing my job, if she's offered it.

He's already pulling agonised faces behind her back by the time I leave the office, so I'm not feeling very optimistic about his chances of having succeeded as I head back there, once I've finished eating my lunch.

As I walk into the lobby, someone grabs me from behind and puts a hand firmly over my mouth. I panic, and *cannot* remember the judo throw Josh taught me, so I resort to kicking backwards instead.

'Hrmph,' I say. 'Grff!'

'Ssh,' says Greg. 'And stop wriggling. In here.' Then he pulls me into the loo. The men's, for goodness' sake.

'What the hell do you think you're doing?' I say, shaking myself free. 'And why do men's toilets always smell so bad? It absolutely *stinks* in here.'

'That's why it's the only place where Vicky wouldn't think to snoop,' he says. 'And the smell is not important, in the scheme of things. Look at this. It arrived half an hour ago by Special Delivery – for you.' He hands me a parcel and says, 'Open it, quick!'

'You already have by the looks of it,' I say, contemplating the flap that is no longer stuck down.

Greg shuffles his feet, then claims he was protecting me from anthrax attacks.

'So what is it, then?' I say. 'You might as well tell me, then we can get away from this horrible smell more quickly.'

'I don't know,' says Greg. 'I thought opening the actual box might be taking things a step too far. But *that's* labelled "Tiffany" – of Old Bond Street, no less.'

Oh, my God. Even *I* have heard of Tiffany. I open the package to find a turquoise box wrapped in ribbon, along with a card on which is typed:

> *Lara*
> *For you, to remind you of me. I don't need to be reminded of you, as you're on my mind more than is good for me. It's very annoying indeed.*
> *See you at the end of next week. Wear this, and nothing else at all.*
> *Zhivago x*

Inside the box is a pendant on a heavy gold chain. It's deep green, figured like malachite, and looks exactly like a miniature Fabergé egg. Greg stares at it, open-mouthed – which is not a good look when one is in the process of eating a Twix.

'Bloody hell,' he says. 'That looks expensive. From Russia – with love, I presume?'

'Um, yes,' I say. 'I suppose you could say that, though perhaps it's not *that* expensive.'

Greg looks at me as if I have entirely lost my senses as I stash the box containing the necklace in my bag.

'It's probably one of those replicas,' I say, as we take the lift upstairs, to avoid being seen. 'Or a convincing fake, like that stuff they have on QVC. Diamonique, or whatever it's called.'

'Don't be daft,' says Greg, pausing to prop the weeping fig back up. 'Johnny's an oil baron. He's not likely to do his shopping on QVC.'

I don't know about that. Johnny's always saying how bored he gets in his hotel rooms.

There's no time to discuss it any further now, anyway – or Vicky will probably report me absent to The Boss. She's lounging on the sofa in the Oprah room and completely ignoring the phone, even though the extension is ringing right next to her head.

'Get that, Molly, will you?' she says. 'I'm far too busy to bother with constituents, and it's about time you did some work.'

'Oh, for God's sake, Vicky,' says Greg. 'Stop picking on Molly. It wasn't *her* fault about Mr Fran—'

I cut him off, just in time.

'Hush, Greg,' I say, sitting down at my desk. 'It's fine, Vicky. I'll deal with it.'

I pick the phone up, before Greg can attempt another self-sacrifice on my behalf.

'*Hal*-lo, Miss Molly,' says a very loud voice. '*Dobry dzen!*'

'Oh, hello, Igor,' I say. 'And *dobry dzen* to you, too. Or however you're supposed to pronounce it. Russian isn't one of my strengths, I'm afraid. I had to look up what it meant on Google, the first time you said it.'

Greg raises his eyebrows at this, and then slaps himself on the forehead, sits back down at his computer and types something into the search bar. Then he stares at the screen for a few moments, before gesturing at me to get rid of Igor.

This proves difficult, as Igor seems to have got it into his head that his wife has fallen in love with one of the

Mafioso keeping her under surveillance and is completely distraught as a result. By the time I've finished reassuring him that he's imagining it, and he's finished thanking me, Greg is practically jumping up and down.

'What on earth's the matter with you?' I say, as he quietly closes the door to the Oprah room. 'You look even more manic than Igor sounds. Which is *really* saying something.'

'I've found out how much that necklace cost,' says Greg, in a whisper. 'Come over here, and look at *this*.'

With that, he points to exactly the same egg charm as the one attached to the necklace Johnny sent me. It's on the Tiffany website, and its price is £815:00. Just for the charm.

'Holy shit,' I say. 'How the hell am I supposed to explain *that* to Max? The roses were bad enough.'

'Tell him an over-friendly expat gave it to you,' says Greg. 'Then you're not really lying, and Max will think it was Igor – *if* he even notices it.'

I say nothing to this, and when Greg spots my expression, he tries desperately to cover his tracks.

'Oh, God,' he says. 'Don't start crying again. I didn't mean Max wouldn't *care*. I just meant that you always say that he never takes any notice of what you wear.'

He doesn't, but I'm pretty sure he'd notice *this* – and he'd probably call it vulgar, too. I might even agree with him.

**THURSDAY, 21 OCTOBER**
'I'm not as much of a liability as you and Molly think

I am,' says The Boss to Greg, when he phones this morning. 'At least I didn't employ a Russian researcher when I was on the Select Committee for Defence. Not like that idiot LibDem MP. *His* assistant's just been picked up by MI5.'

'Don't count your chickens,' says Greg. 'I've got a bad feeling about Vicky, you know.'

The Boss tells him not to be silly, but Greg decides to investigate further anyway. He picks up a new notebook, opens it to the first page, and then walks towards the Oprah room, pen poised at the ready.

'Got any Russian relatives, Vicky?' he says, subtlety never having been his forte, along with tact.

'Don't be ridiculous,' she says. 'Why d'you ask?'

'Something Slavonic about your cheekbones. *And* you look like a woman who'd know how to make a man tell you anything.'

'Thanks,' says Vicky, as if Greg had meant it as a compliment. She obviously hasn't a clue what he's really talking about, probably because she thinks keeping abreast of current affairs means revealing as much cleavage as possible. I keep hoping that she'll catch pneumonia like Mum always warned me would happen if you walked around with your bosoms hanging out all over the place. (In those days she used to wear knickers, so was still in a position to comment.)

'What about Russian friends?' continues Greg. '*Close* friends? Take your time before you answer.'

'I don't need to. I don't *know* any Russians, apart from Igor.' Vicky rolls her eyes. 'Now do you mind letting me get on with what I'm doing – *finally*? I've got to finish this, then go and see a constituent, on Andy's behalf, so I'm in too much of a hurry to waste time answering any more of your stupid questions.'

Greg makes a great show of writing *that* down in his notebook, but Vicky doesn't seem to notice, as she's busy concentrating on trying to mend another of her horrible nails. When she decides that the task is beyond her, she phones for an 'emergency appointment' at the nail bar and buggers off.

I breathe a sigh of relief, but then Greg sits down opposite my desk, and starts staring at me. 'Of course, we already know we have *someone* with Russian connections in this office, don't we, Molly?' he says. 'And I don't just mean Igor, even though he does think the sun shines out of your arse.'

Greg follows this statement with one of those meaningful looks he usually reserves for when The Boss makes one of his wilder claims to the media. It's easy to see why being jailers went to people's heads in that 1970s prison experiment.[39]

'Oh, for God's sake, Greg,' I say, leaving him at my desk and heading for the relative safety of the kitchen. 'I hardly think one disastrous date with a UK citizen who just *happens* to work in Russia counts as exposing myself to bribery and corruption. And, anyway, Johnny takes

---

[39] The Stanford Prison Experiment: A psychological experiment carried out at Stanford University, which seemed to prove that we all have it in us to become completely power-mad. Some of us more than others, I suspect.

441

absolutely no interest in my job whatsoever. He's as unimpressed with it as I am. More, probably.'

'Ah, yes – but you *have* always wondered what a man as rich and successful as he is could possibly see in you, haven't you?' says Greg. Somewhat insensitively, if you ask me.

'Thanks,' I say, though not in the same tone of voice as Vicky used earlier.

'Just some food for thought,' Greg says. 'And that Fabergé thing could easily be construed as a bribe.'

I add salt to his coffee, which I then spill on his trousers when I pass it to him. He accuses me of doing it accidentally on purpose, but it does shut him up for the rest of the afternoon, until it gets dark.

Vicky's only just come back, so God knows how long fixing her nail has taken. Now she's moaning about how she's going to cope if any more of them break over the next few days.

'My nail technician has decided to take a few days' holiday, with no notice at all!' she says to Greg, who's pretending to take an interest in order to save my job. 'She's going away until the end of next week, so I don't know what she thinks I'm going to do while she's gone. I can't walk around with my nails in a state like Molly's.'

Greg says, 'Oh, my God – no, you can't. That would be terrible. *Insupportable.*'

When Vicky does a double-take to check if he's being serious, he panics and suggests she go home early, as she's 'had such a busy day'. She seems impervious to *that* particular piece of sarcasm.

When she's gone, Greg comes back into my office and walks to the window. He peers out for a while, then dives to the floor. 'Get down!' he says, in a very loud whisper. 'They're out there, Mol – waiting for you.'

'Who?' I say. He could mean any one of a horde of demented constituents as far as I'm concerned.

Fear *is* contagious, though – and Greg's is palpable – so I slide under my desk, knocking the printer onto my head in the process. I stay on the floor for a few minutes, saying, 'Ouch' and looking for blood, until I realise that Greg has stood up, and is looking through the window again.

'MI5,' he says. 'Look – dark car, and a man in a dark suit, speaking into his sleeve.'

When I've managed to disentangle myself from the printer lead that caused all the trouble, I stand up and approach the window myself. Very carefully, in case I'm seen.

'For Christ's sake, Greg,' I say, after a cursory glance outside. 'That's Phil Ashbury, the guy from Joan's union. He had a meeting with her at 5:00pm, probably to discuss the way The Boss keeps treating her. And he's putting his *gloves* on, not speaking into his sleeve.'

'So he'd like you to *think*,' says Greg. 'But some of us are not so easily fooled.'

He'd be a lot more convincing if he wasn't also laughing, but I'm a bit unnerved, anyway. What if MI5

443

*are* suspicious of anyone with a connection to an MP, and to a Russian? And what if they're reading my emails, and followed me and Johnny to our hotel? They're bound to have nominated us for one of those Bad Sex Awards if they did.

They might even suspect that my necklace was Johnny's way of softening me up. If it was, it's already worked a treat. I told him *all* about Andrew's views on LibDem sex scandals earlier today.

**FRIDAY, 22 OCTOBER**
'You might have to help me with a CV,' says Max, over breakfast. 'As well as Josh. There are rumours there's going to be a big announcement at work on Monday, and I doubt the news is going to be good.'

'Okay,' I say, 'though you'll need to get home a bit earlier in the evenings than you have been doing, if you want to get it done before next weekend. I can't understand how this Mrs Bloom can need so many late calls, all of a sudden.'

I still haven't seen any evidence of Mrs Bloom's *existence*, and nor have I seen Ellen much this week. Or not when Max is 'working late', anyway.

He gives me one of those 'don't start' looks, just as I realise that the top of the Tiffany box is protruding from my handbag and make a lunge for it.

God, that was close. My blood pressure won't take much more of this, so I shall post the necklace back to Johnny at lunchtime today – before it gives me a heart attack.

'I'll need to write a CV for myself, as well as for you,' I say, 'if Vicky carries on the way she's going. Even though I'm really trying to be nice.'

'Try harder, then,' says Josh, who's sounding more and more like the parent in this relationship of late.

When I arrive at the office I do intend to follow his advice, but then Vicky joins Andrew in the Oprah room, and Greg and I don't see either of them for the next couple of hours. They must be whispering, as we can't hear them either when we wander casually past the door for no reason every few minutes or so.

When they finally come out, The Boss announces that Vicky's going to accompany him into surgery today.

'Why?' says Greg, before I can ask the same question myself.

'It'll be useful experience for her,' says Andrew, though he doesn't say for what.

Greg doesn't make any further comment, but scribbles something on a piece of paper, which he shoves into my hand as I pass his desk on my way to the kitchen. I need another, stronger, cup of coffee.

'Here's that number you wanted, Mol,' he says, pulling his meaningful face. 'Put it somewhere safe, so you don't risk losing it again.'

I read Greg's note as I wait for the kettle to boil. 'That proves it, Molly,' it says. 'Vicky's after *your* job. Surgery's usually your responsibility, except for when Andrew plays silly buggers and makes me *Goldenballs*. So we need a survival plan for you – and *fast*.'

When she comes back into the office after surgery has

finished, Vicky looks as if she needs one more than I do. Her face is unusually pale, even through all the foundation she wears, and she's chewing the side of one of her precious nails.

'You all right, Vicky?' I say. Now I can tell Josh I really *am* trying to be nice, though the effort's killing me.

'Of course she's all right,' says Andrew, helping Vicky put on her coat with a rather excessive flourish. 'Cope with anything, can't you, Vicks?'

'Well, I can't,' says Greg. 'I need to go the chemist and get something for this persistent nausea.'

Andrew offers to do it for him, as he says he's taking Vicky for lunch 'very close to Superdrug', but Greg says he needs some fresh air and stomps off ahead of them. I stay at my desk, trying to think of the best way to word a 'Thanks for the egg, but no thanks' email to Johnny. It sounds *much* simpler than it is.

I'm still on draft one when Greg returns. 'Christ,' he says, before throwing himself onto the sofa in the Oprah room and closing his eyes as if he's in pain.

'What on earth's the matter?' I say. 'And get off there before The Boss and Vicky come back and decide that you've been sleeping on the job.'

'I shall just tell them that I have had a relapse of PTSD,' says Greg. 'Caused by the trauma of encountering Steve Ellington at the pharmacy counter in Boots. Is it too much to expect constituents to keep their bloody distance when you're on your lunch-break and engaged in a sensitive transaction?'

'Yes,' I say. 'I mean, no. Well, you know what I mean.'

Greg nods. MPs' staff should be like teachers and live anywhere other than the town in which they work. You never know who's going to pop up and start demanding to know what the point of the United Nations is, right at the moment when you're trying to read the instructions on a tube of KY jelly – not that that's ever happened to me. It's just a hypothetical example I thought up off the top of my head.

'What were you buying?' I ask. 'Something embarrassing?'

'Imodium,' says Greg. 'I can't tell you how much fun Steve had with that, but suffice it to say that it involved lots of increasingly tedious references to politicians' tendency to verbal diarrhoea. So I've come up with a cunning plan to camouflage ourselves while we shop, in future and I've bought you something to help. Pass me that carrier bag.'

I do as I'm told, and then wait while Greg rummages through endless packets of Imodium, two cans of Red Bull and three bags of Haribos. After what feels like hours, he finally says, 'Got it!' and chucks something towards me.

I catch it, without even trying. It's automatic, thanks to Josh. When he was about two, he went through a rather lengthy and dangerous stage of saying, 'Catch!' at the same time as throwing hard objects straight at Connie's head.

So now I'm staring at the shapeless thing that's landed in my hand, and which seems to be knitted from thick black wool. 'Um, thanks,' I say. 'It's very nice. But why are there holes in it, and what is it for?'

'It's a balaclava, you fool,' says Greg. 'I bought myself one, too. We just put them on whenever we leave the office – and then we can stay incognito wherever we go. Brilliant, eh? Let's try them on, and see how we look.'

That idea may have been a mistake, in retrospect – judging by how Andrew and Vicky react to the sight of us when they walk back into the office. Vicky starts screaming and The Boss pulls her in front of him, as if she were a riot shield.

'Who are you, and what do you want?' he says.

'Whapf?' says Greg, which is a significant achievement with a mouthful of Haribos. My teeth are so firmly stuck together that I'm incapable of making any sound at all.

The Boss drops his voice and pulls Vicky closer to him, before continuing: 'Are you the Russian Mafia? If so, I'm not Igor Popov – but I do know where he lives.'

'Nompf, you foof! S'mee,' says Greg – twice, before he gives up and removes his balaclava, and gestures at me to do the same.

Some people have no sense of humour at all. Even after Greg's pointed out that terrorists and Mafioso don't usually fill the time spent lying in wait for their victims by typing letters, The Boss still can't see the funny side. He doesn't speak to us for the rest of the afternoon, and Vicky doesn't speak to us, *or* him.

'Why's Vicky giving The Boss the silent treatment?' I say to Greg, when we sneak off to the Labour Party's office to get away from the chilly atmosphere pervading ours.

'Didn't you hear what she said when Andrew finally released his grip on her?' says Greg.'

'No,' I say. 'I was still trying to pull my balaclava off, so I couldn't hear anything at all. It's a bit tight and I couldn't get it over my ears.'

'Yeah, I spotted that,' says Greg. 'You looked a bit like Colonel Gaddafi crossed with a meerkat who'd joined the Special Forces. Anyway, Vicky called Andrew a spineless coward for hiding behind her – so maybe she's not as daft as she looks.'

Or as me and Greg look, when we're wearing our new shopping kit. Greg reckons it's worth it, if we've finally managed to put Vicky off stealing my job.

## SATURDAY, 23 OCTOBER

I get up very late to find Max making poached eggs on toast for him and Josh while listening to the radio. It is playing James Blunt's new song, so I turn it off.

'I don't see why you hate James Blunt so much,' says Max. 'Most women seem to love him.'

'Well, you wouldn't understand why I'm not one of them, would you?' I say. 'Seeing as you're such a fan of the blonde female version next door.'

Max just huffs at that, and then there follows one of those uncomfortable silences. Josh decides to try to break it by taking an interest in politics. 'What do you think of this Daylight Savings Bill,[40] Mum?' he says.

---

[40] Daylight Savings Bill: Proposal to advance UK time by one hour 'for all or part of the year'. I've never really worked out how that differs from what happens at the moment, and The Boss certainly hasn't.

449

'I'm against it,' I say. 'The less daylight I have to look at myself in, the better. How about you?'

'I'm against it too.' Josh sounds as if he's actually given this some thought. I am very impressed and settle myself for a long discussion. Another mother-and-son bonding session coming up.

'I was only joking,' I say. 'I'm in favour, and I thought you'd think it was a good idea, too. Why don't you?'

'I don't like change,' says Josh.

He looks meaningfully at Max and me. I squirm, while Max says, 'Why not?'

'Because change brings pain,' says Josh. 'Oh, and did I tell you Connie's coming home for the weekend? She should be here in a bit.'

Max and I look at each other, then both shake our heads. How does Josh know something about Connie that we don't? They must have spoken to each other on the phone, though that's so rare as to be almost unheard-of.

'I wonder what they were talking about?' I say to Max, when Josh has disappeared upstairs to play on his Xbox.

'I don't know,' he says. 'Maybe about what's going on with you.'

'What do you mean with me?' I say. 'What about you?'

'Well, with *us*, then,' says Max, as the front door opens and Connie comes in.

'I'm hypothermic,' she says, when asked how she is. She looks perfectly all right to me, which is a bit worrying, with one case of Histrionic Personality Disorder in the family already.

'Don't exaggerate,' I say. 'You sound like Dinah.'

'I'm not exaggerating,' says Connie. 'I nearly died of cold during the night.'

Given that she made Max and I buy her a million-tog duvet before she left home, I somehow doubt that – so I say as much.

'Yeah, well, I couldn't use it, could I?' she says, as if I should have known.

Children may think their parents are psychic, but when I ask Connie why she couldn't sleep under her quilt, things are still as clear as mud.

'Because of the spider,' she says. 'On the bedroom ceiling.'

Connie is terrified of spiders due to some unspecified childhood trauma, which probably had something to do with Josh. Most things trace back to him, as far as she's concerned – but, even so, I'm still confused and so is Max.

'What's that got to do with your duvet?' he says. 'You usually just trap spiders under a glass and wait for someone else to get rid of them.'

Connie explains that she couldn't get to sleep while the spider was walking around above her head, so she decided she had to get it down somehow. This was a challenge, as Connie has the same trouble with reaching high ceilings as I do but, eventually, she managed it.

'I flicked it off the ceiling with a pair of tights,' she says. 'But then it landed on my bed.'

'Well, why didn't you just flick it off that as well, then?' says Max. 'Job done.'

451

'That's what I was *going* to do,' says Connie. 'But you know I don't like hurting anything – so I wrapped it up in the quilt and tried to shake it outside instead.'

'Well, for God's sake, Connie, there was no reason why you couldn't use your bedding once the spider had gone. Even Dinah wouldn't have made that much fuss.'

'She would have done if she'd dropped the f*cking quilt out of the window as well,' says Connie. 'Into a puddle.'

As Max and I digest this information, Connie says that she's going upstairs to see Josh, for 'a brother and sister bonding session'. This lasts for an unusually quiet half an hour, and then they come back downstairs and say that they are inviting us to join in.

'Let's have a take-away tonight,' says Josh. 'And some beers. Me and Con will pay. Then we can play Monopoly, and remind ourselves how lovely it is to be part of a nuclear family.'

'Subtle, our children aren't,' says Max, much later, as we cuddle up on the sofa, rather drunk. 'But we *will* be okay – whatever happens with our jobs -- as long as we stick together, you know.'

'I know,' I say, kissing him.

## SUNDAY, 24 OCTOBER

God, I've got a terrible hangover. Why on earth did I decide to drink beer instead of gin last night?

Josh is in an even worse state than me, though he denies that it has anything to do with a hangover and claims that he's just sleep-deprived. He may be, but join the club, as Max would say.

I'm having a lovely dream in which Max and I are renewing our vows, floating on a cloud above a Caribbean island to the accompaniment of a heavenly choir led by our children, when Connie comes barging into our room.

'Mum!' she yells as loud as she can in my ear.

Max is still asleep beside me – so why is Connie picking on me? 'Ouch,' I say, swatting her away and pulling the pillow over my head. 'Shush, Connie. My head really hurts.'

'You've got to do something about bloody, bloody Josh, Mum. And do it now!'

'What?' I take the pillow off my face, and try to open my eyes, but the light makes them hurt, so I shut them again.

'Con,' I say, 'Josh is probably still out cold, like I was, so I really don't see the urgency.'

'My new shoes,' she says. 'They're probably ruined. I come home for one night, for the first time in ages, and he does *this*.'

What is she talking about? I sit up in bed, decide fast moves are a very bad idea and lie down again. Very slowly.

'Connie, I have a terrible hangover and I feel like death, so just tell me. What have your new shoes got to do with Josh?'

'They're in the tree outside his bedroom,' she says. 'Come and look, if you don't believe me.'

She keeps on until she's woken Max up, too, and then

she insists that we follow her downstairs and out into the garden. Once there, we stand and stare upwards in disbelief – at Connie's new shoes, which really *are* in the tree. Still in their box, though this doesn't seem to make Connie feel better.

I leave Max trying to shake them down, and head back inside and straight up the stairs to Josh's room – which smells of teenage boy and far too much beer the night before. Now I feel sick, as well as having the head-ache from hell.

'Josh,' I say, shaking him. 'Josh! Wake up! Why are Connie's new shoes in the tree?'

'Oh, yeah,' says Josh. 'I threw the box out there about four o'clock this morning. Now go away and let me go back to sleep. I'm *very* tired.'

'Why?' I say, at the same time as Connie and Max, who have now arrived in Josh's room.

Josh opens one eye, glares at all of us, then sighs as if the answer should be obvious. 'Because the bloody birds were singing too loud, and the shoebox was the first thing that came to hand,' he says. 'Connie shouldn't have left it in my room.'

'I'll get dressed and go and get the ladder,' says Max. 'Good morning, one and all.' There's a definite *tone* to the way he says it, which sounds like the giving-up of hope.

Josh is still asleep when Connie leaves to catch her train, weighed down by a heavy-duty sleeping bag as a temporary replacement for her quilt, and still furious about her shoes.

'They looked all right to me,' says Max, carrying the ladder back to the shed. 'Though it's a good job it didn't rain. Don't pull that up, Mol – it's not a weed.'

I've just remembered that it's Sunday, when the bins are due to be put out, so I'm trying to find an excuse to remain in the garden as long as Max does. I'm not having a naked Ellen ruin the *rapprochement* our children seem to have worked so hard to help us achieve.

I look up at Ellen's bedroom window, just to check, but there's no sign of her, naked or otherwise – though she could have dived behind the curtains if she'd spotted me. Probably best not to take any risks.

'How's the garden doing, Max?' I say, wandering casually around, and then trying to hide myself in a rather attractive purple shrub, out of Ellen's line of vision, just in case.

'Be careful,' he says, at the same time as I say, 'Ow.'

That's just typical, isn't it? The only plant big enough to provide cover for a very small person, and it has to be a berberis. Prickles everywhere, unlike Ellen's bloody cactus.

'What are you doing, Mol?' says Max. 'You know that plant's spiky. It's why we planted it – to deter Steve Ellington from burgling us again.'

'Allegedly,' I say – referring to Steve's part in the burglary, and not the planting of the berberis.

I wish we hadn't planted it now, seeing as it's just ripped my skirt and a pair of my new lacy pants – not that Max seems to notice *them*. He's too busy looking at me as if I am mad, so I dab the blood off my leg with the hem of my skirt and look around for inspiration. There must be another plant big enough to lurk behind.

'What the hell is this?' I say, picking up a tangled brownish mass of foliage that appears to be comprehensively dead, albeit one that's still encased in a rather nice pot.

'Oh,' says Max. 'Ah. Um – that's the plant you bought me for our anniversary. I think I may have forgotten to plant it. Or to water it, actually.'

I look at him, then down at the dead plant, then back at him. I'm trying to avoid recognising this latest metaphor for my life, but the bloody things just will not stop making their presence felt.

'So,' I say, very slowly. 'I buy you a passionflower for our anniversary. And then you kill it – by neglect?'

Max winces, as he nods his head, and all Josh and Connie's efforts go to waste.

## MONDAY, 25 OCTOBER

Well, if today is anything to go by, there's no *way* these NHS reforms are going to work. Not that I should care, given that I probably won't have a job in politics for much longer, thanks to those bloody GPs at Silverhill Surgery. Talk about people not wanting to take responsibility!

The Boss phones from Westminster, just after 11:00am. 'Molly,' he says. 'I'm faxing you a copy of a letter I've just opened. Phone me back as soon as you've got it – and be ready to explain yourself.'

He sounds so angry that I head for the fax machine

straight away and then stand there fretting while it prints out a five-page letter. The damn thing seems to take forever.

I've only just begun to read it, when Andrew calls me back. 'Stop the delaying tactics,' he says, 'and tell me what the hell you thought you were playing at? You've only gone and upset an entire medical practice, you bloody idiot.'

'What?' I say, still trying to make sense of the letter. I can't believe what I'm reading – which is saying something, given the total lunacy of fifty per cent of the mail we receive on a daily basis.

The Practice Manager accuses me of irresponsibility, and tells Andrew that the Practice does not appreciate its doctors being made 'apologists for systems created by politicians'. For God's sake.

Apparently, it was completely unacceptable for me to have suggested to Mr Franklin that his wife should go back to see her GP if she thought her condition was worsening – so that the GP could then advise the hospital, if *he* felt she needed to see a consultant more quickly.

'But, Andrew,' I say, 'I don't understand what's so bad about what I did. *I'm* not a doctor – and nor are you. Mr Franklin wanted us to *order* the hospital to see her more quickly. How was I supposed to know if that was justifiable or not?'

'That's not the point,' says The Boss. 'You've pissed off every doctor in the whole practice. They've all signed the letter of complaint, individually!'

They *have*, which makes me almost as cross as Andrew, though for different reasons.

'That's ridiculous,' I say, 'I didn't put it in the way that they're saying I did, anyway – and, seeing as they're doctors, they must *surely* be able to tell that Mr F is a total nutter, who'd tell anybody anything to get what he wants.'

Andrew doesn't say anything, but I can feel that he doesn't give a damn whether I'm being unjustly accused or not. He just wants the problem solved – as usual.

I'm so furious that I can't let it go though, so I carry on regardless: 'I would have thought that someone from the Practice would have phoned to ask me what I'd *actually* told Mr F before they kicked off like this, if only out of professional courtesy,' I say. 'That's what I would have done in their place. I *always* try to check the facts before I accuse anybody of anything.'

Even Josh and Connie would agree with that last statement, but it cuts no ice at all with Andrew.

'I don't care what your excuse is, Molly,' he says. 'I can't afford to have a vocal bunch of bloody doctors against me, so you will write to them today and apologise. Grovel, in fact. And I want you to fax me a copy of the letter before you post it, so I can see whether this was only a one-off cock-up, or if you're as crap at your job as I've been hearing you are.'

'From Vicky, I suppose,' I say, as I notice that she's standing in the doorway, listening in and smiling.

I glare at her, which sends her scuttling back into the Oprah room, and then I type the most over-the-top apology anyone has *ever* written, while swearing under my breath and willing all her stupid nails to fall off.

Greg gives me a questioning look, but I'm not saying anything else that Vicky might overhear – so I just hand him the letter from the surgery, together with a copy of my reply. He winces as he reads them both, then sucks air in through his teeth.

He's obviously about to say something he shouldn't, so I put my finger to my lips and shake my head, at which point he starts scribbling on a piece of paper. Then he holds up the result for me to read.

'Total f*ckers,' it says.

That analysis makes me feel a lot better, so I'm much calmer by the time The Boss phones back again, after I've faxed him a copy of my apology.

'Right,' he says. 'Get it in the next post – I don't want this hanging around until the end of the day. Let's just hope it does the trick. I can't be doing with a posse of bloody GPs fomenting trouble in Lichford at the moment. They're far too damned articulate at the best of times.'

'Oh, I should think they'll be too busy to worry about you soon,' I say. 'Seeing as they're going to be running the entire NHS, if the Coalition gets its way."

'They're going to find *that* a bit of a challenge, aren't they?' says Greg, as I put the phone down. 'If they can't even handle justifying their own diagnoses to their patients.'

I don't reply, as that seems the safest bet with Vicky still in earwig mode. Instead, I run downstairs to post the letter – and to smoke a cigarette.

You'd think I'd want to avoid doing *anything* that might make me need a doctor after what's just happened – but every unhealthy drag feels like sweet revenge. Smokers' logic is seriously warped. A bit like that of some GPs.

When I return to the office, Vicky's still gloating. 'That's why Andy needs *me*, Molly,' she says. 'Because I am so much more trustworthy than you.'

'Rubbish,' says Greg. 'And I knew I should have pushed that horrible Franklin man off the pier when I had the chance.'

Vicky tuts, as if this is further proof of the total incompetence of Andrew's longest-serving staff, and office morale hits an all-time low. It's still there at lunchtime when Vicky goes to the hairdresser and Greg to the pub. Then Mr Sampson phones about his long-standing and complicated legal case. The one he told me he'd lost, when I last spoke to him, well over a year ago. Maybe he's planning to appeal.

'You were supposed to be sending me something in the post, urgently,' he says, 'but it hasn't arrived.'

This is news to me, so I ask Mr Sampson who he last spoke to.

'That new girl,' he says, 'when she visited me, last week.'

'Oh,' I say. 'I don't know what she meant, I'm afraid. I didn't know there had been any new developments, and there are no recent updates on the computer. Just hang on a moment – I'll get your file.'

I put Mr Sampson on hold, and head for the filing

cabinet. I look through it twice, then on my desk – and in the Oprah room, but there's no sign of the file anywhere. I promise to phone Mr S back, and search again, still without success. I'm rifling through the paperwork on Greg's desk when he walks in and asks me what I think I'm doing.

'Trying to find Mr Sampson's file,' I say. 'Can't see it anywhere. Have you had it?'

'No,' says Greg. 'Haven't talked to him myself for ages, but Vicky did visit him last week, now I come to think of it. I remember her moaning that his file was too big when she broke a nail trying to cram it into her briefcase. You'll have to ask her what she's done with it, if she ever deigns to come back to work.'

Another hour goes past before Vicky finally does return from having her hair done, and then she claims she gave the file to me. She looks me straight in the eyes while she says this, not that *that's* ever a reliable indicator that someone's telling the truth. Steve Ellington *always* does it.

'It was so that you could do the photocopying,' she says, while smirking. Fishily – if there *is* a fish that resembles a Madame de Bouffant.

'What photocopying?' I say.

'Mr Sampson gave me a pile of documents to take copies of. Then *you* were supposed to return them by post.'

I look at Greg, who looks back at me. Neither one of us wants to ask the next question but, as usual, I cave in first.

461

'Vicky, *please* tell me that these aren't *original* documents we're talking about?' I say.

'Oh, I should think so,' she says. 'Otherwise the constituent wouldn't be so anxious to have them back, would he?'

Does she *have* to look as if she's enjoying this quite so much? Sometimes I fully understand axe-murderers – and their motivation.

Greg makes a seemingly endless series of V-signs behind Vicky's back while I answer the phone to The Boss, who's now even crosser than he was earlier. Apparently Mr Sampson has given up waiting for me to call him back and has just phoned the London office.

I take a deep breath, and then explain.

'Well, Molly,' says Andrew, 'this is obviously yet another example of your unbelievable incompetence. You'll just have to explain to Mr Sampson that *you've* lost his file, and apologise. Profusely.'

'Me?' I say, abandoning my resolution to be nice to Vicky to save my job. 'It's not my fault! Mr Sampson gave it to—'

'Collective responsibility's the thing,' interrupts Andrew, before hanging up on me. Now it's my turn to make V-signs – and mine are even more extravagant than Greg's.

'Now what?' I say, more to myself than anyone else, but Greg replies anyway.

'Holding manoeuvre,' he says, in a whisper. 'Buy some time, so we can find the file.'

He's right, so I brace myself, then phone Mr Sampson. I cross my fingers, firmly, and tell him that Andrew's just realised that the file was in his briefcase, which he's taken

462

with him to London. 'I'll have to get the paperwork sent back from there,' I say. 'I'm *very* sorry for the delay, but there's really nothing to worry about.'

I hope there isn't bad karma for white lies or I am buggered in the next life, as well as this – apparently.

## MONDAY, 25 OCTOBER (LATE EVENING)

Vicky still insists she gave me the file, so I'm clinging to the hope that Greg and I will find it and solve the problem, but it's already almost 10:00pm and we're still searching the office, while Fish-Face is long gone.

She's probably refreshing her fake tan tonight, or doing something equally important, whereas Greg and I won't be going home until we've found what we're looking for.

There's paper everywhere and the place looks as if it's been ransacked. We haven't even had time to discuss what on earth we're going to do about the most serious problem: Vicky. I don't know why, but I'm *sure* she lost this file on purpose. So is Greg.

'Never underestimate a hair-flicker,' he says, as we admit defeat and lock the office up for the night. 'That's the lesson we need to learn.'

'Or a piranha,' I say. 'Did you *see* the way she smiled at me?'

'Yes,' he says. 'It's the first time *I've* ever heard the theme from *The Twilight Zone*. I used to think you made that up.'

## MONDAY, 25 OCTOBER (MIDNIGHT)

I didn't think white-lie karma moved so fast. I've just

got home, to be told by Max that he was made redundant this morning.

'I need to go back to the office now, in that case,' I say. 'It's even more important that I find this file, if I'm the only one of us with a job.'

Max persuades me to get some sleep first, but he's being a bit optimistic about my chances of achieving *that* . . .

**TUESDAY, 26 OCTOBER**
I finally dozed off at about 6:00am, and now I'm awake again, less than two hours later, so I suppose I may as well go into work right now. At least then I can carry on searching for Mr Sampson's file in peace and quiet until the office opens to the public – and without Vicky watching me while I do it.

So much for that brilliant idea. When I arrive at the office, who should I find sitting in the Oprah room? Only Madam Vick the Flicker of the Hair. Her smile still looks like a piranha's, too.

'Morning, Molly,' she says. 'See you haven't visited a beauty salon overnight.'

I make several attempts to kill her using the power of thought, but none of them work, so then I stalk into my office and slam the door. Or I *try* to slam it anyway – but The Boss has left a pile of papers in the way, so the door just hits those and then rebounds and whacks me firmly in the face.

I'm digging around in the fridge for another ice-pop to stop the swelling, when Greg arrives.

'Morning, all,' he says, sorting through the mail that I abandoned half-way through dealing with it, when the egg on my forehead began to form.

He gives Vicky a particularly menacing smile, which she repays in kind, and then grabs a parcel from the top of the pile and shouts, 'Take cover! Parcel bomb!'

It says something about my state of mind that I do as he tells me, without even panicking, but Vicky doesn't. She stands up and then stops dead in the middle of the Oprah room as Greg throws the parcel – overarm – directly onto the sofa that she's just vacated. It bounces off a cushion, hits Vicky's cleavage-enhancing bra, and rebounds straight back into Greg's outstretched hand.

'False alarm,' he says, tearing off the brown paper to reveal a video cassette, while Vicky's screams slowly subside. 'It's not dangerous – unlike people who shaft their colleagues. Or so I hear.'

'Oh, honestly, Greg,' I say. 'Don't be so flippant. And thank God you were right about that parcel. You could have blown the whole building up if you'd been wrong.'

'He's an irresponsible *idiot*,' says Vicky as she pushes past Greg and heads out of the office, probably on her way to the loo.

He sticks his tongue out at her as she storms off down the corridor, then lowers his voice and says, 'The corner of the paper was already ripped, Mol – so I could see what it contained before I threw it.'

He winks, then volunteers to make the first round of coffee. We're going to need plenty of *that* today, given how knackered we are. I'm about to start searching for the file again, when I realise that I haven't checked my email at all, not once since I heard that Mr Sampson's file had gone missing.

My inbox is full of new messages, but the first one I open is from Johnny, telling me that I can give him the necklace back when we meet on Friday. *If* he hasn't managed to persuade me to keep it by then, which he says he's still determined to do.

I tell Greg, who looks me up and down several times, then says, 'That man is obviously maddened by lust, though God knows why. You look *appalling*.'

'Thanks,' I say. 'But I can't keep the necklace, can I? What sort of person would I be if I accepted a gift as expensive as that?'

Greg shakes his head in mock-despair, as I notice that the fax machine has jammed, and try to kick it back to life.

'An intelligent one,' he says. 'What's the point of having a so-called affair with an oil baron when you don't get any money out of it?'

'Or any sex,' I say, kicking the fax machine again, even though it's already begun to work.

It stops again, presumably in protest, and then remains on strike for the rest of the day; as does Vicky, as far as we can tell. She never returns from her trip to the loo, much to Greg's irritation.

'I need to search her briefcase,' he says, when it gets to closing time, and we still haven't found Mr Sampson's file. 'I'm sure she's hiding it in there, just to spite us.'

Joan agrees with him. 'She's capable of anything, that

woman,' she says, when she comes in to ask why Greg and I are working late again. 'Pete Carew told me he overheard her telling Andrew he couldn't trust anyone *months* ago, after GC one night. So it's probably her who's been making him paranoid, all along.'

'She's having that effect on me,' I say. 'Though it's probably not paranoia if something bad is *guaranteed* to happen to you, is it? Such as me losing my job, if I don't find this bloody file.'

Joan tries to reassure me that *that* won't happen, but I'm pretty sure it will. 'Andrew'll be even crosser, if he finds out that Greg and I have been so busy searching that we haven't done any actual work today,' I say.

I still haven't responded to a single email, including Johnny's, or any messages on the answer-phone, and nor has Greg. I haven't even phoned Dad back after he left a voicemail on my mobile, saying he needed to 'discuss something important, urgently'. I don't have time, so I text Dinah, and ask her to ring him instead.

She texts back to say that he didn't answer, but that she's emailed him the details of the kitchen worktops she thinks he should choose, anyway, as 'that's bound to be what he needed to know'. She adds that she told him to choose ones containing glittery bits, to satisfy any future cravings to become the leader of the Glitter Band. This makes me laugh, then makes me cry. HPD may run in families.

'Don't worry, Molly,' says Joan, giving me a hug. 'I know you're stressed, but you can rely on your friends at times like this.'

Now she's helping in the search, but it's already really late and we *still* haven't found the file. We've checked every cupboard, every drawer, and emptied all the filing cabinets. And the archive boxes – twice.

Greg's almost torn the Oprah room apart, and the kitchen cupboards too. We can't think of anywhere left to look, so finally both he and Joan admit defeat and say goodnight. I am doomed, but too knackered to care, so I'll think I'll sit down, just for a minute . . .

## WEDNESDAY, 27 OCTOBER

Bloody hell, the sofa in the Oprah room's uncomfortable to sleep on. I've got a terrible crick in my neck, and God knows what time I finally got home last night, once I woke up from my accidental nap. I probably shouldn't have bothered leaving the office at all, as now I'm going to be late for work.

'They're using printer cartridges to try to blow up planes,' says Greg, who's reading the breaking news online when I finally arrive at 9.15. 'So I think I'll leave the job of changing the next one to our mutual friend, Victoria.'

That's not a bad idea, but I am a bit worried about the risks to other less-annoying people, such as Johnny, for example.

'Maybe you shouldn't fly to the UK on Friday,' I say to him, in an email marked 'high priority'. 'It sounds as if it could be dangerous.'

'Don't be daft,' he says when he phones me, to avoid the need to type a reply. 'I'm not going to have our meeting messed up by anything, this time – certainly not

468

by a terrorist threat. Don't forget I've worked in all the major trouble spots of the world. *They're* usually where oil is found.'

'Well, don't mention that to Scotland,' I say. 'Or you'll have Alex Salmond[41] after you.'

Johnny laughs at that, for far longer than I think necessary. Then he says, 'Why *are* Scottish politicians all named after fish? Isn't there another one called Sturgeon, or something like that?'

Then he asks me if I like caviar. I do wish he'd take politics a bit more seriously sometimes.

'Anyway,' he continues, once I've confirmed that it tasted nice, on the one occasion that I've eaten it, 'you should be flattered that I'm willing to risk my life to see you again. *And* suitably grateful, once we finally get into bed.'

On that note of shameless emotional blackmail, he rings off, leaving me in the middle of what I'm sure would qualify as a *very* hot flush. I open the window, stand in front of it and flap my jumper up and down in an attempt to maximise the breeze.

Greg asks what the hell I think I'm doing, so I tell him that I feel very odd indeed.

'It's a panic attack, you fool,' he says. 'Probably due to all these adrenalin-fuelled late nights, looking for Mr Sampson's bloody file. Go and lie down in the Oprah room for a minute, until you get a grip.'

---

[41] Alex Salmond: First Minister of Scotland. Or 'Mr Smug', as he's affectionately described by Greg.

*That's* not going to happen, unless there's a miracle and the file turns up, but I do feel a bit better after another brief, sofa-based snooze – until I stand up again. Then I start thinking about what Johnny said, and what he's expecting us to get up to in forty-eight hours' time, which doesn't leave me very long to work out if Max really *is* having an affair with the Botox Queen, before we do.

'No wonder you still don't know if Max is up to something,' says Greg, 'seeing as your investigations have been totally half-arsed, so far. You should have let me stalk him. I have a talent for covert ops.'

'*Edmund Beales* is better at keeping a low profile than you are,' I say. 'Even *he* wouldn't refer to a Semtex Surprise, in a public place.'

Greg claims Mr Beales probably *would*, 'if he had the imagination to come up such a witty phrase', but I don't reply. I'm too busy thinking about what would happen if I *did* get photographic proof that Max is guilty. Then I'd *definitely* be entitled to have a fling – as long as said fling was metaphorical, and didn't involve Johnny falling over any more stationary objects – but what about *after* that?

What would become of Connie and Josh if Max and I split up? I don't even want to think about that, let alone consider what would become of me. It's not as if spending the rest of my life with Johnny would be an option, even if I wanted to.

For one thing, I'd be bound to fail the training course for oil company wives, seeing as I can't even eat a canapé without getting crumbs all down my front. Now I'm *definitely* having a hot flush.

'It's another panic attack, you muppet,' says Greg. 'You're losing your mind.'

'Thanks so much,' I say. 'Where's your empathy gone?'

'It's burnt out. Well-known problem with MPs' staff. You need some Valium.'

I suppose Greg could be right, so I decide I'll ask my doctor for some when it becomes clear that I'm going to have to meet Josh at the surgery anyway.

'Mum, I think I've broken my hand,' he says, when he calls at lunchtime. 'Can you take me to A&E when you finish work?'

'No,' I say. 'I am not spending any more of my evenings there this month. Especially not when I'll have to go back to work afterwards, to carry on hunting for this bloody file. You'll have to make do with an ordinary doctor for now.'

This approach is vindicated when the locum GP feels Josh's fingers and says that he doesn't think that they're broken, but to come back in the morning if the pain and swelling get any worse.

'I didn't expect the Hallowe'en lantern to be quite so hard,' says Josh.

'And how did you find out that it was?' says the doctor, in a tone that suggests that he doesn't much care.

He seems even more unimpressed when Josh explains that he brought his fist down on it, at the same time as yelling to Robbie, 'You know the band, The Smashing Pumpkins? Well, here's their greatest hit!'

I've got a horrible feeling this doctor may also cover Silverhill Surgery, judging by his humourless reaction, so I decide not to ask him about the Valium. He'd probably go back and tell his colleagues I'm a drug addict if I did. Then they'd write another letter of complaint to The Boss.

'Josh, do you *never* learn?' I say, as we walk across reception towards the exit. 'That was really awkward.'

'Just playing it for laughs, Mum,' says Josh. 'Just for laughs. That doctor should try it some time. The miserable bugger.'

I don't react, as I have just noticed a poster, printed on bright pink paper, detailing 'other services' offered at the surgery – including Botox injections at £150 a throw.

'So that's where Ellen gets hers done,' I say, to no one in particular, as Josh turns left to head for home, and I turn right to return to the office.

I shall have to save up for some of those myself if these late nights carry on. I look exactly like my great-grandmother, shortly before she died. Or maybe shortly afterwards.

## WEDNESDAY, 27 OCTOBER (VERY LATE)

I look even more like Great-Gran when I leave the office again, at almost midnight, as I still haven't found that bloody, *bloody* file of documents. I get a taxi home, as Max doesn't answer when I call to beg him for a lift. Probably because he still hasn't returned home himself.

When I ask, Josh says Max hasn't phoned him either.

'Maybe he's popped round to Ellen's,' I say. 'To re-light

her fire, I mean *boiler*, again. I'll just go and have a look.'

I almost break my neck in the attempt, as Ellen's house is in complete darkness and I walk into her whirly washing line when I try to sneak up close to the windows. There's definitely no one in though – so, if she's with Max, it must be at a hotel somewhere. Probably the bloody Marriott, now I come to think of it. Max knew exactly where *that* was, didn't he?

I'm about to phone reception and demand to speak to him when in he walks, looking even worse than I do.

'You're losing your job this week, so please don't claim you've been working until this time of night. Where the *hell* have you been?' I say, or rather, shout at him.

He makes a shushing motion with his hands and says, 'The hospital.'

Then he takes off his jacket, and sits down heavily on the sofa, while I say the first thing that comes into my head. 'Oh, the *hospital*. Did Ellen need an emergency Botox injection, by any chance?'

'Mol, I'm tired and I have no idea what you're talking about,' says Max, closing his eyes. 'I've been with Mrs Bloom since six o'clock.'

I am *so* fed up of the obviously fictitious Mrs Bloom. Time to do some calling of bluff.

'Right,' I say. 'If that's true, then give me her number, now. If you're sure she'll be able to confirm your story – to your wife.'

'She can't confirm anything at the moment, Molly,' says Max, speaking very slowly, as if to a child. 'She was unconscious only a few hours ago. Some sort of diabetic coma, the doctors said.'

'Oh,' I say, mainly because I'm not sure whether to believe him or not.

It does sound credible, though, when Max starts to explain. He says that Mrs Bloom called him just as he was leaving work and asked him to pop in on his way home to fix a curtain pole, which had fallen off the wall. When he arrived, she didn't answer the door, and then he spotted her through a window, sitting slumped in her chair and not moving at all.

'So I broke the window, climbed in and realised that she was unconscious,' he continues, 'and then I phoned an ambulance.'

Max says that he waited with Mrs Bloom until it arrived – intending to come home once it did. But Mrs Bloom had regained consciousness by then and was terrified, so she begged him to ride in the ambulance with her and then to sit with her in A&E. Not wanting to add to her distress, he did as he was asked – or so he says.

'She's got no family, you see,' he says. 'So I didn't have the heart to abandon her.'

And I yelled at him, for *that*. God, I really am unreasonable.

## THURSDAY, 28 OCTOBER

I go into work early again this morning, in a last-ditch attempt to find Mr Sampson's file, so I don't get to apologise properly to Max, who's fast asleep when I leave the house. I might as well have stayed in bed with him a bit longer – seeing as I still haven't found the damn thing by the time the mail arrives, along with Greg and Vicky.

I do wish mad constituents hadn't given up using lurid green ink. Now everyone's got a computer, it's much harder to work out which letters to be careful about when you're opening them, although funny-coloured envelopes are usually a reasonable indicator.

I'm sorting through this morning's delivery when I spot a lavender one, so I decide I'll leave that until last, on the grounds that it may ensure that I remain alive for as long as possible. Then I use my non-patented letter-opener-stabbing procedure, the one that involves half-turning my back.

The tension is contagious, and Vicky chooses that moment to vacate the office – on what she calls an urgent mission.

I keep jabbing and tearing for another few minutes, until finally – *success*! I'm still in one piece, and my technique's obviously improving, as so are the contents of the envelope.

'What is it?' says Greg, from underneath his desk.

'Oh,' I say, then, '*Aw.*'

'What? *What?* Can I come out, or not?'

'Yes,' I say. 'You'll never guess what it is, anyway.'

'As long as it isn't any more bloody white powder and my man-boobs are safe from being put on public display again, I don't care *what* it is,' says Greg, sitting back down in his chair and wiping his forehead on his sleeve.

'It's a *thank you* card,' I say. 'Believe it or not.'

Greg chooses the latter option. 'Piss off, Molly!' he says. 'Don't be ridiculous.'

'See for yourself,' I say as I pass the card to him, which then renders him speechless for at least a minute.

He can't remember the last time a constituent said thank you after we'd got them a result, and neither can I – not that I think you should get bonuses for doing your job, but a word of appreciation never goes amiss. (Igor's not a constituent, so he doesn't count.)

It's not as if this thank-you was even deserved, seeing as all I did was to sort out ambulance transport for that lovely man, Mr Bradley – which the hospital should never have forgotten to arrange in the first place. Not when they were the ones who'd chopped his leg off.

Anyway, Mr B writes that, since he finally managed to attend his out-patient appointment, he's now had his prosthetic leg fitted, is 'managing very well', and that he and his wife will be 'eternally grateful' for what I did for them.

'Makes you think, doesn't it?' says Greg, dabbing at his eyes, while claiming to be suffering from a bout of winter hayfever.

'What does?' I say, pretending I believe him.

'How some people are so reluctant to ask anyone for help, no matter how much they deserve it, and then this lot of bloody whingers—' Greg gestures at the files and letters strewn across his desk.

'I know,' I say. 'But at least there's some hope, while there are people like Mr B around.'

After Mr Meeeeurghn phones to complain that his neighbour is still sniffing him at every opportunity, and Miss Emms calls to say that her guinea pigs are now suffering from cannabis anti-motivational syndrome, I'm starting to change my mind about *that*.

'Big Ears Beales is still stalking that poor policeman, too,' says Greg, slamming his phone down at exactly the same moment as mine begins to ring again. 'Taking photos of the poor man everywhere he goes.'

'*Ssh*,' I say.

I am on the phone to Carlotta, who sounds as if she's about to have a heart attack. Apparently she's been trying to get through to us for well over an hour.

She's only just managed to say, 'Andrew – on his way back – early – furious' when the man himself walks in, accompanied by Vicky, who's been absent from the office ever since I opened Mr Bradley's card.

Andrew's clearly in a towering rage, while Vicky's smiling like a well-fed piranha yet again.

'Explain this, Molly,' he says, slamming the lunchtime edition of the local paper down on my desk.

The front-page headline reads, 'Local MP to be sued by constituent'.

The article itself begins with my name, and is followed by phrases like 'loss of vital documents', 'incompetent' and 'negligent'. The 'negligent' bit is directed at The Boss for employing me, the incompetent who lost the documents – according to the 'whistleblower' who advised Mr Sampson that this had happened, earlier on today.

'You've done it on purpose, Molly, haven't you?' he

says. 'First you set all the doctors in Lichford against me, and now you do *this*! It's bloody sabotage, that's what it is.'

Andrew's face is the colour of a prune. God knows what his blood pressure's doing.

'But—' I say, when Andrew interrupts.

'Give all your work to Vicky – *now*,' he says. 'She's the only one here who knows what she's doing.'

'Thanks so much,' says Greg, glaring at The Boss, who glares right back at him.

'You should watch *your* bloody step as well,' he says. 'You're *all* dispensable.' With that, Andrew walks into the Oprah room and beckons for Vicky to go and join him.

'Don't stand for this, Mol,' says Greg. 'If you won't tell him who had that bloody file last, then I damn well will.'

I'm too stunned to do anything at all, so Greg throws his hands up in frustration, then asks to speak to Andrew in private, i.e. without Vicky being present. Andrew says he's not putting up with any more sneaky behaviour, so Greg's forced to tell him that Vicky was the last person to have the file – while he's standing in front of her.

'*And* she hasn't spent one single minute helping me and Mol to look for it,' he adds. 'When we've been here until God knows when for the last few nights, the two of us. Even Joan tried to help, but Vicky didn't.'

At this, Vicky bursts into tears, very decoratively – no hiccups or runny noses for her. Then she says that Greg and I have been bullying her ever since she started work, because we resent her for watching Andrew's back.

'Andy, you *know* I'm the only one you can trust,' she says, dabbing at her eyes.

Her mascara isn't even smudged, which – for some reason – finally gives me a kick in the butt. 'Ah,' I say. 'So *you're* the one who's been telling Andrew that everyone here is against him, are you?'

'They are,' says Vicky. 'Especially you. I'm the only person who appreciates him. Aren't I, Andy?'

The Boss looks backwards and forwards between me and Vicky as if in a daze, then shakes his head and says, 'I'm sick of not being able to trust people. If I were you, Molly, I'd go home – right now – and consider your position. Seriously.'

Greg starts to protest, but I have had enough. 'Oh, I will,' I say. 'And I suggest you consider yours too. Nice earrings, by the way, Vicky. I see Andrew gave you back the one you lost down the side of the sofa – there's probably another pair embedded in Joan's hedge.'

I feel quite triumphant as I grab my coat and bag and head for the door but, by the time I've arrived home, I'm a mess and in no doubt at all about what my position is: absolutely bloody buggered. It's karma, for planning to meet Johnny tomorrow and being horrible to Max when he was just being kind. Or 'a star' – as Sam would put it.

'I'm calling to say thanks for the invite to Max's birthday party,' he says, when he phones early evening, while Max is still at work. 'Wouldn't miss it for the world. Is the man himself available for a chat?'

'No,' I say. 'He's working late a lot at the moment, even though he's just found out that he's being made redundant.'

'Good God,' says Sam, proving yet again that he and Max hardly ever speak to each other.

You'd swear phone calls between male 'best friends' were limited by law to four a year. By the time I've finished explaining what's happened to Max's job, Sam is late for yet another blind date, so I don't have time to tell him that I may have just lost mine as well.

'See you on Saturday, then,' I say. 'Want me to give Max a message, when he gets home?'

'Yes,' says Sam. 'Tell him I meant to thank him for that fantastic excuse he gave me to escape from Shona. Worked a treat. I even got out with my saintly reputation intact.'

When he tells me that Max suggested that he should claim that his grandmother had gone into a coma, I start considering my options, as well as my position.

'It was a diabetic hyper, or a hypo,' Sam continues. 'I can't remember which now, but I got the right one at the time. Anyway, it was a brilliant cover story – so good, Max almost had me convinced when he described it to me.'

'Yes,' I say. 'He's good at that.'

### FRIDAY, 29 OCTOBER
Well, that's just typical, isn't it? I get sacked, and – on the very same day – two of the most annoying birds in Lichford get killed, with one particularly well-aimed

480

stone. Metaphorically speaking, of course – not that *that's* much bloody comfort.

I'm just preparing to line Charlie's litter tray with the front page of yesterday's paper, when I spot an article on page two headed, 'Animal lover discovers cannabis factory on her doorstep.'

One of the accompanying photographs shows Mr Meeeeurghn being led away by several police officers (all wearing high-vis jackets). The other features Miss Emms, his 'vigilant neighbour'. She's grinning like a maniac and holding several guinea pigs in her arms. She looks far more psychotic than they do.

I'm still banging my head on the table when Max appears and asks me what I'm doing.

'Thinking how lucky some people are,' I say, meaning Greg and Vicky, whose workload's just been cut by half.

Max waits for me to explain – but, when it becomes clear that I have no intention of doing so, he changes the subject. 'Why did you go to bed so early last night?' he says. 'I thought you'd still be up when I got home from the hospital. Mrs Bloom's doing really well.'

He almost believes in that made-up woman himself, doesn't he?

'Oh, good. I'm *so* glad,' I say, which earns me a sigh and a funny look from Max, who decides that now might be a very good time to take a shower.

When he comes back downstairs a little later and finds me still sitting at the table in my pyjamas, drawing a handlebar moustache on Mr Meeeeurghn, he asks why I'm not ready for work.

I say that I'm not feeling well, and leave it at that. My options will stay far more open if Max has no idea that I'm considering them – or of what they might be.

''Bye, then,' he says. 'See you later?' He makes it sound like a question but, again, I don't answer. Who knows where I'll be, by the end of tonight? I certainly don't, not that Dinah cares. She's only bothered about Dad's whereabouts.

'Molly,' she says, when she calls my mobile, towards the end of the afternoon, 'why the hell aren't you at work? I phoned your office because I thought that's where you'd be.'

'Ah, well, that's because—' I say, when Dinah interrupts.

'It doesn't matter now, you idiot,' she says. 'You won't believe this!'

'Oh, I probably will,' I say. 'Nothing surprises me any more.'

This is obviously not the right answer, as Dinah huffs in outrage. I keep forgetting she has a legitimate medical reason for being dramatic.

'Stop talking,' she says. 'And listen. It's Dad. I've just been to visit him.'

She pauses, but I'm doing as I'm told, so I don't say a thing.

'Are you still there?' says Dinah, so then I compromise and make a number of vague but encouraging noises. These seem to do the trick, and so she carries on: 'He's not there. I had a feeling he was up to something again!'

'He's *always* up to something,' I say. 'DIY, at the moment, and fishing, apparently.'

Or apparently not, when Dinah finally gets to the point. 'There's a "For Sale" sign outside his house!' she says. 'And he's gone back to bloody Thailand again – to live, this time. His next-door neighbours knew *all* about it.'

I'm still getting over the shock of that, when Dinah makes a choking sound.

'You okay, Di?' I say.

'No-o-o,' she says, gasping and snorting. 'We've lost him all over again, Mol. How many times is this going to happen? I'm *tired* of not having a normal family with only two parental figures!'

I know what she means, but I wish I didn't. Now all I can think of are Connie and Josh, saying the same thing – when Max either runs off with Annoying Ellen, or I bugger off to Russia to be with Johnny.

'People are supposed to *mean* their marriage vows,' says Dinah, before sobbing gets the better of her and she hangs up.

I haven't heard her cry like that since *her* mother and Dad divorced. It's disconcerting, even allowing for the HPD. I consider emailing Dad to try to find out what's going on, but then decide I can't be bothered, when faced with the contents of my inbox: about twenty-five emails from The Boss, and the same number from Greg, all telling me to contact the office. Greg has sent a similar number of texts, as well – all during the relatively short time that I've spent talking to Di.

There's no time to read any of them now, even if I wanted to, as I've got to get ready. Johnny'll be arriving at his hotel in just over an hour.

'No second thoughts?' he says in a text, responding to mine imparting the news about Dad. 'I hope you're not going to change your mind.'

I'm not, though Josh is trying his best to change it for me. You'd almost think he *knew* what I'm planning to do.

'What are you so dressed up for?' he says, as he walks past and sees me checking my reflection in the wardrobe mirror.

'A meeting,' I say, poking at what appears to be a stray chin hair, but turns out, on closer inspection, to be an eyelash that's fallen out. 'With an energy supplier.'

'Hmm,' says Josh. Then, 'Where's Dad? Wouldn't it be nicer to spend an evening in with him? It'd make a change, after the last week or so.'

'I thought you didn't like change,' I say, neatly side-stepping both his questions. I have no idea of the answer to either.

'I don't,' Josh says, then turns away, mumbling something which sounds oddly like '*That's* my point.'

I'm spared the need to reply when my taxi arrives and the driver honks his horn. Josh doesn't answer when I shout upstairs to say goodbye.

The cab hasn't even reached the end of the road before my mobile begins to ring.

'Mum,' says Connie. 'Josh says you're going out without Dad. *And* that you look really nice.'

I wish I could see what she's doing, right now. I *bet* she's talking into her sleeve.

## FRIDAY, 29 OCTOBER (LATER, THOUGH GOD KNOWS WHEN)

Johnny greets me in the hotel lobby as if we really *are* meeting for a discussion of the price of oil. He even shakes hands, before leading me into the lift and waiting until the doors have closed. Then he takes my face in his hands, and kisses me, very hard.

I stop the kiss before it really gets going, as I can't breathe properly. The lift just keeps on going up and up.

'Sorry,' I say. 'I hate lifts. I'll be all right again, once we get out.'

I'm not, though, not once I see the suite that he's booked. I'm completely overwhelmed. Plate-glass windows overlook one bank of the River Ease, and I can see the lights of Lichford stretching away on the other side. I can even see the office, and make a good guess as to the roof of my house.

I turn my back on the view and look instead towards the table, which is laid with starched white linen and a number of plates hidden beneath shiny, domed metal covers. They glint like the polished cutlery, and the antique silver candelabra. It holds five thin, tapered beeswax candles.

As Johnny lights the first one, there's a very loud *bong*. It's as if he's taking part in a religious ritual.

'What's that?' I say, as there is another *bong*.

'I don't know,' says Johnny, his words followed by *bong, bong, bong, bo-o-ong*. 'I think it might be church bells ringing.'

*Bong, bong, bong, bong. Bong, bong, bong, bong. Bong, bong, bong, bong.*

Oh, *God*. They must be practising for a wedding tomorrow.

'Did *you* have a church wedding?' I say to Johnny, who looks at me as if I am insane.

'Yes,' he says, 'but I don't want to talk about the past tonight. I want to talk about the future. *Our* future, specifically.'

'Ah,' I say. I didn't have a church wedding, but I assume the vows are the same, wherever you make them. Johnny waits for me to elaborate, but when I don't, he raises his eyebrows, then pours me a glass of champagne.

'I thought we'd stay in the suite this evening,' he says. 'So that's why I ordered a buffet. That way we can decide whether to eat first . . . or afterwards. Listen to this. I brought it with me specially.'

He walks over to a very sophisticated wall-mounted stereo system, and presses a button. Music begins to play, almost drowning out the sound of bells.

'Recognise the song?' he says, putting his arms around my waist, and pulling me close. I nod, and then he says, 'Dance with me.'

I put my head on his shoulder, and we start to sway. It's like the end of the fifth-form disco again, but without the Babycham-fuelled nausea.

'You're even more beautiful than you were then,' says Johnny, into my ear. 'And *I* am even more turned on.'

'What's different about you?' I say, standing back to look at him. 'Oh, it's your glasses. Where've they gone?'

'Contacts,' he says. 'Seemed the safest bet. I get to see

your face clearly when I kiss you, but without any more accidents. Let's put the theory to the test.'

He starts to kiss me but, when I open my eyes to look at him, it's not his face that I see. It's Max's, though *his* eyes are firmly closed – thank God. I blink several times, to make him go away.

I keep my eyes shut when Johnny begins to kiss me again. 'Turn round,' he says. 'I want to undress you, bit by bit.'

He pulls down the zip of my dress, and then everything starts slowing down, except for my thoughts. *They* are racing everywhere.

By the time I'm down to my underwear, my tights left in a ball somewhere behind the sofa, and my dress abandoned God knows where, we've made it across the suite and into the bedroom.

The lights are lower in here, which is obviously a good thing due to Johnny's bloody contact lenses. I bet he can spot even *microscopic* hairs with those.

'How good are they close up?' I say. 'What exactly can you see?'

'This,' he says, turning me around so that we are both facing the mirror above the dressing table. 'The stuff of fantasy.'

He can't be seeing what I'm seeing, then. Connie and Josh's faces have just popped up, behind our heads. Their mouths are open, in big round 'O's, like cartoon characters, and they look *appalled*. So am I.

'Bugger off,' I say. Aloud, by accident.

'What?' says Johnny.

'Not you,' I say, turning my back on the mirror, and doing some more furious blinking. 'Sorry. I was just worrying about something.'

Johnny pulls me down to sit next to him, on the bed. 'Well, stop it,' he says. 'I'm serious about you, you know that. This is not just a fling for me.'

'Hm,' I say, covering myself with the sheet, though I have no idea why. Then I add, 'Sorry, Johnny. I'm just not used to having sex, that's all. Well, not outside my marriage, you know.'

Nor in it recently, but it wouldn't be fair to tell him that.

He hugs me, as if he understands what I mean anyway. 'I know,' he says. 'But, if it's any comfort, I just got my AIDS test results back last week.'

Now it's my mouth that's forming a giant 'O', while I look at Johnny, look away, and then look back again. Several times.

'What?' I say, once I get a grip. '*What* sort of test? What are you talking about?'

'An AIDS test,' says Johnny. 'Like I said. I have them every year. What are you doing?'

He tries to stop me as I bounce off the bed, but I wriggle out of his grasp and race out of the bedroom.

'What the hell does it look as if I'm doing?' I say, as he follows me, and then stands still, watching while I try to untangle my tights. 'I am *out* of here.'

'Why?' says Johnny, to the accompaniment of those bloody bells. 'What have I done?'

I'm hopping now, partly with rage, but mainly because,

although I've got one leg in my tights, I can't seem to get the other in. They're all twisted out of shape, which could easily be a metaphor.

'Well,' I say, continuing to hop, 'what sort of man – who has apparently never cheated on his wife before – and is only doing it now because his marriage is dead and he's fallen in love with me, ha ha – needs an AIDS test – *every year*?'

'But—' says Johnny, as I finally get my other leg into the tights.

'But nothing,' I say, pulling my dress over my head and zipping it up. 'You must think I was born yesterday, though God knows it should be all too clear that I wasn't, if the optician got your prescription right.'

Johnny says nothing as I shove my feet into my shoes, grab my coat and open the door. When I look back at him, just before I slam it, it's *his* mouth that's in an 'O'.

Much like those of the people in the hotel lobby. I only realise why when I walk outside to get into the cab and find that my dress isn't pulled down properly at the back.

My mobile rings all the way home, but I'm too busy crying to answer it.

## SATURDAY, 30 OCTOBER (DAYTIME)

My bloody phone still will *not* stop ringing, but I don't want to speak to either of the buggers who keep calling it – The Boss or Johnny 'AIDS Test' Hunter. I'm too busy bursting into tears every time anyone attempts to speak to me. I wish they'd all stop staring at me, too.

'What on earth's the matter with you, Mum?' says Connie when she arrives. 'Josh said you looked weirdly good when you went out last night, but now you look absolutely *terrible*.'

'I don't know,' I say. 'It's probably my hormones, or something like that.'

'If you say so,' says Connie, sounding as if she doesn't believe a word of it.

She and Josh take Max out for a long, birthday lunch straight after that – to keep him away from the party preparations – so at least I won't be under scrutiny for the next few hours. Dinah's on her way here to help, but she won't notice *anything*.

'I've cheered up,' she says, when she walks in, carrying the cake she's made and holding Damian, I mean Jake, by the hand. 'If Dad dies while he's living in Thailand, or something else happens to him, I've got a plan to help me cope.'

'What?' I say. 'How can you possibly find the prospect of Dad dying in Thailand something to be cheerful about?'

'Well,' says Dinah, pausing to slap Jake's hand, to stop him poking the cat with a stick, 'you know how you hate flying, so you said you didn't want to have to go and get Dad if anything happened to him while he was there?'

'Yes,' I say, removing the stick from Jake's hand, given that Dinah's presumably illegal slap had no effect at all.

'Well, *I* will do it, instead – so you don't have to face your cowardly fears.' Dinah takes the stick from me, and pokes Jake with it, to make him let go of the cat, before

490

she carries on: 'But only if you agree to one *very* important condition first,' she says.

I go to fetch a plaster for Jake's hand, which Charlie has now scratched, while Dinah drums her fingers on the table, waiting for me to accept the deal.

'What condition?' I say, on my return.

'That we split the costs,' says Dinah, 'and I get to take two weeks' exotic holiday, before I bring the body back. You can look after Jake while I'm away.'

That's *three* conditions, isn't it? Dinah doesn't wait for me to agree to any of them, so hopefully none of them will ever arise. Especially not the last one she mentioned. I'm starting to wonder about Jake's scalp myself.

I check it, by virtue of a supposedly affectionate mussing of his hair, but there's still no sign of the number 666. Maybe it develops gradually over time, like a slow Satanic Polaroid.

'Aw, your aunty Molly loves *you*, doesn't she, Jake?' says Dinah, when I reach the end of the covert hair-checking operation. 'Give her one of your extra-special hugs.'

Jake looks even more horrified by this idea than I am, so I recall that I have to check my emails, urgently.

There are stacks of them from Johnny, all of which I delete without reading them first. I'm even more annoyed with him than I am with Dad. *He's* sent me three messages, too – presumably from various internet cafes along his route across Thailand to Porn-Poon's village in the North.

In the first one, he says that he *tried* to tell me that he was moving to Thailand before he went, but that I

491

was always 'too busy looking for some silly file' to talk to him. In the second, he instructs me to tell Dinah that he didn't inform *her* that he was going because, if he had, 'she'd only have made more sarky comments about glittery worktops'. He describes these as 'completely uncalled-for', which is pretty much what I'd say about the subject line of his third and final message.

It just says, 'Hot and wet.'

God knows what I'm going to say to the guests, when they start arriving. Seeing as now I'm wholly lost for words.

## SATURDAY, 30 OCTOBER (EVENING)

Well, God knows how I did it, what with Dinah and Jake's so-called *help*, but the house is ready, so now it's my turn to be tidied up.

It only takes ten minutes, seeing as I'm not worrying what I look like any more. When you're job-less, lover-less and probably soon to be husband-less, fretting about appearances seems a bit of a waste of time.

I put on my little black dress, the one that makes my body appear decades younger than my face, according to Max, and give Dinah a free hand in applying my make-up. The result is better than I expected, and clearly much, *much* better than Dinah did.

'You look *quite* good,' she says, standing back and appraising me. 'Considering the state of you before I started.'

Max seems even more impressed than Di when he

arrives home to find most of the guests already assembled.

'You look gorgeous,' he says, as I hand him a glass of champagne, supplied by Sam. I think he's about to kiss me when the doorbell rings.

I open it to find Ellen slumped against the doorframe, obviously already drunk. She doesn't look anywhere near as shiny as usual.

'Molly,' she says, swaying slightly as she moves in to give me a hug. 'Jush the person I need to talk to. Important thingsh to tell you. Ver, *ver* important thingsh.'

She gives me a meaningful stare as she tries to focus on my face, and then she makes a grab for my hand when I try to lead her along the hallway to join the others at the back of the house.

'No,' she says, pulling me towards the stairs instead. 'Ish private schtuff we need talk about. Men, relationship schtuff. *You* know.'

Oh, my God. This is *it*, isn't it? The moment when Ellen tells me all the things I don't want to know. I look around frantically, willing someone – *anyone* – to appear and offer a chance of escape, but there's no one in sight, and all I can hear are excited voices and loud laughter emanating from the kitchen, which might as well be miles away.

'Sshit down, and less talk,' says Ellen, yanking at my hand, which she's still clinging onto as if her life depended on it.

*Bang*. The letter-box opens and shuts, nearly making me jump out of my skin, and now there's a big piece of dog poo on the carpet. Ellen and I both stare at it, but neither one of us says a word.

Then the letter-box opens again, really slowly this time, and a voice booms out, '*Sur-prise!*'

I yank open the door, and Greg immediately falls into the hallway, landing squarely on top of the piece of poo. I laugh at that, but then so does he.

'It's a fake,' he says, picking up the poo and pocketing it. 'I wouldn't post a real piece through *your* door, Mol, even if you have been ignoring me. Now take me to where the alcohol is – *and* the birthday boy. I've got *tons* to tell you about The Boss.'

This sounds a lot better than whatever it was that Ellen was about to tell me, so I usher Greg down the hallway and get him a drink.

'Why the *hell* haven't you answered any of my messages?' he says. 'I've been trying to get hold of you for the last twenty-four hours. Andrew has been, too.'

'Huh,' I say. 'Why would I want to talk to *him*?'

'Because he's sacked Vicky,' says Greg, clinking his glass against mine.

My legs feel funny, so I sit down, while Greg explains. 'Andrew took a phone call yesterday, while Vicky and I were out at lunch,' he says. 'From Vicky's nail technician. *She'd* just got back from her mini-break.'

I don't say anything to that. I'm too busy watching Ellen weaving her way unsteadily through the room in search of another bottle of wine.

She keeps looking at Max, then at me, with a very

peculiar expression on her face. Maybe she wants to rip all Max's clothes off, and is only waiting until she's drunk enough to do it. He *does* look very handsome tonight. As well as very tall.

'Earth to Molly,' says Greg, waving his hand in front of my face. 'Are you listening to a word I'm saying?'

'Yes,' I say. 'Vicky's nail woman phoned up. What's that got to do with me?'

Maybe I could get Connie and Josh to guard Max, until Greg finishes whatever he's going on about.

'She said Vicky'd left something behind in the salon during her last appointment,' he says. 'And guess what *that* turned out to be?'

I forget to answer, as I'm still watching Ellen and wondering where she's off to now. Probably upstairs to the master bedroom, to check how much closer she could get the bed to the window once she moves in here and takes my place.

'The *file*, Molly,' Greg says, or rather, shouts. 'This is important, so listen to me! Vicky left Mr Sampson's file at the nail bar, for f\*ck's sake – and Andrew went *mad* when he heard about it. He fired her as soon as she got back from lunch.'

It's odd how being vindicated makes you want to rush to the loo – only to find that someone's already using it. I jiggle about on the landing, cross-legged, until the door opens and Ellen comes out.

'Molly,' she says. 'I schtill wan' talk to you. I wan' you tell me wha' your secret is.'

I stop jiggling, and freeze instead. *My* secret? Oh, my God. She knows about me and Johnny, and she's going to tell Max.

'I'm just going to the loo, Ellen,' I say. 'I feel a bit sick. Stay there – I'll be back in a minute.'

Max will think he can justify leaving me for Ellen now, won't he? It won't even matter that I haven't had any sex with Johnny – and *won't* be having any in future, either. And *why* can't I actually be sick? I'm sure it'd make me feel a whole lot better.

I run the tap and gulp down several mouthfuls of water before I open the bathroom door. Ellen's sitting on the top step, waiting for me as instructed.

'What secret?' I say. Might as well get this over and done with.

'To a happy marriage,' says Ellen. Then she snorts, and I want to punch her for finding this funny.

'Don't take the piss, Ellen,' I say. 'Isn't what you've already done to my marriage bad enough?'

'Wh-a-a?' she says, before starting to snort again. Playing the innocent, like every mad constituent I've ever met.

She carries on snorting while I glare at her, until I realise that she isn't laughing. She's crying, very messily – so I hand her some toilet roll, then wait for her to calm down and blow her nose.

'He was going to propose, back in June, when we were in Germany,' she says. 'I *know* he was.'

'Propose?' I say, fighting another wave of nausea. 'How the hell can he propose? He's still married – at the moment.'

'No, he isn't,' says Ellen. 'He's *never* been married. He's far too young for that. Or that's what he says now, anyway. That's why he dumped me earlier on today. He wants children, and I've already got more than enough.'

Max has, too, given that one of them is Josh, so I'm shaking my head in confusion, when Greg appears at the bottom of the stairs.

'I'm still waiting for you to come back, Mol,' he says. 'I haven't finished telling you about what happened with Vicky.'

'Oh, sorry,' I say, stepping over Ellen, who's still emitting the occasional sob. 'I'm coming now. It's time we all sang "Happy Birthday" to Max anyway, I suppose.'

Max – who definitely *isn't* too young to be married. And *is*, anyway – to me. God, I'm slow.

I turn back towards Ellen, and bend down so that I can whisper in her ear. 'By the way,' I say, '*who* was it who was going to propose?'

'Alex,' she says, 'of course. The one I met at salsa class. Who did you think it was?'

'Oh, him,' I say. 'Alex, I mean. The salsa man – yes, obviously *that's* who I thought you meant. I'm just no good with names, or sports. I thought you two met at kick-boxing.'

I pat Ellen on the shoulder, as I like her a whole lot better all of a sudden – as well as the salsa-dancing Alex.

'You joining us?' I say to her.

She nods, stands up and starts to follow me down the stairs, wobbling unnervingly. Greg raises his eyebrows as she finally reaches the bottom and walks straight into him.

'Ah, Greg,' I say, 'have you met Ellen, by the way?'

'No,' says Greg, turning to face her. 'But I feel as if I already know you *very* well.'

Ellen stops crying, brushes away her tears and licks her lips, before giving him a beaming, perfectly veneered smile, which doesn't move her eyebrows one iota.

'You look like that guy in *American Psycho*,' she says. 'The one with the interesting sex-life, I mean.'

'That's me,' says Greg, squaring his shoulders and sucking in his stomach. I feel sick again.

'On that fascinating note, shall we go and join the others?' I say, not a moment too soon as it turns out.

Dinah's already furious with me, when I find her in the kitchen. 'Where the bloody buggery have you been, Mol?' she says, flicking ash all over the place while stabbing candle holders into the cake. You'd swear we didn't have a rule about never smoking in the house, and God knows what Health and Safety would say.

She throws her cigarette out of the back door when she sees my expression, then continues: 'It's about time we lit the candles on this beautiful cake that you asked me to make for Max, and that neither one of you has bothered to comment on. *If* Max can be arsed to get off the phone in time to blow them out, that is. He's been talking to someone for hours and hours. God knows who.'

If God does, I certainly don't, but there's no time to ask for divine guidance now, not when Dinah's on the warpath, so I send Connie off to check on Max. When she comes back she says that he isn't on the phone any longer, so then I light the candles and carry the cake through to the living room while everyone sings 'Happy Birthday'.

Dinah's put Josh in charge of the video camera, which she says will be safer than leaving him teaching Jake to skateboard in the garden. She's even crosser about Jake's newly missing second tooth than she is about the cake, even though Josh says the accident was entirely Jake's fault for 'failing to follow clear landing instructions'.

'Smile, Dad,' he says, zooming in.

Max blows all the candles out in one fell swoop, then closes his eyes to make a wish. He doesn't say what he wishes for, though he gives me a very peculiar look when he opens his eyes again.

'Speech, speech!' says Sam – so many times that Max eventually agrees to oblige.

He begins by thanking everyone for coming, and says that he hopes his mid-life crisis is now over, rather than just beginning. Then he raises his glass, and says, 'And now I have two very important people to thank. Number one – Mrs Bloom.'

Oh, shit. Mrs Bloom. Who *is* she, if she isn't Ellen? And why is *she* number one? Maybe I've been looking in the wrong place, yet again. No wonder I can never find a thing.

Max waits for ages before continuing with his speech, until someone yells at him to carry on. I don't *think* it was me, though I suppose it could have been.

'Mrs Bloom is my favourite ex-customer,' he says. 'She can't be here tonight, as she's in hospital, but she's just phoned, to make me an offer.'

Presumably to go and live with her. Now he's going to say, 'So I am leaving my incompetently faithless wife for someone she thought was a work of fiction.' *Argh*. Why doesn't he just hurry up?

I nudge him as he takes a mouthful of wine, so that just delays things even further. Max is still wiping himself down with a towel when he says, 'She has just offered to set me up in business, working for myself, effectively. So I am no longer middle-aged *and* redundant, just middle-aged.'

Everyone claps and cheers again, apart from me. I am still processing what Max has just said, and what it means. He puts his arm around my shoulders and carries on with his speech.

'And the other important person I need to thank is my lovely wife. She may be last on this occasion, but she's never *least*, or not to me, anyway.'

He turns to face me, and raises his now-empty glass.

'Thanks for arranging this great party, Mol, and for – well, everything, really. Even though I take you for granted far too much.'

'You do,' says Sam, much to my surprise, though apparently not to Connie or Josh's.

They are both nodding at Max, in approval. Then he winks at them.

'I may not buy you enough roses, Mol,' he says, as he moves in for a kiss, 'but you know you mean *everything* to me. You always will.'

I kiss him back, despite a sudden bout of hiccups. Then several times more when I spot Greg and Ellen sneaking out of the back door, hand in hand.

## SUNDAY, 31 OCTOBER

I don't even have a hangover this morning, and Max and I have earned two gold stars! We might be about to earn another one, too, if only my phone would stop beeping for long enough.

'Who is it who keeps trying to contact you?' says Max. 'Your phone kept making noises half the night. Nearly put me off more than your hiccups did.'

'It's probably The Boss,' I say. 'Who I'm ignoring, since he fired me. Or at least since I *think* he did.'

'*What?*' says Max; I forgot I hadn't got round to telling him I might be unemployed – though he doesn't seem too bothered, once I've finished explaining.

'Well, it's probably a good thing,' he says, 'if Andrew's so stupid that he trusts that woman over you. And, anyway, you'll get a better job, easily.'

I don't know why he thinks that, when there aren't exactly hundreds of Labour MPs needing caseworkers since the election. Maybe I *should* find out what Andrew's got to say for himself.

'No need,' says Max, as I pick up my phone to check my texts. 'Have you forgotten Mrs Bloom's investment? When I set myself up in business, I'm going to need a good PA.'

Now my phone's ringing, not just beeping. It's only Greg, though, so I decline the call. I am being interviewed for a job, which is much more important – if quite unusual, when in the nude.

'So,' says Max, 'that means that you can tell Andrew to shove his job, if you want to, even if he didn't mean to fire you. I couldn't possibly be a worse boss than he is . . . could I?'

'I have no idea,' I say, 'though I'm pretty sure he'd wouldn't ask me important questions while naked. I'll think about it.'

There's a crash outside our room, on the landing, and then Connie and Josh start yelling at each other. Some things never change – like casual sexism, now I come to think of it.

'Why do *you* have to be the boss?' I say to Max. 'Why can't I be in charge, for a change?'

He laughs, then says, 'You can't spank your boss. I was planning on you playing the Maggie Gyllenhaal role in *Secretary*, if you really want to know.'

'Ah,' I say. 'Well, that sounds a lot more interesting. Want to have a test run now?'

Max nods, then there's another crash, this time right outside our door, and Josh yells, 'Ow!'

'Later, I think,' says Max, getting out of bed. 'When I've taken Connie to the train station, and found a way to evict our beloved son.'

He manages the first, but not the second, so we leave Josh at home when we go out for a late lunch, just the two of us.

'Are you *sure* Josh hasn't broken his foot?' I say. 'He did kick the banister rail ever so hard.'

'Yes,' says Max. 'Though he's going to have a hell of a bruise. When *will* he learn that Connie always ducks?' He leans across the table and takes my hands. 'Now let's stop talking about our bloody kids,' he says, 'and talk about us, for once. Are we going to be okay, d'you think?'

I look at him – at the lines around his eyes that I've watched develop over years of wincing at Josh, at the glint of the few grey strands that are starting to appear in his hair – and I think about what he's just said. No one else would know that Connie always ducks. Johnny wouldn't, and nor would Ellen.

'Yes,' I say. 'I think we're going to be okay. Do you?'

'I hope so,' he says, 'though I dread to think what you've been writing about me in that diary of yours. Maybe I should take a look? To see what your over-active imagination has been conjuring up.'

'Oh, nothing important,' I say, my fingers firmly crossed. 'Just a record of the daily grind. And that's going to change now, anyway – isn't it?'

'Yes,' says Max, though I'm not sure either of us knows what changes I'm referring to. All I know is that I'm going to burn my diary as soon as I get the chance.

With that in mind, I light a fire as soon as we get home, using a whole box of firelighters in an attempt to get it going as quickly as possible. It's excessive, but it works, and Max and I are just snuggling down together on the sofa, admiring the flames, when the bloody doorbell rings. Neither of us wants to move, so we both look imploringly at Josh, who shakes his head and pleads his latest 'disability'.

When the doorbell rings again, for a very long time, I groan, then admit defeat.

'Hurry up,' says someone, silhouetted against the glass of the door. 'Let me in. I'm bloody freezing.'

It's Greg, who looks even more like Patrick Bateman than usual.

'You'll never guess where I've just been,' he says, heading into the kitchen and turning the kettle on.

I raise my eyebrows but don't make any attempt to guess. I already know, given that Greg's still wearing the same clothes that he had on last night: at Ellen's house. If I encourage him, he'll probably tell me her favourite sexual position, or what she's saying when she yells like that, and I am trying *not* to feed my imagination any more.

'The police station,' says Greg. 'To collect The Boss. He was arrested in the early hours.'

'Oh,' I say, once I've got over the shock. 'So *that's* why you phoned me this morning.'

'Yes, you idiot, but you didn't answer. As usual, these days. I don't know what's wrong with you.'

'I don't want to know stuff about a job I no longer have,' I say. 'Is that *so* unreasonable? Anyway, you're here now, so you may as well tell me – what did Andrew do?'

'What did *who* do?' says Josh, who's just come hopping into the kitchen to get more ice to put on his foot.

'No one did anything,' says Greg, before turning his back on Josh and mouthing, 'Tell you in a minute', at me. 'When we're in private.'

Then he makes himself a coffee, and scatters sweeteners into it, like confetti.

He's on his second cup by the time Josh has finished telling him about how annoying sisters are, as well as how unsympathetic girlfriends can be to boyfriends who are 'slightly accident-prone' when dealing with those sisters – and I am rapidly losing the will to live. If it gets much later, Max will fall asleep and we won't manage to test our *Secretary* scenario tonight. There must be some way to persuade Josh to bugger off.

The box of chocolates that Max got for his birthday does the trick.

'Thank God for that,' I say to Greg as Josh finally hops out of the room, chewing a hazelnut and almond praline, one of Max's favourites. 'I thought he'd be here all night, going on about his self-inflicted injury. So what was Andrew arrested for?'

'Drink-driving,' says Greg. 'But that's all I'm allowed to tell you about what happened. He says you are to read tomorrow's paper, as he's sent you a hidden message, to show you that he's not really a bad guy, and to persuade you to come back to work.'

I don't know what to say to that, so I don't say anything. I just eat a truffle, absent-mindedly.

'You don't look very happy about it,' says Greg.

'I don't know if I am,' I say, 'though you're looking *very* pleased with yourself. Something to do with Ellen, by any chance?'

Greg looks surprised for a second, until I gesture at his clothes.

'Ah,' he says. 'So that's how you knew. Well, let's just say James Blunt has a certain appeal.'

'Christ,' I say, then illogically, 'Judas. You're supposed to be on *my* side, Greg. That woman almost brought my marriage to its knees. God knows what was going on between her and Max.'

'*Nothing* was going on,' says Greg, rolling his eyes. 'I can promise you that. Ellen says Max is far too old for her liking. She likes them young and fit, like me.'

I'm so stunned that I don't even react to the word 'fit' being used in relation to Greg. I'm more concerned about the slur on Max – and what it says about me.

'Ellen's the same age as Max, for God's sake,' I say, '*and* me. And what was all that mad sex talk about, whenever she saw him, and all those nudges and winks? She kept making meaningful comments about him to me, every time I saw her – you know that.'

'I know,' says Greg, with a pained expression. 'I did ask her about that, in a roundabout way, but you're not going to like what she said.'

I probably won't, but I still *have* to know. 'Tell me,' I say. 'And I'll try my best not to over-react.'

It must be bad, because Greg pats my hand before he speaks. He doesn't even shake hands with ministers, without using hand sanitiser afterwards.

'She said, "Molly's so easy to wind up",' he says. '"She gives me hours and hours of fun."'

I'd go and kill her now, if I hadn't promised Greg I'd stay calm, so I eat another of Max's truffles instead. And then several more.

'I almost had an affair because of that, though,' I say,

feeling sick, though I suppose that could be due to the chocolate.

'I know,' says Greg. 'But you didn't, did you? And it's all over with the oil baron now, isn't it?'

'Yes,' I say. 'He was playing me for a fool, just like Ellen was. So I suppose I must really *be* a fool.'

'Hm,' says Greg, as I show him out, before rushing upstairs to bed. Max – miraculously – is still awake.

'Have you been a naughty girl, Molly?' he asks, slapping my hairbrush into his palm, in a menacing fashion.

'Ye-*es*,' I say. 'I think I may have been – but completely by accident. Honestly.'

## CHAPTER SEVEN

# November

(Bonfire of the vanities, as well as of this diary –
I hope.)

**MONDAY, 1 NOVEMBER**

God, it's all very well Max setting up a business from
home, but when the hell am I going to manage to burn
my diary without him noticing? I forgot to do it before
I raced up to bed last night and now, every time I approach
my target – the fireplace – he pops up, like Mr Bloody
Beales' dog. Or Mr Beales himself, now I come to think
of it.

I'm hovering in the garden, still in my dressing gown,
and trying to see whether any of our neighbours owns
an incinerator I could borrow or are building an early
bonfire, when Greg phones me on my mobile – to say
that he bought a copy of the *Lichford News* while he
was on his way to work.

'I'm bringing it round,' he says. 'I'll be there in a minute, so get dressed, now. Then you can come into the office with me, if you want to, once you've seen the article.'

'I doubt I *will* want to,' I say. 'Seeing as reading what The Boss has to say to the local press usually makes me want to resign. I can't see this time being any different.'

'Well, it is,' says Greg. 'You can take my word for that. Put the kettle on.'

Max already has, so I go the window to watch for Greg to arrive, though he seems to be taking ages. Oh, he's just sent me a text.

'Approaching now,' it says. 'Have the door open, ready to admit me. Can't be seen.'

I've just done as he asks when he comes hurtling around the side of the hedge in the front garden, bent double, then drops to his knees and crawls up the path.

'Out of the way,' he says, pushing past me on the doorstep. 'And shut the door – as fast as you can!'

'Is someone following you or something?' I say, as he finally stands up and hands me a totally mangled bunch of flowers.

'From The Boss,' he says. 'Or from Petty Cash, to be exact. Andrew told me to buy you something to show his appreciation.'

I'm not sure what five crushed, scentless – and almost petal-less – yellow roses are supposed to denote, but any appreciation involved seems pretty minimal.

'God, they're a bit tragic, aren't they?' I say. 'And why were you hiding on your way here?'

'Didn't want Ellen to spot me,' says Greg, shuffling his feet. 'She's starting to scare me a bit, she likes me so much. And stop moaning about the flowers. You're just getting cocky because you've had far too many recently.'

'That's true,' says Max, appearing from nowhere, yet again. 'Though the red roses weren't actually *bought* for Molly – were they?'

'No,' say Greg and I simultaneously, and with an excess of head-shaking, to add an air of verisimilitude. I have no idea whether it works or not – but, as soon as Max goes off to make coffee, Greg says in a whisper, 'Is he suspicious about Johnny, Mol?'

'I don't know,' I say, 'but he's being very nice to me if he is. So it's a good job Johnny showed his true colours, just in time.'

'*Yes, it is,*' says Greg, nodding furiously. He doesn't approve of serial cheaters any more than I do, not since his last girlfriend slept with half of Young Labour. Maybe he should introduce Ellen to them, if he wants to get rid of her.

'Anyway,' he says, throwing himself onto the sofa, and dumping the *Lichford News* onto the coffee table, 'shall we have a look at this?'

Andrew's face stares up at me from the front page, captured in the act of blowing into a breathalyser, watched by a policeman, whose face looks oddly familiar. 'Local MP arrested for drink-driving,' says the headline, which is *huge*.

'Oh, my God,' I say. 'What a nightmare.'

'Ignore that, for now,' says Greg. 'It's not important. Andrew says you're to look at the article below the one about him.'

He points at it, while I wonder what the hell he's

talking about. How can *anything* be more significant than The Boss getting himself arrested – and for driving while drunk, of all the stupid, irresponsible things to do? It's a PR-disaster, even on a good day to bury bad news, which this one clearly isn't.

'Here,' says Greg, pointing again. '"A mindless act of vandalism".'

I look at it, then do a double-take, when I inspect the accompanying photograph – which is of a leylandii tree, or what *was* a leylandii tree, before it was cut down. On Silverhill Close, where the Parkers live. Oh, and where The Boss was, at the time he was arrested.

'Holy shit,' I say, to which Greg replies, 'Exactly.'

'Let me see,' says Max, coming into the room with a tray of coffees.

Greg passes him the paper, which he reads for a minute before looking up and saying, 'Andrew did that?'

'Yep,' says Greg. 'Though don't tell anyone he did. He wanted to prove something to Molly, to make her come back. It's lucky he was driving away by the time he was spotted, really – otherwise we'd be reading a headline about an MP being guilty of criminal damage, not just drink-driving.'

'Christ,' I say, unsure whether to laugh or cry.

'Exactly,' says Greg, again. Then we all sit in silence, staring into space, while sipping our coffees.

'But how did Andrew come to be photographed while he was being breathalysed?' says Max, eventually. 'That was bad luck, wasn't it? Did someone tip off the press or something?'

'Good point,' says Greg, picking the paper up, and inspecting it more closely. 'I hadn't thought of that.'

After a few seconds, he passes the paper to me. 'Oh, for f*ck's sake,' he says. 'Look at the photo credit. It's only Edmund Bloody Beales. Talk about sod's law! It's the first time he's ever got all his subjects' heads in shot.'

'Mr Beales – so *that's* where I've seen that policeman before,' I say. 'He's the one who doesn't wear his high-vis jacket.'

'God almighty,' says Greg. 'I need a drink.'

He doesn't believe me when I tell him that there's no alcohol left in the house since Max's party, until he checks all the cupboards for himself. Then he says he's going to the pub, as it's an emergency.

'Will you be at work by the time I've had a few gins, Mol?' he says. 'Has Andrew done enough to convince you that he's still one of the good guys now?'

'I'll think about it,' I say, though I've no idea what my decision will be.

Drink-driving: terrible. Vandalising a tree: normally, also terrible – but brilliant, if it means Mrs Parker sees the sun again before she dies. Why is *nothing* ever black and white?

'Andrew was only *just* over the limit,' says Max, giving me a hug when I groan in confusion. 'If that makes any difference? We're talking about degrees of guilt, you know . . . and whether bad behaviour can ever be justified.'

Now *there's* a profoundly uncomfortable thought.

'Um, yes,' I say, wriggling a bit. 'I suppose we are.'

I'd better focus on only blaming people who are *definitely* at fault, in future – like Johnny, who I wish would stop emailing me all the time. I can't keep on hitting *delete* every five minutes, so maybe I should change my email address.

Oh, but I can't, can I? Not my Parliamentary one, not if I *am* going to go back to work. I'll just have to mark Johnny's emails as junk. That seems appropriate, after all the stuff he tried to get me to believe – like being in love with me. Thank God I came to my senses, just in time.

'I need to deal with a few emails,' I say to Max. 'Urgently, but I won't be long.'

Then I kiss him, properly, and he kisses me back, before I stand up and walk towards the door. On the threshold, I turn around to look at him, and he smiles at me, like he used to, in the early days. I feel like a very smug married indeed.

# *Epilogue*

(Oh, *bloody* hell.)

**From:** Hunter, Johnny
**Subject:** Urgent - re AIDS test.
**Date:** 1 November 2010 07:12:55 GMT+3
**To:** Bennett, Molly

Molly

See below. I have to be tested yearly, to get my work permit renewed. Ask the Russian Embassy if you don't believe me. Not *everyone* tells you lies, you know. I don't.

Johnny

*Decree of the Russian Federation # 1158 from November 25, 1995*

*'On Establishment of Requirements to the HIV Test (AIDS) Certificate, presented by the Foreign Citizens and Stateless Citizens upon their Application for Entry Visa to the Russian Federation for the Period over 3 Months.'*

## REQUIREMENTS
### To the HIV Test (AIDS) Certificate,
**presented by foreign citizens and stateless persons upon application for an entry visa to Russia for a period over 3 months**

1. The certificate should contain:

   – Passport data or those of the substitution document (last and first name of the person examined, date, month and year of birth, number of the passport or the substitution document; the state of permanent or primary residence)

   – Indication of the intended stay in the Russian Federation

   – Information about the result of the AIDS blood test (date of examination, signature of the doctor, who carried out the examination, series of the diagnosticum, with the help of which the analysis was made, stamp of the medical organization, where the examination was carried out, signature of the person examined)

2. The Certificate is filled in Russian and in English and is valid for 3 months from the date of examination.

Polly James is about to chain herself to her desk to start work on her second novel. Before she does, we thought we'd find out a bit more about her, and what the experience of writing *Diary of an Unsmug Married was like.*

## Are there occupational hazards to being a novelist?

There certainly seem to be, as I became horrendously unfit during the writing of Molly's diary. First, I developed an inexplicable addiction to pink shrimp sweets, gained two stone and sent my cholesterol through the roof – and then I became so unfit that I tore the ligament in my right shoulder – just by typing. None of this was particularly helpful, given that I had quite a tight deadline for delivery of the book, and I'm right-handed.

The plan for writing the next book is to stay away from the pink shrimps and to keep some time free for exercise, though I overheard my husband increasing my life assurance the other day – 'just in case'.

## Where do you work and is there anything distinctive about your workspace?

In theory, I work at a beautiful desk that my husband bought me as a gift, and which is in our spare bedroom (though I won't allow the room to be called that, as I still haven't accepted that my daughter really *has* moved out for good, even though she left for university in 2005 and hasn't come back yet).

The desk would look great in front of a window, but I daren't put it there because I'd get so distracted by what my neighbours or passing strangers were up to if I did. (I love people-watching, and am very nosy.) Instead, it faces a blank wall, which *should* serve to keep me focused on writing.

It doesn't, because I'm not working at my desk at the moment. Instead, I'm sitting slumped on the sofa in the living room, in an attempt to find a position in which I can type without using my right arm, because of the aforementioned shoulder injury. This means that I can be distracted by anyone and everything, and often am.

### *What do you keep on your desk and what is the view?*

No view, as mentioned earlier. . .other than of what's on the desk itself. If I turn round, though, I can then see straight out of the window, and right across the small square on which I live, to a street of perfect Georgian houses situated on the other side.

If I wrote historical fiction, this would be a great help as – every time I see that view – I find myself imagining people from the Georgian era coming out of their houses and going about their daily lives (as long as I ignore the pub on my street. . .and the coffee bar. . . and the mini-mart).

On the desk itself, I have a gigantic computer screen a supportive ex-employer gave me to help me with writing the book, as my eyesight's so awful that I was struggling with the small screen on my laptop. Now I just plug that into the big screen, add a keyboard and mouse, and off I go.

That combination takes up almost half of the desk and I tend to use the other half as a dumping ground, so it's often drowning under piles of books, until I lose patience and put them all back into the bookshelves for a while. There are only two books that are allowed to stay on the desk permanently: a copy of 'Elements of Style' and one of 'The Right Word at the Right Time'. (Both are highly recommended.)

Next to those are two index card boxes (which I always intend to use to help me plot things and then forget about completely), and a set of three filing trays labelled 'Book one', 'Book two', and 'Other'. The 'Book two' tray looks worryingly empty at the moment.

There's also a pen pot containing loads of pens (*none* of which ever seem to work); a box of eye drops (for dry eye, the curse of those who spend all day in front of a screen, however large); a copy of my invitation to the Orwell Prize award dinner (to remind me that I *can* write well enough to be short-listed, if I try); and a towering stack of notebooks, yellow legal pads and used envelopes.

I've scrawled ideas on all these things at one time or another, but not in any ordered way, so now none of my notes make any sense, even before I catch the pile with my elbow and send the whole lot crashing to the floor. (This happens at least twice a day.)

Despite the gargantuan proportions of the paperwork pile, and the huge computer screen, the most noticeable thing on my desk is a shocking pink sticky note stuck squarely in the middle of it. On it is scrawled, 'Never sell another book that you haven't already written, you bloody, *bloody* idiot'.

**Molly's always worrying about tempting fate, but are you superstitious, too? If so, what superstitions do you have?**

My first reaction was, 'No, I'm not' but I have a horrible feeling that I am, now I come to think of it – and I *definitely* was when I was a child.

I used to do all that jumping-over-the-cracks-in-the-pavement stuff, throw salt about with gay abandon (alternating shoulders as I could never remember which one I was supposed to throw it over), and try to befriend every black cat in the neighbourhood, only to then reject them when I realised I wasn't entirely positive that they weren't *un*lucky.

When I reached my teens, I decided to fight back by becoming a compulsive risk-taker, so I would deliberately walk under ladders, cross paths with people on the stairs, and put shoes on tables just for the hell of it.

I then became the world's most accident-prone adult, so now I've gone back to being careful – or *superstitious*, if you prefer to call it that!

### What can't you live without?

My husband, my children, earplugs, thermal underwear and piles of books. Oh, and an inexhaustible supply of cups of tea. (I'd have added pink shrimp sweets to the list, but I *refuse* to let them control me any longer.)

### Which five people, living or dead, would you like to invite to a dinner party?

This is a bit of a tricky question as, if you invited a whole load of big personalities to dinner at the same time, that would just be asking for trouble – so theoretically, I should pick some guests who are listeners, not talkers, except no-one's likely to have heard of *them*.

Also, I know you're probably supposed to choose people who've made a massive contribution to the welfare of nations, or who are really saintly and good, but what if they turned out to be tediously boring? Then someone might notice what an appallingly-bad cook I am.

I clearly need to give this careful thought.

<u>Priorities for dinner guests:</u>

- Must be good conversationalists, to divert attention from the food.
- At least one or two should be dead or fictional. Then I won't have to feel guilty if I poison them, and can concentrate on keeping a close eye on the ones who were alive when they arrived.

Prioritising's always so helpful, isn't it? Now I've almost completed my list:

1. Dorothy Parker, writer
2. David Mitchell, comedian
3. Niles Crane from Frasier, psychiatrist (played by David Hyde Pierce, but he has to attend in character)
4. Clive James, writer and critic

I'm stuck on the fifth guest, though, so maybe readers could help me decide who that should be? Here are the candidates:

- Fran Lebowitz, writer ('Ask your child what he wants for dinner only if he's paying.')

- Karl Pilkington, moaner and philosopher ('The Elephant Man would never have gotten up and gone,' Oh God. Look at me hair today.')

- Nora Ephron, writer ('When your children are teenagers,

it's important to have a dog so that someone in the house is happy to see you.')

- Stephen Wright, comedian ('If at first you don't succeed, destroy all evidence that you tried.')

- Paul Merton, comedian ('My school days were the happiest days of my life; which should give you some idea of the misery I've endured over the past twenty-five years.')

- Basil Fawlty, hotelier ('A satisfied customer: we should have him stuffed.')

We thought we'd also include some suggestions for points of discussion for reading groups, so we asked Molly Bennett what she most often asks herself, and then reproduced her questions below.

(She's even had a try at answering them – in brackets – but says your opinions are much more likely to be right than hers.)

### Love and Marriage

<u>Long-term Marriages</u>
- What happens when a marriage is stuck in a rut? (Nothing. That's the point.)

- How much sex is everyone else having? (Much, much more than me. Definitely.)
- Is love cyclical, i.e. can married people recapture their feelings for each other? (God, I hope so.)
- Which is preferable: excitement or contentment? (I must admit, excitement can be very tiring.)
- Do you see the person you're married to as others see them?
- Just because he doesn't talk about it, does this mean he doesn't love you? (It's hard to remember that this may be true.)
- Is *everyone* cheating? (It bloody well seems that way.)
- How often do married people imagine being with someone else? (More than they admit.)
- Is an affair ever worth it? (Not sure, but my guess is no.)
- Is it still love, or just hard labour at the coalface? (How can you tell?)

Divorce
- What are the effects of divorce and stepfamilies on the children, including in their adulthoods? (See Philip Larkin, then multiply by ten.)
- How does divorce affect you: as a child, as a parent, as a married person? (Ditto.)
- Is it ever worth it? (That depends on who you ask.)
- Is it too easy to get divorced? (As above.)
- Is divorce a selfish act? ( " )
- Discuss toy-boys, trophy wives and Thai brides amongst yourselves. (I myself have nothing to add.)

<u>Internet dating</u>

- How realistic are people's expectations? (Do I really need to answer this?)
- Are men trying to find love, or sex? (I'll let you know when I find out, though early indications suggest the latter.)
- How do participants judge suitable candidates? (A picture speaks a thousand words.)
- Does anyone tell the truth when internet dating? (Of course not.)
- Does it really matter if you have shared interests? (D'uh. No.)


## *Family Matters*

<u>Sibling Rivalry</u>

- Why do children agree that their parents are guilty of outrageous favouritism, even though they cannot agree on which one of them their parents prefer?
- Do brothers and sisters ever grow out of sibling rivalry? (Please God they do.)
- How do you balance familial demands, within your immediate and extended family? (Haven't mastered this one yet.)
- Is the family a fixed or a mutable thing? (Note: you argue this one differently if you're trying to justify your own divorce.)
- Why are teenagers capable of such lunacy and yet of giving such sage advice on occasion? (It's a complete

mystery - unless they're watching and learning while you think they're glued to Facebook and the X-Box.)

## Am I a bad mother?

- Why do mothers always feel guilty? (It's part of the job description.)
- Why do mothers always feel responsible? (Ditto the above.)
- Why can fathers sleep through everything to do with the kids? (It's a mystery.)

## Am I a bad daughter?

- Why is it so hard to be sympathetic to your parents, when you're a parent too? (Must try harder.)
- Why is it so easy to forget that your parents are people, even while wishing your own children would envisage you as a human being and not just "Mum"? (See above.)

## *Political Issues*

## The Reality of Politics

- To what extent does the personal affect the political, and vice versa? (Much more than you would think possible.)
- Are politicians really how we envisage them? (Should they be? *Can* they be?)
- How much power do politicians really have? (Answer: much less than they expected, or would ever acknowledge.)

## Care in the community

- How many people are suffering from mental illnesses, whether diagnosed or undiagnosed? (See the usual suspects for further information.)
- What is their impact of the lives of others? (Let's just say that I'd look ten years younger. . .)
- What are the effects of people having too much time on their hands, or of living solitary lives? (De-stabilising, without a doubt.)
- Are MPs policy-makers, or social workers? (In theory, a); in reality, b) - despite lacking any training in the subject.)
- What are the dangers to staff working with the general public? (Under-estimated.)


## *Money Matters*

## The Gap Between Rich and Poor

- How do we even know what life is like for anyone else? (We don't.)
- Is being broke a matter of perception? (The difference between "I can't afford a holiday this year" and "there weren't enough coins down the back of the sofa to buy a pint of milk".)

## Money

- Can *everyone* tell your clothes have come from Primark? (Of course not. No-one here has ever been to Primark.)
- Why do people assume all their friends can afford to

attend weddings in far-flung and expensive locations? And why does the hen party have to be in Cuba? (What *do* these people earn?)

- Am you a bad parent if you don't earn enough, or are your children learning valuable life skills by having to work their vacations, and going to the local school? (Please say yes to the latter option.)
- Will your son inevitably end up in a young offenders' institute because you sent him to the local school? (Required answer: no.)
- Will your daughter's career progression be hampered by your lack of funds, despite the fact that her brain is the size of a planet? (As above.)

### Getting Older

<u>Significant Birthdays</u>
- What do they symbolise? The end of life as we know it – or a new beginning? (God, I hope the latter is true.)

<u>Ageing</u>
- How do we hold back the years?
- Is it worth the effort? (I bloody well hope so.)
- Are women doomed to be replaced by someone younger? (Oh, *don't*.)
- At what stage do women become invisible? (It happened so suddenly, that I missed it.)
- Is it really different for men? (Yes – they have all the luck. Beards hide a multitude of sins, and men are *supposed* to have them.)

- Is hypochondria an inevitable feature of getting older? (God, I hope not.)
- How do you cling on to your self-esteem? (How? *How*?)

## Philosophical Questions

### Success and Failure
- What makes us a success, or not? Career? Relationships? Getting through the day? Doing it differently from your parents? All, or none of the above? (Please don't say money or status, or a smooth forehead.)
- Do others determine whether we are successful or do we decide that for ourselves? (Next question?)

### Life in a Bubble
- Do we ever really know what is going on in someone else's life? (Though would we want to?)
- Can we ever be sure what someone else is thinking? (Note: mind-reading can get one into trouble.)
- Is life always greener on the other side? (Actually, I can't answer this. Given that I can't be in two places at once.)

### Guilt and Innocence
What constitutes cheating? (The answer to this appears to be rather variable, depending on whether we're talking about someone else, or oneself.)
- Is guilt or innocence a matter of degree? (Um…)
- Does it depend on who makes the rules? (Most things do.)